WILD WILD WOLF

Timber Creek
Book 1

B. PERKINS

AIMEE VANCE

Revel Books

Revel Books
Paperback ISBN: 979-8-9882650-9-2

Cover Design and Illustrations
Copyright © 2026 Aimee Vance

Character Art
Copyright © 2024 Mellendraws

www.aimeevancebooks.com

To new beginnings.
They're worth being brave for.

Chapter One

JADE

Propping my phone between my ear and my shoulder, I opened the freezer case and grabbed a bag of frozen chicken.

"You know we just spoke five hours ago."

I grinned at Ruby's voice as I let the door shut, heading over to the discounted frozen vegetables. "Don't act like you weren't counting the minutes."

"How are those job applications going? Maybe once you start working again, you'll leave me in peace."

"It's like you don't know me at all, lil sis," I scoffed. "The first thing I look for in job descriptions is how often I'll be able to step away and text you. You'd think I died if I didn't send you at least a dozen memes a day. It's like our proof of life."

Ruby chuckled, and as always, the sound made something in my chest ease. We joked around, but I took my job as my sister's caretaker seriously, even though she hadn't lived with me in almost five years. She acted like I was an overbearing older sister, but with just the two of us against the world, we'd grown closer than regular siblings. We were each other's best friends, our ride-or-dies, and I'd hunt down anyone who tried to hurt her.

"At what point will you stop calling me *lil sis?* I turn 21 in six months."

"That would be never," I said, hating that I'd miss yet another birthday. "Now, tell me about today's training."

Without missing a beat, Ruby launched into details about her lessons with Brigid Morgaine, the witch she'd been living with in

Deadlights Cove, Maine, for the last five years, working to hone her magic.

I smiled as she recounted hunting down the mysterious wandering coffee van, laughing over where the two quirky owners parked this morning — somehow *inside* the town's gazebo. She chuckled over the seniors tie-dying everything in sight, then a mishap with a local demon that resulted in the whole town smelling like popcorn for days, and the sound of her happiness made my eyes prick. That ridiculous town had ended up being perfect for her — absurd and yet so normal in the way they looked after each other, and especially Ruby.

Almost twelve years ago I'd become her sole guardian after our parents died in a car crash, leaving me in charge of a nine-year-old when I was only 21. Despite the many mistakes I'd made in her upbringing, getting her to Deadlights Cove was one thing I knew I'd done right.

As much as it hurt, I needed Ruby as far away as possible. Trouble always found me, no matter how often I moved.

"Mo let me move out to the carriage house, did I tell you that?" Ruby said, and it pulled me back to the present, away from the memories of my own life at her age — vastly different from her current one. But I wasn't resentful, not after everything I'd put her through.

My familiar guilt threatened to swallow me whole, but I forced it down, feigning excitement for her benefit. "Well, look at you, fancy pants. How is it?"

"Beige, which is just weird considering Mo."

I grabbed a bag of rice off the shelf and forced myself to keep moving, to keep my memories at bay. "Are you going to redecorate?"

"Yeah. She claims it's an early birthday present from her. We're going to get some paint this afternoon. I can't decide if I should go for black-and-white with bright pops of color or something more monotone."

"Neither you nor Mo are monotone girls. I say bright and fun, like you, with some skulls or ominous ravens or whatever you goth kids like these days. I can send you some money for new decor. Make it feel like home."

"You know it won't since you're not here."

"Stab me in the heart, why don't you?"

"Sorry," Ruby sighed. "I just miss you. You know that."

My eyes tingled at her words, the ache for her as deep as it had been since the day I sent her away. "I miss you, too."

This was the longest we'd ever been apart, but this separation was for her own good. We'd get through it.

I wished I could leave our history in the past, could live a normal life with my sister at my side, but it wasn't that simple. We weren't typical wolf shifters.

In fact, if I could give up my powers and wash my hands of the supernatural world for good, I would. Except Ruby, of course.

The rest of them could leave me alone.

Lone wolf, party of one.

I snorted at my own sad truth, even if I'd chosen this path for myself.

"What was that?" Ruby said. "Your sinuses again? Or did you see a hot guy and try to take a whiff?"

"You must be confusing me with your *other* sister."

"Hilarious. You know you are allowed to date, right? I'm all grown up now, Mom. You should try it out."

"No thanks." My tone was sharper than I intended, so I changed the subject before Ruby could keep prodding. "Smooth or crunchy peanut butter?"

"Ew, is that even a question? Smooth."

"Right. Duh." I tossed the jar into my basket, wishing she was here to share with me.

"Are you going to visit soon?" Ruby asked when we'd been

silent for a few beats, and suddenly she sounded exactly as young as she was. "It's been ages since I've seen you."

I sighed, thinking of the exactly $82.46 in my bank account that I'd clean out with this one grocery trip. Plane tickets from Colorado to Maine weren't cheap, and I couldn't swing it. "Soon. As soon as I can."

"I got a job, and I could buy your —"

"You *what?*" I skidded to a halt in the middle of the aisle, and a mom with two screaming toddlers in her cart swerved around me. "When? Where? How? Why would you keep this from me? Oh, my God." I slapped my forehead. "First you moved out and got your own place, now a *job?* What other secrets do you have? Are you married, too?"

"And here I thought you might overreact. Relax, it's just a couple shifts a week at the local bar."

"*Bar?!* You can't even drink!"

"They don't recommend you drink on the job, so that's not an issue. I prep food and clear tables, but I make decent money in tips." She paused, letting me absorb this news. "And I'm not married, but I'm seeing someone."

"She's all grown up," I muttered, deciding, *fuck the budget,* and headed back to the freezer section to throw a pint of ice cream in my basket. If I was going to keep my anxiety at bay over Ruby dating, I needed Rocky Road. Only chocolate and marshmallows could keep my mind from wandering to my own poor decisions. "She's all grown up, and she doesn't need her *selfless,* amazing sister anymore —"

"If you're done with your pity party, his name is Akil," she spoke over my melodramatics and I huffed, waiting for the important stuff.

She waited. I huffed again.

"*And?*"

"*And* he's a fox shifter. His brother Kit is the Alpha here and

Mo's son-in-law. You met Kit and Nimue when you were in town last."

I grumbled in response to that. If Ruby insisted on sticking to the supernatural world, foxes weren't the worst option, even if the idea of my little sister dating *anyone* was enough to make me wish I had the budget to add a bottle of wine to my cart.

"What do you know about this *Akil?* What's his last name and social media handle? Have you done a background check? Any criminal history? Have you seen an STD report? Oh shit, are you having sex?" I cringed. "Don't answer that. How much do you know about his family? What fictional fox does he most identify with? What's his favorite Disney movie?"

Ruby laughed. "Only you would ask these questions. Probably *Robin Hood*, though. And no, no background check, you psycho. I've gotten to know him like a *normal* person does — casual conversations over time, mostly at his family's tea shop in town, sometimes at the library when I'm studying. You should try it some time."

"I think I'll pass." I scrunched my nose at the thought of excess conversation with anyone, but the *Robin Hood* part made me feel better. Ruby needed more Robin Hoods in her life. "Well, I hope you'll let me meet him before you get married. And please make sure you check his references before you sign on the dotted line. If you marry an axe murderer, you can't say I didn't warn you."

"Oh, my Goddess. He's normal, I promise. Let it go."

I paused before the register, listening to my sister's breathing, picturing her red-dyed hair, her dark brown eyes, wishing I could pull her into the world's longest hug. I'd been fooled by what I thought was normal before too, but just because *I* trusted no one didn't mean I wanted that for Ruby. Even if I didn't know Akil, I trusted Morgaine's judgment and knew she'd look out for my girl. It'd be fine, probably.

I gripped the phone a little tighter, trying not to give in to the anxiety threatening to pull me under. "Video chat soon?"

"Tomorrow night?"

"Will you introduce me to your male?"

She gave a noncommittal hum. "Let us date a bit first, okay? I promise if it turns into something, you'll meet him."

"Fine."

"And think about my offer, okay? The money?"

"Ruby, don't worry about me. Just focus on learning what you can with Morgaine. I promise I'll come see you soon."

Silence. Then, quieter, in a voice that cracked my heart, "Okay. Love you."

I repeated the words, and hung up.

Blinking back any lingering emotions, I stepped up to the register, unloading my groceries. As the kid who barely looked old enough to have a job started scanning, I glanced out the front window, checking my surroundings the way I had for years.

Maybe someday I'd grow out of constantly looking over my shoulder, but not today. And certainly not when I found an all-too-familiar male standing in the parking lot, his intense hazel eyes locked on mine.

I should have known he'd find me, sooner or later.

"Kumquats," I muttered under my breath, heart rate skyrocketing as I hastily forked over my whole checking account balance for the groceries. Panic built as I looked around the grocery store for another exit, but found none.

"Everything okay, ma'am?" the kid said, and I ground my teeth together, shaking with the urge to flee.

"I'm not *that* old," I snapped, grabbing the bags off the counter, still watching out the front window.

I hated everything that came with being supernatural, but I couldn't deny the heightened senses were handy, even if mine were dulled lately. Compared to a human, my sense of smell was stronger, my eyesight better, my legs faster, and my punches harder.

Lacing my truck keys between my fingers, I closed my hand into a fist around my grocery bags and pushed through the doors. Willing my heart to steady, I braced for imminent danger, staying alert.

I waited for the low rumble from the other soul under my skin, but my wolf was shockingly quiet, none of her ferocious protective instincts surfacing. Sniffing at the air, I tried my best to sort past the smell of the dumpster behind the store and the lingering scent of oil and tires in the parking lot.

"Really?" I muttered to my wolf. "You growl at a stray leaf, certain I need to flee, but now when I *know* danger is near, you're suddenly absent? Thanks a lot, Balto."

I made a beeline for my rust bucket of a truck, ears sharp for any crunch of gravel. As I neared, I caught movement from behind a huge grey truck parked a row over and I spun, setting my groceries on the ground to free my arms.

"Not today, asshole," I said through gritted teeth, hands up in front of my face, key protruding between my knuckles in a move that would do damage.

"Easy, wolf," a deep voice I wished I didn't recognize said, verifying who was stalking me even if I couldn't see him yet. How two words could contain so much arrogance was beyond me.

It had been five years since I'd met West Larkin on the worst day of my life, but I'd seen the waves he'd made in supernatural society since then. If I was a Lone wolf, West was the opposite. He was involved in *everything*, and I wanted nothing to do with him. That hadn't stopped him from randomly showing up each time I was anywhere in the Rocky Mountains, demanding I join his pack.

"Nope." I threw my hands up, then grabbed my groceries off the ground. No matter how much I hated West, I knew he wasn't a threat to me, which was something I didn't say about *anyone*. Jamming my key in the lock, I twisted it and tossed my bags on the bench seat. "You're more persistent than the car warranty companies, you know that? Not interested, same as last time."

"Jade."

"She's not available, please leave a message," I shot back in my best answering-machine voice, not turning around as I hoisted myself up.

A giant hand clamped down on my shoulder, pushing my feet back down to the ground. And that just lit my fuse.

Nobody manhandled me. Not ever again.

I followed the momentum of his grip, kneeing him in the balls as I ducked and ran for it, leaving the truck door wide open. West wheezed and cursed as he regrouped, then followed me around the corner of the store.

"You can't outrun me, little wolf, and you have to circle back to your car."

Ugh, logic. Who needed it? But if there was one thing I hated — and actually, there were lots — it was being told what I couldn't do.

"We'll see about that, mister," I huffed. Putting on a burst of speed, I shot between a dumpster and the wall, leaping over a pile of trash.

"You can't run forever. Your ice cream will melt."

"Maybe if I run long enough, someone will call the police and arrest you for harassing me," I shouted back without breaking stride.

His laugh rumbled low and dangerous, way too close behind me.

Come on, Balto, I chided internally, hoping he didn't scent the things the sound of his laugh did to me. *Put away your stupid hormones and rip this guy to shreds. Not literally, though, please. I don't want to go to jail.*

My wolf's amusement washed over me, Balto just as stubborn as the wolf on my tail.

At the far end of the building, I slapped my hand out onto the corner, using it to help me whip around faster. I pumped my arms as my truck came into sight, my beat-up sneakers pounding the pavement, but frowned and slowed when I no longer heard footsteps behind me.

There was only one reason West would've stopped chasing me.

He was hunting me.

Fu—

I didn't even finish the expletive in my mind before his body slammed into mine, quickly spinning me until my back pressed against the muddy side of my truck.

"I just want to talk."

West Larkin, Alpha of all Alphas, stared down at me, his hazel eyes glowing faintly in a way only shifters' could, and I willed my body not to respond. No hitch of breath, no change in heart rate.

Absolutely no *anything* south of the border.

Mind over pheromones.

But because I was human — well, not really — my traitorous eyes took in his windswept golden-brown hair and beard, the firm, broad chest filling out his white t-shirt, the huge suntanned biceps caging me in. He moved his feet as he straightened up, drawing my eyes to the cut of his faded denim jeans before I snapped my gaze back up to his. I willed my nostrils not to flare at his woodsy scent with a hint of sweat from our little jaunt around the parking lot, clamped my mouth shut to stop myself from licking my lips when his Adam's apple bobbed on a swallow.

Why couldn't the last five years have been miserable to him? Why did he somehow look *more* handsome than the last time I'd seen him? Why did my stupid wolf tell my stupid body to react like this, every time he was near? All of it was unfair, and I clenched my teeth in annoyance.

West's gaze flicked to the groceries in my backseat, his lip curling slightly in distaste. "Did you buy *frozen* meat?"

I rolled my eyes, an action that made West's pupils flare in response. Of course that was what a wolf-shifter cared about most. The absolute disgrace of having to buy frozen meat.

"Great talk, bye now." I tried to shove him back, but it was like pushing a statue. A warm, well-muscled statue who could probably throw me over his shoulder without even trying.

Nope, did *not* need that image in my head, especially when Balto practically panted at the idea.

I had a real bone to pick with her later. For years she'd flipped out and sent my body into fight-or-flight when anyone came within arm's reach of us, and now, here she was, belly up while West loomed over me.

With his hands braced on either side of my head, caging me in, and my palm on his chest, it probably looked like we were having a romantic moment. And who wouldn't want that? West was by far the most attractive male I'd ever seen, and not just physically. He had a magnetism to him that drew me in like a moth to a flame.

But I wasn't about to get burned again, and I wasn't naive enough to think this was about romance.

This was about dominance.

I pulled my hand off his warm chest, curled it into a fist, and dropped it to my side.

West was trying to make me submit, to lower my eyes and make myself small, like any other wolf of lesser power would do in his presence.

But I wasn't any other wolf. I would *never* make myself small again, not for him or anyone else.

In defiance, I tilted up my chin, rolled my shoulders back, and met his gaze head-on. Little did he know I was a master at staring contests — I'd raised a nine-year-old with wonky magic, after all. I could win a stare off while the trash can exploded moldy spaghetti leftovers all over the ceiling. Just as a random example.

I widened my eyes a little more, just for emphasis. It probably gave me crazy-eyes, but I had a point to prove.

West pressed closer, towering over me, holding himself a hair's breadth off my body. Not touching me anywhere, but making my body buzz with his nearness all the same.

"I'm taking you out to dinner."

I blinked. He smirked. *Damn it. Next time, jerkface.*

"What?" I asked, not positive I'd heard him correctly. Of course he didn't ask — he was an Alpha, after all — but a dinner invitation wasn't what I'd expected him to say.

"I'll buy you dinner tomorrow, and we'll talk." He raised a cocky brow, indicating my paltry groceries again. "A real steak."

I squinted, suspicious of his change in strategy from usual. On the one hand, I wasn't one to turn down a decent meal. I couldn't afford to be picky, and West was relatively loaded. On the other hand, I knew what this bastard wanted to talk about, and I wasn't interested in the slightest.

Still, it wasn't like I'd be the first female to suffer through boring conversation for a good dinner. I'd just tune him out and play *Balto* in my head to distract myself. Sue a girl for having a comfort movie.

"Fine, but I'm ordering extras to take home," I said, the melody of the opening credits already playing in my mind.

The corner of his mouth twitched as he eased back, finally allowing me a breath that wasn't laced with his fresh, woodsy scent.

"Deal."

Chapter Two

WEST

My knuckles went white as I gripped the steering wheel, parked across the street from Jade's apartment complex, tension rolling off me in waves. It was a coincidence I stumbled across her as I was leaving the grocery store earlier, but I couldn't pass up the opportunity to approach her. Since she showed up five years ago asking me to help hide her sister Ruby, I'd kept tabs on her.

I had little to no back story for the Rodriguez sisters, but they weren't part of my pack then and Jade wasn't now — no matter how curious I was, their story was their own. I didn't ask questions when shifters showed up at my door, only helped when I could.

The downside of being the kind of Alpha who helped just because I could? When I saw a problem, I wanted to fix it. *Now*.

Jade's apartment was a problem.

I'd tailed her from the grocery store to make sure she got home safe, and I hated what I found. Peeling paint, trash all over the parking lot in front of the building, cracked pavement, skeevy guys smoking cigarettes by the dumpsters.

I loosened my grip on the steering wheel, my fingers tapping against the leather as I heaved a frustrated sigh. No matter how I tried to deny it, it was more than just Alpha instincts screaming at me that this wasn't right.

Ever since shifters had been outed to the human world five years ago, the number of reported lone shifters gone missing climbed by the day. In a place like this, Jade would be the perfect target. Who would even notice if she went missing?

Me, my wolf said, growling at the thoughts crossing my mind. *We can give her better than this and keep her safe.*

I'm working on it, I tried to tell Togo, but his hackles were still up, impatient as ever.

Every time I saw her, Togo reacted to her teal-green hair and tan skin, her dark brown eyes that held a hint of sadness and so much independence, her clothes that never fit quite right.

I wanted to protect her, the same as I always did for someone in need, but seeing where she lived? Togo paced under my skin.

Jade entered her apartment and closed the door — hopefully locking and barring it — and I rolled my neck, forcing some of the strain from my shoulders. The urge to get out of my truck and stand guard in front of her door was almost overwhelming. It didn't matter that she was smart and capable of defending herself, something she'd proven when she'd sensed my presence, then tried to fight back in the parking lot. All shifters were stronger and faster than humans, but these weren't typical times.

No matter how much I wanted to stay right where I was, I had responsibilities to more than just Jade — I needed to get back to Timber Creek and my pack.

Reversing out of the parking lot, I hit the road back home, my thoughts churning with all the ways I could convince her to join us.

Mountains blurred as I drove, rolling hills covered in pines leading to steep white peaks far in the distance. Taking the exit off the highway, the road became endless twists and turns as I followed the river basin, leading me an hour deeper and higher into the mountains.

Far from prying human eyes.

My phone rang, the screen lighting up with my brother's name, and I answered.

"What's taking so long?" Terran's voice carried over the

speakerphone before I even acknowledged him. From anyone else, the casual greeting would be disrespectful, but Terran was my pack Second and my brother. My family played loose with the rules of obeying my Alpha status unless other pack members were around and, for the most part, I liked it that way. "I thought you'd be back before I put River to bed."

"Pulling onto pack lands now," I said as my headlights flashed over the valley before me. A few minutes outside of town, the river split, running into a smaller creek that rushed with frigid snowmelt, meandering along the road for the last couple miles until it veered off near Main Street. "Everything okay?"

"Yes," he sighed. "River was asking for milk before bed and I switched her to that lactose free one I put on your list. You found some?"

"Bought every carton they had. It's in the cooler in the truck bed."

My brother hummed as I crossed the border of our pack lands, the web of magic tying us together lighting up under my skin. Now, he could *feel* my presence just as I could his, the same as everyone in my pack when we were in close proximity. "Perfect. See you soon."

I slowed as I neared town, taking in the sight of the only home I'd ever known. Even in the setting early-summer sun, most of the stores facing Main Street were closed as the street lights flickered on. Light bounced off the flat-roofed buildings, each painted a different color and looking every bit the Western mining town this once was.

It was my job as Alpha to look out for everyone here, ingrained in my character to be a leader. I loved this town and the supernaturals who called it home, but my head wasn't here tonight. It was stuck in a shithole apartment an hour and a half away, and the stubborn woman who insisted on calling it her home.

As the pack house at the end of the street came into view, my gut clenched at the contrast to Jade's current living situation. Where her apartment was just shy of squalor, my house was just short of splendor.

Lights glowed through the windows of the sprawling mountain lodge, warmth radiating from the house like a beacon calling me home. Originally built with my grandfather's mining money, it had been expanded several times to accommodate the growing pack, and now had a basement that housed just as many as the original house. I was almost never alone, and I wanted for nothing.

At the bottom of the hill, I slowed the truck to type in my access code at the gatehouse, and the wrought-iron warded gate swung open.

"*What's wrong?*" Terran's voice filled my head as I parked by the front steps, his wolf speaking through our pack bonds as he sensed my unease.

"*Meet me downstairs once you get River to bed,*" I sent back as I grabbed the groceries.

Cocking my head as the front door clicked shut, I used the pack bonds to find out who else was here.

The house was open to anyone in our pack, but tonight it was only my family. Terran was upstairs putting his daughter to bed, and my adopted son Leif was in the basement.

Even without the pack bonds, the smell of meat on the grill told me who I'd find on the back porch.

I crossed the slate tile floors and under the archway that led into a spacious open-concept kitchen-living room area, the back of the house a full wall of windows overlooking the valley. A huge deck wrapped around nearly the whole house, and my dad stood at the grill, sporting his favorite *Master Baster* apron.

With a shake of my head, I put the groceries away, then grabbed a beer, popped the cap, and joined him on the deck.

"Remember when you said you were retiring?" I drawled, looking over the elk steak and chicken my dad had on the grill. It would have been enough to feed over a dozen humans, so just about enough for a handful of wolf shifters.

He clinked his can against my bottle. "I left you the good grill here at the house. And somebody has to make sure you slow down enough to eat a decent meal every once in a while."

My dad didn't look much older than my 38 years, although he was pushing 80 — relatively young for a shifter. Like me, Heath stood over six-feet, broad shoulders and lean muscles that fit our wolves, but his hair and beard were more grey than brown, his summer-tanned skin wrinkled around his eyes and mouth. Like always, he wore cargo shorts, a tee, his favorite white New Balances, tube socks, and a cowboy hat. The colors of the tees and hats changed, but the outfit never did. Losing my mother — his mate — 15 years ago had aged him in a way none of us had been prepared for, but we'd pulled together as a family to watch out for him. Especially after he'd abruptly announced he was retiring as Alpha, then moved out of the pack house and bought a ranch just outside of town.

I hummed, taking a sip of my beer as he turned back to the grill.

"Well, that and my Willie escaped again. Can't be trusted to make good decisions on his own, you know. I had to get him put back away where he belongs before he ran rampant through town again."

I stopped mid-sip before slowly lowering the bottle, biting the insides of my cheeks to keep from laughing at the intended innuendo, knowing my father. The male didn't crack a smile though, just flipped steaks like he hadn't said anything out of the ordinary.

One of the many things that kept my dad busy in retirement was his unintentional bison sanctuary — he insisted they just kept showing up, and he named them all Willie.

"Did you at least keep him out of the house this time?"

He chuckled and waved the hand still holding the grill tongs.

"Can you blame him for breaking and entering? He likes the A/C! Who am I to turn down a fella in need? I'm sure he'll leave once the sun goes down."

"Does he know how to open the doors too, then?"

"I left the door open," he said with a deadpan expression like I was the absurd one.

"And the cow patties he'll leave behind?"

"Oh, please." He shot me an incredulous look. "My sweet Willie would never just drop a load. He knows not to do that in the house — we have an agreement."

An agreement with a wild bison, indeed.

"What's on your mind?" he said, flipping a chicken breast and not meeting my eye with practiced nonchalance.

I didn't want to brush him off, but I had a feeling I knew what his advice would be, so I clapped him on the shoulder. "Nothing for you to worry about."

Inside, Terran met my eye with a raised brow from the living room, and I left Heath to his grilling.

Terran grabbed a beer and a stool at the kitchen island, pulling off his faded baseball cap to run a hand through his shaggy, brown hair. The scent of fryer grease and coffee coming off his black jeans and button-down told me he'd been at the restaurant today, as did the general exhaustion emanating from him. Buffalo Willie's was our mother Cora's legacy, and Terran kept the restaurant running behind the scenes.

The sparkly star stickers stuck to his tattooed forearms and beard told me his daughter River had some fun before bedtime.

"What are those furry cows called?" I mused, flicking my gaze to his hair pointedly. "Highland cattle?"

Terran jerked his head to swoop his hair out of his face with a grin and put his hat on backwards over his long hair. "That must be why River doesn't want me to cut it — she loves those damn cows."

"Do you always do what your five-year-old tells you to?"

Terran shook his head. "Funny, coming from the male who's never once said no to River. Hence the one-hundred pack of markers strewn across the floor of my bedroom when I got home today."

I moved around the counter towards the fridge to grab the sides to go with the meat on the grill. "Blame Summer for that one. River said the yellow you bought her didn't match her hair, so she and Summer left to find a different, paler yellow."

He rolled his eyes and I held back the smirk that threatened to escape. Except for our sister Summer, River was raised by mostly men, and even at five, the little girl was a force to be reckoned with. Terran had been a single dad since his human girlfriend dropped a newborn on him and split. No one in town had seen or heard from River's mom since she left, and we all avoided talking about her, Voldemort style. She Who Must Not Be Named.

"Quit spoiling my kid, West," Terran said, but there was no heat behind his words. We all knew how grateful he was for our help — River was our whole world.

"Grill's up!" Heath called, sliding open the back door.

Terran and I brought the sides and condiments over to the large, worn dining table. It was large enough to accommodate my big family and more, but tonight it was just the three of us, at least for now.

We passed platters of food around the table as my dad and brother recounted their days, and I sat back, soaking in the comfort of home. I didn't like to think I took much for granted, but after seeing Jade's apartment and meager groceries, the food turned to ash in my mouth.

"Well I know it's not the taste of my meat bothering you," Heath said. "Did something happen in town today?"

Terran raised a brow at me and I sighed, resting my elbows on the table.

"I ran into a Lone wolf at the store," I admitted. "Jade. That wolf from a few years back. I've talked to her about joining us before, but she's adamant about being on her own."

"You know, some people *like* to be alone," Cooper, my other brother stated as he ambled in from the front door. He'd built a cabin in the woods behind the pack house after he'd returned from active military duty several years ago but stopped by often. Everything about Cooper screamed Wild Mountain Man, right down to his suntanned skin, thick brown hair, and thicker beard. He was bigger and broader than me, but moved with a lethal grace fit for the animal he shared a soul with.

"Wow, look at the time," Terran taunted. "Usually cats beg for dinner two hours early. The mice in the woods weren't enough for you tonight?"

Cooper popped Terran's hat off as he strolled behind him, finding a chair further down the table before pinning an ominous, but playful, glare at Terran. "Make more cat jokes, Fido. I dare you."

I shook my head at their familiar bickering, and brought the conversation back to Jade. "She's barely getting by on her own out there. She's too skinny, her place is a dump, she was buying *frozen meat*."

"Still her choice." Cooper shrugged, but I saw the slight recoil he tried to hide.

Terran shot me a glance, barely stifling a smile.

He was probably thinking this was just my need to save and protect everybody again, but he didn't know the full story about Jade. Hell, *I* didn't even know her full story and it drove me crazy.

"She needs a pack in this day and age."

"Okay." Cooper drew out the word, his brows furrowing. "So, are you looking for strategies? Because if so, just throw her over your shoulder and bring her here. Problem solved."

"If she's really Lone, she'd probably be kicking and screaming, but I doubt she's bigger than you," Terran said, agreeing with Cooper's suggestion as he crossed his arms.

Cooper scoffed. "Knock her out first. Ask forgiveness later."

"I now see why everyone at this table is single," Dad huffed. "Did I teach you boys nothing?"

"Sure." Terran tipped his chair back on two legs. "That Mom was a saint for putting up with us all."

Heath pointed a finger at him, with a wink. "You got that right. But West, women don't want to be caveman'ed. Give her a reasonable argument."

Frustration had me clenching my jaw. Today wasn't my first run-in with Jade, and I was positive it wasn't my last. "I have. She doesn't give a shit."

"What's so special about her?"

There were a dozen answers I could give them.

She's half-witch.

She's hiding from something.

She's starving.

She's alone.

She needs us.

But the truth was a lot simpler, boiled down to two simple words my wolf barked at me, and was completely out of the question to admit to myself or anyone else.

She's mine.

Chapter Three

JADE

My knees ached the next morning as I sat back on my heels, scowling at the tub I'd scrubbed for the last hour. This was the third time I'd cleaned it since I moved in two weeks ago, but no matter what I did, I couldn't get rid of the brown rust stains from the dripping faucet. Why I cared, I wasn't sure. It wasn't like the dirty tub was the only offensive thing in this 400 square-foot studio.

Everything about my apartment was a piece of shit, but I intended on polishing every square inch of this turd. I'd worked hard to get to where I was in life, even if I was currently jobless, alone, and toeing the line with homelessness.

That thought was enough to pull me out of my momentary lull, needing to occupy myself once more. I stood, pulling off my cleaning gloves and grabbing my phone off the counter to check for any missed calls from the restaurants I'd applied to, but nothing. With only two weeks until I needed to pay my first rent check, desperation crept in. Summer was peak tourist season in ski country — I'd thought getting a job around here would be easy, but the clock ticked loudly in my mind.

Idle hands led to idle thoughts, so I shoved my phone in my back pocket and went in search of a snack.

"Control what I can, let go of the rest," I read the magnet on my fridge aloud, repeating the mantra for the billionth time as I pulled the door open and looked at my meager options, then shut it with a disappointed sigh.

Did mantras really work for some people? If so, I was doing it wrong. Maybe I needed to stand naked under the full moon, burning sage and swaying to the music in my soul or something. My mother probably would've known what to do, but I'd buried her over a decade ago.

Swiping the peanut butter from the cupboard, I unscrewed the lid and stuck in a spoon. While it was one of my favorite staples, the first taste was unsatisfying, and I frowned.

Tonight, though, a free meal was coming my way. That was something to be excited about, even if it meant suffering through West's company.

I'd fumed on the drive home yesterday, annoyed by how arrogant he'd been. West had never *asked* me to go to dinner. He'd simply *told* me I was going to dinner with him.

If I hadn't wanted the free meal so bad, I'd punch him right in the junk when he showed up at my door, then slam it in his far-too-handsome face. My stomach rumbled at the thought, unappeased by the spoonful of peanut butter I was currently feeding it.

"A real steak," I mimicked his cocky words, doing my worst deep voice impersonation. My traitorous stomach groaned at the mention of steak and I threw the spoon in the sink, annoyed with myself for not turning him down.

Checking my phone for missed calls one last time to no avail, I got back to cleaning.

I was so in the zone that when a knock pounded on my door, I yelped and whacked my head into the top of the inside of the oven.

"All right in there, Jade?" West's voice rumbled through the door, crystal clear with my shifter hearing.

"Crap on a kumquat," I muttered, pulling myself out of the oven and straightening up to look at the clock. I'd meant to stop cleaning an hour ago to shower and get ready for dinner, but I'd lost track of time.

"If you don't open this door, I'll break it down."

I knew he meant it, so I tore my gloves off and all but ran to the door, yanking it open. "Don't you dare. I'm not paying for those repai—" I choked off the end of my words as I swallowed heavily, taking in the cleaned up version of West. "Holy—"

West in a casual t-shirt and jeans? Drool-worthy.

West in a button-down, blazer, crisp dark jeans, and boots?

I couldn't feel my face. Could I usually feel my face? I could definitely feel other parts of me, though. As that thought crossed my mind, my face flushed as much as my tan skin would allow and West's cocky lips twitched.

"Are you going to invite me in?" West brushed past me without actually waiting for me to extend the invitation, but at least it gave me a minute to pick my jaw up off the floor.

"Well, now I know you're not a vampire."

"All wolf." He flashed a grin with his canines elongated before shifting them back to human. Why did that turn my legs to Jell-O?

West strolled around my apartment, not hiding his blatant inspection. I crossed my arms and frowned.

"Not quite up to your standards, Larkin?"

He flicked on the light over the sink that just so happened to be the one that sparked occasionally, as it did then, and he raised an eyebrow. "Is this up to anyone's?"

"Great, well, you're welcome to fix it while I go clean up." I gestured towards the front closet. "I think there's a rusty screwdriver in there. Hope you get tetanus." With a sugary smile, I walked into my bathroom and closed the door behind me with a thud.

I let out a long breath, trying to quell my racing heart. It was going to be a long meal under the full force of West Larkin's undivided attention.

Chapter Four

WEST

"Ready," Jade said as the bathroom door opened. I put the tools away, having checked and fixed as many outlets and switches as I could, and turned in her direction. Luckily, I caught myself before the low hum of approval slipped free at the sight of her.

While nothing Jade ever wore fit properly, the jeans she had on tonight were practically painted onto what little curves she had. Her green shirt matched the tips of her dyed hair perfectly, hanging loose over her shoulders. The color was faded and grown out, like it used to be all green but she hadn't been able to dye it in a few months, revealing the dark chestnut brown of her natural hair. Paired with the gold hoop earrings, a black-and-white flannel shirt she wore open, and the same worn sneakers she'd had on at the grocery store, the casual look was very Jade. It was impossible for her to be anything but breathtaking, no matter what she wore.

I cleared my throat, holding an arm out towards the door, noticing the four deadbolts. My jaw worked, but I refrained from asking any questions and started towards my truck. She stooped, placing a small rock in front of the door, then turned around and walked down the stairs like her behavior wasn't notable.

She settled into the passenger seat and I pulled out onto the road, her posture stiff.

"How's your sister?" I asked, attempting to ease some of her tension.

It had the opposite effect. She squinted, her nails digging into the seat.

"She's fine," Jade bit out, then turned her body towards the window and shut me out.

Drumming my fingers on the wheel, I mulled over her response. My mission might be more challenging than I thought, but I would only accept one outcome from tonight's dinner.

By the end of the night, Jade would be coming home with me to Timber Creek.

She was quiet the rest of the drive, and I let the silence linger, already having won this first round since she hadn't opened the car door and jumped out yet.

The valet opened my door as we pulled up in front of the steakhouse, but Jade had already hopped out before the other attendant rounded the car.

He scrambled to open the restaurant door for her instead, and Jade paused her stomping momentarily to offer what she surely meant to pass as a kind smile but was definitely more of a grimace.

I chuckled as I handed the valets an extra tip and pulled off my sport coat, tossing it back into the truck. "Thank you, boys."

"Have a great night, sir," the teenager said as he ducked his head, feeling the wave of Alpha power rolling off me even though they were very human.

"I intend to."

Soft piano music drifted in from the bar across the room as the hostess led us to our seats, avoiding Jade's gaze. I was almost positive Jade had no idea how much of a *fuck off* vibe she put out, but it only made me that much more curious.

It was so rare I was challenged like this, and I was more than willing to step up to the plate for her.

Unbuttoning the cuffs of my sleeves, I rolled the fabric up, placing the pack tattoos on my forearms on display. She'd stared at them yesterday in the parking lot, and I wasn't above using her attraction to me against her.

I sipped at my beer as I stared at her across the table once we'd been seated. "Tell me about yourself."

Jade scanned the dimly lit restaurant, constantly on guard, but tilted her head and narrowed her eyes at me. "Was that a question or a demand?"

I smiled, even though her attitude was disrespectful by shifter standards. "I apologize. Jade, I'd love to know more about you. Would you like to share?"

She blinked at my apology, then grabbed her beer and took a sip. "No thanks."

I rested my elbows on the table, working my jaw while I tried to summon every ounce of patience I had to outlast this little power struggle she instigated.

No matter how refreshing her challenge was, I was used to being obeyed.

As Alpha, there was magic laced in my commands that made those under my power jump to do as I said, but Jade seemed almost unaffected by it.

No matter how much Togo wanted to follow my brothers' advice and throw her over my shoulder, Heath's words rang in my ears.

"All right," I said, holding her gaze as she subtly smirked. "Would you like to know about me, then?"

She reached forward to sip at her beer again, but her defiant dark eyes never left mine as she lifted the glass to her lips and paused. "No thanks."

I huffed at her audacity, slowly shaking my head as I asked Togo for the thousandth time why we couldn't just let this woman go.

Mine, he growled in my mind, and I questioned his intelligence.

Before I could come up with anything else to say, our meals

arrived. Jade attacked her steak like she hadn't seen solid food in weeks. I cut into my own, eating slowly but not taking my eyes off her. Like I'd mentioned to my family last night, she was skinny — skinnier than she'd been five years ago when we'd first met — paler, too, with shadows under her eyes. Raking my eyes over her, I noted the wear in her clothing.

I scratched at my beard, pursing my lips. No wolf in my pack would ever live like this.

Jade kept glancing up at me as she ate, her rich brown eyes like the darkest honey full of suspicion, waiting for me to pounce.

Figuratively, of course.

"So?" she said at last, and I hid my smirk. That was twice now I'd won just by waiting her out. Her impatience would be her downfall in the pack, and she didn't even know it.

If I could convince her to join us.

She wiped the napkin delicately over her mouth like she hadn't just inhaled a steak the size of her head, then leaned back in her chair, taking a small forkful of her mashed potatoes. Waving it in the air, she said, "Let me have it. Give me your best speech about why I should join your cult so I can turn you down again and be on my way."

I watched her raptly, something about the moment captivating, and witnessed the ecstasy wash across her face at the flavor. She let out a soft groan of appreciation, and instantly, my jeans were tight. I shifted in my chair. "Sounds like you already have it down pat."

"Yeah, but you came all this way, tracking me down or whatever, right? I wouldn't want to rob you of your big moment," she said around a mouthful of potato, then swallowed and rested her arms on the table. Just that small move had her citrusy scent washing over me, and Togo took a deep inhale, savoring it.

"How *did* you find me?" Narrowing her eyes, she stabbed her fork in my direction. "Have you been stalking me?"

I chuckled, omitting that I had been keeping a loose eye on

her for the last few years, but had no idea she was back in the Rocky Mountains until yesterday. "No."

"Did Ruby tell you where to find me, then?"

"No, I haven't spoken to your sister since I last saw her in Deadlights Cove. I was in town to buy gas and groceries and caught your scent."

Her eyes narrowed even further, full of distrust.

"Call it fate, Jade. This is the closest town to Timber Creek with a good grocery store." For all she fought against joining my pack, she had settled down *mighty* close by. "Or did you forget that's where I live?"

She put her nose in the air, her plate all but licked clean at last, and inspected her nails. "I suppose I must have."

"My *cult*, as you call it" — I leaned forward, bracing my forearms on the table, and her eyes darted down to them and then quickly away — "could offer you protection. Friends. Family. A community." I paused, waiting for her attention to come back to mine, and after a minute, it did. "A good job and a decent place to live."

She rolled her eyes, and I fought the warning that rumbled in my throat at her disrespect. As far as I knew, she'd never lived in a pack. The gesture was disrespectful, shifter or not, but did she know how much the move baited my wolf? I doubted it.

"I don't need your charity, West."

"Really?" I motioned to her plate, then to the two takeout containers next to it. With a pointed look, I silently reminded her I'd seen her apartment. "You don't have to live like this. It's not safe."

"I'm just — it's been — I don't —" she spluttered, trying to come up with excuses, her cheeks heating as she crumpled her napkin and put it on the table, her eyes roaming the restaurant again. "I'm between jobs, okay? That's all. The job I moved here for fell through and I'm working on finding another one." Her eyes snapped back to mine in challenge, and any vulnerability in her voice was gone as quickly as it had come on. "I don't need anyone, or any help."

I leveled a stare at her, since the job thing was yet another reason for her to come to the Creek.

"I'll find another job soon, and everything will be fine. I just had to lie low for a bit after my last one fizzled out."

I raised an eyebrow, issuing a silent command for her to explain that anyone in my pack would immediately follow. When she did, Togo was momentarily soothed.

"There was a drunk customer one night," she started, her shoulders rolling in as she stared at the table.

The change in her posture was enough to catch my attention, my teeth clenching as I waited for her to continue.

Her voice dropped, quiet enough none of the other diners would hear her, and she scanned the restaurant for the fifth time. "He followed me out back when I was taking out the trash, and I sort of lost it on him. Shoved him too hard when he approached and my wolf came forward. My eyes shifted before I could stop it, and he saw."

My entire body went rigid at the thought of some asshole human trying to put his hands on her, but I didn't dare interrupt, afraid she'd withhold any more information.

She cleared her throat. "Anyway, even though he was drunk, he started hollering about me being *one of them shifters* and that he'd report me to the cops. I couldn't take the chance that he'd remember the next day and actually do it, so I took all the money I could from the register and cleared out of town."

"Where?" I bit out, Togo pushing forward in my consciousness.

Jade waved a hand in the air at my question, like it didn't matter, and my teeth ground together. Like she knew if she told me, I'd hunt this loser down and rip his arms off.

Huh. Maybe she had my number after all.

"Relax, West. Nothing actually happened. I can take care of myself."

There was a challenge in there, one I'd have loved to take on and wrestle with until she finally submitted to the idea that I was right and she belonged in a pack where we all looked after and took care of each other. Where something like *that* would never happen to her.

But I couldn't force her to join us. Some Alphas would rope in any wolf who came across their territory unauthorized, but that wasn't the way I ran my pack. When she joined us, it would be because she chose to, not because I threw her over my shoulder and dragged her kicking and screaming to the pack house until she submitted to me like my brothers had suggested.

Even if the thought of that alone was enough to tent my jeans under the table.

"It could happen again," I said, my voice deeper than before.

She lifted a shoulder and finished her beer. "Then I'll know what to do the next time, won't I?"

"This isn't a joke, Jade," I whispered. "Humans are learning more about us all the time. Shifters keep going missing. It's only getting more dangerous to live on your own." My hand curled into a fist on the table as I restrained myself from grabbing her, from putting my scent all over her as the barest form of protection I could offer. But it wouldn't do any good against humans, anyway, who couldn't scent for shit. "You *need* to be with a pack."

"And I should just join yours? Over anybody else's?" She crossed her arms over her chest, raising an eyebrow as she assessed me and seemed to find me lacking. "You didn't even bring me a cake. Besides, I don't see your brochure. How do I know it would be the right fit? What are your benefits like? Does your health insurance cover massages?"

I took a breath, debating if I should say the first thought that occurred to me, and decided even if it was cruel, it was the truth and she needed to hear it. "You should join *my* pack," I said slowly, making sure she heard every word, "because it's not any Alpha who would take you."

Her eyes flashed with hurt at my insinuation, even if she misunderstood my meaning. Alphas wouldn't turn her down because of her current circumstances. Hell, that would probably make them line up at her door, ready to save her just as I was trying to do. But Jade didn't understand pack dynamics, a fact she made evident every time she refused to break my stare, and that caused instability in a pack — something most Alphas wouldn't tolerate.

"Well that's fine with me, since I have no interest in seeking out any Alpha anyway."

I opened my mouth to explain myself better, but she cut me off.

"How's Max?"

How's Max? Togo bared his teeth, not at all pleased to hear Jade asking about another male. How much of her behavior tonight was intentional, just to goad me? Was the question to get back at me after I'd insinuated no other Alpha would want her?

But then I met her eyes, open and full of concern, and I knew she wouldn't do that. Of course she would ask about the literal angel who'd saved her and her sister.

"Is he still living in Timber Creek?"

"He doesn't live there, but he stops in now and again. Which you'd know if you came with me to Timber Creek."

"Pass, but nice try." She paused before adding, almost hesitantly, "Just tell him I say hi if you see him?"

I shook my head with a sigh, handed a wad of bills to our waiter the next time he walked by, then tossed a business card over to Jade.

"When you change your mind, call me. You're welcome whenever you come around."

Chapter Five

JADE

I glared at West's cocky retreating back as he left to go get his truck from the valet — *not* at his ass, or how good his jeans made it look — and crumpled his business card, tossing it across the table.

When you change your mind, he said. Not *if.* Like it was inevitable I'd join him in Timber Creek. It was only a matter of time.

Smug bastard.

Did the promise of a job, a safe place to live, and food on the table sound nice? Of course it did. But I wasn't naive. Nothing good was ever that easy. And besides, I wasn't happy with the way Balto panted in his presence like a needy pup. I had a track record of choosing terrible men, and no matter what my wolf thought of him, I didn't trust West as far as I could throw him.

I let out a deep sigh that betrayed my frustration over the whole evening, wishing I'd ordered another beer before he paid the tab.

West had me so twisted around with his stupid masculine, Alpha scent, I completely forgot to rip him a new one for the whole sending-Ruby-right-into-the-heart-of-danger thing. He'd promised Deadlights Cove was the safest place for her, and look how *that* had turned out.

Next time.

No! There wouldn't *be* a next time. I was never going to see West again, which was for the best. I loved the Rocky Mountains, but maybe this wasn't meant to be. I should have known even over an hour from West was too close to his pack land. Unlike me, his sniffer wasn't broken — he'd find me again no matter where I was around here.

My wolf growled in my mind, baring her teeth and I jerked my head up, looking around the room for what had caught her attention.

Pulling on her senses to try and find that scent I'd been running from for years, I scanned the crowded restaurant for the golden-blond hair I saw in my nightmares. Cataloging every face in the room, I clutched my hands into fists under the table, ready to run. A middle-aged man walked by my table, briefly meeting my gaze, but maybe because I was sitting there sniffing like a lunatic.

"Ready?" West said as he approached, then froze, his eyes flashing a molten gold color for a split second. "What's wrong?"

"Nothing." I pushed back from the table, weaving around him towards the door, needing to get out of here.

Head ducked, I hurried outside and practically dove into the truck. Not until West pulled away from the restaurant did I breathe easily, and even then, I studied the mirrors, checking for cars tailing us back to my apartment.

"Turn here." I pointed towards a backroad that led out of town, a roundabout way back to my place, but was off the main road enough I'd notice any odd cars following us.

"Tell me what's wrong," West demanded, his voice deeper and frustrated enough to draw my attention.

"Nothing."

"Bullshit, Jade. You panicked back there. Your wolf was ready to shift in the middle of a human restaurant to defend you. I don't need to tell you how dangerous that would have been."

I recoiled, scowling at him. "No. I had — *have* her under control."

He sighed so loud it could have served as a backup A/C unit in the truck. "Your wolf is riding so close to the surface, you're a loose cannon, Jade. A starving wolf puts you even more at risk. Can't you feel it? She's ready to snap."

Feeling defensive, I checked the mirror again, relieved to see no one had followed us down the backroad. "You don't know me. Stay out of my business, West."

He let silence fall between us, but I could have cut the tension with a plastic spork. Aside from pointing out directions back to my place, I said nothing.

I hopped out of the cab before he'd even rolled to a complete stop at my apartment, but he threw it in park and rounded the truck before I'd taken two steps, backing me up against the passenger door. His huge body trapped me against the metal, his deadly calm fully focused on me.

"What. The fuck. Happened. Talk to me. Why were you scared?"

I bared my teeth, snapping back in his face as I pushed on his chest, fury moving through me in waves. How dare he insist I spill my guts to him? How dare he think he could just swoop in and fix my sad little life? How dare he be so demanding, masking it as protective instincts?

I shoved him again, harder, and he finally moved out of my way. I wasn't stupid enough to believe I could overpower him. "None of your business, West. I'm not interested in anything you have to offer. I wasn't before now, but this whole alphahole act is enough to solidify my answer to you is *never.* That's when I'll be joining your pack."

"Jade, wait," West said as I was halfway up the steps. "Fuck. I'm sorry."

I paused with one foot in the air, hearing the sincerity of his words, but didn't bother turning to look back at him. "Too late, West. You showed your true colors, and they're shit brown."

Slamming the door when I entered, I threw my takeout bags on the counter and shoved my head between my knees, letting out both the panic I'd felt in the restaurant as well as my anger at West.

I opened my mouth to let out a scream when a small knock sounded at the door. Snapping upright, I spun, heart racing as I looked at the locks I forgot to flip over. I *never* did that.

My hands trembled as I reached for the knife on the kitchen counter, ready to defend myself, my eyes flashing to my wolf's as she readied to take over if needed, when something slid under the door.

Another business card.

I dropped the knife, the metal clattering to the floor as I let out a breath, flexing my fingers to release the tension, a sure sign Balto had been ready to shift my nails to claws.

I stormed over to the door and swiped up the card before tossing it in the trash.

Chapter Six

JADE

"Order up! Hello? Carmen?"

I flinched, then shook myself, remembering the name I'd put on my job application. If Ms. Sandiego could stay hidden, maybe I could too.

Just like I'd told West, I'd found a job here at the Broken Spoke a few days after our dinner. I always got back on my feet.

Shooting Patrick, the cook, a smile, I grabbed the dishes and dropped them off to the patrons with an apology about the wait.

Tonight was a full moon, and Balto was restless, distracting me as she paced in my mind. I'd gone for a long run this morning, trying to work out my excess energy, but my skin still crawled.

The Broken Spoke was a typical dive bar and grill, full of locals in the little mountain town. Everything smelled like fried food and liquor, but the lights were dim and I easily blended in with the shadows in the room when I wasn't serving. The customers weren't bad, and my manager had me working day shifts, which was good because it meant I was done before dusk.

After dark, Balto's instincts were harder to control. Like our canine counterparts, my wolfy urges liked to come out to play at dawn and dusk, and that was if Balto felt normal. I wasn't sure what about this latest move made her so uneasy, but nothing about my wolf felt normal these days.

A quick glance at the neon clock on the wall said I had

minutes until sunset. Tonight was my first evening shift and I'd be working right through dusk on a full moon.

I tried to focus on *Shapeshifting* by Taylor Acorn playing in the bar, controlling my breathing to the beat of the music as I wiped down the counters and kept Balto at bay. A steady *tap-tap* on the counter to my right snagged my attention. My hand stilled as I looked down at the far end of the bar, where a man was waving his empty glass at me.

"Sorry about that, my mind drifted away there," I said, throwing the guy a smile, and swiped his glass. "Same?"

He grunted in the affirmative, and I spun around to make another drink.

"New in town?" he asked as I poured. It was an innocuous enough question, but it raised the hair on the back of my neck and Balto bared her teeth in my mind. I tried to hide my appraisal of him, but nothing about the mid-fifties man stood out. A quick sniff told me he was human, and the tension in my shoulders lessened marginally.

Maybe it was the moon, messing with me still.

"Yep," I said, popping the P, and slid his fresh drink over. The more I studied him, he looked vaguely familiar, but I couldn't place where I'd seen him before. "Are you a regular I should know?"

"Regular enough." He raked a contemplative gaze over me, and Balto paced, teeth still bared in silent threat. His greying hair and wrinkled hands said he was old enough to be my father — not that that meant he couldn't still be a creep, but I wasn't picking up an aggressive drunk vibe from him. The longer his focus stayed on me, the more his scrutinizing gaze bothered me.

Maybe he was a local cop.

Shit. Was there a chance I'd show up on human wanted lists? Max had assured me he'd taken care of all that, but I hadn't followed up on it, removed as I was from all things supe society.

I focused on my breathing again, needing to control the

adrenaline spike that was sure to make Balto worse. As much as I wanted to tuck tail and run, I needed this job more. Feeling the attention of my manager on my back, I reached out my hand and plastered on what was hopefully a friendly smile.

"I'm Carmen. Hopefully I'll be around here a while, Sort-of-Regular," I said, and his hand slid into mine, one firm shake, then detached.

"Bennett," he said, then turned his attention to his phone, and I got back to work.

The rest of the evening passed smoothly, the bar shoulder-to-shoulder at one point since it was a Saturday night, and this was the only watering hole around that wasn't full of tourists and overpriced drinks.

I served other patrons, but I kept an eye on Bennett, nursing his drink. He never chatted with anyone else, glued to his phone until he slapped some cash on the bar and left at about 11:30.

There was nothing particularly alarming about his behavior — he didn't watch me relentlessly, he didn't say anything off-color when I passed, but Balto would not let me lose focus on the man.

I was exhausted by the time we finally closed up around 1 a.m., just me and Patrick.

"Want me to walk you to your car?" Patrick set the alarm, and we walked out the back door together into the crisp night air.

Ahh, Balto turned over and stretched in my mind, scenting freedom soon as the bright moon shone down.

"Nah, I'm good, thanks." I waved as we parted ways and I made for my truck.

"Night."

He made it to his car before I did, and his engine turned over with a wheeze. We waved again as he passed in front of my truck.

Like it so often did, my key stuck in the door, refusing to turn.

I pulled it out, ready to try the passenger door instead when Balto's ears pricked, sensing a presence behind me.

Spinning, my eyes shifted without my permission. Bennett stood forty paces away in the shadow of the bar, purposefully out of the streetlight's glow, his eyes locked on me. And suddenly, in the dim light, I knew where I'd seen him before — he'd been at the steakhouse.

My hackles raised for real this time, canines elongating as Balto prepared for a fight. She didn't care about exposing herself to human society and the danger that would put us in. She had a single-minded focus on our safety. With West's warnings about missing shifters ringing in my ears, I wasn't sure I wanted to fight her on it.

"What do you want?" I called over, my voice steady while my heart raced in my chest. Maybe he'd leave and this wouldn't escalate.

"Not what you think." He didn't sound surprised I could see him over there in the dark. He stepped closer slowly, gauging my reaction with each foot gained.

Sliding my keys through my fingers, I curled them into a fist like I'd done so many times before, preparing for the worst. I tried to shift my eyes back as he got close enough to see them, knowing the way Balto's eyes glowed in the dark would be a dead giveaway, but they insisted on staying wolfed out.

Damn it, Balto, this is not the time to play games!

I blinked rapidly, as though that would help, then stared directly into the streetlight, knowing it would be too bright for her senses.

My eyes shifted back, and I let out a quick sigh of relief before turning my attention back to Bennett.

His scent marked him as human, but my ignorance of magic reared its ugly head. Could scents be masked? I wasn't sure, and my canines elongated at the many possibilities rolling through my head.

Was he a witch? A shifter? His jacket hid his arms — to hide pack tattoos? Or just because it was a chill mountain night?

Six feet away, he lunged for me, and I leapt back, my eyes shifting again as I snarled, teeth bared before I could help it.

That was when I realized my reaction was exactly what he wanted. He nodded, seemingly to himself, then spoke into his wrist like he was playing at being a spy.

"Got one."

I slapped at the sharp prick in my neck before I ever saw the tranq dart coming.

Gravel bit into my knees as I crumpled, and the world went dark.

)))●(((

The edges of the world were blurry when I woke up, my hands bound in the back of a van.

Shit shit shit.

Had *he* found me? Had he sent these guys? Fuck, this never would've happened if I'd gone with West.

I whimpered internally. Now would be a great time for wolf telepathy to be real.

I bit my lip. *West?*

Nothing. Of course.

Then I realized Balto was unnaturally silent. Whatever they'd had in that tranq gun was enough to dampen my connection to her.

Balto, I reached out in my mind, panic taking over. *Don't leave me now, girl. I can't get out of this on my own.*

She whined, but the connection between our souls still felt blurred.

You need to relax, I reminded myself.

Willing myself to be calm, I took in my surroundings.

Two humans sat in the front seat, but they hadn't noticed I was awake yet, and I aimed to keep it that way.

They had to think they had the advantage. It was the best way for me to pick my moment to get the drop on them.

As silently as I could, I tested the binding around my wrists, and nearly let out a cry of joy when I felt plastic.

Plastic zip ties. Thank the goddess or whatever Ruby always said. *He* hadn't sent these guys. *He* would know better than to use plastic zip ties for a shifter. I had to hope this meant my captors were ignorant on my other shifter traits, too.

I just needed Balto to wake up, and the zip ties would be gone before my kidnappers even knew what hit them.

I looked for other mistakes these idiots might have made. The back door of the van had an interior handle, which was good news for me. Not so good: from the speed and sway of the van, I guessed we were on the highway. It would be a suicide mission to jump out while we were going 75 mph, and I had no idea where we were or how far we'd gone.

While I waited for the van to exit the highway, I tried to gather clues as to who these people were. Some special branch of the NSA or FBI as a best-case-scenario option, but their ignorance made me doubt that theory.

Worst case scenario, I didn't even want to think about. I mentally kicked myself for not asking West more about the missing shifters problem, wondering what I'd accidentally gotten myself into. I tried to hide from supe society, but I hadn't spent much time thinking about hiding from humans, and it had been my downfall.

If there were independent psychos out there trying to track down shifters, I was in far more danger than I realized. Humans had known about shifters for the last five years, and relations were tense at best, but even in my hypervigilance to run from my past, I'd dismissed humans, trusting Balto to keep us safe if a situation came about. This was the sort of thing you always thought couldn't possibly happen to you, like winning the lottery.

My lucky night.

The humans had their music cranked all the way up, so if they were talking, I couldn't hear them over the racket, but at least it hid the rustling as I worked to loosen the ties.

Eventually, we turned off the highway onto a side street. I recognized some of the towns listed on the signs, so at least we were still in Colorado. I just had to get free, then backtrack to grab my cash and split.

I waited until a particularly loud part of the song, then inched my way towards the back door. Not sparing the humans a glance, I used my foot to push down the handle, and ignored their cry of outrage as I leapt out the back and rolled. I ignored the burn of the pavement scraping my skin, pushing past my pain and back to my feet. The van was still screeching to a halt as I took off into the woods.

C'mon, Balto, now's your chance, I thought, hoping the surge in adrenaline would be enough to pull her back to consciousness. She stirred, sluggish, but pulled closer to the surface.

Sweat dripped off my brow as the humans cursed and thundered after me, but even in my human form and half-drugged, I could run faster than them and see in the dark. I put on a burst of speed, getting as far away as I could, then ducked behind a shadowy thicket, and screamed in my mind, *NOW.*

I *hated* shifting, the snap of pain through every single bone, but it was even worse with my hands tied. Still, with Balto's strength, I ripped through the plastic, the zipties falling at my feet, and a moment later, she took over.

Scent filled my nose, the clean pine resin, the clay at my paws. Something was altering my strength, some human toxin, but I was still powerful, my claws still sharp enough to tear flesh.

My lips pulled back as I scented Bennett and the other human on me. I turned, crouching low to the ground as I prepared to fight, but Jade, my human soul, fought me, pulling with every ounce of power she had to turn me away from my retribution.

RUN!

I shook off Jade's command, saliva dripping off my sharp canines as the human prey gained on me.

NOW! *She screamed, and Jade's fear was so overwhelming, I turned my back to the men and we were off like a shadow in the night.*

I ran for what felt like hours, long after I'd lost them, following a tug in my power, a guiding force within me.

I ran until my paws were cut up, my energy drained too much for Jade's healing magic to keep up, my muscles all but giving out. No matter how tired I was, I refused to stop, putting one paw in front of the other until a familiar scent filled my lungs. With a pathetic whimper, my entire body shook with exhaustion and relief and the aftershocks of fear.

I slowed to a lumbering, ambling gait that felt like I was barely moving at all.

But I kept moving forward. One paw in front of the other.

A low chuffing sound stopped me, and I picked up my head, one ear cocked. A giant, storm-cloud grey wolf faced me, just as beautiful as I knew he'd be, his glowing amber eyes locked onto mine.

West's piney scent was unmistakable even deep in the woods, as familiar to me as my own flesh and blood.

Jade tensed, unsure what to do next. We'd never associated with other wolves, and instinct told me I should roll over and show my belly, or bare my neck in a show of respect for the much larger Alpha, but Jade balked at the idea.

Should we shift back? *Jade asked, her voice trembling in a way that made me want to refuse her.* Then we're both naked though, and that's weird.

I huffed at her thoughts. Nudity should mean nothing to her, but she hadn't spent enough time among our own kind.

Instead of letting her take our consciousness back over, I stayed frozen and waited for West to make the first move.

He stalked forward, and something deep inside me purred at the predator in my midst. West was full-wolf, not a halfsie like us, and all my senses told me that in a fight, it would count.

When he was beside me, the top of my head was barely at his shoulder, convenient as he placed his chin on the back of my neck.

A low growl erupted from my throat, my own Alpha instincts balking when confronted with his dominance, even if all he did was stand over me.

That strange chuffing sound came from him again — amusement.

Suddenly, he pressed his weight down on me, forcing me to lie down. I growled again but folded my legs under me, belly to the cold earth as West circled me.

Jade stayed silent, her anger over this display dimmed by pure exhaustion, and for once, she trusted my instincts.

West sniffed my paws, caked in mud and blood, and went stiff as a board.

Between one minute and the next, the hulking grey wolf shifted into a giant naked man.

I yelped, leaping backwards, but he grabbed me by the scruff of my neck.

"Shift," West commanded, and I whimpered at the sheer dominance in his tone. Magic buzzed across my fur while Jade cringed at the implications of what listening to him meant, but I didn't have a choice.

A minute later, Balto's consciousness was subdued again, and I was human. A scrawny, naked human alone in the woods at night with a giant of a male.

"What the hell happened to your feet?" West barked.

"I ran," I said through chattering teeth, frozen with the loss of Balto's downy fur. "Can I shift back now?"

"No. Ran from what? And from your apartment? Jade, that's almost 30 miles. Why aren't you healing?"

I crossed my arms over my chest, even though he'd already seen everything at this point. Balto was amused by my anxiety, but standing around naked trying to have a conversation would never be normal to me.

"Humans kidnapped me, and I escaped. I'm not healing

because I think it's been hours. I'm drained, and I've never healed as quickly as a full-shifter anyway."

His nostrils flared as he leaned over me. Even knowing he was scenting the humans on me didn't relieve the strange mix of emotions I felt with him this close, none of which were fear. Fatigue, I had in spades. Embarrassment, yep. And freaking arousal — that one could kick rocks. Balto grinned in delight.

His chest rose and fell rapidly as anger filled him. "They knew what you are?"

I swallowed, nodding, as West's jaw worked violently.

"Shit," he said at last, then stepped closer.

The heat of his body washed over me, and my body responded by leaning in, wanting to soak in the steady comfort he offered.

Before I could allow something so *stupid* to happen, I forced myself back. He leveled a glare at me.

"I'm carrying you in, and then you're going to tell me the whole story."

"I can walk myself just fine, wolf man."

His lip twitched. "Your feet are all cut up, and it's still a long way back. I'm carrying you." He lurched forward again, but I threw a hand up, clutching the other hand tight across my chest.

"At least let me shift back first." I met his eyes, hoping he could understand what I wasn't saying. What I *couldn't* say.

Comprehension seemed to dawn on him that I might not be quite as comfortable with the whole nudity thing as he was, and he nodded stiffly, turning his back to let me shift.

Balto was all too happy to take over again, ready to rub herself all over West, which made this shift much smoother than the first tonight.

Once Jade settled into the back of my consciousness, West scooped me up into his strong arms, carrying me through the woods in the moonlight. I rested my head on his shoulder as his hand rubbed the fur at the nape of my neck, and I let out a shuddering breath.

"Shh, it's all right now. I got you."

Chapter Seven

WEST

Togo was ecstatic and furious, in turn. Prancing. Howling for joy. Growling and out for blood for the humans I could scent on Jade.

Calm the fuck down, we don't know the whole story yet.

Jade was in my arms. Wasn't that enough? She'd run to *me*. My lands. My scent.

Pack. Mark. Scent. Destroy. Protect.

I nearly stumbled over a root as my wolf's urges barrelled into me. His instincts to make her fully pack and protect her were the sharpest temptation, but there was no way I could mark and scent her now. She'd immediately passed out when I picked her up, her grey wolf form so small in my arms.

I let out an exasperated sigh. I had to turn off those thoughts before I got myself into trouble with her. Jade was on edge on a *good* day, let alone when she'd just run for her life. She'd already shut down at my first Alpha command. I couldn't be like other Alphas, not if I wanted her to stay.

I wanted to take care of her, to make her see the good in the world and protect her from the bad.

Like the asshole kidnappers I could still scent on her.

A low rumble escaped my throat as I thought through everything I needed to do to put an end to this. Supernatural politics were no different than humans — everything moved at a snail's-pace, but the threat to shifters had just knocked on my door, and I was done.

Once I crossed the perimeter onto the pack house property, I called out mentally for Terran.

"Prepare Aspen's room."

I felt his answering confusion. With the full moon tonight, most of the pack was still out running around, connecting with their wolves, but Terran never went far from the pack house where River was left behind.

"I found a — stray. She's injured."

"She?"

"I'll explain when we get home."

Home. Yes, Jade's home now, Togo rumbled contentedly.

Sensing my unease through the pack bonds, several wolves paced the property line, snouts in the air, wondering what was going on.

"Alpha?" Jett, one of the bolder males in the pack, sent. He'd been gunning to move up ranks for a while and I fought back a sneer at the over-step. *"Who is she?"*

I didn't bother with a response, slamming down my mental walls around my connection with the pack and sent a clear message to my brothers and father. It was none of Jett's business, and despite his and the others' interest, my family wouldn't let them come onto the property tonight without my approval.

Not unless they wanted to lose a fight.

As the back of the house came into view, the basement glass door slid open, and Leif stepped out into the night.

"West? Is that her?" His blond hair was rumpled after what was more than likely a quick shift, but as he caught her scent, his eyes sharpened. "She's bleeding."

"Go to sleep, Leif. There's nothing to do until she gets some rest."

"Did you already check her for trackers?"

That was our typical protocol for any strays that wandered in, but I hadn't stopped for that long, needing to get Jade safe and in my domain first. Day one and she had me breaking my own rules and barking at my family — off to a wonderful start.

"Go to bed."

He frowned as we passed by him into the basement, letting out the barest whimper at being unable to help her, but he did as I said. Sliding the door shut behind us, Leif went back to his room, the door shutting softly as I ascended the stairs.

"Room's all set," Terran said when I reached the upstairs landing, looking over the sleeping wolf in my arms with curiosity. "You found her out in the woods?"

I nodded. "She met with some trouble and ran here for help."

Our sister's room still held her lavender scent and her signature mid-century style, even though Aspen didn't live here anymore. Usually, we put injured wolves and stray shifters in the basement, in one of the ensuite rooms like Leif's, but neither Togo or I would hear of having her that far away.

Since Jade didn't belong to a pack, it wouldn't be safe, the logical side of my mind tried to justify itself. As I'd already seen tonight, wolves were nosy creatures. Any wolf passing through would want to sniff her out, to determine her power rank in the pack.

Her room placement had nothing to do with the fact that, if she took Aspen's room, she and I would share a wall.

Terran set a towel down over the comforter to keep it clean before I placed Jade on top, still sound asleep. That alone was testament to how exhausted she was — any other wolf would have woken up at Leif and Terran's presence, alert in case they posed a threat.

I hated to leave her alone, but she needed rest more than she needed me hovering over her right now.

Closing the bedroom door behind me, Terran and I paused in the hall, his eyes full of questions, even if he managed not to ask them yet.

"She was kidnapped."

My brother's brow furrowed instantly, darting a glance at the closed door, then down the hall to the door his daughter slept behind. "By who?"

"Humans. They knew she was a shifter," I sighed, turning and heading towards my own bedroom to grab some sweats.

Terran trailed behind me, muttering a fervent, "Shit."

Shit, indeed.

"What do you need me to do?" Terran asked while I dressed. "Cooper, Atlas, and I could head out tonight —"

"Call Max," I cut in with a frustrated huff. "As much as I want to hunt these bastards down, she thinks she ran dozens of miles to get here. It's too far to track a scent tonight, especially if they're in a car."

Terran paused, standing in the doorway as he eyed me carefully. "Is she the same wolf from last week? The one you took on a date?"

I narrowed my eyes. "It wasn't a date."

"Now feels like a terrible time for semantics, so I'll drop it."

"Call Max." My words were full of Alpha command.

Terran saluted, the small gesture sarcastic even if he had to obey me, then turned to head back to his room down the hall.

Too on edge to sleep, I threw myself onto the couch set to the side in my room and turned on the video game console, muting it so I'd hear anything from the room next door.

It was going to be a long, sleepless night.

Chapter Eight

JADE

"New in town?"

A prick in my neck.

Plastic ties around my wrists.

Running and running and running —

I woke with a gasp, flashes of the night before haunting me.

But I'd escaped. I'd gotten out, and run, and made it to —

Jolting upright, I took a ragged breath, trying to get my bearings in the pack house. Light filtered in through the blinds, but I had no idea what time it was or how long I'd been out. Exhaustion still rode me hard, but after everything I'd been through, that wasn't surprising.

Rubbing sleep from my eyes, I took in the room around me, all too aware West's pine scent was everywhere. This room didn't feel like him, though. It had a feminine touch — funky mid-century modern furnishings, clean floral accents, but nothing to indicate anyone currently lived here. No photos, no knickknacks, no books. On top of the small dresser was a pile of fresh clothes and a water bottle, and beside it a door was cracked open to an ensuite bathroom.

Much as I wanted to burrow down into the blankets, go back to sleep, and hide from all the wolf business that would undoubtedly go down once I emerged from this room, I knew I had to face it.

I must have shifted back to my human form in my sleep, but otherwise my body still wasn't healing quickly, my feet and palms cut up from running on four legs. I peeled myself out of bed gingerly, wincing at my sore muscles, and downed the water bottle in one go.

Everything hurt. Muscles I hadn't even known I had spasmed and thrashed, shouting their protest from the rooftops. My entire body was covered in dirt, my hands and feet bruised and caked in blood, mud, and pine needles. I grimaced at myself before limping into the bathroom to clean up.

Once I'd showered and freshened up thanks to the toiletries left out for me, I pulled on the clothes. The joggers and sweatshirt both had a Timber Creek logo on them, a mountain range silhouette with moon phases above. No shoes, but maybe that was too much to ask. It wasn't like West was obligated to dress me, and I was already indebted to him more than I liked.

I turned and stared at the door. The final step. It loomed at me, seeming huge, or maybe I shrank.

I was the size of a mouse, in a den of wolves. They were going to eat me alive.

Shit, this is why I avoid packs.

Taking a deep, steadying breath, I pulled my shoulders back, bra or no. I wasn't a mouse, I was an *Alpha*, even if I was a Lone wolf who was actually only *half*-wolf and who generally preferred pretending my wolf side didn't exist at all.

But that ship had sailed the moment Balto ran straight here, and I wasn't about to let *anyone* intimidate me. I'd only come here to regroup and warn West that those shifter hunters were nearby, then I'd be on my way again.

Pack, Balto sighed, her contentment flowing through me in waves.

Absolutely not, I shot back, shoving her down in my consciousness like I did every time she rose too close to the surface. Even with her muted, I could feel her smug satisfaction that she'd run until she scented home.

This wasn't home, and Balto wasn't in charge, no matter how much she wanted to be. *I* was.

Ignoring her, I pulled open the door and walked out to find myself on an upper floor landing. To my left was another closed door where West's scent was strongest, so I assumed that room was his, and to my right I scented two unfamiliar wolves. In front of me was a huge, winding staircase, voices drifting up from the ground floor below.

I trailed the voices to a giant kitchen, my eyes bugging out at how spacious and fancy this mountain lodge was. The pewter-dipped antler chandelier in the foyer probably could have paid my rent for six months.

My senses zeroed in on the scent of bacon and I walked blindly towards it, vaguely aware of the voices breaking off. I was pretty sure my eyes turned into glowing hearts like a cartoon, saliva all but dripping out of my mouth, the scent of the savory meat a living, breathing thing calling out to me.

Come eat us!

Oh, don't you worry, bacon. You don't have to tell me twice.

I moved forward, intent on my prize, when a steel bar stopped me across my shoulders.

"Questions first, *then* eat. I saw how incapable you are of talking while eating last week."

I huffed, looking from the steel bar — actually an arm — to its owner, West. No surprise there.

"Two strips of bacon, then questions, then more bacon," I countered as West maneuvered me onto a barstool. His eyebrows shot up. Maybe he wasn't used to anyone trying to negotiate with him, but my stomach refused to cooperate.

"One, *while* we inspect your feet, then your hands, then you can have more."

"Sold." I dove for the plate before he could rethink the offer, swiping four strips of bacon and shoveling them in my mouth before he could stop me. West crossed his arms over his chest, and I smirked, barely containing the moan that threatened to escape. "Possession is nine-tenths the law."

Eyes never leaving mine, West called out, "Leif, First Aid kit."

"Yep!"

Scuffling sounded from my right as someone left the room, but I was locked in a staring contest with a wolf and had a mouthful of fatty deliciousness. I was busy.

"You tracked blood all over my house."

The statement made me blink, ending our stare off as I searched for evidence. Sure enough, streaks of blood dotted the floor where I'd just walked. I swallowed my bite, looking down at my feet and the scabs that had broken open again.

"Sorry about that. I solemnly swear to control my bleeding better next time."

I reached for more bacon, but my hand was slapped down.

"And your hands are bleeding all over the counter."

I frowned at the dark red spots on the light grey quartz, then slumped back in my seat, folding my hands in my lap.

A young guy with shaggy blond hair entered the room with a First Aid kit and sat in the stool next to mine.

"Hi, Jade, I'm Leif," he said brightly, opening the kit and pulling out wipes and bandages. "Right hand."

With a sideways glance at the bacon, I relented to the command. I winced as the alcohol wipe stung my cuts, annoyed at my own show of weakness. "You know who I am?"

He grinned as he set down the wipe and started applying cream. "I was up when you arrived last night, and my dad told me the bare minimum, so pretty much just your name. My room is in the basement if you ever need anything. Happy to help whenever."

Dad? My brow furrowed, looking between Leif, who I guessed was somewhere around Ruby's age, and then at West. It was a safe bet that he was older than me, but to think of him with a 20-year-old son was jarring. They looked nothing alike, making me think there was more to the story here, and I was more intrigued than I wanted to be.

"Jade," West cut through my thoughts, and Leif instantly stopped his charming rambling, his mouth snapping shut as he wrapped bandages around my hands. "Start at the beginning. Everything that happened yesterday."

)))●(((

I went through the whole story between mouthfuls of bacon, waffles, and fruit.

By the time I got to the part where I'd escaped my kidnappers, West sighed, running a hand over his beard. "Finish eating while I call my brothers in here, then we'll need to go through it all again."

Leif hopped off his barstool and headed to the back door while I swiped the last of my waffle through the syrup on my plate, casting a wayward glance towards West's phone on the counter.

"Don't you need to actually pick that up to make a call, or do you just expect Leif to do everything for you?"

West frowned, his head tilting to the side as he inspected me, and I fought the urge to squirm under his scrutiny. "How much do you know about wolf packs?"

I scoffed, letting my fork drop down on my plate with a loud clang, then pushed it across the counter. "Enough to know I want nothing to do with them."

West hummed, but didn't explain further as two men entered the room, one from the back door with Leif, and one from upstairs.

I braced for my familiar panic to ignite at the strangers, at being in a room with four males, but to my surprise — nothing. Even Balto was quiet.

"You rang?" the brother approaching from the foyer said, his nose tilted in the air. "Oh, good. You ate the food I made this morning. How was it?"

I looked between him and West, cataloging the many similarities — same hazel eyes and overall build, similar brown hair though this brother's was a shade darker and shaggier under his backwards baseball cap. His red flannel shirt was unbuttoned over a black shirt with some kind of buffalo logo, the same one Leif was wearing.

At that moment, his eyes slid past me, then widened.

"Leif! You were supposed to open Willie's today and it's already" — he glanced at the clock on the stove — "nine thirty!"

All eyes swung to Leif, whose pale cheeks flushed. "I'm going, Terran, I just wanted to meet her," he mumbled, practically running from the room.

Terran shook his head then moved to pour himself a cup of coffee, but by the amused look he shared with West, I could tell they weren't too upset with the kid.

"Willie's?" I asked.

West nodded towards Terran. "Jade, this is my brother and pack Second, Terran. He runs our family's restaurant in town."

Terran gave a wave and leaned back against the counter.

"And this is Cooper." West gestured to the other male in the room.

Where Terran came across a bit rumpled and friendly, Cooper was… not. A deep-set frown barely showed under his golden-brown beard, his shoulders almost twice as wide as his siblings. The worn jeans, flannel shirt, and dog tags only added to his grumpy lumberjack aesthetic, but his dark gaze felt more intimidating than sexy. Aside from their coloring, Cooper didn't share many similar features with his brothers, and I wondered how this family all fit together. There was more than just genetics at play here.

There was also something about his scent that didn't quite read *wolf*, even to my underused senses.

"Coffee before we get started, Jade?" Terran asked. Even if he was part of this cult/pack, he was already my favorite. First he made me bacon and waffles, now coffee?

"I'd love some." I smiled. I could have sworn West flinched at my reaction to Terran, but I couldn't be sure what had set off the alphahole this time.

We moved to the adjoining living room, and Terran joined us a minute later, handing over a steaming cup of coffee with a splash of milk.

Cooper leaned forward, elbows on his knees, his intense gaze zeroed in on me from across the coffee table. "When you're ready, Jade, we need to hear it all from the beginning." His voice was a deep purr, like faraway thunder, that had me wondering if he was some kind of cat shifter. If so, he was a big cat.

After a sip of my coffee, I sank back into the sofa and started the whole story over.

Each time I told it, new details came back to me, and I had a hard time keeping everything straight.

"Sorry," I said as I drained the last of my coffee, taking a deep breath that was in equal parts due to the story itself and the bottom of my coffee cup. Terran swapped my mug with a fresh one, and I grinned, wrapping my hands around the warmth.

"You did great," Terran said, and set the empty mug to the side. As much as I wanted to find something wrong with Terran so I could instantly dislike him like I did pretty much everyone these days, I came up blank.

West, Terran, and Cooper exchanged silent looks, and my attention drifted to the large picture windows. Rolling mountains and wildflowers stretched as far as the eye could see, sun shining off the aspen leaves dancing in the wind. This was why I kept coming back to Colorado.

"Let's have Zara come up and do a full physical so we can get a better gauge on her healing."

Terran pulled his phone out as he left the room, doing as

West said. Cooper stood to leave as well, some sort of silent communication going on between them all. Maybe it was a brother thing.

"Zara?"

"Local witch, and our best healer in town."

I froze, my heart dropping to my stomach. "No. Absolutely not. No witches, I refuse."

West frowned, crossing his arms. "We don't know what drugs those humans shot you up with, or what else they did to you while you were passed out."

"Um, hello?" I waved my heavily bandaged hands at him, trying to use logic to keep my panic at bay. "Leif took care of it. I don't need a healer. My wolf will take over after I've rested and eaten a few more pounds of Terran's food and I'll heal just fine. I can't feel any lasting effects of the drugs, either. Already out of my system."

West leveled a stare at me. He stood, heading out of the living room. "You're seeing a healer."

Even if my overwhelming anxiety wasn't screaming that it was time to go, that bossy tone wouldn't fly with me.

Hopping up, I limped after him down the hallway to an office. He made his way behind the desk and turned on the laptop sitting open.

"I said no witches." I leaned my hands down on the edge of his desk, my eyes mere slits in my face as I kept my voice even. Anger was easier than fear, and Balto was on my side in this argument.

West's eyes narrowed slightly before they flicked to his computer. "You don't know much about being a wolf, do you?"

I couldn't deny that. "I can't see how that has anything to do with the situation at hand."

"Everything." That hazel gaze settled on me as he placed his hands on the desk, giving me his full attention. I felt the challenge his stare off issued, but I wasn't about to bow down, not over this. "You're constantly disrespecting me."

Ugh, pack bullshit. This was exactly why I stayed away from packs. I rolled my eyes, ready to launch into a tirade about just that, but West cut me off.

"This is bigger than you and whatever your issue with witches is, Jade. You were taken, targeted as a shifter and kidnapped, then managed to escape. If there is even a trace of whatever drugs they used to dull your wolf, we need to find out what it is and how to counteract it to keep my pack safe." He raised a brow, urging me to find some argument against the safety of others. "I need to know with one-hundred percent certainty that they didn't stick you with a tracker and *let* you escape to lead them back to more shifters."

That pulled me up short. I froze, my breaths coming uneven as fear stole the strength from my legs, bringing me crashing down to the chair behind me. "Don't waste your time on a witch, even if she's a healer. Give me some shoes, and I'll be on my way."

West recoiled, all his fierce and commanding nature draining out of him. "I'm not kicking you out. You came to me for help, and that's exactly what I intend to do." He unclasped his hand, reaching one across the desk towards me, palm open. "Let me help you, Jade. I want to, and I think you need it."

Nausea swept over me at the thought of putting more people in danger by lingering here, feeling that same wash of guilt as when I spent time with Ruby. I stared at his hand, not sure what he expected of me, but I couldn't bring myself to touch him.

"Trouble finds me, West. No matter what I do, it's always like this."

"Good thing I have a whole pack for when it finds us."

I dropped my eyes, fiddling with the bandages on my hands as I thought through what would come next.

Us, he said.

It had been a long time since I was part of an *us*, and the last time, it hadn't ended well.

))) ● (((

Zara arrived, a black-haired witch about my age with a punky vibe, thanks to her black leather jacket and boots and heavily studded ears. West had assured me he trusted her, but since I didn't trust West, that meant jack shit.

I met with her alone, giving her questions one-word answers, refusing to elaborate on anything. She must have noticed, but didn't comment, pursing her lips as she hovered her hands over me in a witchy way that I probably should have known more about but didn't. Even when I'd lived with *them*, I'd been kept out of most witch activity, my power too low to do anything.

"You're sure you're feeling okay?" Zara asked, finishing her exam and sitting on the chair in the corner of my bedroom.

"Great," I deadpanned, and her eyes narrowed ever so slightly. I hesitated, afraid to give myself away, then decided I needed to know the answer. "Are you going to document this visit? I don't know how your practice works, but I'd rather not have it listed that I was here."

Zara studied me. "That's fine. I can leave your name out — we have enough visiting shifters coming and going, it won't seem odd. But Jade, I have to ask — are you hiding from something besides those kidnappers? West can keep —"

"No," I cut her off, not wanting to continue that line of thought. "Forget I asked. I'll be on my way as soon as I'm healed. Thanks again."

Zara nodded, packing up the rest of her medical bag, but I felt her eyes on me.

"Drink these electrolytes to flush out the last of the tranquilizer in your system, and your healing abilities should pick up from there once you're more rested," she said before she left the room. I followed her back downstairs to the kitchen where West stood, hands braced on the counter as I took up the same stool I'd sat on earlier this morning.

"All good," Zara said as she slipped a piece of paper over the counter to West. I wanted to grab it off the counter and throw it into the fireplace, but I balled my hands into fists to stop myself.

"She wasn't tagged?" West asked, and I held my breath. I'd somehow forgotten to ask about trackers, too busy being on guard in the presence of a witch.

"No tracker," Zara confirmed, and a breath whooshed out of me. "But it's probably safe to assume they won't make that mistake again." She snapped her bag of witchiness closed, and stood. "Even humans aren't total idiots."

With a final sympathetic smile, she left in a flurry of sage and patchouli.

"Okay, no tracker, drugs will be out of my system soon, my healing should kick in with a bit more rest," I summarized, starting to jabber as West stalked around the island towards me. "So if you could scrounge up an old pair of shoes for me — maybe Leif has an old pair somewhere that might fit — I'll just take a couple strips or pounds of Terran's bacon for the road and be out of your hair before you —"

Stop.

My jaw snapped shut as West's hand landed on my knee, but the word definitely hadn't come from his mouth.

I furrowed my brows, looking from his hand to his hazel eyes in confusion. "What was that? Did I imagine that?" I stifled a groan. "Holy kumquats, I've started hearing voices. This is it. I'm finally losing it. Okay, maybe one more night's rest before I head out? But you'll hardly notice I'm here, I promise."

He shook his head, trying to stop the smile from creeping up his lips. "No, you didn't imagine it, and you're not losing it. You're on my lands now," he paused, as though waiting for me to catch up, waiting for me to connect the dots, but I didn't know what dots he was implying. I didn't even know there *were* dots to connect. "You're on my lands and you came to me for help, for safety." He raised a brow. "That was my wolf, and your wolf heard mine because she thinks you're joining my pack. Wolves can hear their Alphas."

I blinked at him, eyes wide, then choked on a laugh. I plucked at his giant hand on my knee with my thumb and pointer finger, lifting it off and onto the counter instead. "Hilarious, but no. Nope, sorry. I'm not joining your pack." West's gaze intensified, his pupils growing, but I pretended not to notice. "I just needed a place to crash, so —"

"Why did you come here?" he demanded, his voice a low growl that made certain parts of me clench.

"I just told you, I needed a place —"

"No." He shook his head. "Why *here*? How did you know where to go? How far did you run?" He spread his arms, and I looked out the windows, showing miles and miles of mountains. "You could have stopped anywhere along the way and found help, or stolen what you needed. You came *here*, Jade. What brought you here?"

My mouth went bone-dry and I swallowed, realizing what he implied.

Scent.

Balto followed an instinctual pull to him, his scent.

She ran and ran until she smelled *him*, because to her, he was home.

His lands. His pack.

Even worse, I hadn't just run blindly to Timber Creek, I ran directly to West, finding him in the woods.

His gaze landed on my rapid pulse, and he smirked. My face heated — from rage — and I crossed my arms over my chest.

"Contrary to what you might think, it's not a great idea for a young woman to stop and beg for help just anywhere in the middle of the night," I snapped. "This was the nearest place with anyone I knew."

A low hum emanated from his throat that sounded like disbelief, but I didn't care. He didn't have to believe me. He just had to let me leave — once my feet were healed up a bit more. And I had a way out of town. And a plan for what to do next, now that my new job, my car, my apartment, and my town were compromised.

He leaned back, his heavy scrutiny lifting off me as he dug his phone out of his pocket. "Max is here. He needs to hear your whole story as well."

I clenched my teeth, the name of the angel I'd never forget causing my heart to race. "Don't you have it memorized yet, West?"

His jaw tightened as he tracked the movement of my eyes, and I realized a beat too late that eye-rolling might be on the list of disrespect he'd mentioned before. Too bad for him — I didn't care about wolf etiquette.

"He needs to hear it straight from you."

I sighed. Of course he did. "Great, the more the merrier. I love telling it. It's my new favorite bedtime story. I'll probably make it a recording so I can play it for myself every night. Now, let's go see dear old Massimo."

Chapter Nine

WEST

My hands clenched into fists at my sides as I led Jade to the deck off the kitchen, reminding myself to relax.

Togo was pissed we didn't argue further with Jade, but more than once she'd pulled back if I pushed too hard. I had to keep that wall from slamming down between us again.

How could she still think she was better off alone after that had gotten her fucking *kidnapped*?

Anything could have happened to her if those asshole humans had succeeded. Would she have been assaulted? Subject to testing? Sold to the highest bidder? Left in a ditch to die? Every terrible outcome ran through my mind on a never-ending loop as Togo howled in outrage at her defiance and yearned to charge off into the woods to hunt her captors down.

And she could already hear my wolf. Yet she still didn't think she was joining my pack?

With a steadying breath, I let her pass me onto the deck, then slid the door closed behind us.

Terran was already here with Max, the dark and broody angel who'd left Jade on my doorstep five years ago. He stood against the railing, his black wings draped over the edge. His dark wings and dark hair set him apart from the other white-and-silver angels I knew, as did his casual white t-shirt and black ripped jeans. Sunglasses obscured what I knew to be sharp blue eyes that missed nothing.

Jade hitched a breath when she saw him, and my gut

clenched. Was she just reacting to seeing him again, or something more? Maybe I'd dismissed her questions about his well-being at our dinner too soon, but something about the tension in her demeanor said she was more nervous than interested in the male.

But like flipping a switch, Jade straightened her spine, shoving her nervousness away as she gave a mock-bow.

"*Salve, Dux* Massimo," she offered. "Angelic fascism seems to suit you."

Max flicked a glance my way, amusement tilting up the corner of his mouth, and I wanted to pummel his pretty face.

"You know what they say, a couple years in prison can do wonders for your complexion," he shot back, making no move to stand up straighter or shake her hand.

Jade faltered slightly, tilting her head. "Prison?"

"Was that Latin?" Terran cut in, saving Max from having to answer that one.

Jade lifted a shoulder. "I thought that would be, like, an angel thing. You're supposed to be the stuck-up formal supes, right? Especially with that name." She waved a hand to indicate Max's entire person, and he snickered.

"Blame my dear old dad for that one."

Terran pressed his lips together to hide a smirk, meeting my eye. "Guess it's not just you she's got a problem with, brother. It's everyone." He pushed off the railing, heading for the back door, and I frowned.

"Where are you going?"

"To find more food to ply her with. Do you know how rare it is for a middle child to be the favorite? I can't let this go." He raised his eyebrows in a taunt before disappearing into the house.

"Maybe prison is the wrong word," Max mused. "Have you heard of Omega Level?"

Jade's eyes widened, confirming she'd heard of the angels' rumored prison in Headquarters.

Hesitantly, she asked, "What's Omega Level for?"

Max scratched his jaw idly. "Corrections. Traitors. Angels who can't follow orders."

Jade's tan face paled, a rush of guilt flooding her I sensed through the wisp of a pack bond forming between us. What the hell had happened five years ago that Jade somehow felt guilty for Max's imprisonment?

"I didn't know you had black wings," she changed topics as she approached him, and I looked between them, trying to remember everything I'd heard about Jade. "You usually had them glamoured. This color is beautiful."

A muscle in my jaw twitched at the casual, familiar way she interacted with him. *Usually?* How often had they seen each other?

Max, smug as ever, let her approach, flipping his sunglasses up onto his head, his azure eyes glittering. "Seen many angels lately, *tesoro*?"

"Just the ones in Deadlights Cove," Jade admitted. "They had white wings, so I assumed all angels did."

"Most do."

"Yours aren't totally black, though, are they? More like that sort of, opalescent all-dark night-shimmer that ravens or starlings have."

She reached up, like she was going to stroke one of Max's feathers, and the fucker smirked directly at me, daring me to put a stop to it. Jade, clueless to supernaturals as she was, probably had no idea that angel wings were incredibly sensitive. That with one stroke of her finger, she could probably get Max hard.

I cleared my throat not a second too soon, and Jade spun, putting her hand down and leaning back against the railing next to Max.

"How is Ruby?" Max asked, the taunting expression wholly gone from his face, replaced with genuine concern.

I waited for her to lash out at the question, the same way she had at me, but instead, Jade fiddled with the hem of her sweatshirt.

"She's doing great now." Swallowing heavily, she met Max's eyes, some unspoken emotion passing between them as she rasped out the quietest, "Thank you."

And something about that hurt more than any of their other interactions. I wanted to be the one she trusted like this, and I was prepared to fucking earn it.

"Start your story, Jade."

With a quick nod, she moved towards the patio set, and we followed. I put myself between her and Max, something she didn't seem to notice but Max did.

Max worked with the Paranormal Regulations and Inter-species Council, also known as the PRICs, a group of supernatural leaders with representatives from each species that regulated us and held all supes to our set of laws. His specific job was hush-hush, but he'd spent more and more time in Timber Creek the last five years, and I didn't hate him — except maybe for right now.

The more Jade talked, the deeper Max's brow furrowed in concern as he leaned forward, elbows on his knees. "This was last night?" Max clarified once Jade had finished, and she nodded. "And you got a good look at this Bennett, or at both of them?"

"Just Bennett. I never saw the other guy."

"Great. May I?" Max shifted to the edge of his seat, reaching his hands towards her.

Jade recoiled. Togo grinned, and I fought not to mirror his expression when she glanced at me — for *support*, or so I told myself.

"I don't want my mind wiped."

Max huffed, and again I wondered what the hell had happened in her life to make her jump to that conclusion.

"He wants to access your memories to see Bennett's face," I

explained, and Jade's eyes widened. "He's not going to wipe your memory."

She snapped her attention back to Max. "You can do that? Don't erase their faces. I need to remember everything I can. Can you just make a copy of the whole story so I can quit telling it, though? This is getting old."

Shaking his head, Max said, "You wouldn't want me in your head that long, sweetheart."

She pursed her lips, but Max was already standing, moving around the coffee table towards her.

"You won't feel anything," he said, sitting on the edge of the table in front of her. "I just need you to focus on Bennett's face, any details you remember about him, and I'll see it too. Can you do that?"

A mischievous glint I didn't like entered Jade's eye and she tossed her half-green hair over her shoulder. "Sure, no problem. Have at it, *Massimo*."

"I really hate that name," Max muttered, and placed a hand on Jade's forehead.

Jade squinted one eye, lips twisted in concentration, and a moment later, Max barked a laugh.

Jade grinned, and turned to me. "I showed him how I kneed you in the balls when you tried to corner me at the grocery store."

This was the first genuine smile I'd seen on her, and my breath caught in my throat. The joke was at my expense, but I didn't care when it made her that happy.

I stared a beat too long, memorizing every gorgeous line of her face. Her smile slipped, a wrinkle forming between her brows, then she cleared her throat, looking back at Max.

"Okay, I'm ready for real now."

Max's hand went to her forehead, and less than a minute later, he moved back with a nod. "Got it," he said, then turned to me. As he did so, his knee *accidentally* brushed Jade's, which she didn't react to.

My wolf fucking did though. And I knew Max did it on purpose. Why he'd decided to make it his mission to piss me off today, I had no idea.

"I'll let the Council know," Max continued. "They might want to speak with you themselves, Jade, so you should probably stay around here for now."

She frowned, sitting back. Even though that broke the contact between their knees, I hated that she was this repulsed at having to spend some time here with us. "For how long?"

Max shrugged. "I'm not sure. It depends on what else they have on their plate right now. But I'll be in touch as soon as I know anything."

She nodded, and Max stood, moving away from us. In a single bound, he landed easily on the porch railing.

"Always a pleasure, West." He gave a cocky, two-fingered salute before bending at the knees and launching into the air, dark wings snapping open a moment before his glamour hid him from sight.

Jade stared at the spot where he'd disappeared, mouth agape, before shaking herself. "Can you imagine being able to just vanish like that? Damn."

She pushed her chair back, heading back inside. Terran met my gaze through the glass, his wolf responding to my edginess at Jade's open admiration for another male.

Only because Togo wanted her as pack, wanted her to be that comfortable and impressed with *us*, and didn't want her attaching herself to some other Alpha-supe in the meantime.

That was the only reason.

Chapter Ten

JADE

"Who are you?" a little girl said as I stepped through the sliding glass doors into the house. Her blonde hair was in a lopsided ponytail skewed heavily to the right, but her rosy cheeks and hazel eyes were the same as the Larkin men.

"Jade," I answered as West slid the door closed behind me. "And who are you?"

"River," Terran said, hands on his hips, his voice full of authority I recognized immediately as Dad Voice. A sandwich stacked high enough with fixings it required toothpicks was on the kitchen island in front of him. "I thought you were going with Papa today. Does no one follow the schedules I make?"

"He's downstairs fixing things and I'm hungry." River pulled open the pantry, heading for a bin on the bottom shelf. She grabbed two handfuls of gummy fruit snacks, the small bags overflowing from her closed fists as she moved to shut the door again.

"You know you're only allowed one of those a day." Terran stared at her and River stared right back, gaze unflinching as one of the packs fell from her little hands and landed on the floor with a plop.

"The rest are for Papa," she said with a level of confidence I smiled at, no matter my inner turmoil over having to stay in town. She was lying through the skin of her teeth, and dammit, I was in love with this kid already. "Here, Jade. You can have one."

She reached out and handed me a pack of the fruit snacks as

she walked by, not sparing a glance at the two intimidating males at my back.

I chuckled as I ripped open the bag and popped one of the fake cherries in my mouth, enjoying the burst of sweetness. "You sure told her who was boss, Terran."

I turned back to face them just in time to see West shake his head at Terran, whose forehead crinkled in exasperation. With a heavy sigh, Terran trailed after his daughter, picking up the bags of dropped snacks as he went, adding, "Sandwich is all yours, Jade."

"What was that?" I popped in another gummy, and pointed to where Terran had been standing and then where he'd gone.

West slid the sandwich across the counter to me, his mouth a thin line. "Another wolf thing."

"Got it. I used the salad fork for my waffles this morning. What. An. Embarrassment." I took a huge bite out of the sandwich, my eyes sliding closed as I savored the avocado chicken BLT. "Son of a kumquat, can I request bacon with every meal? This is heavenly."

West cleared his throat, staring down the hallway towards where Terran went, and I swallowed. Whether I meant to or not, I was messing this up.

"Is there any chance you have a manual or something? That way I'd at least *know* I'm doing something wolfy wrong, even if I decide to do it anyway?"

His attention shifted back to me, the hazel gaze glowing gold for a moment. "Your wolf knows exactly what to do, but you shove her so far down in your consciousness you can't hear her. Ask her to help."

His brow rose in a challenge, begging me to tell him he was wrong or explain my weird balance with my wolf, but I shoved the sandwich back in my mouth and ignored him. He might be helping me out by offering me a place to stay, but that didn't mean I owed him my story.

A yawn escaped me before I could stop it, and West nodded towards the sandwich.

"Finish that, then go rest. We'll chat more later."

As much as I wanted to ignore his commands the way River had her father's, there was no way I was leaving this sandwich unfinished, and I was tired. It didn't hurt that the chances of accidentally pissing off more wolves was significantly less in a room by myself upstairs.

He left me alone in the kitchen, and by the time I cleared my plate, exhaustion pulled at me. Even if I wanted to buck West's orders, I couldn't resist the need to lie down again.

I trudged back up the spiral staircase, headed towards my room. As my hand rested on the thick wooden door, Balto surged in me, forcing my head to turn towards the door down the hall that smelled so much like West.

Balto whined at me to go there, to let the smell of him wash over us and wrap us in his protectiveness as we rested, but I wasn't an animal. No matter how much she wanted to give in to him, had already given in to him, I wasn't driven by her instincts. *I* was in control, and I refused to let some man swoop in to save me. Not again.

With a sigh, I pushed open my door and shuffled to the bed. Plopping face-first on the mattress, I closed my eyes and was asleep in seconds.

)))●(((

The room was dark when I came back to consciousness. My stomach groaned, insistent as any alarm clock. I had no idea what time it was, but there was no way I could go back to sleep with the bottomless pit that was my stomach.

Wishing my shifter senses were stronger, I strained my ears to hear if anyone else was up. I didn't want to creep around the kitchen alone like a raccoon in the night, but it might be preferable to getting caught by someone.

Hearing nothing, I ventured into the darkened hall. From the total lack of lights or sounds, it must have been even later than I thought.

I slipped down the stairs, making for the kitchen until a soft glow caught my attention. A door stood open at the end of the hall, and when I crept closer, I found a set of stairs leading down. The faint sounds of a TV drifted up.

Someone was awake.

I hesitated, torn between my curiosity and hunger. Who had West said lived in the basement?

"You coming down or are you going to stand at the top of the stairs all night?" came a low voice from below, and I sighed. Of course it was West.

Part of me wanted to turn around and ignore him out of spite, but asking if I could help myself to food would ease my conscience. Wolves were not trash pandas.

The stairs opened into an expansive basement, a TV taking over most of one wall with shelves on either side full of books, board games, and video game consoles. A leather sectional couch big enough to seat at least 20 sprawled in front of it, pillows and blankets strewn over it in a way that was more homey than messy.

A game room led off from the main space — pool, foosball, ping pong, air hockey… you name it. I cocked a brow at the wall of vintage arcade games, their colored blinking lights coaxing you to spend every last quarter.

"Damn, is this a teenage wasteland or what?"

Was I trying to avoid looking at him? Maybe, not that it was possible. Sprawled across the couch in a white t-shirt and grey sweatpants, West was positively lickable. His hair was messy, like he'd been running his fingers through it, and suddenly mine itched to do the same. To trace the lines of the geometric pack tattoos that covered his arms. I tried not to ogle, but the hint of amusement in his hazel eyes said I failed.

West huffed. "With all the shifters we've had coming and going in recent years, we moved all our rec room stuff down here and out of our main family spaces upstairs. Bored, drifter wolves are a recipe for fights, so" — he gestured at the many activities around the room — "we keep them busy."

I circled the couch, sitting on the far end away from West, and pulled my knees up to my chest, hugging them. "Makes sense. Why don't you have them stay somewhere else if they're such a hazard?"

He eyed me a moment, and I wasn't sure he would answer. I didn't know why I asked — I shouldn't be curious, shouldn't encourage any sort of connection between us. But something about the stillness of the house, that nighttime hush and darkness, made some of my usual defenses crumble.

The next moment, a video game controller hit my thigh. "I'd rather have them right under my nose than roaming around pack lands unsupervised. But we've been getting more and more recently, and now that River lives here full time…" West let out a deep sigh laced with exhaustion. "We're looking into alternative housing options."

The shadows under his eyes seemed to darken as he closed them, rubbing a hand through his hair.

"Why do they all come here? Or are wanderers a nationwide problem?"

"I have a well-known open door policy," West said as he fiddled with the remote, then met my eye. "Any shifters are welcome here, no questions asked. That invites a lot of shifters with shady histories, but we haven't had major problems so far. Most people just need a safe place to breathe and they'll thrive."

I blinked, needing to break the intensity of his gaze as his words hit me straight in the chest. Learning this made me rethink the whole *"not all Alphas would take you"*, and I fidgeted with the controller in my lap. It was easier to ignore the pull to West when I thought he was a bossy jerk. If he was actually genuine about accepting and protecting *anyone*, I might have to reevaluate my opinion of him. And that could be dangerous — for me.

So why was that so hard to remember right now, when it was just me and West and the stark honesty of the deep night? Why did he have to seem so normal, so *human* tonight?

Needing a distraction, I lifted the controller and looked at the screen. "What are we playing?"

The opening credits for *Super Smash Brothers* rolled across the screen, and I sat forward, unable to stop a smile from breaking over my face.

"My name is Jade Rodriguez, you took my bacon, prepare to die." The smack talk rolled off my tongue before I could stop it, honed from years of practice with Ruby. As I clicked around the screen with expert precision, I shot a quick glance at West, unsure how he'd react to my taunt. Once upon a time, sass like that wouldn't have gone over well.

"Really?" West snorted, unfazed in the least, and I relaxed a little. "Kirby? I'll take my chances."

I *tsk*ed as West picked Link for his player. "Cliché."

West frowned at me. "How?"

Battle began, and I didn't bother saying he had a hero complex, always needing to save the lost princess. He knew it as well as I did, even if he wanted to ignore it.

"C'mere, little elf — let me eat you and win my hat." I charged after him as fast as my tiny character would allow, and West sat up straighter, alarmed at my amazing skills.

"What the hell —"

"Aha!" My Kirby ate his Link, popping the character back out as a little green hat appeared on mine. "Never underestimate the underdog, wolfie. They say Athena wanted to create the perfect warrior after her failure with Achilles, so she created Kirby."

As West stared at me, awestruck by my wisdom, I went for the kill. The screen showed my win, and I flashed him a smile. "Because Kirby has no ankles."

His forehead wrinkling, West shook his head. "That is the most ridiculous thing I've ever heard."

A soft laugh escaped me as my stomach groaned again. "And yet the proof lies before us."

West's eyes dropped to my stomach. "Hungry?"

"Kind of." It groaned louder, calling me a pathetic liar.

"You did sleep through dinner." He picked up the remote, clicking off the TV. "C'mon, midnight snack time, Kirby."

I followed West up the stairs, nearly tripping over my own feet as his perfect, grey-sweatpants-clad ass met my eye-line, and gripped the railing for dear life as a wave of lust swept through me.

West twisted and saw me miss a step, a small smile on his face. "You all right?"

"Peachy!" Crap. Peaches, *asses*. Would that give away I was staring at his butt? No, that was crazy. West probably didn't even know that was what the peach emoji meant. Right? He didn't strike me as a big emoji-user. I averted my gaze with my will of steel and got my cool back on by the time we entered the kitchen.

"Do you always play kids' video games at" — I glanced at the clock above the stove — "two in the morning?"

West scattered a handful of tortilla chips on a tray before sprinkling a healthy amount of shredded cheese on top, then slid it into a toaster oven. "Hey. The rating is ages ten *and up*."

"My mistake. So, what, it's your secret shame? That's why you hide it? Or are you training to settle a vendetta?" I raised my eyebrows. "Is River bullying you? Blink twice if you need help."

Biting his lip to silence a laugh — and I absolutely did *not* track the way his teeth grazed over his skin — he shook his head before answering. "I don't always sleep well. Dumb games help me shut my mind off for a bit."

I blinked at the honesty, not having expected him to open up, then shook myself as the oven beeped. A moment later, he slid a plate over to me.

"Just me?" I pointed at the single plate. "Now I feel weird. Surely a strapping young wolf like you *also* needs a snack."

"Strapping?" West raised an eyebrow and I nearly fainted. Growly, demanding West was obnoxiously hot, but flirty, playful West? Every pair of panties in a 10-mile radius burst into flames.

I blushed, grabbing a chip and shoving it in my mouth to keep myself from saying anything else stupid.

West chuckled, and the sound affected me way more than I cared to admit as he scooped some of my chips onto a plate of his own, then topped everything with a generous scoop of guacamole. "Let's eat outside."

On the deck, it was like a weight left West's shoulders, his muscles visibly loosening from the tension he usually carried. We each took an adirondack chair overlooking the valley, cool night air drifting around us heavy with the scent of pine resin and honeysuckle. Stars dotted the sky, constellations bright as they shone down — my favorite part of living in the Rocky Mountains.

We fell into a comfortable silence as we ate, enjoying the crickets chirping and owls hooting in the distance. When we were done, West stacked our plates on the coffee table, and I leaned back in my chair, watching the stars.

Maybe it was the blanket of darkness that made me bold enough to ask, but I found myself wondering aloud, "A fellow insomniac, huh? What sorts of things keep you up at night, then?"

"Shifters going missing, for starters," he offered with a flick of his eyes my way, before easing back to look up at the sky too. "Assimilating all the new ones coming into town, or into the pack, without causing too much drama. They're not all wolves, so it can be tricky with different dynamics."

"You accept non-wolves into your pack?" I'd never heard of that before.

"Well, they don't partake in *every* aspect of pack life, but we try to make them feel part of our community. My brother Cooper is a cat. Our parents adopted him when he was an infant, but he's always been one of us, just like if he were a wolf. We look out for each other up here."

I just barely resisted an eye roll. That was certainly his mantra.

"Then there's my own family, but I won't bore you with all their problems," he sighed, and I swallowed down the dozen questions I immediately had about *that.* "Do you know what's going on with the Paranormal Regulations and Interspecies Council?"

"The PRICs?" Sure, I'd heard of them, but I didn't track supe news much.

"There's been all sorts of political upheaval the past five years, and sometimes they ask me to be a part of it. To be a voice for shifters." He drummed his fingers on his chair before continuing. "Then there's this rogue Lone wolf who refuses to join my pack even though she keeps getting herself in danger."

"Hey, I hear she also gets herself *out* of danger just fine."

West snorted. "Sure."

His words hung in the air as he let the conversation drop, and it dawned on me just how much West had to deal with. His pack, his family, the entire council, stray shifters — what the hell was he thinking trying to add me into that mix?

I must have voiced the last bit out loud, because a low growl came from West's throat.

"What?"

"Jade, you —" he let out another growl, his jaw working as he seemed to struggle with his words. Sitting up and turning to face me, he licked his lips, and my mouth parted at the sight. His irises flashed amber, his wolf just under the surface, before he pulled himself together and started again, enunciating each word pointedly. "You are just as worth protecting, caring for, as every single shifter and supernatural here."

I stared in stunned silence as he rose from his chair to place his hands on the armrests of mine, leaning his huge form down until his nose skated the sensitive skin below my ear. His woodsy scent invaded my senses, overwhelming, and a shiver ran through me as I clamped my thighs together. I fisted my hands at my sides to stop from reaching out, from gripping his shirt and pulling him down onto me.

The ghost of his lips traced the shell of my ear as he said, "Don't for one second think I'll give up until you accept that."

He pulled back just enough to meet my eyes, his own gone full gold again. Once I gave him a shaky nod, he stood, putting space between us so I could breathe.

"You should go to bed, Jade. Your body still needs rest."

He took the plates, leaving the sliding door open for me to follow, and I finally allowed myself a whimper as my mind wandered to all the *other* things my body needed.

Chapter Eleven

WEST

Jade followed me back inside and headed for the stairs with a quick wave goodnight. I forced myself to stay in the kitchen, mostly so I didn't chase her up the stairs and herd her into my room. Every tic, every tell, every hitched breath she took, I noticed, and I fucking savored.

Jade might not want to be here, but she didn't hate me, and I could work with that.

Gripping the kitchen counter, I reined in my urges, needing to get a hold of myself. Prior to our impromptu game night, I'd been reading through reports of other kidnappings and needed to drown out the heaviness of my thoughts. The last thing I'd expected was for Jade to waltz into the game room wearing our pack sweats like she belonged, then demolish me in *Super Smash Brothers*. I'd underestimated her, but had learned my lesson the hard way.

Everything about her was surprising. I wasn't used to having anyone outside my family defy me the way she did, but I was already starting to crave it.

For that hour with her, I was just West, not the pack Alpha, not a **PRIC** representative, not anything but *me*.

I couldn't remember the last time I'd felt that free.

Dropping my chin to my chest, I breathed deeply, but it only emphasized her sweet citrus scent still lingering in the kitchen, tantalizing me.

It had been a long time since I'd felt this desperate for anyone, if ever.

Her door clicked shut upstairs, and I let out a deep sigh. Brushing a hand through my hair, I climbed the stairs two at a time and rushed to my room, closing the door and heading straight for the shower. I needed to get her out of my system if I ever wanted to sleep tonight.

))) ● (((

Birds chirped in the tree outside my window the next morning and I shoved the pillow over my head, trying to drown them out.

No matter how much I wanted to sleep in, the phone dinging on my nightstand demanded attention. With a yawn, I reached blindly across the bed, grabbed my phone, and pulled it towards me.

"PRICs never respect time zones," I muttered as I scrolled through the emails already in my inbox even though it was only six in the morning. Skimming through several general notices, I paused on one with updates on yet more kidnappings. My stomach dropped even from the preview of the message, and I decided I needed caffeine before I read it. Throwing the blankets aside, I rose from the bed and grabbed some sweats, then went downstairs to start the coffee.

The house was quiet as I made my way to the kitchen, enjoying the stillness before everyone else woke up. Shaking coffee grounds into the machine, I leaned back on the counter as it percolated, the bittersweet scent waking me up.

Steam curled from the pot as I poured myself a cup, then slid the back door open and took a seat in one of the adirondack chairs. Cool mountain air brushed against my skin, a refreshing contrast to the first hot sip of coffee. Two yellow warblers flitted between the trees near my bedroom window, and I stared at the window next to mine.

Jade was up there, probably still asleep, but this morning would be so much better if she were here at my side. It was a stupid, selfish thought — she needed sleep, and I had never been one to need company in quiet moments of solitude. But I wanted it, just the same.

My phone vibrated in my pocket, and I pulled it free, glancing down at the report.

Paranormal Regulations and Interspecies Council North America:

Confirmed missing supernaturals: 28

Shifters: 17
Hybrids (part-shifter): 8
Nymphs: 2
Witches: 1

I scrubbed my jaw, the number 17 standing out like a flashing beacon. Twenty-eight supernaturals were currently missing. Jade would have been 29 if she hadn't showed up at my door.

Togo paced under my skin, raging at our inability to find every single offender. With 28 supernaturals missing, this couldn't be considered coincidence. Were they laying helpless, tied up and drugged like Jade had been?

My chest tightened as adrenaline worked its way into my system, feeling the pressure to *do something.*

As though he could sense my unrest, my phone buzzed with an incoming call from Cooper, and I swiped to answer it immediately.

"Anything?" I asked, no preamble. Cooper preferred it that way.

"We found where Jade got away," he said, and I squeezed my phone, canines already lengthening. Once Cooper had heard her story, he'd taken off with Atlas, our best tracker in the pack. If there was anyone who could hunt down Bennett and the other kidnapper, it was those two. "Like we thought, we lost their trail once they took off in the car again."

I cursed softly, and Cooper grunted his agreement.

"West," he started, then huffed before continuing, "We're a good fifty miles out. Your girl's a hell of a runner. She must have run for a whole day."

I'd already wondered this, but hearing it confirmed made my chest puff with pride. Even in her wolf form, that was remarkable.

For Jade's wolf to find mine over that kind of distance, for her magic to sustain her stamina that long to reach me…

Cooper's weighted silence spoke volumes, but he didn't push. I knew my brother well enough to know that he'd bring it up again later, preferably when he could level his unrelenting cat stare on me until I answered his questions.

I changed the subject. "Update from the PRICs."

"How many?"

"Twenty-eight."

"Fuck."

"There were two reported missing in the Rocky Mountains, but neither were names I recognized. Still, we need to tighten up security." I rubbed my temple, already adjusting my never-ending to-do list. "I'll get the others in for a meeting, see if we can figure out who else to place on patrols —"

"Make Terran do that."

My brows furrowed. "Terran is busy at the restaurant today, and then River —"

"No," Cooper cut me off the way only he could. If he'd wanted to lead his own pack, Cooper was certainly Alpha enough to make it happen. "Terran can make time. *You* have other shit to do today."

Frowning, I rubbed the back of my neck. He wasn't wrong. That was one of Cooper's more infuriating traits — he rarely was. My tone was sharper than I intended when I responded, "I need to be there and make sure my pack's safety is taken care of."

"Trust Terran. You have to take care of your m—" — a low growl in my throat slipped free, and Cooper smirked — "Jade. Send Dad with him if you're really worried."

I sighed, the most I'd verbally concede to him, but even with one meeting off my list, my mind instantly filled in the other things I had to do today. "Call a town meeting. It's not just shifters missing, so I need everyone to be aware of what's happening and taking precautions. I need to call Max too, see if he has any news on his end about Jade's case. And Aspen —"

"I'll call Aspen," Cooper said. "You handle Max. Have Summer contact the Coven and the other stray supes to set up the town meeting, then she and Atlas can host it tomorrow."

I nodded, even though he couldn't see me. It made sense to delegate, but damn if it didn't make my skin itch not to handle everything myself. Still, even having the plan made my shoulders feel a little lighter.

I cleared my throat. "Thanks, Coop."

"Jesus fuck." He hung up on me, and I chuckled. Cooper was allergic to sentimentality.

I dropped my phone down on the chair and stood, taking my coffee to the railing as I looked over the valley. With each sip, I ran through the extra measures I could put in place to protect my people better, even if my pack wasn't the most likely to be targeted with how remote Timber Creek was.

My phone chimed on the armrest, but I ignored it, needing a break from the world. It chimed again a few minutes later, then again, and again.

"Freaking group texts," I muttered as I grabbed my phone and swiped it open.

SUMMER

Wait. Leif said there's a girl in the house.

Who has a girl in the house?

Terran??

TERRAN

Why are you up? It's too early for this. And River is the only girl in my life forever. Stop asking.

LEIF

I met her. She's pretty.

TERRAN

Agreed. River is pretty, just like her dad.

SUMMER

Hitting on yourself is a new low. You really need to get out more and stop hanging out with Cruz.

TERRAN

Maybe you're right. Should I ask New Girl out? I am her favorite, after all, and she's smoking hot with that green hair and tan skin.

SUMMER

So she's there for you?

TERRAN

Nah. I'm just saying I can appreciate beauty when I see it, right West?

ASPEN

Men. You're all the same. I hope you can feel me slapping you on the back of the head. Good morning, you animals.

COOPER

Not the insult you think it is, sis. And some of us have been up for hours.

TERRAN

hiss

COOPER

I don't hiss.

SUMMER

You absolutely hiss. It's a weird sound coming from an animal as big as you. Even weirder when you do it in human form.

COOPER

I. Don't. Hiss.

TERRAN

Thou doth protest too much.

ASPEN

Ten bucks you literally hissed that.

HEATH

What are you hooligans doing blowing up my phone so early? You're disrupting my morning Willie time.

ASPEN

Dad. We've talked about this.

SUMMER

I just threw up in my mouth.

TERRAN

IDK morning Willies are a sign of virility. Good to know Dad's still got it. Good sign for us, West. Maybe not so much for Cooper and Leif.

LEIF

Leave my Willie out of it. I'm in my prime.

ASPEN

Now I'm throwing up in my mouth.

Aspen has left the group chat
Terran added Aspen to the group chat

TERRAN

Nice try. Can't ditch us that easily.

Summer has left the group chat

TERRAN

Should we torture her and make her wait? How long before she snaps and sends one of us a private message, asking to add her back in?

ASPEN

Let her sweat.

HEATH

And your mother always said for twins, you two had nothing in common.

Leif added Summer to the group chat

SUMMER

I hate you all. Except you, Leif.

Did I miss anything?

COOPER

Nothing. What are you baking this morning? Should I stop by when we get back?

SUMMER

Sure, I've got cinnamon buns in the oven. I'll save you one.

SUMMER

BACK TO THE GIRL

TERRAN

YEAH WEST. BACK TO THE GIRL.

SUMMER

Who is she?

West has left the group chat
Aspen added West to the group chat

ASPEN

Don't think so, brother. If I can't leave, neither can you.

WEST

I hope you all have an awful day.

HEATH

If only your mother were here to see the love in this family.

SUMMER

Love you, Dad.

HEATH

Love you too, sweetie. Love ALL of you pups and I hope you have a glorious day. Off to tend my Willie.

ASPEN

Please stop saying it like that.

I shook my head as I put away my phone and headed back inside, ignoring the continued buzzing that indicated Dad was probably doubling down on his terrible word choices, as usual.

The world might be going to shit, but my weird family was an endless source of entertainment and I loved them for it.

My calendar for the day was booked solid with meetings, but I couldn't bring myself to start any of my tasks until I'd seen Jade.

Chapter Twelve

JADE

"Any word yet?"

Sitting at the kitchen island, West glanced up from his phone as I walked in to the smell of fresh coffee.

"Nothing helpful," he said, his eyes catching on my hands and feet as he gave me a quick once-over. I raised my palms, now fully healed, and he tilted his coffee mug towards the pot. "Help yourself."

I grabbed a mug, filling it then adding a splash of milk from the fridge. Part of me felt weird making myself at home like this, but the other part of me felt… good. Right.

By the stove was a tray of breakfast sausages and a bag of bagels, and I made myself a plate, then remembered how West had served me last night. I made him a plate too and brought both over to the island, sliding his over as I took the stool beside him.

Those hazel eyes flicked up from the plate to my face, and it was a good thing I'd already sat down because my knees would have given out.

I'd laid in bed for a long while this morning, wondering how to address that *moment* we'd had last night. The one where I almost thought he would kiss me, then he didn't. Until now, I'd convinced myself it was a wolfy thing I didn't understand, but the heat in his gaze made me doubt that.

Grabbing my bagel, I shoved it in my mouth and stared at

the counter, unable to continue this sexy stare off this early in the morning.

"Okay, but you wouldn't withhold information because you want me to stay here, right?" I picked up my coffee mug and peered at him over the rim as I took a sip, but his focus turned to something on his phone.

A muscle in his jaw twitched under his beard, the sign I'd quickly learned meant I broke some shifter norm and he was restraining himself from mentioning it.

While his gaze was on his phone, I allowed myself a moment of weakness to take him in, the way his biceps pushed the limit of his dark green t-shirt, the flex of his corded, tattooed forearms as he twisted his mug, the casual strength radiating off him. Was his golden-brown hair as soft as it looked? It was just the perfect length to run my fingers through, to grip onto during a passionate —

With a jolt, I nearly choked on my latest sip of coffee as I remembered what West said after he'd projected his words into my mind. Shit, could he see *my* thoughts too, or just sometimes hear them? Did I need to consciously project them for it to work? I needed that wolf-shifter manual ASAP, the Cliffs Notes version. Better yet, a quick video on Shifter 101 I could put on 2x speed. The crash course.

"No, Jade. I wouldn't lie to you." His hazel eyes met mine when he said it, an underlying intensity to the words.

He absolutely knew what I'd been thinking about.

I broke eye contact and cleared my throat, distracting myself with another sip of coffee. A soft chuckle came from his throat, and I realized too late I was losing terribly at our stare offs this morning.

Man, I was rusty. Where was River? I needed to practice my staring contest skills, stat.

"Do you have any idea how long it'll be until we hear back from Max?"

With a click, he turned his phone off and set it on the counter. Turning to face me on his stool, his knees were close enough to my thigh, I could feel his heat. "In a rush? Because last I checked, your job and home were compromised, so where exactly is it that you have to be?"

His words hit like a gut punch, even if they were true, and I ground my teeth. "Don't trap me here, West."

He leaned back, his eyes wide like I'd slapped him, and I frowned, not understanding what I'd done to upset *him*.

Turning his focus to the windows, he took a heavy breath, and why was his lack of attention worse than the weight of his gaze?

"I have no intention of trapping you or anyone here, Jade. I wouldn't dream of taking away your free will, but I do plan on protecting you if I can." With a sigh, he turned back to me, the weight of the world showing in the deep lines between his brows. "Headquarters operates on its own timeline. I wouldn't be surprised if it takes quite a while for the Council to get back to us. They've had a lot on their plate since shifters were outed."

"What's *quite a while*?"

He tilted his head. "A month? Seven? Their Premier Malachi is an angel, Jade. Practically immortal. Angels' sense of time doesn't compare to ours."

I groaned, rubbing a hand over my face. "And this whole time we're waiting, these humans could be taking more supes. Probably already have."

West grunted in the affirmative, returning his focus to his phone.

"That doesn't bother them at all? Bother *you*?"

He didn't look back up, but that same muscle in his jaw ticked. "Of course it bothers me. But until we know more, there's not a whole lot we can do except stick together and stay vigilant."

I tried not to roll my eyes at the *stick together* bit, since I knew that gesture was on his list of annoyances. "And I have to stay here that whole time? I can't just leave my contact information with you in case they have more questions?"

"What contact information? You're homeless and you lost your phone, remember?"

Anger flared this time at his blunt words, and I jerked up, straightening my spine. He was trying to rattle me, and I was going to prove to him that I was unrattleable. Whatever the opposite of a rattlesnake was, that was me. A manatee, maybe. They seemed chill. I'd be chill as a freaking manatee.

"I can get a new phone." I smiled at him, oh so sweetly. "And leave you my number then be on my way. Better yet, just give me Max's number, and I'll text him mine when I have one, and then we don't have to involve you at all."

That caught his attention.

West's eyes flashed gold at my words, though I couldn't tell if it was because I wanted to leave, or if mentioning Max pissed him off.

"What's your plan, then?" He crossed his arms over his chest as he met my eyes head-on. Being on the receiving end of his full attention made Balto roll over and show her belly, panting happily, but human-me was less than thrilled at his tone, knowing where this was going. "What's your bank account look like? Can you afford a phone? What about after you get your phone, where are you going to go? Do you have enough cash to rent anywhere? To *go* anywhere? You can't go back to your apartment or your car. If they found you at work, they'll find you again."

My cheeks flushed, something akin to shame creeping up uncomfortably, even though I knew I was doing my best. It was hard for shifters out on their own right now and — okay, that was his whole point. I realized that. But it didn't make the truth sting any less.

Worse than that, he was starting to make me question myself, and *that* was something I refused to do again. I would *not* let him keep me here under the guise that it was all *my* idea because I needed him to look out for me. I glared, readying to launch into him, but his next words caught me up short.

"You're not under house arrest, Jade. I won't make you stay here. All I want is to help you, but think long and hard about what your options are if you go back out on your own."

West stood, towering over me enough that I had to tilt my head up to maintain eye contact — and I'd be damned if I let him win *again*. He raised a hand, and before I could stop the reflex, I flinched. Immediately I wished I could undo it when his eyes widened slightly, tracking the movement.

Instead of turning away from me, he slowed his movements, holding my gaze calmly as his fingers reached a stray lock of hair that had escaped my messy bun. My heart raced as I fought to control my reaction, hating myself for this weakness. To him, to touch, to men. All of it.

When I didn't pull back again, he gently pushed the strand back, his fingertips ghosting over the shell of my ear, sending tingles all the way to my toes. His thumb brushed over my temple again, repeating the motion, and I forgot to breathe, locked in his thrall.

He blinked, swallowing heavily, then stepped back. Grabbing his plate and mug, he walked them over to the sink, then left the kitchen without a backwards glance.

Like always, clarity didn't hit me until after he left the room. He'd said he *wouldn't* make me stay here, which implied he could, if he wanted to.

While I might not know a lot about shifters, I *did* know wolves had to follow orders from their Alphas. If Balto was already starting to think of him that way, he absolutely *could* make me stay here.

"Nope," I said aloud, even though it was just me here now. "Ain't happening."

Grabbing my dishes, I hurried to the sink and rinsed them off before putting them in the dishwasher.

I had to get out of here.

Except… I didn't have my phone. My wallet. Any of my credit cards. I could potentially hitch hike back to my town, break into my own apartment, and grab some stuff and my cash tips. My purse was surely long gone, left on the seat of my open truck door in the bar's parking lot. By now my account would be drained by some scammer or locked down.

I racked my brain, trying to remember how much money I had in cash at my apartment.

Maybe $200? Shit. I was so screwed. I wouldn't get far on that, especially without my truck.

Gripping the counter, I hung my head, suddenly thinking I might need something stronger than coffee to get through this day.

"Everything all right?"

I picked my head up to see Leif slink into the room, eyeing me uncertainly.

"Just peachy." I grinned, showing far too many teeth. "I don't have any money or clothes and my home is probably compromised and I'm stuck here for the foreseeable future while I wait an indeterminate amount of time to see if some mythical angels need to talk to me about being kidnapped by some evil human shifter-snatchers for kumquat only knows what reason and there's nothing I can do about any of it for now. Thanks for asking."

Leif blinked, tilting his head as I spoke, looking eerily like a dog trying to understand a weird sound. A bubble of laughter escaped me at the thought, and at the current hopelessness of my situation.

"I'm sorry, I didn't mean to unload on you. You're a nice kid, and it's not your problem."

He moved closer, resting his elbows on the counter.

"Well, *most* of that you can't do anything about yet, but the clothes thing I can help you out with."

I snorted, then walked over to him. As he straightened up, I leveled my hand on the top of my head and then moved it towards him, meeting his collar bone.

"I don't think we're quite the same size, bud, but thanks for the offer."

He rolled his eyes. "Not *my* clothes. I mean there's a shop in town. It's small, but I'm sure you could find something to fit you better than this."

"Hey!" I pointed up to his face. "*You* get to roll your eyes? West keeps giving me shit!"

Leif laughed, shaking his head. "I'd pay good money to see you roll your eyes at West. Did he flip out?"

"Not exactly, but he definitely doesn't like it. And *West?* You call your dad by his first name? How Gen Z of you."

"West adopted me when I was 7, but he was only 25, so we kind of grew up together. Calling him *Dad* is weird, but he's the only father figure I've ever had." Son of a bitch, that pulled at my heart strings and I hated it. I didn't want to have anything in common with West, least of all this. "And don't roll your eyes at your Alpha. It's rude."

I shot him an incredulous look, these shifter rules like a whole other language. "He's not *my* Alpha. He's not my anything."

"Come on." Leif jerked his head towards the front door with a grin. "West will give you money for some clothes."

The thought of accepting money from West twisted my gut, but I didn't have much choice.

We found West in his office, and he agreed to foot the bill, passing a handful of cash over to Leif despite my huff of protest.

I planted a hand on my hip. "You know, females are actually allowed to carry money themselves now, old man."

"Leif is going with you." West's tone brooked no argument, but argue I would.

"What? Why?" I scowled. "You said this town is all supes, so that's got to be pretty safe, and I can see the town from the front door. I promise I won't get lost."

West shared a look with Leif, and I clenched my jaw, growing tired of all the telepathic mumbo-jumbo going on around here. With a nod, Leif turned and headed out, calling back, "Meet you out front."

"Leif's going with you because you're a wolf without a pack in a town of wolves, a lot of whom are fairly—" West paused, running his tongue along his teeth, a movement I tried and failed not to track, "—assertive. New blood in a pack sometimes means ranks change, and that makes everyone uneasy. They're not going to know what to make of you, but Leif's presence says you're associated with me, even if you're not pack. It'll keep them from sniffing around too aggressively."

Maybe he had a point there. Or maybe he was making it all up, what did I know? I had to pick my battles with West, though, and Leif had readily answered my questions so far, so I figured this was one I could lose.

"Fine." My conscience prodded me, or maybe that was the almost-forgotten voice of my late mother, and I added, "And, thanks. For the money. Letting me stay here. Everything."

If my gratitude pleased him, he didn't show it. He merely lifted a shoulder and said, "We take care of each other here. That's the whole point."

I could sense this was about to get preachy again real quick. Instead of dwelling on that, I decided to push my luck while he was being generous. "Any chance there's enough cash in those money-bags for a new phone, then?"

He gave me a flat stare. "Will you run off the second you have it?"

"...No?"

Sighing, he shook his head. "None of the shops in town sell phones, but I'll order you one."

I blinked. He'd order me one? Just like that?

No, I told myself harshly. Just because he was being a decent person did *not* mean I got to feel emotional.

Before I could overthink that too much, I made for the front door to meet Leif.

"Oh, and Jade," West said from behind me, and I turned to see him leaning against the door jamb of his office, arms crossed.

Holy kumquats, why was The Lean so sexy? And how much Spandex was in that shirt for it to plaster to his muscles like that?

"I talked to Brigid Morgaine this morning. Ruby is doing fine, and she knows you're here. I told her to contact me if she needs anything and that you'd give her a call later today."

Tears pricked my eyes, relief swimming through me at his words. I'd pushed worry for my sister to the back of my mind, refusing to acknowledge it, but he'd taken care of it for me. Fortunately for all parties involved, I didn't start sobbing standing there in the foyer. I simply nodded, then offered a small smile. "Thank you."

"Of course. I understand how much she means to you. She's family."

Family, indeed. The only person in my life that mattered, and he'd thought to check on her for me.

Like the non-asshole he might be.

Shit.

I spun on my heels so fast I nearly toppled over, needing to get out of this house and away from West.

Chapter Thirteen

JADE

Leif stood out front, holding a pair of slide sandals for me. I slipped them on and we walked down the winding drive towards town.

At the gate at the bottom of the hill, we passed through the booth, and Leif pointed at an intercom as he closed the door behind us.

"If you're ever out on your own, hit the buzzer and someone will let you in."

"How many of you live at the pack house?"

"Right now, there's you, me, West, Terran, and River. Sometimes my aunt Aspen when she's in town — she and Terran are twins. The other rooms in the basement are set up for visitors, but we don't have anyone here currently, besides you. Pack members will stay with us if they get injured so West can keep an eye on them, and he houses the strays who show up needing a place to stay. Summer comes over a lot, and Cooper is in and out, but he has his own place in the woods. "

As we crossed the street, an auto shop with Cruz Motors written in a graffiti spray-paint style above the red garage doors caught my eye. The sound of a wrench and Latin pop music drifted out the open bays, a guy in dirty ripped jeans lying underneath a car, half-hidden from view.

"That's Cruz." Leif pointed to the guy under the car. "You'll meet him eventually. He's Terran's best friend and hangs out with us a lot.

"Summer, West's youngest sister, owns the bookstore slash bakery over there" — he pointed to the opposite side of the street to a shop called Love Bites, painted bright yellow with multi-colored wildflowers covering every square inch of available space between the sidewalk and the window — "and Terran runs Buffalo Willies, our restaurant down the street."

As we continued strolling down the street, it struck me that the Larkins didn't just live here. This was *their* town, more than I'd ever realized, and way more than just West being this pack's Alpha. Timber Creek stretched out in a line before us, most shops situated on this main street, but I'd seen from the house that a grid of streets clustered around it on either side.

Leif gave me the full tour, including the long-standing history of the pack, dating back to the late 1800s. He knew more about the people of this town from a hundred years ago than I knew about my own parents.

"They should have just named this Larkintown."

Leif grinned. "It takes some getting used to a family this big, but not a day goes by that I don't know how lucky I am that West chose me."

For a moment, I wondered what that would be like. Siblings and family in and out of the house all the time, always having someone to hang out with, to talk to. Or would it feel more like never having a moment to yourself? Having people track your every move?

"West seems over-protective," I ventured, wondering if Leif would take the bait and give me the inside scoop.

"He is," Leif agreed, and nodded towards the next shop door, reaching for the handle in front of me. "That's his job."

Inside, he pointed to the women's clothing section to the left while he made his way over to a small shelf of video games to the right. Apparently this was a one-stop-shop for mountain dwellers.

I turned down the next aisle and started looking through the racks of shirts, then realized I had no idea what sort of budget I was working with. As I turned to wave Leif over, a woman appeared out of thin air beside me and I let out a shriek of alarm.

The clothes hangers rattled as I bumped into them, my hand over my racing heart. "Holy *crap* what the hell was that! How did you — what was —"

"I'm so sorry, I saw you come in with Leif so I assumed you were a supe, too — you are, aren't you?" She swept her waist length copper waves over her shoulder, gold bracelets jangling on her wrist. Her loose patchwork skirt dusted the floor, turquoise cowboy boots peeking out from beneath the brightly patterned fabric. She had a mustard yellow t-shirt with a buffalo on it tied in a knot at her waist, and I admired her relaxed but funky style, even as she attempted to — sniff me? "Yeah, you totally are, so why…"

"Are you a shifter?" I tried to use my own super sniffer to figure out what *she* was, but I was stumped. All I could detect was something vaguely smoky, but that could have been from the incense wafting around the shop.

The woman laughed, her black irises twinkling in amusement. "No, no, not a shifter. *Definitely* not — not that there's anything wrong with that! I'm a demon. Indigo, but you can call me Indi. This is my store, Provisions and Provocations" — she waved a hand around the space — "everything you need, even more you don't."

"Oh, wow." My eyes widened. "Sorry, I'm Jade. I haven't met a demon before — I mean, as far as I know."

"Most of us are your run-of-the-mill troublemakers, but none of that *rose from the pits of hell* nonsense. Minus the fire powers." Flames licked at her fingertips, then disappeared just as quickly, and I couldn't hide my reaction fast enough. Indi tilted her head. "Are you new to the pack?"

"Um." I met Leif's eyes briefly across the store. "Not exactly.

But I'm looking for a few outfits to get me out of" — I gestured to my pack shirt and sweats, not to mention the too big slides on my feet — "this for the foreseeable future."

Indi hummed, taking in my appearance, and nodded. "Well, my selection isn't the broadest, but from your vibe I'd guess…" Without finishing her thought, she twirled and flitted around the store, gathering an armful of items and pushing them at me, then steered me into a dressing room. "Take your time! Anything you want a second opinion on, just pop out."

The curtain for the dressing room closed behind me and I looked at the clothes Indi pulled for me. A plaid shirt, solid tees in grey, black, and green, two pairs of jeans and two pairs of cutoff shorts — everything I would have picked for myself. Anxiety clawed at me as I turned over the price tags, mentally tallying up the total. I couldn't afford this, and the thought of repaying West was daunting.

No matter how terrible my finances had been in the last decade, I'd never left debts unpaid, but this one… If I let West buy me these clothes and a new phone, I wasn't sure I'd be able to repay him.

As if sensing my distress — maybe that was a wolf thing too — Leif's footsteps shuffled closer to the dressing room. "He's not going to make you pay him back. In fact, he'd probably be insulted if you tried."

"I don't like handouts," I whispered, but I should have known that was pointless with another shifter around.

"Then join the pack," Leif said as nonchalantly as if he was choosing what to eat for lunch. "It's not a handout when everyone does their part. It's just taking care of each other."

"Great," I scoffed as I pulled the first shirt over my head. "So you're communists. Does that mean West is the dictator? Kind of makes sense."

"I think the word you're looking for is *family*, but okay. Just pick some stuff for now and let's go — I never ate breakfast and Terran will make us lunch at Buff's if we hurry."

I almost swallowed my tongue as Indi rang up my purchases, but the jeans I had on felt like butter compared to anything I'd ever owned. In addition to the three shirts, jeans, shorts, a jacket, yoga pants, and underwear, she'd insisted I take not one, but two pairs of shoes, so I had on the checkered Vans and a simple v-neck black top she'd picked for me as we left.

"One more thing!" Indi called, and appeared right in front of me holding out a pair of hoop earrings with a green stone hanging from the center — jade.

I started to shake my head, but she pulled them off the card and reached for my ears, clipping the hoops in place before I could resist.

"A welcome gift from me to you." Indi smiled and pulled me into a hug, my body nearly frozen against hers, but she released me just as quickly. "See you around!"

We left the shop and before I could register his actions, Leif pulled the bags from my hands.

Leif seemed to know everybody in town, waving and calling out to people as we strolled down the street.

Across the road was a shop called Moonrise Emporium, its windows filled with hanging plants, crystal displays, and moon phase symbols, and goosebumps exploded across my skin.

As much as I'd been avoiding my wolf in recent years, I'd burned whatever witchiness was left in me at the metaphorical stake.

I swallowed, trying to release my unease at all of the familiar objects in the window. Several people moved within the shop, one woman watering the hanging plants in the window, but I ducked my head, all but cowering at the reminder of my past.

"Is that a witch supply shop?"

"Yeah. We have a Coven here in town. With the popularity

of witchcraft among humans these days, they don't even have to hide half the stuff in the back anymore."

I'd known Zara was a witch, but it still surprised me to hear there were enough here to warrant their own shop. Making a mental note to avoid them at all costs, I asked, "So, wolves, witches, angels, demons apparently. Anybody else here in town?"

"Well, Max is the only angel, and he doesn't live here, just stops in to see West occasionally," Leif said. "Indi and Cruz are the only demons since, you know, having too many of them in one place can be a bit overwhelming." I didn't know, but I nodded to keep him talking. "Mostly shifters and witches, though there are a few sea nymphs who live out by the lake. Oh, and Ryker, when he's in town. He's a dragon."

"Seriously?" I gaped. I'd heard of sea nymphs from Ruby but I had no idea they could live away from the ocean. "But it's fresh water."

"Nymphs are adaptable. They can shift into a bunch of forms."

I tried to absorb that information as Leif opened the door to Buffalo Willies, holding it open for me.

"Oh, and there's also —"

"Table for two?"

I started as the waiter silently appeared out of thin air right beside me, then started again as I got a good look at him. There was nothing obvious marking him as a supe, but the kid's flat, dark-eyed stare immediately marked him as *other*. The sleeves of his hoodie were pushed up to reveal colorful tattoos down his skinny, pale arms, and when I blinked, he'd moved imperceptibly closer to us both — no, to Leif. He was drifting towards him like they were opposing charges.

"Yeah, thanks Q." Leif smiled, clueless to or ignoring the host's attention. Without blinking, Q spun on his heel and headed for a table by the window.

"Drinks?"

"Water, and menus, please." We slid into the booth Q indicated, and I noticed he tracked Leif's every move before he left
without another word.

"What kind of —"

Two glasses clinked down in front of us, and I jerked back,
snapping my mouth shut. Q was gone again before I even had a
chance to thank him.

Leif didn't seem nearly as surprised by Q's behavior as I was,
taking a sip of his water. I peered towards the kitchen door, and
Q watched us through the pass-through window. When he realized I'd caught him staring, he moved out of sight.

I turned back towards the table and took a sip of my water.

"Q — Quentin — is a vampire," Leif said casually, and I spit
out my drink.

"He's a *what?*" My voice had gone incredibly high and
squeaky. "You're pulling my leg. Vampires aren't real, every supe
knows that. Even this one" — I pointed my thumb at myself —
"who is basically a failure at all supe things."

Leif gave me an uncharacteristically stern frown. "You're not
a failure. You just had a different upbringing than most of us.
And vampires are new to all of us. I mean, they're not *new*, but
they've been hiding their existence for centuries. We've only
known about them since all that stuff went down a few years
ago."

"What's their deal, then? Do they really drink blood?" I
gestured to the window beside us, bright Colorado sunlight
streaming in in full force. "Obviously he's out in daylight, so I
guess that one's made up." I caught sight of Quentin back out on
the floor of the restaurant, carrying a tray of food to a far table.
"Is he immortal? Does he eat? Breathe? Sparkle? Sleep in a
coffin?"

Leif chuckled at my endless stream of questions, shaking his
head. "They've kept it pretty hush-hush, even after their species
was outed. But I'm pretty sure they do drink blood."

At that, Quentin looked over at us, his eyes darkening at the word *blood* as he met Leif's gaze.

A moment later, he was at our table again, handing out our menus.

"Just so you know," Quentin said, lowering his voice as two canines snicked out from his gums, revealed in a bright smile that negated the threat his teeth posed. "We do drink blood."

I inched closer, eager to hear more. "What about all the other stuff?" But he wasn't listening to me, too busy staring at Leif's carotid artery pulsing in his neck as his cheeks flushed.

I blinked, and suddenly Quentin whispered something in Leif's ear before he hurried away again, gone in a silent flash.

Leif turned from pink to beet red at whatever Quentin said, purposefully not meeting my eye as he picked up his menu.

I slapped it down. "*What was that?*"

Leif cleared his throat. "Nothing."

"He wants to drink your blood, doesn't he?" Leif didn't answer, but his eyes darted over to where Quentin had disappeared back into the kitchen again. "*Oh my God!* He does! Are you going to let him? Is shifter blood okay for them?"

"Keep your voice down!" Leif adjusted the collar of his shirt. "I'm sure shifter blood works fine for them, but it doesn't matter. He probably says that to tons of people."

"Uh-huh." Quentin was staring at him again from across the room. "Dude, he is *into* you."

Leif blushed again, a shaky laugh escaping him. I was almost positive that teasing him was against the wolfy code I needed to learn, but it was too fun.

Damn, first video games with West, now getting lunch with Leif, and I'd had more *fun* in two days than I'd had in years.

Still, I could be merciful, so I picked up my menu and let the subject drop.

"So," I said, drawing out the word. "What's good here?"

"Everything." Leif set his menu down, looking relieved at the change in subject. "This was Cora's restaurant — West's mom — and apparently she was the best cook. Terran runs this place mostly off her old recipes and only lets the best dishes stay on the menu. Just whatever you do, don't order —"

"I'll have the buffalo burger," I said as Quentin reappeared with a notepad.

A dish shattered behind us and all conversation in the restaurant ceased. Every head whipped to our table.

A dozen pairs of eyes stared daggers into my skull.

A deep grunt that sounded a lot like a dying buffalo echoed down the valley as a small child burst into tears two tables over.

I cleared my throat. "Something I said?"

"You *never* order the buffalo burger!" Leif hissed under his breath.

Quentin nodded sagely, pointing to the taxidermied bison head on the wall. "The buffalo is sacred."

I leaned forward, lowering my voice. "Then why is it on the menu?"

But Leif, Quentin, and everyone in the room were shaking their heads at me.

"Forgive her Willie," Leif murmured to the bison head on the wall, crossing himself and then putting his thumbs against his temples, hands clutched into fists with his pinkies out — horns. "She knows not what she says."

"Okay"— I put my hands up — "a regular burger it is."

A collective breath of relief whooshed through the room, and after Leif placed his order for the same, Quentin vanished again.

"Ever since Heath — West's dad — started running his accidental buffalo sanctuary a few years ago, it became an unspoken rule not to actually *order* the buffalo burger," Leif explained quietly, but my attention had shot to the door, where West entered with a man who looked like West in twenty years — Heath, presumably. "It was Cora's specialty though, so no one can bring themselves to take it off the menu. Heath thinks it's a sign the buffalo just keep appearing here. Cora's way of making sure Heath doesn't give up on life without her."

That was romantic in the strangest way, but apparently the whole town bought into it, so I noted never to order buffalo again.

Leif kept up a steady stream of chatter about the town and the latest gossip, but I couldn't tear my gaze from West as he made his way around the room. He stopped to chat with *every-body*. He knew every single person in the room, greeting everyone with a smile and genuine interest in what they were saying.

From the tidbits of conversation I caught, half of the people he spoke with had a problem they wanted him to fix, and he listened intently to each one. The other half just wanted to catch up, or share the latest news from their own businesses and lives.

How could he keep track of all that? How could he keep up with managing all these people's issues and solving all these tiny problems? It would be exhausting. His insomnia made so much sense.

West's eyes caught mine, even though he didn't break from his conversation with the table in the corner, and I was para-lyzed. Caught like a rabbit in a snare, the air pulled tight between us.

I only snapped out of it when Leif tapped my hand.

"What?"

"You know a stare off is a challenge to another wolf, right?"

I blinked, and realized Leif was glancing between West and me discreetly.

I shuffled in my seat so it would be easier to keep West out of my line of sight. "He started it."

Leif raised an eyebrow to show just how much he believed that, but let it go.

"Leif, my boy, you didn't tell me you were into cougars," came a boisterous voice, and Heath clapped Leif on the shoulder with a grin at me as Leif went bright red again. He held a hand out to me. "Heath Larkin, pleasure to meet you."

I stood to shake his hand. "Jade Rodriguez. I'm Leif's — what's the opposite of a sugar daddy? A sour mama?"

Leif mumbled under his breath, but Heath barked a laugh and, unexpectedly, pulled me out of the booth and into a tight hug.

"Oh, I like you already, Jade."

"Dad, let her breathe."

Heath pulled back at West's words, but not before giving my shoulder a squeeze.

"Oh!" Heath clapped his hands together, already back-tracking towards the kitchen. "Stay right there, Jade! I want an unbiased opinion on my balls. You two" — he snapped his fingers at Leif and West — "do *not* turn her against me!"

The kitchen saloon doors swung shut behind him.

"He — say *what*?" I spluttered.

West shook his head and gestured for me to return to my seat, sliding into the bench beside me.

"Not what you think," he assured me as his thigh grazed mine under the table. I forced myself not to react to it, but the tiniest touch had Balto losing her shit, belly up and panting for more.

"It's worse," Leif muttered, then clamped his lips shut as Heath reappeared with a small plate of what looked like meatballs.

"You don't have any allergies, do you, Jade?" Heath asked, sliding in beside Leif and pushing the plate towards me. "Wolves never do, but I don't know how it works with witches and I know you're half."

"Oh." I was surprised he knew about me, but West must have told him everything. "No allergies, no."

"Great! Have one, have one!"

Leif shook his head subtly until Heath elbowed him hard in the ribs.

"Hey, what did I say about leading the witness?"

"Is she on trial?" West turned to me. "You do not have to eat that."

Despite West's warning tone, Heath beamed at me with uninhibited expectation, and for some reason, I found myself not wanting to let him down.

It couldn't be that bad, right? I'd once eaten a dirt cup Ruby made me with gummy worms and chocolate pudding, not realizing she put *actual* dirt in it.

As Leif cringed and West held his breath, I popped one of the mysterious balls in my mouth, Heath's eyes widening as he awaited my judgment.

At first, it wasn't too bad. A little gamey. But then the second wave hit.

I coughed, my eyes stinging and tearing up immediately as my throat burned.

"Oh, shit," I wheezed, and Leif wordlessly slid his water over to me as I chugged my own and slammed the empty cup down. "How is it — so spicy — and yet — so sour?"

"Pop Rocks," West and Leif said in unison.

Heath hummed, lips twisted to the side as he tapped his fingers on the table. "I'll tweak it a little more."

"No amount of tweaking will ever make those edible," West said. "Pop Rocks and Carolina Reapers will never cancel each other out."

"Ye of little faith, my son." Heath clapped West on the shoulder, then made his way to the kitchen.

"You're one of us now, Jade," Leif offered grimly. "You survived the Balls."

"Is this surviving?" I indicated my watery eyes and the sweat still beading on my brow. Was I frothing at the mouth? It sure felt like it.

Quentin set our burgers down, and I shoveled in a fistful of fries to chase the taste out of my mouth as Leif and West laughed.

People dropped by to chat with West while we ate, and even though his food went cold, he gave every one of them his time and full attention.

At one point, a couple guys came over to chat about some construction work, their eyes drifting over to me repeatedly until West casually stretched an arm across the back of the bench behind me. I hadn't realized I'd curled in on myself, trying to shrink away from their attention, until the warmth of West's arm fed me reassurance.

"We should be ready to start construction soon if the plans are ready, Alpha," the tallest one said. I eyed him warily, taking in his a grey t-shirt, jeans, and workboots. His black hair and beard were neatly trimmed and combed, his freckled skin showing the effects of being out in the sun a lot. Nothing about his posture was meant to be intimidating but I hated how his dark eyes trailed between me and West, a question and a challenge waiting just beneath the surface.

Part of me, maybe Balto, urged me to meet his eyes, to challenge him right back and memorize his features so I could report him if needed. The other part of me just wanted to run away and hide somewhere until he left.

"I'll get in touch with Aspen and have her send them over. Thanks Jett."

The conversation was over, but the guys still stood there, all but staring at me. The second guy felt a lot less intense than the first one, his hands casually in the pockets of his sweatpants, though he was just as built as most shifters. His black shirt only enhanced his naturally brown skin, and his hair was cropped close to his head. He offered me a polite nod before Jett asked, "Who's she?"

I opened my mouth, about to snap that he could ask me

himself if he wanted to know who I was, but West's arm slid from the back of the bench onto my shoulder, squeezing gently in warning.

"With me, Jett," was all West offered, staring him down.

After a tense moment, the other guy tugged on Jett's shirt, and once he blinked, he muttered an apology to West and let the other guy steer him away.

As soon as they left, West removed his arm from me, and the tiniest part of me missed its warmth and weight.

I shook it off. "Who were they?"

"Jett and Zion. They're pack Shields — just below Terran in rank. They just wanted to sniff you out." West shook his head.

"Is everyone here in your pack?" I asked, not missing the way West's eyes narrowed ever so slightly when I said *your* pack.

"Not everyone, but most. The rest are other types of supes."

West and Leif proceeded to point out the various members of the pack to me that were in the room, including their various pack roles.

I tried to keep up, but I hadn't even known there *were* pack roles. Other than Alpha and Second, anyway. But apparently everyone here had some designation or another — Trackers, Shields, and other titles I didn't even understand.

The more they talked about how everyone contributed and played their role, the more I was convinced I'd never belong.

Even if I wanted to join the pack, what could I possibly do? Half-assed bartending? Wait tables with barely-functioning anxiety? I couldn't track or guard or any of the other stuff they rattled off like it was no big deal.

Hell, I couldn't even use my nose to scent a demon when one was right in front of me.

"Jade?" West's voice drew me out of my spiral, his brows furrowed in concern. He raised a hand like he wanted to place it on my shoulder, but at the last second set it back down.

"What?" I shook myself, trying to clear the self-pity that wouldn't do me any good, and forced a smile.

West inched imperceptibly closer. "You just got all — my wolf felt yours —"

"All good, West." I patted his hand awkwardly. "Just trying to think of the best mnemonic to remember all these names and whatnot. Did you know mnemonic has a silent m? Weird, right? Those used to be my favorite to whip out on Scrabble night with Ruby —"

West's hand curled around mine, the heat of his palm radiating through me, but I plowed right on, ignoring it like a champ.

"Pterodactyl, tsunami, gnome — oh, my God, Ruby refused to believe gnome. She tried three dictionaries —"

"Jade?" A new voice cut through my babbling, and in a way, I was relieved. Leif was already looking at me like I'd lost my marbles.

There was something eerily familiar about that voice, though. I twisted around to find its source, and my heart leapt to my throat.

Chapter Fourteen

WEST

My hackles rose the instant I set eyes on the newcomer, for three reasons.

One, I didn't know him. I knew everyone in this town.

Two, he *terrified* Jade. She'd stopped breathing as she stared at him, her eyes wide and pulse racing.

Three, he smelled wrong. I couldn't put my finger on it, but there was something off about him.

"B-Bram," Jade croaked, her eyes darting around the room as her face drained of color. She squeezed my hand so tightly, my fingers ached. If it made her feel even the tiniest bit better, she could break my fingers for all I cared.

Togo bared his teeth, snarling and ready to snap, the sharp scent of Jade's fear all we needed to run this asshole out of town. But, like the adult I was supposed to be, I fought to keep my cool.

For now, Togo answered.

I had to agree.

I closed my eyes, counted to three, then pulled myself to my feet, offering him my hand.

"I don't think we've met. West Larkin."

Bram sized me up, no doubt taking in the height difference between us and the good 50 pounds of muscle I had on him, and took my hand.

Did I grip his a little too hard? Maybe.

Even if I couldn't smell the witch on him, Bram dressed the part like a cliché. Head to toe in black, with his ripped skinny jeans and black eyeliner, witch marks and runes tattooed over his pale forearms. His dark hair was cut short, and while he looked to be in his mid-twenties, you never could be sure with witches.

Inhaling his scent and cataloging it in my memory, I grinned, letting the barest hint of my canines show. Luckily for him, his scent didn't match the two humans who'd kidnapped Jade or I'd rip him to pieces in the middle of my family's restaurant.

To his credit, Bram didn't back down easily. "Bram Rasmus," he offered, then nodded to Jade. "Haven't seen you around in ages, Jade."

Jade slid out of the booth, and when she dropped my hand, I couldn't help sidling up to her, pressing my side into hers. She had no idea what that meant, and at the moment, I didn't mind.

Stepping forward with a hesitant glance my way, Bram reached out for Jade, who awkwardly met his arms in a hug.

I narrowed my eyes. Why was Jade hugging this guy she was so scared of?

"You two know each other?" I asked, waiting for one of them to clarify what was going on here. Togo was running out of patience.

"We used to," Jade stammered, stepping out of Bram's arms and scanning the room again. "Are you here alone?"

Bram took a healthy step back, just enough for my wolf to stop snarling at him. Clearly *he* knew a thing or two about shifters.

"Just passing through. I had an order to pick up at Moonrise Emporium."

I sensed the anxiety ratchet up again in Jade, her entire body starting to shake. Togo reared again, more irritated than before.

Jade was clueless the rest of the pack had tuned in to this conversation, their awareness drawn to Togo's heightening emotions. I raised the walls around my mental connection, but didn't close them entirely in case a fight broke out.

"You're still there? With… *them?*"

Bram stuffed his hands in his pockets, rocking back on his heels. "Yeah? Listen, we've all been wondering where you went for years. You and Ruby just disappeared, never to be seen or heard from again. We thought maybe you died in the attack, but couldn't figure out why they'd leave so many bodies behind but not yours. Thaddeus will be relieved to hear —"

"No!" Jade's hands went up in a *Stop* motion, her fear spiking to a near paralyzing level as her wolf surged forward, eyes glowing and ready to shift. Did she even notice her nails lengthening to claws? "You can't tell him you saw me. You can't tell *anyone.*"

As close as I was to losing control, Jade's shaky balance with her wolf was frightening. Whatever was going on here, her wolf thought Jade was in mortal danger. My canines descended fully, Togo insisting we shift and take a chunk out of this guy, but I ground my teeth together, hiding them until I could get myself under control.

Confusion was clear as day on Bram's face, his forehead wrinkled as he squinted at Jade. Then his gaze slid to me, to my arm still touching Jade's side, and he let out a derisive snort. "Oh, I get it. You ran off and left Thaddeus for this guy."

Anger flashed through Jade's eyes. "That is *not* what happened —"

"No, it's cool, Jade." Bram's hands went up. "I won't say anything. I wouldn't want to be the one to tell Thaddeus you broke your engagement and fell into the lap of the first Alpha you found, anyway."

"Don't be like this," Jade snapped at him, but I was done listening, and so was my wolf.

My voice was low as I stepped in front of Jade, several members of my pack appearing silently at my side and behind Bram, circling our prey. "I don't know who you are, but you've got about thirty seconds to get out of my town."

"I've got her," Leif called to my mind, and I took a deliberate step forward, forcing Bram back towards the door.

"Hey, man, I was just here picking up an order," Bram shot back as he backed away, bumping into the door, then through it as he moved out onto the street.

"Then why are you still here?" Terran said from behind him, having circled the building and come around front when he sensed trouble. Bram bumped up against Terran's chest and spun, his head swiveling between Terran and me as he realized the number of shifters who'd quickly formed a circle around us.

"What are they doing?" I heard Jade ask Leif as she pushed through the door to join us on the street, but I couldn't focus on her now.

Bram glared at Terran, but didn't turn his back on me. Maybe he wasn't a total idiot. Like a cornered animal, he lifted his arms, preparing for a fight he had no chance of winning. "I can't eat at a public restaurant? Last I heard, Timber Creek was one of the most inclusive towns in the Rockies, but I guess I heard wrong. This is some bullshit." He spat on the ground, and Terran licked his teeth, cocking his head at me in a silent ask for permission to strike.

"Bram." Jade stepped forward, but I put my arm out to stop her, keeping her behind my back. "Just go."

The witch flexed his hands, curling them into fists, and I took back any previous thoughts that this male wasn't an idiot.

"Are you kidding me right now, West?" Jade scoffed, side-stepping my arm and I fought the urge to bare my teeth. A ripple of shock went through the pack bonds as everyone watched her blatantly disobey my orders. Even if I hadn't said them aloud, my body language had been clear — at least, to shifters. "All that's missing is the tumbleweed rolling between you two and we could call this a saloon fight. He's not going to hurt me."

"Hey Jade," Leif called, his voice nearly shaking. The whole pack was buzzing, ready and waiting for a fight, and now even more on edge with her confusing them. "Let's… go this way."

"No," the infuriating female said, all sense of self-preservation gone as her small hand shoved my shoulder. "Let him go, West."

Sensing my father behind me, I didn't break eye contact with Bram as I moved Jade right into Heath's waiting arms. "Get her out of here, now."

"What?" Jade snapped, indignation making her voice high and sharp. "This is ridic—"

Her words cut off in a gasp as Heath threw her over his shoulder, marching down the street towards the pack house.

"This is going to backfire, son," Heath sent to me, but I ignored him, refocusing on the witch. I needed this asshole taken care of, now.

"Actually, Bram, before you go" — I nodded to Terran, who whipped his phone out in a heartbeat, typing away — "we have one more person we'll need you to meet. Well, two, technically, but we might have to wait a tic for the second one."

With a flash-bang theatrical enough to wow any half-rate magician's audience — and decidedly unnecessary — Cruz flickered into the midst of our showdown, grinning ear to ear. His dark hair was as messy as his grease-stained shirt and jeans, but then again, that was how Cruz always looked.

"I hear there's a witch for me to —"

I pointed at Bram, who barely had time to register the demon's presence before Cruz's magic lashed around him, tackling him to the ground and binding him in place, keeping the witch from reaching any of his own magic to fight back.

Cruz let out a whoop, and sprinkled a shower of sparks down on Bram's writhing body as he fought the magical bindings, hissing as the sparks met his skin.

"Fuck, it's been ages since you needed me to go all *Bad Cop* around here." Cruz grinned, rolling his shoulders. "I like it."

Chapter Fifteen

JADE

"Heath, I know you're following orders, but if you don't put me down *right* now, I'm going to shred this shirt until you do!"

Heath only chuckled — *chuckled* — and kept walking with no indication he would do any such thing. What happened to the nice old man with horrific taste in food?

"Have at it, sweetheart, I never liked this shirt. But I'm not putting you down till we're inside. Don't worry, we're almost there."

I growled in frustration, my body bouncing awkwardly against his back. "I can walk, you know. If you put me down, I promise I'll be good."

"In case the white hair didn't tip you off, I wasn't born yesterday. I raised five teenagers who were just as terrible at lying as you are."

"What are they doing to him? Who was that guy that showed up?"

"That's Cruz. And they're going to do what they have to do to keep you safe."

I gasped. "They can't *kill* him!"

"No! No," Heath assured me, typing in the gate code and letting us in, starting the climb up the winding driveway. "They'll hold him for a bit and make sure he won't talk. Not my boys' first rodeo protecting someone on the run."

Back in the house, Heath finally set me down on my feet. My

world spun, black spotting my vision as the blood rushed from my head.

"They won't hurt him?" I took a deep breath as my body regulated itself upright again. "And I'm not on the run," I added after the fact, not even believing my own words.

Heath eyed me cautiously, but didn't prod. "Not unnecessarily. C'mon, let's grab a drink. I have a feeling you could use one."

Too stunned by everything that had just gone down to disagree, I followed Heath to the living room, where he poured us both a finger of whiskey.

))) ● (((

Twenty minutes ticked by agonizingly slow as I stewed, pacing the length of the living room and feeling no less settled despite the whiskey in my system. By the time the front door crashed open, my teeth were about to become powder if I ground them any harder.

"And that's my cue to leave. Good luck, sweetheart," Heath said, grabbing his whiskey off the coffee table, and retreating out to the back patio.

I planted my feet as West stormed through the house, stopping right in front of me.

"Where is Bram?" I asked, ice coating my words. "What did you do to him?"

West's jaw clenched, his head tipping to the side as he closed his eyes in frustration. "You don't get to ask the questions right now, Jade."

I jerked back at his tone. Was he seriously angry at *me* right now?

"I sure as hell do when you go all Big Bad Wolf on my friend!"

"Your *friend?*" West stepped up into my space but didn't touch me, forcing me to tilt my head back to meet his eye. "The one that made your scent sharp with fear? That made your heart race, your body shake? That made you panic at what information he could relay to some *Thaddeus*? That friend?"

I curled my hands into fists, but I didn't have to answer him. My relationships with Bram *or* Thaddeus were none of his business.

"Here's what's going to happen next, Jade. We're going to sit and have a long chat about Bram, and Thaddeus, and whatever the hell it is you're running from. I need to know every secret, every potential risk you pose to my pack, every threat that could head our way while you're here."

"No."

West raised an eyebrow. "I wasn't asking. Consider this your first Alpha order."

I seethed. "Ironic, coming from the male who told me his pack is different because they accept everyone, *no questions asked*. I should have known it's because you don't *ask*, you *order*. Too bad I never asked to join your pack. You're not my Alpha, and I take no orders from you or anyone else, asshole."

West shook his head, pulling in a long breath. "You're right, I'm not your Alpha. But seeing you that afraid, that *terrified*, is something I can't tolerate. I thought your heart was going to give out, it was racing so fast. Every single member of my pack was ready to rip Bram apart because my wolf was losing his fucking mind, and I barely held control over the crowd, even before you disobeyed me. I can't have that happen again, and I can't protect you if I don't know what the threat is."

I reared back as if his words had physically slapped me. Tears burned in the back of my eyes at his words, but I refused to give him even an ounce of my emotions. Of course, how dare I disobey the great *Alpha Larkin* in front of his pack. "Fuck you, West."

Shoving at his chest, I pushed my way out from under his

looming frame and towards the back door. "We're not done discussing this, Jade."

But *I* was done. I pushed the door aside, running right past Heath, down the steps and into the forest beyond.

Wind ruffled my hair as I sprinted away from the pack house, needing to put as much distance between West and me as I could. I wasn't sure if he was following — probably — and I didn't care.

I'd made plenty of mistakes where men were involved, Thaddeus being the most glaring example, and today proved I needed to get the fuck away from West. While his kindness towards his family and town was unexpected, he'd shown his true colors today — a controlling Alpha, just like I knew he was. I saw it at that first dinner, and I saw it again now. Fool me once, shame on him. I refused to be fooled twice.

Needing to distract myself from the hurt of his words, I sniffed the air, searching for any signs of Bram but found none. I never wanted to see Thaddeus again, but Bram was mostly innocent of the Coven's many crimes.

He was the highlight of my years with the Coven, his friendship the one thing I didn't regret about my time there. In the end, I still wish he'd seen the harm Thaddeus was doing and defended me, but I couldn't blame Bram for that either. He was just as blind to it all as I had been, maybe he still was. Ruby's and my safety was far more important than Bram's and my friendship, though.

Until he cut ties with the Coven, any hope of rekindling a bond with Bram was impossible. Just the idea of him sharing where he'd seen me urged me to move faster, feet pounding on the earth to put distance between me and Timber Creek.

The temperature dropped drastically, and I looked up at the sky, the heavy grey clouds matching my thoughts as the first fat raindrop landed on my cheek. More followed, the storm worsening as quickly as it had appeared. I ducked under the cover of the trees, but had to keep moving even though my clothes were soaked through.

Even if West hadn't acted like an asshole, I couldn't go back. If there was even the slightest chance Thaddeus could catch wind of my location, that place wasn't safe. I'd been running for years, and I'd been a fool to think I could stop now.

I picked up a new scent as I skirted around a line of boulders, but it wasn't one I recognized. Once again proving I was useless as a wolf, and better off pretending I wasn't one.

When a giant mountain lion stepped into my path, I shrieked.

Chapter Sixteen

JADE

Skidding to a halt, I stopped only a few feet from the huge cat. I didn't know much about real mountain lions, but this one was way too big to be natural, and its eyes glowed the same as a shifter's.

Suddenly, the cat shifted, and became a giant naked man instead.

Why did this keep happening to me?

"Now's not the time to run off, pup," Cooper said gruffly. He looked a hell of a lot different naked than when I'd seen him on the back porch a few days ago, barrel chest hidden beneath his plaid shirt. Were all shifter males this ripped? Maybe I'd been doing myself an injustice avoiding my kind.

He took a step closer, and I shuffled backwards. He paused.

"We can do this the easy way or the hard way, Jade. Either you come back to my place willingly, or I can shift back and carry you in my teeth." He shot me a pointed stare. "They're sharp."

I huffed. Leave it to all those muscles to momentarily distract me from how domineering shifter men were. What was it with them and carrying me?

Still, I'd had enough of being thrown around like a sack of potatoes for one day and had no doubt he'd do as threatened, so I took the barest step forward to show him I would comply.

In a blink, his human form was gone, the large cat in front of me once more as he turned, tail flicking casually as he led the way through the forest.

If he wasn't twice my weight and three times as fast, I might have contemplated running, but I knew my chances of escape were next to none.

I wrapped my arms around myself, cold quickly seeping into my bones now that I was drenched. Cooper kept up a steady, loping gait I struggled to match in my wet shoes, hardly able to see through the rain.

Smoke rose from the chimney on a small A-frame cabin, almost hidden in the dense aspen grove we trekked through. Cooper walked right up onto the porch, shifting in front of the door. He opened it and reached for something inside while I tried and failed not to stare at his muscled ass. Tossing a hoodie towards me, he headed inside, leaving the door open for me.

The arrogance in his movements — he didn't insist I follow him, he just *knew* I would — annoyed the hell out of me. I begrudgingly pulled the hoodie over my head, and it fell down to my knees. Even in human form, Cooper was huge.

Too cold to stand outside, I went in. His rustic cabin was nothing like the main pack house, the first floor all one room, with a loft above that was presumably the bedroom.

I crossed my arms as I stood just inside the door, not sure what to do now we were in here. "So, what, I'm a captive now?"

Cooper's head peeked out from the edge of the loft as he pulled a shirt over his head, already having found pants. "I could tie you up, but you don't seem like that kind of girl."

My jaw nearly fell open at his words. "Excuse me?"

Not bothering to apologize or explain himself, Cooper made his way back down the steps towards me, now fully clothed.

Cooper said nothing, proceeding to his kitchen to open the fridge, studying its contents before grabbing a few things. He worked in silence, pulling pots and pans from the cabinets as he threw together ingredients with a confidence I'd never felt in the kitchen.

"Do all of you cook?" I asked, curiosity getting the best of me as meat sizzled in a pan, the scent of chili seasoning reaching me. "Is this a thing with the Larkin family?"

He glanced over his shoulder at me as he pointed to the barstool on the other side of the counter from him. "Sit."

I arched a brow in challenge, but Cooper didn't wait to see if I obeyed his command. Apparently he wasn't as concerned about Alpha dynamics as West was, although no way was this male not also an Alpha. Were all cats Alphas, for that matter? From what I knew about wild mountain lions, they were lone creatures, not traveling in a pack, so maybe the same could be said for the shifters. Yet another thing I had no idea about.

Frustration and annoyance at my own ignorance drove me to sit where Cooper had pointed, not a need to follow his order.

He worked with quick precision, whisking some sort of sauce in a pan as he flipped the meat in the skillet simultaneously. It was fascinating to watch, especially considering the way his large, very muscled back flexed when he moved.

"Quit staring at me," he said, and I snapped my eyes up to the back of his head — how'd he even known?

"I can see you're the friendly brother," I said, sarcasm dripping from my words, but Cooper didn't rise to the bait. He was as stoic as they came.

He flipped off the burners and slid the chicken and rice covered in a red sauce he'd made onto two plates, then pushed one across the counter to me. "Eat."

"I just did in town." I nudged the plate back towards him, even though I was kind of hungry after my flight through the forest. I didn't want to accept anything else from these people.

Cooper pushed the plate back my way again, reached across the counter to grab my hand and placed a fork in it. "Eat."

Stare off number seventy-two since I'd arrived in Timber Creek commenced. But then my traitorous stomach rumbled and I looked down at it. Realizing what I'd done, I looked up just in time to see satisfaction lit in Cooper's eyes.

I lost, by a long shot. Did anyone ever win a stare off against a cat?

With a deep sigh, I stabbed at the chicken, swirling it in the sauce before I put it in my mouth. Cooper focused on me until I swallowed, the glare almost eerie in its intensity.

"Cora cooked all the time," Cooper said as he cut into his own chicken. "Our mom."

I looked up, a little surprised by the olive branch Cooper was offering. "Leif said the restaurant was hers before she passed," I said between bites to encourage him to keep opening up. I'd wanted to refuse him, but this was delicious and I couldn't stop myself from shoveling it in. "Did she teach you guys how to cook?"

He nodded. "She was constantly making something and we all fought over helping her. With five kids in the house, you had to be scrappy if you wanted one-on-one attention, but Mom always seemed to have a moment for all of us. I never under-stood how she could make us all feel like we were her favorite, simultaneously, but she did."

Emotion tugged at me, feeling the power of his words. What would it have been like to grow up in a house full of that much love? Cooper wasn't even her biological child, and yet, by the way he talked about her just in those few words, I knew that never mattered to Cora.

I only had Ruby, and I hoped I'd made her feel like she was my favorite, but I drowned myself in guilt for all the times I'd struggled to feel like *anything* was my favorite. Refusing to let myself spiral into that depressing thought, I cleared my throat. "She sounds lovely."

We finished our meal in silence, and Cooper reached across to grab my plate after I was done, turning to the sink.

"I can help with dishes," I offered, feeling useless sitting at the counter. But Cooper waved me off, apparently done talking.

I rose from the chair, pushing it in as neatly as it had been before, and spun, taking in the rest of the small space.

"West said you might want to call your sister," Cooper said as he stood at the sink. I paused, squeezing my eyes shut as I fought back the emotions that overcame me at his words. "My phone is on the table — you can use it."

"Okay." My voice cracked, but I grabbed his phone and walked towards the front door. "Mind if I sit on the front porch?"

He turned towards me. "You're aware I run much faster than you, correct?"

I tipped my head up towards the ceiling to hide the eye roll, but gave him a thumbs up.

Pushing through the door, I sat in the rocking chair, pulled my knees up to my chest under the oversized hoodie, and dialed my sister's number. Rain flowed off the roofline, the water creating a barrier between me and the outside world.

"Hello?" Ruby answered on the first ring, tone slightly panicked. "Jade?"

"Yeah." Tears itched at my eyes at the sound of her voice. Why was I such a mess today? "Hey sis."

"Holy crap, I've been so worried about you. Mo got a call that something happened to you, but you're safe and in Timber Creek, but that's all I've heard. Spill it, now. What the heck happened?"

I puffed out my cheeks, feeling the weight of the last several days in a way I hadn't allowed myself to until this moment. "I was picked up."

The line went silent for several seconds before Ruby said, "Like, *kidnapped*, picked up?"

"Well, I'm 32, so I don't know if kidnapped is the correct term anymore, but I guess. *Attempted* kidnapping." In a sudden rush, I couldn't hold it back anymore and the whole story spilled out of me: the new job, the humans who knew what I was, escaping and somehow shifting into my wolf, running blindly to fall right at West Larkin's feet, my time in the pack house, the tour of town, all of it.

Well, not *all* of it. I didn't tell her about the almost kiss because Ruby would focus on that, romanticizing it into something much larger than it was. And besides, West was dead to me now.

"I'm so glad you're okay," Ruby said, her voice shaky.

"Don't cry, please."

"I'm sorry," she sniffed, "you know I'm the weepy one of the family."

"If you cry, then I might cry, and I really don't want to cry right now. I'm out in the middle of nowhere at West's brother's house, and he already thinks I'm insane. I don't need to become a blubbery mess. You know how puffy my eyes get. It's not a good look."

Ruby giggled, tears seeming to dwindle. "Okay, but why are you at his brother's house?"

Conveniently I'd ended the story before bringing up Bram's sudden appearance. Ruby and I didn't talk about our years with the Coven for a reason — she didn't remember most of it, because I'd made a deal with Max to erase her memory.

Everything was glossed over in her mind like a distant childhood memory even though she'd been a teen when we lived with them. Max had erased or manipulated the worst of our time there, while I remembered every painful moment. I had to — it was my penance for the mistakes I'd made to lead us there in the first place.

I'd failed her so terribly.

Tears slid down my face and I wiped them away as fast as they fell, blinking rapidly to clear my vision.

"It's a long story, but I can't stay here anymore. I need to move on again."

"I thought you said you lost your phone, cards, everything. Even your truck is compromised — they know your plates now."

Ruby was quiet for a minute, then whispered, "I don't think that's a good idea, Jade."

"Not your decision to make, Ruby." I hated how harsh I sounded, but between the fear the Coven would find me again and how controlling West had been, I couldn't stay here. It was bad for both my safety and my heart.

"You have no idea how much I worry about you, do you?"

My sister's words pulled me up short, stopping the logistical planning that had already taken over in my mind. "What?"

"*I* need you to stay there, to figure out a better plan before you just take off again. You always do this. If something feels like it might be too good to be true, you run. Maybe Timber Creek is like that for you."

"Ruby," I sighed. "If something seems too good to be true, it almost always is."

"Deadlights Cove isn't."

"Says the girl who was possessed by a demonic curse while evil villains tried to destroy the town. Not sure that's what I'd call *good*, sis."

"Whatever," Ruby said, sounding every bit like the teenager I'd raised. "You never listen to me anyway. Just stay safe, okay? Call me when you get settled wherever you end up."

The defeat in Ruby's voice was hard to hear — once again I'd disappointed her. I hung my head, indecision racking me. "You know I will."

"Love you."

"Ditto."

She hung up, and I put the phone down, staring at it. The rain had let up while we talked, and birds chirped in the trees overhead, life moving on as if the world hadn't been rocked by the worry in my little sister's voice.

But it wasn't her life I was living — it was mine. I needed to make the right decision for me, whatever that was.

I dropped my feet to the deck, moving back inside. Cooper

was nowhere to be seen, but I wasn't dumb enough to think he'd left me here alone after his comment about outrunning me.

A worn deck of cards sat on the coffee table and I walked over to it, dropping onto the couch. Driven by muscle memory, I set up a game of Solitaire, just as I'd done thousands of times before. My mind calmed as I went through the motions, sorting cards, strategizing how to get them all to their designated place when Cooper dropped into the chair across from me. I glanced up for a split second, but didn't say anything — Cooper was a quiet guy and that was fine by me.

I finished the game quickly — easy to do when I'd played dozens of hands a week for years — and picked up the cards, shuffling them back into a neat stack.

"War?" I asked as I shuffled the cards again, and Cooper held out a hand for the deck. I passed them to him and he dealt two neat stacks, passing me one.

I leaned forward, fighting back a smile at the comfort of the simple game. Ruby and I had played War almost nightly, but it had been years since I'd had anyone to play with.

Neither of us spoke as we moved through the cards quickly, flipping numbers so fast they blurred.

"Wow," I commented nonchalantly. "You're almost as good as my little sister."

Cooper paused for a split second, then tilted his head. "Oh, gonna be like that, is it?"

The corner of my lip twitched when his eyes flashed with amusement.

The size of our stacks alternated as we went through hand after hand. Cooper only had four cards left in his hand when we both threw down queens. My heart raced as we silently put down two face-down cards, then flipped the last one. His was a three, mine an ace.

"Ha!" I yelled out, then pumped my fist in the air, grabbing the cards off the table, adding them to my pile as a shit-eating grin took over my face. "You lose, sucker."

Cooper sat back in his chair. He held out one hand, opening and closing it before he pointed at the deck. "Best out of three."

I scoffed, shuffling the cards on the table, flaring them out to exaggerate how adept I was with cards. They were cheap and endless entertainment, both wins in my book. And anything was better than being lost to my own memories. "Being a sore loser must also be a Larkin family trait. Either way, you're going down, Whiskers."

Chapter Seventeen

WEST

I paced the length of the living room, fists clenched so I didn't lash out and hit something. Togo slammed against the thin barrier in my mind, furious I wouldn't let him out to hunt Jade down. He wanted to drag her back, to lock her in the bedroom upstairs and refuse to let her out while we hunted down anyone who'd ever hurt her, but I couldn't do that.

I'd seen her face when she'd run out the door — looked like I could add myself to the list of people who had hurt Jade now.

Fuck.

"You're going to wear a hole in the carpet, brother," Terran said as he strolled in the room with a sleeping River in his arms. Only the sight of the peaceful little girl kept me from pulling Terran out into the yard for a shifted fight to work off some of my aggression. I knew he'd do it, too, but he needed to keep his strength up.

With Jade's display in the street, it was only a matter of time before some of the cockier wolves came looking for a fight, champing at the bit at my perceived moment of weakness. As my Second, he'd be the one responsible for keeping them from getting to the door.

"She *ran*."

"No, really? The girl scared shitless of alphaholes ran when you ordered her around?" Terran shook his head, moving towards the stairs. "Have you seen yourself? You're not helping anything. What did you say to her when you got back? Did you at least apologize for telling Heath to throw her over his shoulder?"

I paused, thinking through our whole conversation. Shit, I really had messed up. I hadn't apologized for anything. Instead, I'd demanded she tell me every secret she'd ever had, thrown every bit of Alpha power into the command, and somehow, she'd still denied me. Which led me to my next question — just how powerful was her wolf?

"Well, from that eloquent answer, I'm gonna go ahead and guess you dug yourself a nice big hole to jump into," Terran said, a hint of amusement in his voice as he reached the top of the stairs, turning to River's room. "Good luck, man. Bring a ladder."

The mocking tone was something no one outside my family would dare take with me, a familiarity not allowed or proper with an Alpha, especially not one of my rank, and something that always wore on me. Seeing the easy friendships others had, their joking, playful banter — I wasn't allowed those things. Every conversation was a business transaction, someone needing something from me, and I gave it every time.

But Jade didn't care about any of that.

She rolled her eyes at me every chance she had, refusing everything I'd done to try to help her. Why was that both infuriating and invigorating?

In my pocket, my phone buzzed.

COOPER

Located your fugitive.

His choice of words didn't help assuage my guilt. I was about to strip, shift, and run out to meet them when a second text came through.

COOPER

Maybe hang back till she cools down. I'll keep her here.

Shit, now even Cooper was giving me advice? About a *female*? The male was a recluse, had been since he was a kid. As far as I knew, he hardly talked to anyone outside our family. While I was sure he wasn't as celibate as Terran and I gave him shit about, no one in our family had ever seen Cooper involved with a female, ever. At least, not since —

A *thump* sounded from the deck, and looking up from my phone, Max gave a wave through the windows as he straightened from his landing, already tucking his black wings in against his back.

"You wolves are getting pretty needy," he snarked as I joined him out on the deck. "What now, Larkin?"

With a grimace, I explained the situation with Bram and Jade. His eyes darkened as I spoke, a flash of recognition at Bram's name, and I clenched my jaw, biting back the order to know more.

"*Just* erase his memory?" he clarified, shadows seeping out from his boots, growing and rising like a black fog, twitching in a mirror of his unrest. "How much has Jade told you? Do you know what happened? Bram is—"

I shook my head, refusing to give into the curiosity eating at me. As I'd suspected, Max knew exactly who Bram was to Jade, their history, but it wasn't my place to ask him, just as it wasn't my place to insist Jade tell me everything about her past. Trust had to be earned, not taken. "Whoever he is, Jade says he's a friend. Erase his memory of seeing her here and send him on his way. Please."

"A *friend?*" Max snarled, and stared at me. "West. Do you want to know…" he trailed off, but I shook my head again. Even though Max could fill in a lot of the blanks about Jade, it was her story to tell when she was ready. "All right, where is this idiot?"

"There's one more thing." I fought down the possessive urge that wanted to keep any and all other males away from Jade. She and Max had history, so I had to hope he could help her out. I explained — briefly — the current situation with Jade and where she was. "Try to talk some sense into her? You know she's safer here with me than anywhere else."

"After this, I expect not to hear from you guys for at least a month," he grumbled, and followed me out to the large garage where we'd stowed Bram. At the door, Max held up a hand to stop me. "I have a few questions of my own for the witch first, if it's all the same to you."

I raised a brow. "Whoever he is, Bram is my responsibility while he's in my town. I'm coming in there."

Max's eyes hardened for a moment, before a wicked glint entered them instead. "What exactly do you think I'll do to him?"

I met his gaze, though I didn't have a good answer for him. Did I trust Max? Enough to ask for his help from time to time. But I'd never gotten the impression that everything Max did was above-board, prison sentence aside. There was a lot I didn't know about the dark angel, which seemed to be exactly the way he wanted it.

As I led the way into the garage, his dark chuckle was enough to confirm my concerns.

A lightbulb flickered overhead, casting the large room in an eerie glow as we walked towards the storage room Cruz had left Bram in. I pushed the metal door open, and Bram looked up, anger written on every line of his face where he sat tied to a chair in the center of the room. "You can't keep me here. I didn't do a damn thi—"

His words cut off as his focus shifted to my right, where Max stood casually leaning against the door jamb.

Lunging forward as much as his binds would allow, Bram's lips pulled back in a snarl. "*You* —"

With a lazy snap of Max's fingers, Bram's words cut off. He

coughed, doubled over and gasped for air, his face turning red. Suffocating.

I whirled on Max, ready to bark at him to knock it off, but at my expression Max sighed and relented.

"Spoil sport," he murmured.

Bram sucked in gulps of air, slowly sitting upright again to seethe at Max.

In one smooth movement, Max conjured a chair out of nowhere and spun it around to straddle it. He draped his arms over the back and leveled a cold stare on Bram.

"Here's how this is going to work," he began. "I ask questions, and you answer them. If I like your answers, I won't rip into your mind to find them myself. How's that sound?"

Bram opened his mouth to answer, but no sound came out, whatever magic Max had set on him apparently still in place.

Max smirked. "Oops." With a wave of a finger, sound returned to the witch.

"You haven't changed a bit," Bram rasped, his voice hoarse as if he'd been choked by an invisible hand. "What the fuck is wrong with you people —"

Another snap, and Bram's speech left again.

I expected Max to be smirking once more, but instead, his gaze was as icy as I'd ever seen it, his voice low and lethal as he hissed, "You're one to talk, Rasmus. Still sitting by and watching your friends be abused to within an inch of their life?"

My back teeth ground together at his words, puzzle pieces forming in my mind to a picture I did not want to imagine.

Bram opened and closed his mouth, gasping for air as Max toyed with his prey. Crossing my arms, I stood against the wall, showing Max he was running the show when I called over, "Get on with your questions."

"If you insist," Max purred, his moment of rage vanished. "I'll make this simple, witch. I have but one true question for you." I could have sworn the shadows in the room grew, flickering at the corners as Max paused, ensuring Bram's full attention was on him. "*Where are they?*"

Bram blinked at the question, and I frowned.

Who was he talking about? Thaddeus, and whoever else Jade was hiding from? Or was Bram somehow involved with the kidnappers?

"Like I'd ever tell you that," Bram spat.

A blink, and Max was on him, his palms pressed to either side of Bram's head.

I pushed off the wall. "*Max —*"

I didn't make it two steps before an unseen force shoved me back, and held me pressed into the wall. Togo raged against the force, but whatever power held me was far greater than my own.

Darkness crept up Max's arms, snaking from his hands up his forearms like ink in water as Bram screamed between his palms.

Whatever magic Max possessed seeped into Bram, the whites of his eyes streaking with black as Max's skin had until his irises clouded over.

I pushed against the magic holding me back, but it was iron-clad.

Bram let out a whimper, and Max snarled as sparks shot off him, raining from his dark wings like an unholy storm.

"*MAX—*"

With a roar, Max wrenched back from Bram, pure loathing in his eyes. Bram's head lolled against his chest, the witch dazed after Max's assault on his mind.

"*Spelled,*" he rasped.

I stumbled forward as Max released his hold on me.

"What the fuck, Max," I growled, my muscles shaking from having been coiled so tight at the restraint. "What the hell was that?"

Max let out a shaky breath, his wings twitchy and still sparking as he flexed them to loosen some of his tension.

"Don't worry, Larkin," Max said, but his tight voice revealed his agitation. "Only a moment more to wipe his memory, and you can send this useless witch on his way."

Steadying himself, Max gave one final shake of his wings before approaching Bram again.

JADE

As we were finishing our third hand of War, the front door opened and Max strolled in.

"I always forget what a charming little hovel you have here."

"I regret ever allowing you to know where it is," Cooper muttered, the words holding a deep rumble that sounded a lot like his cat as he threw his cards down on the table, all but admitting defeat. I'd been about to win again.

I bit my lip to keep the smile at bay, seeing the poison in Cooper's glare as Max joined us on the edge of the couch, pulling his dark wings in tight between his shoulders.

"Did you handle the situation?" Cooper said, changing the subject as he collected the cards, shuffling them back into the neat pile they'd been when I first found them.

Max nodded, meeting my eye. "It's done. Bram's gone and has no recollection he saw you here. As far as he knows, he stopped in town to pick up his order from Moonrise, and kept right on moving. Jade can go back to the packhouse safely now."

"No thanks." I snorted, shaking my head. "Nope. I'm not going back."

Both males stared at me, silent. But somehow that was worse. I was prepared for them to strongarm me, to argue. Silence I had no idea what to do with.

"West is a jerk who only cares about his stupid pack status."

Cooper crossed his arms. "If you actually believe that, you're dumber than I thought."

"Okay, rude. I thought we bonded over how terrible you are at cards, but I guess we're back to frenemies now," I said, then turned to Max for support, waving a hand in Cooper's direction. "Do you hear these guys? No way am I going back to live with West and his family when this is how they see me."

"You misunderstand." Max leaned forward, his elbows resting on his knees. "Right Cooper?"

Cooper sighed, cracking his neck as he eyed me. "He doesn't give a shit about his status for himself — but when shifters are on the verge of losing control to their wolves, the only thing that can stop them is their Alpha. An Alpha that can't control his pack is useless — that's how you end up with dumb pack fights and pointless deaths." He let the word linger, and I swallowed heavily.

I certainly didn't want deaths on my conscience, and I knew all too well how easy it was to lose that fight with your wolf. But Cooper wasn't done.

"You're a liability to West, whether you're here in Timber Creek or out on your own. His wolf has claimed yours as pack, even if you haven't accepted the bond yet, which means no matter where you are, he'll feel compelled to care for you. To protect you, even if it's nearly impossible. To fight for you, kill for you... whatever needs to be done."

"That's —" I paused, trying to think through his words as my heart raced with a mixture of anger and hurt. "That's ridiculous. His wolf can't just decide I'm pack without my consent or his. And I certainly don't have to accept it. Besides, West *does not* want me as part of your pack — I heard the resentment in his words. He doesn't want to have to deal with me. He feels *sorry* for me, and that's a big difference. He sees a princess in need of rescuing and has to come in on his white horse, saving the whole world one lonely wolf at a time. Too bad I'm no damsel, and I've been saving myself for years. I don't need him, or you, or any of this."

But Max shook his head. "I can't let you leave, Jade," His blue eyes pleaded with me to understand. "Not until we can resolve this situation. I need you to stay with them. Stay out of trouble, and lay low."

Somehow, that hurt worse than anything else. The one time I'd needed saving, Max had been the one to swoop in and rescue me. I'd built him up to this god-level worship in my head, the dark avenging angel arriving to slay my enemies. But even he was asking me to stay, and didn't trust me out on my own.

And Ruby — shit. I'd heard the worry in her voice.

"Two weeks," I whispered, defeat weighing heavily on my shoulders. "I'll stay for two weeks. Find me a phone, get me cash so I can get out of here, and clear up whatever you need to on your end, Max."

"Six," Cooper grunted, brow raised in challenge as he sat back in his chair.

I glared, hands balling into fists under the long sleeves of the hoodie. "One."

He huffed. "I don't think you understand how bargaining works."

"A month," Max countered. "Give me a month to get this straightened out, to make it a little safer for you out there on your own, and I'll help you get settled somewhere new. Deal?"

I sighed, teeth grinding together. "Fine. A month, and then I'm gone. But I don't see why I have to stay at the packhouse — there's got to be somewhere else in town that would be just as acceptable." I glanced at Cooper, since he presumably knew the town better than Max did, but he shook his head.

"No way West will let you stay anywhere else."

I groaned in frustration. "No, I'm telling you, he does *not* want me in his space."

Max's lips pursed into a line that looked suspiciously like he was fighting a laugh as he and Cooper made eye contact, something passing between them that I, yet again, was left out of.

"West might be upset right now, but not enough to throw you

to the wolves. Literally." Max smirked before continuing, "He could barely force himself to ask me to come talk to you."

My brows lowered. "What do you mean?"

Waving a hand, Max smirked. "Forget it. You'll understand soon enough."

Cooper's head swiveled to the door. "Speak of the devil."

The door swung open to reveal a once again naked — seriously, shifters? — West, his hazel eyes laser-focused on me.

He didn't give the two other males in the room so much as a cursory glance, his gaze dropping to the sweatshirt wrapped around my body as his jaw clenched.

"Have you had enough time to cool off?" he bit out, one hand still gripping the doorknob hard enough, it looked seconds away from being ripped out.

"Have *you?*" I shot back, nodding pointedly at his white knuckles. He released the doorknob, flexing his hand at his side.

"Jade," Max admonished, and his expression silently reminded me of the agreement I'd made only moments before.

"Fine! Fine, I'm going." I threw my hands up and stood, making for the door. Then, remembering my manners, I spun on my heel to face Cooper. "Thank you for your hospitality." Maybe there was a hint of sarcasm in my words, but I mostly meant it. Cooper had shown me kindness when he really had no reason to.

The cat shifter blinked. Knowing that was all I would get from him, I followed West out onto the porch, and he slipped on a pair of shorts and a shirt from a bin on Cooper's porch.

"We're walking home." West didn't even look at me as he went right back to ordering me around.

I scoffed, crossing my arms. "Seriously? This again already? West —"

Suddenly, his hands grasped my shoulders, the muscle in his jaw twitching as his nostrils flared. "Jade. I'm sorry I had Heath carry you out of town. I'm sorry I yelled at you for not understanding pack ways when you have no basis for them. But if you spend one more second than necessary wearing Cooper's scent, I will *not* be sorry for ripping this off you myself. We need to go."

West closed his eyes in a grimace as he pulled away, stepping back just enough to give me room to maneuver.

I wasn't sure if I'd expected to ever get an apology from West. Maybe someone had told him what an idiot he'd been. If I had to put money on it, probably Terran.

West stepped off the porch, then stopped, back flexing as he curled his shoulders up then released them with a heavy breath. "Your shoes are drenched. How are your feet? It's not far, but I can carry you if you don't want to walk."

The last thing I wanted was to touch West the whole way back, so I strode past him, letting my silence answer for me.

We walked for several minutes in silence, but with each passing moment, the tension between us seemed to ease. That kept happening with him, and it was infuriating. I should be livid with him, holding a grudge to last a century, and yet Balto was ready to forgive and forget. The conflicting emotions between my two souls were getting exhausting.

West cleared his throat, and pointed through the trees to the right. "There's a watering hole to the right where the pups like to play." I glanced up at him, recognizing the peace offering for what it was, then followed the line of his arm to peer through the woods, though I couldn't see any water.

"My sisters had a secret hidey hole up on the left when they were young," he continued, and huffed a laugh. "No males allowed."

He kept up a steady stream of commentary the whole way back to the house, pointing out the places he and his family and pack had history all around us.

What would it be like to have roots like that — to know the land so well, it was like its own character in your past? As someone who'd constantly been on the move, I could hardly wrap my head around it. Something about it made my chest ache.

Was that what *home* felt like?

Did I want that? I'd never even let myself consider it. But I had to admit it might be… nice. To know every rock and tree and creature, and all that.

Probably just a Disney fantasy.

Before long, the packhouse loomed above us again, and I fought a disgruntled sigh. I was really starting to dread the sight of it.

West must have heard me, because he stopped, turning back to me.

"Go ahead in and get changed, then meet me in my office. We still have some things to discuss."

I tried — I really did — and failed not to roll my eyes. "You got it, Tyler Lockwood."

Pleased I left him confused with my Vampire Diaries reference, I sauntered past him and slipped inside.

Once dressed in my own clothes, I met West down in his office as requested. Well, *ordered*, but who was keeping track?

Me. I was.

To my surprise, West had a simple map of the town laid out on his desk, waving me over to look at it with him. He gave the briefest glance to my clothes, seeming to relax a fraction when he saw I was back in my own.

"Max filled me in on your deal," he said and I jerked my head up, eyes widening. Crap, what had Max told him about my past?

West must have sensed my panic because he clarified, "A month here. And Leif mentioned you're concerned about money." He indicated the map again. "There are a number of family businesses you could work at for some cash."

I blinked at him, but his gaze was trained on the map. Was he actually being considerate, or did he just want me out of his hair so he didn't have to see me moping around the house all day every day for the next month?

"What, not another lecture about respecting the great Alpha Larkin?" I teased hesitantly because, well, I had thought he would bring it up again, and I needed to know where we stood.

West's shoulders tightened, only fractionally but enough I could see it. "I meant it when I said I'm sorry how I handled that. I'm not used to" — a muscle in his jaw ticked — "I don't usually have to explain myself to anyone. And you —"

"Mess everything up?"

He frowned.

"Cooper maybe explained it a little more," I offered, then bit my lip. I wasn't quite ready to say I was *sorry* exactly, but I did want him to know I understood. "I didn't mean to endanger anyone out there. I won't do it again."

West met my gaze steadily, assessing, before giving me a nod.

He indicated the map again with a wave.

"You know Buffalo Willie's." He tapped the restaurant on the map. "You said you've done some waitressing?" I nodded. "I'll be honest — it wouldn't be my first choice for you. After what the pack saw today, Jett won't be the only one trying to get his paws on you, and waitressing would have you out on the floor, circling among the public. It'd be easy for him or anyone else to get to you."

"Isn't Terran there most days?"

"Usually, but he's got his own stuff to do and he hardly ever leaves the kitchen or the office."

I frowned, seeing his point even if I didn't like it.

"A better option might be Summer's shop — bakery, book-shop, and cafe." He slid his finger to another location a little ways down the street from the restaurant. "You could work in the back, or even if you're out stocking shelves or something, it's a quieter crowd."

"I don't know anything about baking," I admitted.

"Can you read directions?"

I shot him a flat stare, and for the first time since our argument, his expression softened, the corner of his mouth tilting up.

"Then you'll be fine. Summer can teach you."

I nodded hesitantly, imagining every worst case scenario, but anything was better than sitting around here all day, and I did need money if I wanted to stop taking handouts left and right. "Okay. I'll do it. When do I start?"

Chapter Nineteen

WEST

Fog rolled over the mountains in the distance as I sipped my coffee the next morning, the pink hues of sunrise giving the view a happy glow. The bakery opened early every morning, and Jade's first shift started in 20 minutes.

My eardrum was still recovering from Summer's screech of joy when I'd called to ask about Jade working with her last night.

Footsteps sounded on the stairs behind me, and Togo sat up, already sensing Jade's presence.

"Oh." She skidded to a halt under the archway into the kitchen, staring wide-eyed at my bare chest. "I didn't realize you'd be up already."

I arched a brow, but couldn't keep a smile off my face, her presence and increasing comfort here. If she kept staring at me like that, no way in hell was I going to wear more clothes around the house. In fact, I was sure I could find endless excuses to be shirtless. "Trying to escape our agreement already?"

Her eyes narrowed, the hint of a smile she'd had before vanishing into nothing. "I said I'd stay, didn't I?"

Setting my coffee cup down, I swiped my truck keys off the counter and moved towards her. Instinctively, Jade stepped back, and I fought to hide my frown. "I trust you, Jade. I was trying to be playful, but you saw the worst in me yesterday, and I can see why you're not ready for that yet." Holding my keys up, I shook them. "I'm up early because I thought I could drive you to town for your first day and get you started on a good foot."

She huffed, crossing her arms over her chest as she stared hard at my shoulder, not meeting my eyes. "I can walk fine, West. Just because I agreed to lay low here doesn't mean I need a babysitter. Leif pointed out her shop yesterday. It's not that far."

I rubbed my jaw, scratching my fingers through my beard as I tried to find a way to get this woman to understand I *wanted* to help. Not because I thought she needed it, but because I felt this unending pull to be around her, this intrinsic need to lay the world at her feet if she'd only let me.

I got this, my sister's voice rang in my head right before the front door burst open and Summer swept in like a ray of sunshine.

"Good *moooooorning!*" she sing-songed as she beamed a bright smile at Jade, never looking my way. "I was so excited when West called last night and said you needed a job! I'm Summer by the way, in case you hadn't figured that out yet. West's youngest and nicest sister. And you're my soon-to-be new best friend."

If I thought Jade was wide-eyed when she saw me this morning, then this was a new level of surprise. "Jade," she said, sticking her hand out to shake.

Summer chuckled, then pulled her into a tight hug, her long golden-brown ponytail swishing with the movement. "I'm a hugger. Nice to meet you, Jade."

Finally turning in my direction, Summer grinned. "Rumpled is an interesting look for an Alpha. You've got that weird hair-shelf thing going on on the right side of your head."

"Where's my happy greeting?" I said, fighting the urge to fix my hair.

"I'll give you good morning hugs when you stop having women thrown over shoulders like some tyrant. Do better tomorrow."

Jade's head whipped between Summer and me, her mouth slightly open. I nodded at my sister, keeping the focus there, but needing Jade to hear my response.

"It was a mistake, and one I will try my best not to repeat."

Summer nodded, then slipped her arm through Jade's, tugging her out the door.

After they left, I went into my office, but instead of sitting at my desk like I'd planned, I stood at the window, watching them walk into town.

I had no doubt Summer would call me if they had any trouble. None at all. And yet yesterday's drama made me uneasy. No matter how Jade tried to brush off her reaction to Bram, she'd been terrified, and my protective instincts were still in overdrive.

Should I send Leif to watch over the bakery? No. That would be overkill, right?

Maybe I could ask Cooper to tail Jett so I at least have one less concern.

I kneaded my knuckles into my forehead, wishing some of the tension would ease, when my phone rang.

"Aspen?"

"I'm not moving home," my sister began with no introduction, to the point as usual.

A grin escaped me at her words. Aspen was the only one of us who'd left town, something we all repeatedly told her was a mistake.

"Stop smiling," she grumbled, like she could see me.

"I'm not." I was. "So, when will you arrive? There's someone staying in your room right now, but —"

"I'm staying at Summer's," she cut in. "I read between the lines of that group text and I'm not touching any of that with a ten-foot pole. Cooper said there was drama yesterday too."

"Does this family keep no secrets?" I sighed, watching as Summer and Jade passed the gatehouse and into town, disappearing out of sight. "And is there a secret group text that I'm not in where you all discuss me?"

"No. And of course there is. You mean to tell me there isn't one about me?"

There definitely was, but I kept that to myself.

"I'm taking your silence as a yes and choosing to ignore that I now know this. Anyway, Terran said you've been acting like a real caveman since you ran into this girl at the grocery store."

"Rich coming from the brother who told me to throw her over my shoulder and drag her here. At least Jade showed up here of her own free will."

"Then what happened with you ordering Dad to throw her over his shoulder yesterday? Or was Summer mistaken?"

"Hey, I asked him to get her out of there, he improvised the *how* on his own."

"Uh-huh. Sure. Anyway, I should be in later tonight. I'll meet with your guys tomorrow to go over the plans, and I need to go see the site in person."

"You'll come to dinner tonight?"

"Is Dad grilling?"

"He will be when he hears you're coming home."

Aspen let out a groan. "I am *not* 'coming home.' I'm *visiting*. Do not tell Dad I'm back for good. I know where you sleep at night, Westly." With that thinly veiled threat, she hung up.

The calendar app on my phone dinged, pulling my attention from the window where I'd long since lost sight of Jade. It was time to go speak with the pack.

Now that it was settled that Jade would be here for a month, I had to let everyone know at least the bare minimum of what was going on. Otherwise, they'd just keep sniffing around until, eventually, someone got hurt.

I sent a summons through our pack bonds for my Shields to join me in the meeting room in the barn behind my house, the first time any of them had been allowed on the property since Jade's arrival. Our pack was divided into sectors, mostly based on power, and the Shields were our highest tiered Alphas, just below Terran on the power scale.

The barn was set a few hundred yards from the house, along the treeline. It was a simple structure, housing several snow mobiles as well as all of Heath's old workshop and a meeting room we used for pack business.

I reached the building at the same time as Nova, who gave me a nod before following me inside. As we passed the storage room we'd held Bram in, I went over the questions yesterday had unlocked.

Whatever Max and Bram's history was, it wasn't pleasant. And even more concerning was Max's mention of abuse. I'd always known Jade was hiding from a past she never wanted to confront again, but the thought of someone hurting her made me want to rip the world apart until I found everyone responsible.

The lights flickered on as Nova and I entered the meeting room, moving around the massive, twenty-seater round table. The walls were white, like any boring conference room, except the back one where Terran had painted a mural of a wolf howling at the moon. We didn't need the huge space for the six of us, but it wouldn't hurt to leave a little room for the amount of energy that would be in here in a moment.

"This about the new wolf?" Nova ventured, leaning against the wall, arms crossed. Like most of my pack, his arms were covered in geometric tattoos, black against his pale skin. He had a more punk look than the rest of us, but he'd moved here from California and wasn't as accustomed to the laidback mountain life as we were. I didn't care how gelled his dark hair was if the male could defend my pack.

I nodded. "We'll wait for everyone else."

Before long, the other Shields showed up. Jett, who was on my shit list at the moment, wisely kept his mouth shut as he took up a spot next to Nova, kicking a muddy boot up against the wall. Atlas and Drea showed up together, glancing around at the others before taking seats nearby, then finally Zion and Terran slipped in last.

I gave Terran a once-over, my brother sporting a few scrapes and bruises but nothing too serious. Unease had run through the pack yesterday after the encounter with Bram, and Terran had dealt with some troublemakers.

His eyes flicked to mine, jaw tightening. *"It's fine. Taken care of."*

I nodded my appreciation, then turned to the others in the room.

"You're all aware of the new wolf in town," I started, knowing full well they were. They'd all been sniffing around the property line over the last couple days, and Zion and Jett had seen her in town. "Jade is going to be staying here for the next few weeks." I shot a look at Jett without conscious thought. "She's to be left alone."

"Is she joining the pack?" Maybe Jett had a death wish.

"What do you need from us, Alpha?" Drea said, shooting a sideways glance at Jett that shut him up quickly. Her long brown hair was tied up in a ponytail, and she was dressed casually in ripped jeans and an oversized white tee. At just over five-foot, Drea's size should have prevented her from rising in the ranks of our pack, but she was scrappy in a fight and never backed down from a challenge. She was the newest Shield to join our ranks, and I was happy to have her calm confidence in a room of hotheads. Didn't hurt that she worked at the medical center either.

Atlas followed her lead, nodding in agreement as he waited for orders. The tall blond male had returned home with Cooper after a tour together in the military several years ago and joined our pack shortly after. Sitting next to Drea, the full extent of his size was evident — twice as wide and towering over her, even seated. In his black tee, camo shorts, and dog tags, he looked the same as he always did, but I liked that about the male. He was constant. The sight of him was enough to send most people running for the hills, even though Atlas was one of the friendliest guys I'd ever met.

"This isn't to leave this room." I put Alpha command into

the words, forcing everyone to sit up straighter. "Several days ago, Jade was captured by humans not far from here. They knew she was a shifter and had targeted her, prepared with drugs meant to incapacitate her. Fortunately, something didn't work properly and she escaped, finding her way here."

"Is this the wolf Zara saw?" Drea asked, then finished the sentence in my head. "*The one who wasn't healing?*"

"Yes," I answered both of her questions aloud, but didn't elaborate on the last part for the males in the room. Feeling defensive of Jade, I didn't want to publicize any weakness of hers, especially after I suspected how strong her wolf was. The last thing we needed was a dominance fight to break out.

"And who was that guy we sent packing yesterday? One of the kidnappers?" Zion asked, and a low growl rumbled through the room, all of our animals on edge.

"No," Atlas answered for me. "Coop and I hunted them down, and this guy didn't match their scents. Doesn't mean he's not involved, but he wasn't one of Jade's original abductors."

"*Find me anything you can on Bram, regardless,*" I sent to Atlas, who gave the briefest nod in answer.

"Like a lot of us" — my gaze drifted to Jett, then Drea — "Jade's past is a mystery. Bram, the witch from Willie's yesterday, is someone from her past. I don't know the whole story, but we all felt her fear. Anyone who spikes that much of a reaction from a wolf under my care isn't welcome here."

Everyone nodded, knowing the lengths I'd go to protect what was mine, and Jade had quickly fallen into that category. "Spread the word about Jade's presence, but that she shouldn't be bombarded." I hesitated before telling them the next bit, but if I couldn't trust my Shields, who could I trust? "Jade didn't grow up in a pack. She doesn't know most wolf etiquette — I don't want anyone starting trouble with her over perceived slights she doesn't know she's doing."

"Didn't grow up in a pack?" Atlas' voice was full of concern

— being packless was typically unheard of for young shifters. Some adults chose to be Lone, but children and teens were always adopted by a pack, like I'd adopted Leif. We took care of our own.

I nodded. "All of this — being in town around so many of us — it's all new to her. I'm hoping my sisters can help ease her into it."

"It sounds like you want her to stay," Drea said carefully.

"I do," I admitted. "The reports I'm getting from the Council are upsetting. The number of supes going missing grows by the week, almost all shifters. This isn't a good time for Lone shifters, no matter who they are. And with what Aspen's coming here to build for us, this is the best option to give Jade the freedom she's used to while she figures out what she wants to do."

"So, we should be welcoming, but not overbearing," Atlas said.

"And *nobody*" — Drea cut Jett a sharp glare — "should try any funny business."

Jett put his hands up. "Hey, I'm not going to start humping her leg, or anything, but if she's unclaimed and willing, where's the harm —"

"Consider her claimed," Terran barked at him for me.

Jett looked him up and down, eyes narrowed. "By you? You finally coming out of your pity party over Naomi leaving you?"

"If the Alpha says she's off limits, she's off limits," Drea cut in before Terran could rip him to shreds, his canines already elongating.

Jett tilted his head in my direction. "Did you say that? If so, I must have missed it."

"I'm saying it now." I could barely contain my temper as I stared Jett down. Both my wolf and I didn't like how much Jett was pushing this. It should have been a one and done, order given, message received.

Feeling the wave of my Alpha power aimed in his direction, Jett ducked his eyes, nodding briefly. "Anything else?"

Atlas leaned forward. "Even though we lost the kidnapper's trail, I think we should check in with other packs in the surrounding regions. I can make some calls, see if they've had similar situations."

"Yes," I agreed, glad to have him on my team. "Take care of it."

"On it," he said, patting his hands against the table.

"I'll meet with the Trackers and make sure they know not to let any humans through the town lines," Zion said.

"Good. Dismissed."

Terran lingered as the rest of the pack left, his eyes tracking Jett until the male left, then he turned to me. "How'd last night go? Did you kiss and make up?"

I turned a hard stare on my brother. "She's still here. That's enough for me."

A loud bark of laughter escaped Terran before he slapped my back and left the room. "Keep telling yourself that, brother."

Maybe if I did, I'd start believing it too.

Chapter Twenty

JADE

"Shoot, shoot, shoot." I wrenched open the oven door, fanning away the smoke with a towel before reaching in and pulling out the flaming muffins. Tapping the door closed with my foot, I hurried over to the counter to set down the tray.

Summer appeared in the doorway while I slapped a cookie sheet over the tray to smother the last of the dying flames.

"Okay, well, this is still progress from the last batch." She bit her lip to hide her grin. True to her name, Summer was possibly the sunniest person I'd ever met, and I'd found myself instantly at ease with her. Her long, caramel blond hair was pulled into a high ponytail for work, and under her pink apron, she wore a casual marigold-striped t-shirt dress that she somehow made look elegant.

Lifting the cookie sheet, I gaped between her and the charcoal pucks that were supposed to be lemon poppyseed muffins. "How?"

"Last time they never even made it into the oven."

I groaned, remembering the last batch I'd dropped on the floor — after accidentally swapping the sugar for salt anyway. I was truly hopeless at baking, and my focus was anywhere but the task at hand. Seeing Bram yesterday, then the argument with West, then everything after left me off-kilter. "I swear I followed your instructions."

Summer drifted over, inspecting the mess, then glanced at the stacked commercial oven. Rather than the traditional stainless steel commercial kitchen appliances, everything was yellow and had a funky retro feel to it, a cheery contrast to the dumpster fire I was making of it.

"Oh."

I was right beside her, trying to see where it had all gone wrong.

"Okay, you had it on broil." She pointed to one of the many buttons on the oven — I hadn't even known I'd pressed it. "So, next time — don't do that."

"How are you so calm? I am *ruining* your bakery. No one is going to want to buy pastries when this entire building smells like burnt sugar and despair!"

"Oh, please." Summer turned the oven off. "Trust me, the people in this town who want pastries aren't going to abandon the shop for a few mishaps. They don't have any other options. Supply and demand, my friend. I hold all the supply."

The front door bells jingled, and we both looked out the window into the cafe. "See? What did I tell you?"

I frowned, hearing her words but not believing them as I followed her towards the door. By all rights, I should be fired.

"Oh, hey Krista!" Summer said, a fake cheerfulness taking over her tone as she pushed through the door and behind the counter. "I didn't know you were in town."

Balto growled deep in my throat and I paused with my hand on the door. While my wolf was always prickly, she hadn't reacted as often here in town, so I heeded her warning, staying hidden.

"Yeah, back for the summer again," Krista said, her voice holding a rasp that sounded somewhat familiar. Maybe she'd wandered through Buffalo Willie's the other day. "Are you working alone here today?"

"Slow day today," Summer said, and I took that as confirmation to hang back. "How's Max?"

Max? I frowned, then ducked down below the kitchen

window, working my way across the kitchen where I could stand behind the appliances but see into the cafe.

"Oh." Krista laughed, and the haughty sound grated on my nerves. "We're not together right now."

"I'm sorry to hear that," Summer said, sounding anything but. I peeked out the window, catching the barest hint of long black hair blocking most of the woman's face. "Anyway, what can I get you?"

"I was hoping for peach lemonade. Any chance it's my lucky day?"

"Peach season isn't until later this summer, so not until then. Raspberry okay with you?"

Krista flicked her hair behind her shoulder, her gaze darting towards the window, but I pulled back just in time to hide myself.

I fought back Balto's rising agitation, willing myself to calm down when the front door bells jingled again, and Summer came back through the door.

"Sorry about—" she stopped, tilting her head as she looked between me and the front of the shop.

"Is she still there?" I peered around the corner, and sure enough, Krista stood just outside the shop, drinking her lemonade through a neon pink straw, staring right at me. "Fuck."

"Do you know her?" Summer asked, and I wrung my hands, trying to explain myself. I knew my reaction to strangers was uncalled for and abnormal, but the panic was very real, especially after yesterday.

"No," I sighed, willing Balto to the back of my consciousness. "I don't think so."

"Her loss, definitely not yours," Summer said, turning back to the counters and wiping them down as if my overreaction was nothing notable. If I hadn't loved her before, I definitely did now.

"Do you not like her?"

"She's not my favorite."

I chuckled, the last of the tension leaving my body. "I'm a little shocked. I kinda figured you liked everyone."

She turned towards me, resting her hands on the counter behind her. "I respect loyalty above all else, and that witch has none. She's cheated on Max more times than I can count, and he deserves so much better."

I hummed, wondering if her being a witch was enough to set Balto off.

"Time to shelve books?" I attempted to change the conversation. "I can't mess that up, right?"

Summer hesitated briefly before smiling, but that momentary hitch was enough to tell me shelving books wasn't an option.

"West told you not to let me out front, didn't he?"

She scrunched her nose, not quite scowling but not the happy smile she'd worn all day either. "Not exactly in those words."

"But the same meaning, right?"

She huffed. "Yeah, pretty much. I'm sorry."

I waved off her apology. "I'm the one who's been ruining your kitchen all day. You don't get to apologize to me."

"You have not been ruining my kitchen. You've just been experimenting, somewhat unsuccessfully. But that doesn't mean you should give up."

Eyeing her skeptically, I asked, "Are you always this optimistic?"

"Usually, yes." She laughed, her infectious smile back. "I opened this bakery and bookshop because it's *fun*. The books I stock mostly have happy endings, except for that dark corner in the back, but I avoid it at all costs. And that's why I never bake the same menu — I bake what makes me happy. Today that was lemon poppyseed muffins, but apparently they don't make *you* happy."

I threw the towel at her, hitting her in the middle of her pink apron. "Rude."

Not missing a beat, she grabbed a handful of M&Ms,

throwing them back at me. "I'm never rude. You must be thinking of Aspen. She's the blunt sister, never afraid to speak her mind."

I opened my mouth and caught the last M&M she threw at me, chewing as I smiled back at her. "All right. Other than clean up this mess, what else should I be doing?"

"Check the expiration dates on the fire extinguishers?"

I laughed, my jaw hanging open as Summer winked, then headed back towards the cafe. "Maybe we can find some oven-free recipes for you to try."

Since the store was empty, I followed her out front. "Did you already forget the salt for sugar debacle? I think you need to keep me out of the kitchen entirely."

Summer hummed thoughtfully, resting her elbows on the register counter as she surveyed the shop. I joined her, mirroring her pose, and sighed in hopelessness.

"Well, you can pour coffee, right?"

We both looked over to the vacant seats in the cafe section of the shop.

"Is it always this dead in here?" I asked before I thought through my words, then winced at how rude it sounded. Summer didn't take offense though, her brow furrowing in thought.

"No, it's not. In fact" — she glanced behind us at the vintage romance novel cover calendar on the wall, and frowned, even at the sight of Fabio's hair blowing in the wind — "the book club should have been here twenty minutes ago."

"Ugh, see? I knew it. I'm ruining the business."

"*You're* not, no, but I have a sneaking suspicion I know who is." Mouth set in determination, Summer pulled out her phone and started a call.

I heard the familiar rumble of West's voice the minute he picked up, and pretended the sound of it didn't make my stomach flutter.

"What's wrong?"

"What's *wrong*, brother dearest, is that you scared off all my customers."

There was a long pause before he answered. "I did not."

"Did too!"

I crossed my arms, trying to hide my amused smile at their antics. "Children."

"I *may* have mentioned something—"

"Aha!"

"Summer —"

"No, you listen here. This is *my* shop and I will not have *my* customers run out because of your paranoid delusions! You fix this now, or so help me, Westopher, I will poison you. It may not be today, it may not be tomorrow, but *some*day, you will eat something of mine and *it will betray you*. You will break the toilet bowl, you will sing high notes you've never reached before as you cry out for the Goddess, knowing she'll never answer you for the terrible things you've done. Mark. My. Words." Summer paused, letting her threat sink in. "Have I made myself clear?"

A long-suffering sigh sounded down the line before West muttered something in acquiescence, and hung up.

"Westopher?" I laughed, and any hint of annoyance left Summer's face.

"That's not really his name, but Aspen and I love to annoy him by calling him anything but West when he's being an ass."

"I like it. Maybe I'll have to try that next time."

"Do it." She nodded, then untied her apron, pulling it over her head and hanging it on the hook behind the register. "You know what? Let's close up for the day. Help me organize my guest room before Aspen shows up and has a hissy fit over the mess. We can make mojitos and dish about how controlling West can be."

She grinned at me expectantly, and I met it with one of my own. "Well, I'll never turn down a mojito."

)))●(((

Summer's apartment above her shop was like an exhibit in pastel sunrise decor. Her light cream sofa — I made a mental note not to drink anything other than water anywhere near it, and under no circumstances to eat on it — literally had a sunrise rainbow pillow on it, as well as six others in varying shades of pink and orange. The sherbert orange walls cast the whole room in a warm glow, inviting even though it was almost the polar opposite of how I would decorate, if I ever had the cash. Everything was tidy and cute and bright, just like Summer.

Past the living room was a kitchen similar to the one downstairs, all the appliances retro-style, and Summer went right to the fridge.

"Can you grab some mint from the patio?" she called, already in mojito-assembly mode.

"Sure." Spotting sliding doors, I opened one to find a green witch's paradise of a patio garden. One entire wall had hanging pots of herbs, large colorful pots housed several varieties of citrus trees, and vines of tomatoes and beans and I didn't know what else ran up the railing and a trellis on the other wall. I stepped over to the herb wall, tapping my chin. "Mint, mint, mint," I muttered to myself, scanning through the rows of plants, finally spying the mints along the bottom row. I picked off a few stems with good leaves and rejoined Summer in the kitchen.

"That's quite the little garden you have out there."

She smiled as she took the leaves from me, quickly rinsing them and adding them into the tumbler. "I like fresh ingredients for baking or for cooking. There's more on the roof."

Adding a measure of rum to the tumbler, Summer squinted at me a moment before tipping her hand again, adding a little more. "Ice is in the freezer if you want to fill the glasses."

She stirred up the drinks while I grabbed ice, then poured us each one, topping both with another sprig of mint.

"To knowing one's limits," I said, holding my glass in toast.

"To trying new things," Summer countered, and we clinked, then each took a sip. "Okay, I seriously need your help with the guest room, where all my past ADHD hyperfixations go to die."

"Oh —"

Summer was already tugging me down to the last door in the hallway, then grimaced as she paused in front of it. "Brace yourself."

With a flourish, she flung the door open, and my jaw dropped. Summer winced.

"I know. Aspen's gonna kill me."

The room looked like a craft store had thrown up. Fabric littered the floor, some pieces cut and pinned, others a jumble, and others in a pile of scraps. The bed was covered in a dozen skeins of yarn — knitted, crocheted, and loose. Stickers and scissors for scrapbooking overflowed from a basket wedged in the corner. A clothesline was strung from the window to the closet, tie-dye t-shirts and aprons hanging from it.

"I'm much better at starting things than finishing them," Summer commented, sipping her mojito. "The dopamine rush from starting new things is too good, and then I get bored. And in my defense, my sewing machine was out to get me."

I set my glass down on the only available surface — on the floor in the corner. "I see we have our work cut out for us. We're going to need three bins — trash, donate, and keep. Do you have a label maker?"

Summer turned wide eyes on me like I was an alien descending from the cosmos. "No, but I could get one."

"Absolutely not." I waved a hand. "We're not buying anything else. If this view is any indication, you would just make labeling your next hobby."

Summer huffed but denied nothing.

"Markers and masking tape will do just fine."

Summer turned, presumably to go find the items I'd

requested, though I could have sworn I heard her muttering *"But the aesthetics"* under her breath as she went.

"Aesthetics are rewards for good little wolves who get their shit organized," I shot after her.

"Every party needs a pooper, that's why we invited you, Jaderade."

I rolled my eyes, but Summer reminded me so much of Ruby I grinned. "Now I'm getting nicknames, too?"

"Of course you are." She reappeared with masking tape and a rainbow assortment of Sharpies in hand. "You're one of us now."

I nearly choked on my tongue, my heart squeezing at how easily she included me. Whether she meant part of her family or her pack, I wasn't sure, but did it matter? I was only here for a month — not to stay. The clock was ticking, and I needed to keep myself detached.

"I didn't mean to scare you off," Summer said as she sat on the floor next to me. "I've been told I'm pretty intense with how quickly I latch on to everyone."

"No." I reached over, patting her leg briefly. I wasn't much of a hugger, but I hated hearing that comment come out of Summer's mouth, even if she *was* intense. She was also infectiously happy and loving, qualities I didn't think I could embody if I tried. "You didn't scare me off. Just surprised me, that's all. I'm not great at the whole girl bonding thing."

"Well, help me fix this mess before my sister yells at me and I'll consider you the best friend I ever had."

I smiled, something I'd done a lot today, and nodded. "Let's do it."

)))●(((

It took about fifty rounds of some variation of *"Do you really need this?" "Yes!" "Are you sure? Are you ever going to crochet again?" "I guess not.*" before the room finally started to look livable. Summer's first instinct for everything was to keep it *Just in case*, but when I'd discovered some of these items had been in here for literal years without her touching them, there was no more Ms. Nice Girl. The Donate pile was now larger than the Keep pile, and the trash bin held everything that couldn't reasonably be used again.

I shoved the Keep bin at her. "Okay, you go deal with this — somewhere in *your* room where *you* will have to see it and deal with your choices — and I'll put the other bins by the door."

Now that we could actually see the bed and the floor, the next steps were easy — vacuuming, new sheets, hiding the potentially evil sewing machine, and voila. A whole new room.

"Where have you been all my life?" Summer sighed wistfully, looking over the room once we finished before we headed back out to the living room. "Seriously, Jade, you can never leave. I'll have this place looking like a disaster zone again within twenty-four hours after Aspen leaves."

"For the next month, consider me your clutter accountability partner."

I drained the last of my mojito and rinsed the glass in the sink as Summer plopped on the sofa, throwing pillows aside to make room.

Not sure what to do next, I stood at the edge of the room near the door. Should I leave now that we were done cleaning and she didn't need me working in the shop? She hadn't said anything else, but without a designated task, I felt like an intruder.

Even though she'd said I was *one of them,* I was hyper-aware that I wasn't a part of any of this. Not this town, this pack, this family.

"Sit." Summer patted the sofa next to her. "We have an hour before we're supposed to be at the house, and I don't want to go early and get roped into their monthly cleaning day."

"Monthly?"

Summer waved a hand. "Believe me, monthly was hard won. But I'm sure you'll experience the joy of a pack house cleaning day eventually."

I perched on the sofa, still overly aware of how clean the light cream fabric was and afraid to get it dirty.

"Relax, I just get one of the witches over here to magic any stains out," Summer said. "Trust me, this couch has seen more tomato sauce than I care to admit."

Just then, there was a thud outside the door a second before it burst open, a young woman who looked a few years older than Summer shuffling a duffel bag forward before dropping several armfuls of tote bags on top of it. They had similar features — the shape of their eyes, the slope of their noses, the full bottom lip — but everything about Aspen was a shade darker than Summer. Chocolate brown hair and the same hazel eyes West had — though set behind round, wire-frame glasses — made their family resemblance undeniable.

"Okay, who told Dad I'm coming home to stay? Was it you, Judas?" She stepped over her stuff, closing the door behind her, before plopping onto the sofa next to us, waving a lazy hand at me. "Hello, you must be Jade, nice to meet you, I'm Aspen, etc, etc. *Summer!* Look at this!"

Aspen held up her phone to a text message, scrolling up and up and up to show incoming message after incoming message.

"Oh, dear." Summer laughed, and Aspen glared at her.

"*Aspen, when will you be here? How long are you staying? Do you want Cap'n Crunch for breakfast? Do your old waders still fit? When was your last oil change?*" she read from her phone. "On and on and on, all day! This is ridiculous, even for him. I nearly hit an elk, I was so distracted by all his texting."

"So turn it off!"

"Oh, don't I wish!" Aspen rolled her eyes. "Sure. Then I get phone calls. *Aspen, did you drive into a ditch and die?*' Whatever, I'm putting my stuff in your guest room and so help me, I will burn any half-finished crafts I find in there."

I raised my eyebrows at Summer as Aspen dragged her many bags down the hallway.

"I told you she says what she's thinking," Summer murmured.

"Heard that!" Aspen shouted, opening the guest room door, then added, "Holy crap, Summer — are you possessed?"

After several thumps indicating she'd set her bags down in the room, the door closed again and she joined us back in the living room.

"What happened in there? Who are you and what have you done to my sister?"

"Jade helped me organize a bit. She made me *give things away.*" Summer shuddered.

Aspen stabbed a finger at me. "Never leave, Jade. I like you already."

Chapter Twenty-One

WEST

Dad was in rare form at the grill with at least five different options, and enough for everyone to have one of each. Today's apron read *I rub my own meat*, which I refused to acknowledge.

Summer might be his baby and Cora's spitting image, but Aspen had our mother's personality — organized, logical, productive. Cora had been the calm to Heath's storm, and the pair had been unstoppable together. He always got himself psyched up when Aspen visited, sure *this time* would be when she chose to stay for good.

"Oh!" He snapped his fingers. "I should have grabbed those elk and jalapeño sausages she likes!"

"There's plenty," I assured him. "And she's here for more than one night."

"Right, you're right," he muttered, flipping a steak. He handed me a tray of chicken that was already done, and I brought it inside. River stood on a stool at the counter, stirring the salad as Terran added chopped vegetables.

He quirked a brow, looking towards the door. "Where are the girls?"

"Probably running late —"

"*Ex*cuse us." Aspen appeared in the doorway to the front hall, hands on her hips, and flanked by Jade and Summer. "Is that any way to welcome your long lost favorite sibling?"

"Aspen!" River leapt from her stool, sending it toppling, and ran to Aspen to wrap her little arms around her legs.

Aspen patted River's head awkwardly. "How do you do, pup?"

"Aspen is River's favorite because she's the least competent with children of anyone I've ever seen," Summer whispered to Jade, who bit her cheeks to contain her smile, but the happiness in her eyes eased every worry I'd had today. "I swear the kid does it on purpose, just to make Aspen uncomfortable."

River let out a demonic laugh before returning to her station, righting her stool and hopping back up.

Heath flew through the door, dropping a platter of meat on the counter before he wrapped Aspen in a hug so tight, her feet left the ground.

"Hi Dad," Aspen said as Heath hugged her for several seconds. "You're going to have one less daughter if you don't let me breathe soon."

"Oh, don't be so dramatic." He set her down again.

"*I'm* dramatic? Says the man who thought I was dead if I didn't respond to his texts within two minutes today."

"The mountain roads can be tricky! What if you got lost? Who knows if you even remember how to get home with how much you store in that big brain of yours?"

Continuing their squabbles, Aspen followed Heath back outside to catch up and bring the rest of the food in. Summer already had Jade helping her get glasses and water for everyone, so I went to help Terran with the sides.

Jade looked at home here, smiling at something Summer said and helping River down from the stool. Everything about it was domestic and familiar in a way it shouldn't be yet, but it felt *right*. But I was apparently the only one who felt that way because I noticed how she avoided eye contact. Looked like we still weren't on friendly terms.

But she was here, so that was something.

"How'd today go?" I asked when Summer walked by.

"I don't think baking is in Jade's future," Summer said as she placed a pitcher of water in the middle of the table for refills. "We had a great day though, didn't we, Jade?"

Jade's head popped up, swiveling in my direction before she looked at Summer instead. "Yeah, it was fun."

My sister pulled out her chair, then the one next to it, urging Jade to sit down with her. "She organized my hoard."

"Seriously?" Terran coughed from the island. "Many have tried, none have succeeded."

"Hey, it was organized chaos, *my* way," Summer retorted, chucking a dinner roll at him. He caught it, then threw up in the air again and River snagged it in her teeth with a giant grin.

"If she can do that, we should sic her on Dad's hoard next," Terran continued like nothing had happened, but a loud gasp from the sliding door answered his statement.

"My own son!" Heath pretended to sob, clutching his chest. "The betrayal!"

"Don't tempt me with a good time," Jade said with a flick of her eyebrows.

Cooper walked in the back door behind Heath, tugging at the hem of the shirt I'd left for him on the patio, knowing he'd shift to run here. My brother was quiet, waving at everyone as he looped around the table and gave Aspen the smallest side-hug I'd ever seen. "Good to see you, sis."

"Same," she said.

"Wow, that was beautiful." A slow clap came from the doorway to the front hall, where Cruz now stood, having flickered in silently. He wiped a fake tear off his tan cheek, then smiled brightly, teeth flashing in amusement. Instead of his usual grease-stained clothes, he had on a light grey tee and black jeans, his dark hair tucked under a snapback, and face freshly shaved.

Aspen scowled, rolling her eyes. "Terran invited *you*?"

"Define 'invited.'" Cruz grinned, then charged forward and scooped a squealing River into his arms, swinging her around upside down while she giggled. Cruz had an open invitation to any family events as Terran's closest friend, despite not being a shifter. The male had been there for my brother in any way he needed from the minute River's mother bailed. *"Hola chiquita! How's my favorite little girl? You didn't have Papa bring you by my shop this week."*

"He said he was *working*," River said as he set her down, putting so much emphasis on the last word it sounded sarcastic. "I was out at Grandpa's ranch."

"Did you practice that buffalo call I taught you?"

"Oh, you mean the one where you told her to bellow at exactly 11:47 every night?" Terran deadpanned and I fought back a laugh. "That one?"

Cruz smiled, tugging one of River's pigtails, then grabbed a bowl of potato salad off the counter and brought it over to the table. "It works, I swear. Keep trying, *cariña*. And make sure you come by my shop before I eat all the candy I bought you."

Pulling out the chair next to Jade, Cruz sat down and stuck his hand out, flashing his megawatt smile. "We never officially met, though I gotta say you look better right-side-up. I'm Cruz, the only male you need to know in town."

Despite his flirtatious words, even Togo knew Cruz was full of it and had no reaction.

"Ugh," Aspen scoffed from across the table. "Has that line ever worked for you?"

Cruz shifted his gaze, and part of me was glad to see him move his attention elsewhere. "Never hurts to keep trying." He winked.

As the rest of the family took their seats, I kept one eye on Jade a few places down from me, a slightly amused smile on her face as my siblings descended on the piles of meat like — well, like a pack of wild animals.

As Alpha, it was my job to see everyone got what they needed, so I waited until everyone had served themselves before touching the food. From the other end of the table, my father did the same, smiling and listening to River chatter while everyone else began to eat.

Suddenly, something the little girl declared had Terran groaning.

"Not this again," he muttered, earning a beaming grin from his daughter.

"What?" Aspen asked.

"I want a puppy!" River shouted.

There was a beat of silence before everyone except Terran burst out laughing.

"Living with these old dogs isn't enough for you, *Río*?"

"Jade's not old!" River beamed. "She's living here, too, right Uncle West?"

I fought not to turn in Jade's direction, to watch her reaction to River's words, but smiled at my little niece. "For now, yes."

Terran slapped Cruz upside the head, popping his backwards hat off his head, and I sent a quiet rumble of gratitude through our mental link for not letting the focus linger on Jade and her status here.

"Call us dogs again," Terran snapped, but he was fighting a grin before he turned back to his daughter with a much more serious expression. "No puppy. Same as the last twelve times you asked."

River frowned, sticking her bottom lip out in a dramatic pout.

"A puppy would be terrified of our wolves, River," Aspen told her matter-of-factly, and River glared but dropped the pout. "They're part of the canine family, like us, but would be able to sense we're the top predators. It wouldn't be a good environment for a puppy."

The conversation shifted to talk of dad's crops and how he planned to tweak his new balls recipe, which none of us volunteered to taste test.

"Jade?" he asked, turning his pleading eyes her way. "Want to try the next batch? I tried dialing down the heat with kumquats, so it's a sweet and spicy mixture. KumBalls."

Cruz cackled while Terran got up from the table to walk away, gripping his side. Cooper took a sip of his drink, and I bit my cheeks to keep from laughing. This was exactly what my father wanted — a reaction. His little innocent act fooled no one.

"What's so funny?" River demanded, grinning despite not getting the joke, then shouted, "Kumballs!"

"Dad," Aspen scolded him, just like our mother would have. "You are the worst."

"I'm saying no for her," Leif volunteered, and Jade held a napkin over her mouth, but I saw her shoulders shaking. "Don't trick her twice. That sounds absolutely awful."

"Trick?" Heath jerked back. "I would never. I think I'm really onto something this time. Might even be good dipped in a special sweet cream."

Water sprayed from Cooper's mouth, dousing Aspen, who shot him a glare that promised revenge as water dripped off her chin.

"I'll help, Dad," Summer said, always the bleeding heart of the family. How she hadn't incinerated every last tastebud from being his designated taste-tester was beyond me, but I loved her devotion to Heath. "But you have to promise me never to call them that again."

"Knew I could count on you, sweetheart." Heath reached across the table and kissed her forehead.

After dinner, Cruz, Cooper, and I took care of clearing the dishes while Heath and Terran got out one of the many scent training games for River in the living room.

"No peeking, now," Heath said, and River threw her arms over her eyes. She'd climbed into Jade's lap after Jade sat down, but she didn't seem to mind my niece's affection, her hands set loosely on River's thighs as the little girl squirmed in excitement.

"All right, let's see what you got, pup." Heath slid the tray across the coffee table to River. On it were five upside down wooden cups, under which were five different scents for River to identify — a common game with shifter children to help train their senses.

Most full-blooded shifters began transforming around age two, but River's fifth birthday had just passed, and there was still no sign of her wolf. Since she was half-human, none of us knew exactly how her shifter genes would manifest, but so far she'd shown enough aptitude at the scent games that we hoped she might be able to shift one day.

I moved to join them once all the dishes were clean, taking an armchair. River sniffed each cup, her little face scrunched in concentration.

"Pine needle, black pepper, rosemary, lily," she said, tipping over each cup as she went to reveal their contents. Jade's eyes popped open when she saw that there was only a speck of each content. At the fifth cup, River cringed. "Blegh! Daddy's dirty sock."

"Really, Dad?" Terran grabbed said sock as Heath and Jade laughed, tucking it in his pocket.

"You knew it was his?" Jade's nose scrunched as she inspected the game. "And you can tell what each of these are from such a tiny amount? I'm so impressed, River!"

I gaped at her, as did Heath and Terran. Summer and Aspen halted their conversation at the island, coming over to stare at her also. Even Cruz stopped drying the last dish he held.

Jade's hesitant gaze darted between us. "What?"

"Can you — can you *not* scent those?" Terran asked at last, his eyes sliding to mine for a brief moment.

"T, don't be a dick," Aspen shot at him, and he held up his palms.

"Just asking."

Jade bit her lip, realizing she'd revealed something personal. "You all — can? Scent them?"

"Hey, it's no big deal," Summer assured her, joining her on the sofa and looping an arm through Jade's. "If you want, I can help you practice. We can have you scenting like a pro in no time."

Jade nodded, though she shifted her weight uncomfortably on the couch.

"So Aspen," Heath said, intentionally changing the topic, for which I was thankful. Jade was pulling back, curling in on herself before my eyes, and I hated it. "Tell us about the project West has you working on and how long it'll keep you here."

Aspen rounded the couch, dropping to the ottoman next to Heath's chair as they strategized her next build and how it would impact the town. But I couldn't focus on their conversation, not when Jade stood and moved to lean against the wall beside Cooper, the two of them slightly removed from the group. He'd been silent all night, but that wasn't unusual for him.

I could have tuned my hearing in to what they were saying, but I forced myself not to, focusing on everyone else in the room. Then Cooper smiled at something Jade said, and she laughed in response, and I couldn't take it anymore.

Somehow in the span of only a few days, she'd won over Cooper, become fast friends with Summer and River, and was well on her way to befriending Aspen — a feat in itself. Leif followed her around like a puppy, waiting for attention, and Heath had included her all night like she was one of us. Even Terran and Cruz seemed fond of her, but that duo loved anyone who was sweet to River.

Mine, my wolf said as I left the room, needing space. But my human side was all too aware of how much I'd have to work to earn her forgiveness for that to ever happen, if I even wanted it.

Mine, he insisted, dismissing the doubt in my thoughts. *Mine.*

Chapter Twenty-Two

JADE

"I think I'm going to head up to bed." I pulled away from the wall as I watched West leave the room, a frustrated expression on his face I didn't understand. "Tell Summer thank you for her offer to help me."

"Tell her yourself." Cooper crossed his arms over his broad chest. "You're here for a month and the offer was genuine — you have nothing to be ashamed of, Jade."

I nodded, even if I wanted to hide my embarrassment. The few days I'd spent here in Timber Creek had made it painfully obvious how behind I was as a shifter. River, a five-year-old half-human, was more advanced than me, and that stung more than I cared to admit.

With a sigh, I climbed the stairs, headed up to my room. Was it also the same direction West had gone? Sure. But his room was right next to mine — it didn't mean I was *following* him.

I'd seen his frown when I admitted how poorly my senses worked. No doubt he wanted to fix this for me, too. The thought alone made my eye twitch.

The saying about old dogs and new tricks came to mind, making me wonder if it was hopeless to try to understand my wolf better at 32. But I'd never had help learning these things before, and now I was surrounded by a family of shifters who would jump at the chance to help me, if I could swallow my pride and embarrassment to ask.

And there was the kicker, wasn't it?

Asking for help was like a root canal. Sometimes necessary, and always painful.

The wooden floorboards creaked as I reached the landing, staring down at the family below me. As much as I didn't want to let anyone in, part of me was starting to think maybe I *should* try, for once. To use this month here with the Larkins as an opportunity to better myself.

No matter how much I wished I could will away my supernatural genetics, I couldn't. Hindsight is a real bitch, and I saw the night I'd been kidnapped in my mind on replay.

If my connection with Balto had been clearer, would I have been able to interpret her warning better? If my senses had been sharper, would I have noticed Bennett sooner, and avoided the kidnapping altogether? If I had been stronger, could I have fought back? Probably not, but I couldn't stop my mind from pointing out all the ways I'd failed myself.

Knowing we were in peril, Balto had taken over, something I'd only allowed once before, and that first time had been so scarring, it featured regularly in my nightmares. But Balto hadn't attacked this time. She'd run straight here, right to West's feet.

She trusted him implicitly. I, the *human* Jade, trusted no one, living up to my high school nickname, *Jaded*.

My feelings were clouded when it came to West, torn between his bossy demeanor and his kind actions. But tonight, he'd seemed so removed from his family, so much quieter than I'd expected through dinner. As someone who spent the majority of my time alone, I understood better than anyone what it felt like to be lonely in a crowd, and I wondered if part of West's attitude wasn't about me at all.

Trust him, Balto urged in my head, and I jerked to a stop. She rarely spoke in words to me; usually it was grunts, growls, and general emotions. I blinked, trying to recover as I stood in front of my bedroom door, my gaze drifting to where West's door was slightly ajar.

Light spilled out, but I didn't hear anything from within. My feet refused to move, stuck in the hallway staring at his room as Balto pushed me forward, urging me to take this leap of faith, to trust West to help me.

He was nothing like Thaddeus, and I was a different person than I'd been nine years ago when I'd first met the witch and fallen under his spell. Just because I'd been burned the last time I let someone help me didn't mean everyone was out to get me.

Seconds ticked by, my heart racing, my familiar anxiety taking over as I tried to convince myself that was true. Tried to reason with myself past my knee-jerk emotions. Clenching my fists in frustration, I shook my head, giving way to my stubbornness as I pushed my own door open and went inside.

Trauma was a fickle thing, and even though I knew I needed to get the fuck over it, to stop letting it rule my life all these years later, that was easier said than done.

The door clicked shut behind me, and I threw myself on the bed, sinking into the plush mattress, and let myself wallow in all of my failures, just for tonight.

))) ● (((

My heart raced as I wandered through the halls of the main Coven building, checking my phone for the fifteenth time. I hadn't heard from Ruby in three hours, and Balto was surging forward in a panic. This wasn't the first time she'd clawed at me lately, insisting something wasn't right, but this was the first time I recognized it as instinct. Maybe this was even a pack bond.

For all I'd tried to pretend Balto didn't exist, that I could rely on my mother's witch heritage and fit in with Thaddeus and the Coven, I couldn't. Ruby's wolf was as wild and untamed as they came, and I had to keep my own close to the surface to manage her. This was my responsibility as her Alpha, as her guardian, as her sister, even if I had no idea what I was doing on all three fronts.

I dialed again, listening as it rang several times. "Answer, dammit," I growled. Gripping the phone tighter, I picked up my pace as I raced by dorm rooms and any of the common spaces I thought she might be. There weren't that many places she could have gone.

Over the last several weeks Ruby had been getting worse — fits of teenage rage forcing her to shift, her wolf taking on a violent edge I didn't know how to calm. Maybe I needed to shift, to exert dominance to bring her to heel, but I didn't know how to do that. I didn't blame my father for bringing me up without a pack, but now Ruby needed some pack structure and I had no idea how to help her.

That same niggling feeling got worse as I moved towards the back of the common building, Balto damn near howling to be released.

Something was wrong. Ruby was in trouble, and I needed to find her.

My phone rang in my hand, and I answered it without looking at the screen. "Ruby?"

"No," Thaddeus said, sounding annoyed. "Where'd you run off to? We were supposed to head out to work on your spellcasting today."

"I can't find Ruby. She's not answering her phone."

"Relax," he said, and I clenched my teeth. That was always his solution when I was stressed — to relax. Gee, thanks, hadn't thought of that. "She's not a little kid anymore, Jade. She's fifteen — a teenager. Maybe she finally found a friend and is off doing things kids her age should be doing."

I shook my head, wanting to believe that was possible, but I knew it wasn't true. Ruby, as bright and wonderful as she was, had no friends here. It was a constant source of guilt for me, and it broke my heart. I'd chosen to move us here to make my life easier, and had ruined hers in the process.

"I'm sorry, Thaddeus," I said, knowing I'd have to deal with his anger later. He didn't understand my need to hover over Ruby, but I loved my sister more than anything. I had to find her. "Raincheck. Tomorrow, okay?"

"Fine."

"I love y—" But he hung up before I could finish the words.

I sighed, stopping to drop my phone back in my pocket as I drew in a deep breath. This wasn't the first time I'd been torn between Ruby and Thaddeus, and it wouldn't be the last. Raising a young teen wasn't for the faint of heart on a good day, let alone dealing with magical powers and grief at the same time. They were both a part of my life, and eventually he'd get over it. Or so I hoped.

Frustration rose in me as Balto pushed at the barrier holding her in check, her agitation making my heart pound. My wolf had developed a hair-trigger temper over the past few years, the equivalent of a dog barking at falling leaves. After Thaddeus had teased me about her overreacting the first handful of times, I'd learned to tune her out.

Today, she refused to be ignored.

"I'm going," I said aloud to my wolf, which was dumb even by my own knowledge of shifter powers.

I let an inkling of my shifter magic take over, and Balto guided me forward, right to the main chambers at the back of the Commons. Confusion clouded my thoughts as I pushed open the doors of the ceremonial hall I'd only ever been in once — when I'd been inducted into the Coven three years ago.

The room was dark, only lit by several flickering candles in the center of the room. Smoke curled in the air, smelling of frankincense as the door closed behind me, locking me in. The ceilings rose 20 feet into the air, the only windows stained-glass skylights far above.

I waited for my eyes to adjust to the darkness, faster than a human's thanks to my wolf, then studied the white pentagram tiled permanently into the floor. It didn't look any different than last time, but a hint of power lingered. Recent magic had been performed here.

That alone was odd as it took a dozen or more witches to power a pentagram of this size, and I hadn't known of any ritual taking place today.

As I moved closer to the candles, I realized the lump between them was a pile of dirty clothes. The air sucked out of my lungs as I knelt, finding a clump of hair tied together with a string atop the clothes — black hair, with red-dyed tips.

"Ruby," I whispered, my heart thundering in my chest. Ruby's witch powers were almost non-existent — why would she have anything to do with a spell, let alone be in the chambers? And what was going on for this much magic to be focused on her? Unease clawed at me, Balto demanding I shift, *insisting I charge into battle to protect her, but I didn't understand what I was fighting.*

My fingers shifted to claws without my consent as Balto physically turned me towards the outer walls, cloaked in darkness. Arches ringed the main chamber, a hidden walkway behind it allowing for witches not participating in a spell to watch.

My muscles spasmed as Balto urged me to shift, but I fought her back, moving in the direction she urged. My breaths came quick as adrenaline built, Balto sharpening her senses, preparing for a fight.

The faint ring of metal on metal.

The taste of salt in the air.

The sharp tang of copper.

Blood.

"Ruby?" I called out, the sound echoing back to me as I stumbled under the archway, my movements jerky as Balto and I wrestled for control of my body. Stepping into the darkness, I broke into a clumsy jog as I shouted for her again. "Ruby!"

My feet pounded on the tiles, loud against the eerie silence of the space as panic pushed me faster, convincing me I was already too late.

"RUBY!" My voice broke, needing her or someone to answer me, to explain this overwhelming feeling I had to kill anyone who crossed my path.

Something was ahead of me in the darkness, and I slowed my steps, the scent of blood growing stronger. That same sound of metal on metal rang again and I rushed forward, right up against the bars of a steel cage.

The metal stung my palms as I gripped it, but the pain was nothing compared to my heart when I saw what lay within.

)))●(((

A choked sob escaped me as I pulled myself from the same dream I'd had a thousand times over the last five years, wetness pooling beneath my face on my pillow. I gasped for air as I curled in on myself, emotions overtaking me.

Panic. Fury. Guilt. *So much guilt.*

I pushed the heels of my palms into my eyes, willing it all back to the recesses of my memory where it stayed as a lesson learned.

Nothing mattered more to me than Ruby. Not then, not now, not ever.

No matter how much I told myself I'd been young, I'd done the best I could, I'd done what I thought was right, we'd gotten out in the end — it never fully erased the all-encompassing guilt.

My sister would never access her wolf again, and it was my fault. Her witch magic was all messed up, and it was my fault. Years of her childhood memories had been erased, and she didn't even know it, and it was *all. My. Fault.*

Reaching blindly for the nightstand as another sob shuddered through my chest, I patted the table, looking for my phone before remembering I didn't have one.

I groaned, wiping the snot from my face as I sat up in bed. Already my head was pounding, but I knew there was no way I'd be able to go back to sleep until I heard Ruby's voice.

I needed to find a phone.

After splashing some water on my face in the bathroom sink, I opened my bedroom door. It was well past midnight and the house was quiet as I went downstairs, towards West's office, hoping he had a desk phone I could use.

The office was dark like the rest of the house, but the moon shone brightly through the windows, illuminating the space — no phone in sight.

Feeling defeated, I turned back towards the stairs when I noticed the blue light coming up from the basement, just as it had two nights ago.

Someone was down there. And maybe that someone had a phone.

Chapter Twenty-Three

WEST

My ears pricked up the moment Jade's foot hit the top of the basement stairs. I smiled, already hoping for another night like we'd had a few days ago as I set my controller aside, pausing the game on the screen.

After I'd been too pushy the other day, I needed more one-on-one time to show her a different side of me if I wanted to gain her trust. My mind spun as I thought through how I could get closer to her tonight until I heard the muffled sniffle. I stood just as she came around the corner into the room.

"Jade? What's wrong?"

Even disheveled from sleep, Jade was gorgeous. Her green-tipped hair hung over one shoulder, and my wolf rumbled his approval that she'd chosen to sleep in the Timber Creek logo sweats I'd given her.

Her lower lip trembled faintly as she raised wide eyes to meet mine, and without conscious thought, I stepped forward, into her space, and guided her chin up with my finger.

"Hey." I hoped my tone came out soft and soothing, not freaked out that she might not let me help her, *again.* "Talk to me. Please?"

She closed her eyes for a breath before opening them again, looking steadier as she took half a step back. My hand fell to my side, and I tried to hide my disappointment that she'd backed away from me again.

"Can I borrow your phone? I need to make a call."

I frowned. "Are you sure?" I glanced at the clock, sliding my phone out of my pocket and handing it to her. "It's one in the morning."

"I'm sure," Jade said, already typing a phone number as she headed for the door to the backyard. "I won't be long."

"Take your —" but she was gone before I could finish my sentence.

I stepped up to the door to watch her pace in the backyard, phone clutched to her ear, but I tuned out my hearing. If I wanted to earn her trust, I couldn't do it by eavesdropping on her, but the thought of her outside alone had me on edge.

After a moment with the phone to her ear, some of the tension smoothed from her bunched up shoulders as she mouthed, *"Ruby."*

My wolf settled at the knowledge she was talking to her sister, and as she'd said, it wasn't long before she ended the call and came back inside.

Jade handed my phone back to me, a steady if small smile on her face.

"Sorry, I just — had a nightmare and needed to hear Ruby's voice," she said as she sat on the couch and wrapped her arms around her middle. "Dumb, right?"

"Not at all. Do you want to talk about it?"

Jade let out a sigh, but shook her head as she pulled her knees to her chest and rested her chin there. "I'd rather just forget about it."

I searched her eyes, wondering what she wasn't saying. What nightmare would induce enough panic to call her sister in the middle of the night? I was sure, in my gut, it had to do with seeing Bram and whatever history that had stirred up for her, but I wouldn't push it again. Not until she was ready.

Instead, I tilted my head towards the TV and sat on the couch next to her — not touching, but closer than we'd sat last time.

"Super Smash?"

Jade quirked an eyebrow and held her hand out for a controller. "Game on."

))) ● (((

After a few battles, Jade yawned, her shoulders relaxed as the memories of whatever nightmare haunted her dissipated.

"You lose. Again," She tilted her head back against the couch, eyes closing. "Never underestimate the power of an angry pink marshmallow."

I smiled as I reloaded the game, preparing another fight. If she couldn't tell I'd intentionally let her beat me all night, I wasn't about to ruin that for her. I'd been ready to head up to bed when she came downstairs, but no way in hell was I leaving before she quieted her inner demons.

The fight reloaded and I looked over, about to say something, but she'd fallen asleep, controller in hand. Her head tipped my direction, body slumping towards me, and I was satisfied with this small win.

Jade was one of the most guarded people I'd ever met. For her to feel comfortable enough to fall asleep meant she trusted me to *some* degree. Or, at least, her wolf did.

The soft blue light from the screen cast shadows over her face. Her eyes were still puffy from crying before she joined me down here, and that thought alone was enough to drive me half-mad.

She hummed in her sleep and moved, sliding further down the couch as her head almost fell in my lap, strands of her hair falling over my thigh. I stiffened, afraid to move and startle her even as Togo cried out in excitement at her proximity.

Minutes ticked by, my mind torn as I contemplated letting her sleep on the couch, but I didn't think she'd be comfortable waking up in the open down here. Besides, my wolf growled at anyone but me seeing her vulnerable as she slept, even if it was only Leif down here tonight.

In a split second decision, I scooped her up and headed for the stairs. She didn't stir, only nuzzled closer into my neck, and a shiver ran through me as I padded up the stairs to our rooms.

I nudged her door open with my foot, and laid her gently on the bed. Not until her head hit the pillow did she wake, her eyes opening sleepily as they found mine.

I held my breath, soaking in the warmth of her gaze as I waited for her to react. While I'd done nothing but carry her upstairs, I knew how fiercely independent Jade was — maybe she'd begrudge even this small act of kindness. I didn't dare to move, not wanting to mess up this fragile peace we'd found tonight.

"Thank you," she whispered, the barest hint of a smile tipping up her lips. "For your phone, for the distraction… all of it."

I smiled, her words meaning more to me than she knew. "Of course. Anytime, Jade."

She nodded, the motion sending several strands of hair down over her forehead. Before I could stop myself, I reached forward, and brushed them back, fingers tracing across her skin tenderly, wanting to do anything and everything to take care of her. Jade sucked in a breath at the small touch, and I pulled my hand back, stepping away from the bed as if I'd been shocked.

My wolf was insistent we should stay and keep an eye on her — that we should, in fact, crawl right into that bed with her, wrap our arms around her, and nuzzle her hair to fill our nose with her scent. But that would be crossing a line in a big way, so I forced myself to leave her room and shut the door behind me.

Patience, I assured Togo as he glared at me.

I closed the door to my own room, leaning back against the wood. My head fell back as I sighed, trying to follow my own advice.

With only a wall between us, it was hard not to barge back over and soothe all of her fears and worries, hard to keep the big picture in mind. Even an hour later, I could feel the panic that had ridden her hard when she'd crept downstairs to join me. As much as I wanted to know if there was anything I could do to help, I had to dig deep, to be patient. She'd agreed to a month here with us, so I had a month to prove I was worthy of her trust. That I *wanted* to help, without an ulterior motive.

She'd run once already. I wasn't fool enough to believe she wouldn't again if I messed this up.

Mine, my wolf said at the thought of her leaving, and I pushed off the wall, headed for bed.

Not helping, I answered.

But he didn't care. Jade was ours, whether she knew it or not. I just needed to earn her trust. And I knew how to do that, starting tomorrow.

Chapter Twenty-Four

JADE

I assumed I was headed back for another terrible day at the bakery, when Aspen waltzed into the kitchen and set me straight.

"You're with me today, Jade," she stated, pouring herself a generous travel mug of coffee and swiping a strip of bacon from the kitchen island.

I said, "I am?" the same moment West said, "She is?"

We exchanged a look, and the slight curl of West's lips as he fought a smile had me trying to smother one of my own, something fluttering in my stomach at the sight. Sleep had eluded me after West tucked me in, his hands lingering on my face as he brushed the hair from my eyes. Nothing about the small move had been sensual, and yet his touch was electric. All morning I'd snuck looks in his direction, afraid to make eye contact for fear he'd realize how affected I was by last night.

His sharp words from days before should have stung still, but the gentleness he'd shown last night reminded me nothing about West was simple.

"Yep, Summer fired you, or should have but she's too nice, so I'm firing you for her and hiring you for me," Aspen explained rapid-fire and I forced myself to focus on her, not her brother. "After the miracles you worked on Summer's apartment, I'm sure you can help me get my office up and organized. I need a dedicated space while I'm here overseeing the build."

I didn't miss the way Aspen's gaze slid to West, didn't miss the almost imperceptible nod he gave her, approving this change of plans. I swallowed down my snort — this brief moment only more proof being in a pack meant your every move was micromanaged. Lovely.

The front door opened and closed, and Leif joined us in the kitchen, his blond hair windswept today, small plastic bag in hand.

He raised the bag, announcing, "Got it!"

West waved him over to me, and Leif set the bag next to my coffee mug.

"New phone," West answered my unasked question. "Take it with you, and you can get it up and running while you're with Aspen today."

It hit me like a gut punch, and I fought not to gape at him, at the bag, at this gift or what seemed like one. My heart warred with itself — on the one hand, swelling with gratitude for the gift, and on the other, sounding warning bells that this was too good to be true. That there was some as-yet uncovered nefarious plot at hand that I was, once again, too naive to see.

I slid the box out of the bag, taking in the brand new, current model phone. I'd *never* had the newest model of anything, and here West was just giving this to me, no strings attached.

Unless this was a Trojan horse.

"Thank you," I managed around the lump in my throat and forced a smile. "Guess this means I won't have to interrupt your gaming sessions anymore."

West stood to go, but paused at my words. He stepped closer to murmur, his breath ghosting across the back of my neck, "Interrupt me anytime, Jade."

Aspen purposefully busied herself fixing her coffee as warmth crept up my cheeks.

"What do you mean, that was the only space available?" Aspen snapped at Terran, hands on her hips. We were in the back office of Buffalo Willie's, where Terran had handed Aspen the keys to an office space located nearby. Apparently, right over Cruz Motors.

Terran crossed his arms and sat back in his chair. "That was the only space for rent in town. Take it or leave it."

Aspen gaped at her twin. "There's no way we can work there. Are you insane?"

"What's the problem?" I asked, hoping to find a solution. I excelled at creating plans A through Z for any circumstance, then I started on the Greek alphabet.

Aspen huffed. "The *problem* is Terran's hetero life mate tries to drown out the whole block with his music all day. And even if we talked Cruz into some kind of noise ordinance agreement, the fumes will be terrible."

"If you just ask Cruz to turn down the music, I'm sure he would," Terran shot back. "You're being dramatic just because you've never liked him. But hey — you don't have to work there." He threw his hands up. "There's a perfectly good dining room table at the house."

"You know I can't work with *people* in my space," Aspen grumbled, narrowing her eyes. "Coming and going and interrupting me constantly. I need to *focus*. In a calm, quiet, *fume-free* environment."

The twins stared at each other, Terran in resigned disinterest, Aspen in a rage.

Finally, Aspen groaned and swiped the keys off the desk. "Fine! But if we get the black lung working there, it's on *your* head."

"Good thing I have so many spare siblings." Terran waved us out of the office, and Aspen all but slammed the door on our way out.

We left the restaurant and as we headed up the street, Aspen turned to me. "Do you have any brothers, Jade?"

"Nope, just the one sister."

"Well, consider yourself blessed. Brothers are a whole other kind of headache, and I have three."

Aspen stopped in front of Cruz Motors, frowning at the closed garage door, fists clenched at her sides.

I checked around the corner for another door, but didn't find another entry besides the ones currently sealed shut. "Is there an exterior door to access the office or…?" I trailed off as Aspen shook her head.

"There's another door inside that leads up to the office, which I'd guess is what this key is for." She sighed, then glanced at her watch. An evil glint lit in her eye. "It's ten in the morning, so he's probably dead asleep. Let's rudely awaken him, shall we?"

Before I could answer, Aspen stomped down the street towards a row of small houses facing Main. Each was painted in a different color, but the houses were identical — likely catalog-ordered in the 1800s. Aspen stopped in front of a red Craftsman, hands on her hips as she chewed on her lip.

I stepped up beside her. "Should we knock?"

"That's far too civilized for this brute," Aspen said as she dropped her hands and peered around the side of the house. Several windows were open to let in the summer breeze, and Aspen grinned, the sight damn near frightening in its intensity. She held a finger up to her lips, then crept around the house. In a matter of seconds she was back, a garden hose in her hands.

Squinting one eye closed, Aspen held up the hose and pulled the trigger, shooting a jet of water straight through the open upstairs window.

"Wake up, asshole," she shouted loud enough to wake the dead, water still streaming into the house. I spluttered a laugh, glancing sideways at Aspen as I evaluated my new friend.

"You're insane, aren't you?" I said, then regretted it when Aspen's vengeful stare snapped in my direction.

"Only when I need to be."

I was about to offer to take a turn with the hose when a garbled yelp sounded from inside the house, and Aspen's eyes expanded. "Oh shit," she said, dropped the hose, grabbed my arm, and ran.

We were hardly back to the sidewalk by the time the front door flew off the hinges, a sopping wet Cruz standing on the porch in only a pair of very small, very fitted, very *wet*, black boxer briefs. Steam rose off his skin as the water evaporated quickly.

My jaw unhinged as I gaped at the male, muscle lines on his abdomen I didn't even know existed, and a set of other muscle lines pointing in a V right down to his —

"*Mis ojos están arriba, amiga.*" Cruz grinned, pointing two fingers at his eyes.

The arrogance in his posture had me fighting the biggest eye roll I'd ever eye rolled. "I don't speak Spanish, *muchacho*. Take it up with my dead dad or my *gringa* mother if you have a problem with it," I retorted.

Aspen shook herself out of the stupor she'd also fallen into to add a helpful, "Yeah."

Cruz laughed, swiping his wet hair off his face as he reached above him to grab the door frame, confident as ever even though he looked like a contestant in a Speedo contest. "Though I'm sure staring at my sizable package first thing in the morning is every girl's dream, is there some secondary, much less important reason you two decided to try to drown me in my own bed?"

Aspen narrowed her eyes. "Three things, demon. One, it is not first thing in the morning, it's ten. That's decidedly, objectively mid-morning. Two, your 'package,' if you want to call it that, could be mailed with a standard postage stamp and wouldn't even rank in my top ten. And three, you wouldn't know the first thing about girls' dreams if you could astral-project straight into them."

Aspen and Cruz stared off, Aspen with her hands on her hips, seething, and Cruz just barely not flexing his biceps, clearly fighting another grin.

"And we need to get into the office above your shop," I added, feeling like the worst third wheel in the world.

Cruz broke, bursting into laughter so hard he doubled over, hands on his knees. Aspen rolled her eyes, muttering under her breath as she pivoted on her heel and stomped back towards the shop.

I hesitated, not sure if I should follow Aspen or stay here and try to talk Cruz into letting us into the office. Cruz regathered himself, taking a few deep, calming breaths.

"Damn, *chiquita*. I think she likes me, no?" He chuckled with a flick of his eyebrows, before disappearing on the spot.

I blinked, still unused to demons flickering like that, but about thirty seconds later, he was back and dressed in a t-shirt and loose shorts.

"Come on, next thing you know she'll break down the door," he tossed at me, throwing a Cruz Motors trucker hat on backwards as he strolled after Aspen. "Don't want to miss the show."

I shook my head, barely containing my laugh at the broad grin on Cruz's face. He didn't seem deterred by the idea of her breaking down the door. If anything, he was excited by it.

Cruz shoved his hands in his pockets, whistling as he sauntered through town, waving good morning to everyone we passed, completely unphased by Aspen's anger and prank.

"You aren't mad?" I asked, baffled by his reaction. "About the water? Or the potential break-in about to happen?"

"Eh." Cruz shrugged. "I gave up on anger a long time ago. No room for it anymore."

I squinted at his broad back, confused. "I… don't think it works that way."

"Sure it does," he said, spinning to walk backwards. "I write my own story, and it's full of happy endings." He winked, and this time I didn't hold back my snort.

Cruz laughed, the sound booming and so full of joy I couldn't stop my own chuckle. He spun back around, throwing an arm around my shoulder. "I think we'll be great friends, you and me."

I surprised myself by not recoiling from his touch, instead asking, "And why is that?" Despite Cruz's flirtiness, nothing about his arm around me felt romantic or sexual — more, familial. Was this what having a brother was like? I didn't hate it.

He leaned down, whispering in my ear, "You're gorgeous when you laugh, and I happen to be very funny."

I shoved him, pushing him out into the street, which only made him laugh harder.

By the time we made it the two blocks back to his shop, Aspen was nowhere to be seen.

"That can't be good," I said, scanning the area for her.

Just then, the garage door moved, screeching as it was forced open from the inside. A second later, a small plastic rock shot out from inside, and Cruz caught it against his chest.

Aspen scoffed. "Really? A fake rock?"

Cruz tossed it to the side of the shop. "Hey, if someone's going to steal from me, I don't want to have to replace the windows, too."

Aspen stared at him. "That's the stupidest thing I've ever heard. How about installing some actual theft deterrents instead? Do you even have cameras on this place?"

Cruz shrugged, and Aspen rolled her eyes.

"Ridiculous," she muttered, turning and heading inside the shop again. "Let's go, Jade. We have an office to set up."

Cruz offered me a teasing salute as I passed him, and I followed Aspen upstairs.

⟩⟩⟩●⟨⟨⟨

Unlike her sister, Aspen was already pretty organized, and we quickly had a system in place for her office. Since she was only in town to work on this build for the pack, she didn't need more than the bare essentials for the office, which Leif and a few other young pack guys brought in shortly after we'd arrived.

We set up two desks, hung up a dry erase board, and cleaned off a large table, which she quickly covered in sketches and blueprints.

While Aspen reviewed her plans, I set up my new phone and programmed Ruby's number into it. I didn't know anyone else's numbers, but was unsurprised to find all the Larkins, plus Cruz, had already been programmed in.

I shot off a text to Ruby, following it up with six hello GIFs so she could be sure it was me, like my own calling card.

"We should go see the site after lunch," Aspen announced later, sitting back in her office chair.

I put my phone down, spinning in my own chair, and nodded my agreement. "Sure." Truthfully, I felt a little useless now that the office space was set up, and unease sat heavy in my gut. "I know you're trying to help out and give me something to do, but are you sure you need me?" I gestured around the room, where everything was nicely in its labeled place. "You seem like you'd be fine on your own."

"Trust me, once we get up and going, I'm going to need someone who knows my whole system to help keep me sane. I'll be back and forth between Timber Creek and my other offices, so having you here is perfect," she said, scribbling on a scrap of paper. "You're not charity, you're my therapist-alternative. And before you try to ditch me, this is what I typically pay my assistant per month." She slid the paper over to me before opening up her phone. "What do you want from Willie's?"

I barely registered her question, all my focus narrowing on that scrap of paper. I didn't know what I'd expected to be paid from these family jobs, but the number in front of me was so far out of the scope of my imagination, I could only blink at it.

"Jade?"

"Um," I swallowed heavily, still trying to process. "Whatever you're having is fine."

My brain was a whir of numbers, calculating all the things I could do with the salary Aspen was offering. I could visit Ruby. I could look for a new car. I could pay West back for the phone and the clothes and any other expenses I racked up. Even if I only worked for her for a month, I couldn't remember the last time I'd had access to this much cash. Maybe never. If I stayed past that? This was a life-changing dollar amount.

"Great, Leif will bring it over in a bit." Aspen went to set her phone down when it buzzed again, a new call coming in. Whatever the screen showed turned her expression resigned, and she glanced over at me before swiping to answer the call. "Hey, Matthew. I thought we said we'd chat at 7 tonight."

I stood to excuse myself, sensing this was a private call, but Aspen waved at me to stay.

"Yeah, we'll talk later," she said, not one ounce of inflection in her voice. "Yes, I'll remember this time. Okay. Bye." Ending the call, Aspen set her phone down and breathed out a long exhale, massaging her temples.

"So, Matthew?" I raised my eyebrows, leaving it open for Aspen to share if she wanted to.

"My boyfriend — well, fiancé, I guess."

"You… guess?"

Aspen shrugged. "We've been dating for three years, and Matthew said statistically that's the most successful time to get engaged. He didn't officially ask me or anything, but it was understood when he left a ring on my nightstand. I don't wear my ring on the job, though. It's too flashy — more his taste than mine."

Holy red flags. I studied Aspen, trying to work out how she felt about that. Unlike when she'd been furious with Cruz earlier, now she was a closed book, and I didn't know her well enough to read her yet. Trying to offer the benefit of the doubt, I asked, "How did you two meet?"

"He was an investor for one of my builds," she said. "He's in finance. He asked me to dinner once the build was concluded, we had an acceptable evening, and that was that."

I stared at her, but she was opening her laptop, already getting back to work. Shaking my head, I muttered under my breath, "Just like a fairytale," right as Leif came into the room, carrying a takeout bag from Buffalo Willie's.

"Don't do that," Aspen chided as she took the bag from Leif, whose eyes expanded as he glanced between me and Aspen. "Muttering. Any shifter in a half-mile radius can hear you, even if you whisper."

Leif pointed at the door, then practically sprinted through it.

Shame crept over me from my sarcastic comment. "I'm sorry." Here she was offering me a job, helping me when she had no reason to, and I was acting like a jerk. "If you're happy, that's all that matters."

Aspen nodded, handing me my food as she set out napkins on the desk. "No need to apologize. I don't care, but others will. The rest of my siblings will probably tiptoe around telling you how you're supposed to act in a pack to protect your feelings, but I can tell you're tougher than that."

"Thank you," I said, frowning down at my sandwich. "I think."

"Only way to learn, right?"

I bit into my sandwich, thinking over her words as I ate, the green chili smothering the chicken bringing just the right amount of heat. If I was going to survive here for a month, I needed to understand the way this world worked, even if I planned on leaving it again when this was all over. "Tell me what else I need to know."

Chapter Twenty-Five

WEST

Behind the garage, I walked up the still-dirt road to the future dorm site, rounding a turn to find the whole space cleared and leveled. The aspen grove that had sprawled over the land was gone, chopped into stacks of firewood.

A year ago, a Lone wolf stayed with us at the pack house and picked a fight, and I'd never forgiven myself for letting it happen in the same house as my niece. That next morning, I'd called Aspen and the plans for the dorms had begun.

Here, anyone needing a place to stay would be close enough for me to oversee, but far enough from River to keep her safe.

I waved to Jett and Zion, who I'd put in charge of the construction zone. Jett, because I hoped giving him a little authority might help appease his Alpha wolf, and Zion because he had actual construction experience. A number of other pack guys were scattered around, prepping for the foundation pour.

"Progress looks good," I said as I reached Jett and Zion, shaking their hands. "When are you getting started on the forms for the foundation?"

Jett nodded. "Aspen said she's coming by later to look things over and make any final changes, then we should be good to keep working."

"And materials?"

"We have the lumber and rebar on hold in town," Zion answered. "We can pick it up once we know the final measurements. Concrete is set for next week, but the guys need to work on leveling the roads first so the trucks can get back here easily."

"Good. Sounds like you have it under control." The conversation turned to ideas the males had for the new dorms and I listened intently, giving them my full attention. As easy as it would be for me to step in and take charge, I had enough on my plate right now without taking on this build too. I needed to trust they could handle it on their own.

The second Jade stepped onto the site, I knew.

I turned from Jett and Zion as Aspen and Jade strolled up the trail, talking and laughing together. That in itself hit me like a gut punch — Aspen had grown more and more serious since our mother died, less likely to let people in and joke around. And yet, here she was, already embracing Jade like Summer had.

Jett nodded to Aspen as they reached us. "Glad you could make it."

"Show me what you got, boys," Aspen said, clapping her hands together. "Where's that sexy rebar I love to see?"

Zion chuckled as he held out a hand for Aspen to follow him. "We only just finished grading, but if it's steel pipe you're looking for — *oof.*"

Aspen cut off Zion's harmless flirtation with an elbow to the ribs, and together they wandered off to check the site, Aspen whipping out her tablet as they went.

"How are you settling in, Jade?" Jett asked casually, and I tried not to bristle. He was allowed to talk to her. Theoretically.

Togo had other opinions.

Jade turned her brown eyes on him and gave him a polite smile. "The Larkins have been very welcoming."

"Where did you say you were from again?"

Her eyes narrowed ever so slightly. "I didn't. But I've lived all over."

"Hey, I think they want you over there," Jett said to me,

pointing across the field to where Aspen raised her brows, hands on hips. I'd heard her same as Jett, but Togo was on edge.

I wanted to stay and chaperone Jett and Jade, but they were adults. With a nod to each of them, I strode across the field to see what Aspen needed.

"So, the original drawings included around 20 rooms for incoming or visiting shifters," she started, showing me a blueprint mockup on her tablet of the dorm-style building I'd commissioned. Much as I tried to give her my attention, I kept one eye on Jett on the other side of the field, still talking to Jade. "But we hadn't finalized whether you want all the rooms to have kitchenettes like studio apartments, or just put in one common area kitchen. If we did one kitchen, then I could make room for more common spaces, like a living room area, or an office lounge."

Jett took a step closer to Jade, and my hand clenched into a fist. She didn't step back, but I saw the hint of a flinch with his proximity, and Togo growled. "Westothy."

I blinked. "What?"

Meeting my sister's unamused, steely glare, I forced myself to look at her tablet. She swiped between different images showing a few options for how to set up the dorm. "Choose. Dorms or apartments."

"Both," I said, needing to make a decision though I couldn't focus on anything other than the two wolves in the distance. "Do a few full studios on the top floor, for people living here long term." *Like Jade*, my wolf rumbled, *until she comes to live with us.* "Then the main floor, keep the rooms simpler and do the common kitchen and living room."

Aspen squinted at her tablet, examining her sketches before nodding. "We can do that. I'll sketch the new layout tonight, but the foundation will be the same size as my original blueprints, so you guys can frame that for now. I'll have rough plumbing locations for you tomorrow, so we can get concrete poured as soon as possible," she added the last part for Zion, who nodded.

My phone buzzed in my pocket as they started up construction talk again, and I pulled it out to see Drea calling me. "Drea? Is there a problem?"

"Atlas and I found something you'll want to see for yourself," she answered. "We're at the northern territory line. Can you come out here?"

I shot Jade another glance, where she was still talking to Jett. Why did the male have to be so long-winded? He'd never been my favorite, but his wolf was strong and I tried not to shut anyone out without good cause. When Jade smiled at something he said, he went down several notches in my book. Maybe it was time to look harder for *good cause.*

As much as I didn't want to leave her out here with him, I knew she'd be fine. And Aspen was here, too — my sister may have been book-smart, but she was also ruthless in a fight. Nothing would happen to Jade on her watch.

"I'll be there in twenty minutes."

)))●(((

At the territory border, I followed the pull of pack bonds to Atlas and Drea, their animals' uneasiness already putting mine on alert before I reached them. Crunching over pine needles and skirting boulders, I found them in a clearing, concern on their faces.

"What is it?"

"Two things," Drea started, and waved for me to follow. We climbed over a row of boulders we used as the northern line of the territory, and she stopped about fifty yards past the border, pointing up into a tree. In it was a well-hidden camera, and not one of our own.

My hackles rose instantly.

"How long has that been there?"

Atlas grimaced, hands in his pockets. "We patrol the border regularly, but beyond it?"

Shit. I jerked my head towards the camera. "Is it still on?"

"We assume so."

"Any others?"

"Nova and his scouts are checking now," Drea said. "So far they've found two more."

"I assume no scents we recognize."

Atlas shook his head. "All we can tell is they seem to have been put there by humans; there aren't any shifter scents on the cameras or in the area."

"Were the other cameras also looking onto pack lands?"

"Yes. And they were all about the same distance from territory borders."

Togo snarled. That sounded like we had a traitor in our midst, or some other shifter was out there, helping these humans by scenting our lands for them. Either way, my wolf wanted blood.

"Take the cameras down immediately. Bring them to Aspen and see what she can find out," I ordered, and Atlas was up the tree in a flash, ripping the camera out of the tree before effortlessly dropping 20 feet to the ground. "And we need to leave enough scent on the scene that if they do have a shifter with them, whoever they are, they know we're onto them."

Atlas nodded, already texting Nova the directions as I spoke.

"You said there were two things?"

Drea nodded, and motioned for us to head back onto our lands, Atlas following behind as he texted.

Clambering over the boulders again, we hopped down on a different section further east, and I smelled copper.

At the base of a boulder, nearly passed out, lay a male shifter. I didn't recognize the scent enough to identify what kind he was, despite the amount of dried blood covering his face and chest. He looked to be in his mid-twenties, but that didn't mean much with shifters.

"Who are you?" I asked, and the guy opened a swollen eye to blink blearily at me.

"Rob Yeung," he rasped, trying to lift his hand in a lazy wave. "Call me Robbie."

"Robbie. What are you doing here, and what happened to you?"

"To be totally honest, I don't know where I am, so I'm afraid I can't answer that first bit, boss," Robbie said, then winced and gripped his side. "Some dudes — *big* dudes, man, I mean, I'm pretty big, you know? But these guys, they even lift, bro — anyway, they jumped me."

I exchanged a long look with Atlas, and knew we were thinking the same thing. More shifter kidnappings.

"Next thing I know, I wake up in this cell," Robbie continued. "I don't even know how long I was there, but eventually they needed to move me somewhere else. I broke out and ran for my fucking life. Think I broke a few ribs and who knows what else crashing through the window. It should have healed by now, but —"

"You broke through a window?" Drea gaped at him.

"Yeah," Robbie coughed, grimacing again. "No cake-walk either, lemme tell ya. It was that kind with the embedded strips of metal?" He indicated his face, which had healed but was still covered in dried blood. "My bear is strong, though."

"You're a bear," I repeated for confirmation, thinking through the dens I knew of in the area. Atlas shook his head, his dark eyes meeting mine briefly before he looked back at the kid.

He waved a dazed hand again. "Panda."

My line of thinking came to a screeching halt at that.

"Did you just say you're a *panda* shifter?" Atlas asked, stealing the words from my mouth. "I didn't even know that was a thing."

"Not many of us left," Robbie said as he pushed to sit up, gripping his side. "And I'm half. My mom was a witch."

"Where are you from?" I asked, my mind finally catching back up after this shocking revelation.

"Cali," he said, then looked around the forest. "Where am I?"

"Timber Creek, Colorado. You're a long way from home." Unease gripped me as I looked back to where the camera had been, wondering who was watching us. "Any idea how far you ran?"

"Honestly, I don't remember any of it," Robbie said as he stood up with a wince, brushing leaves off his very naked, very large body. He rubbed a hand over his black hair, then seemed to realize Drea was standing next to me and clapped a hand over his junk, eyes wide. A blush rose on his tan skin and I decided I needed to take several years off my age estimate.

"Nothing I haven't seen before, buddy." Drea smiled, and Robbie blushed even harder.

"I hate to be a burden," he turned his eyes to me, "but maybe I could trouble you guys for some clothes?"

Drea and I made eye contact again, communicating through our pack bonds everything that needed to happen next. Contact Max, have Zara come out to the house to check for trackers, let Robbie rest and get his strength back.

"Until we have you checked out, I'm afraid we can't bring you all the way into town." I crossed my arms. "But I'll have someone bring you some clothes when our town witch comes to see you."

Robbie's eyes went wide. "Town — w-witch?"

I nodded. "I need you checked for tracking implants before we bring you in. As long as you're clear, you can regroup in town as long as you need."

"Trackers?" Robbie gulped, and started frantically patting his body. "Oh crap, it could be anywhere! This is what people who get abducted feel like! They violated me! Crap, is this it? I found it!"

Robbie whirled around, pointing to the back of his neck as he broke out in a dripping sweat.

Drea pursed her lips to hide a smirk. "I think that's a vertebra, big guy," she teased. "I'll get Zara out here. Don't worry, Po, we'll get you sorted out in no time."

Robbie breathed out a slightly relieved exhale, before tilting his head as he whipped his gaze back over to me. "Wait a second, Timber Creek?" I nodded. "Then you're West freakin' Larkin?"

Atlas gave an amused snort, taking in Robbie's giant, naked, bloodied form like this was just another Tuesday for us.

"He is indeed West freakin' Larkin," Atlas said with a bemused expression.

"I saw you on the news, bro! You're, like, shifter royalty!" Robbie cupped his junk with one hand and extended the other to me to shake. I hesitated — it had *also* recently been on his junk — but Robbie wasn't offended, only chuckling again. "Right, sorry. We can do a more formal introduction when I'm not all — y'know." He gestured at himself, and I hummed in agreement. Then his expression went almost sheepish as he bit his lip and added, "And maybe I could get your autograph? Mr. Larkin, sir?"

Atlas' booming laugh filled the woods, and he clapped Robbie on the back hard enough to have the giant guy wincing again. "This kid with the sweet talk, huh?"

"Hey, my Ma taught me to respect my elders," Robbie said.

"Elders?" Drea asked. "How old do you think West is? How old are *you*?"

"I'm 23, but Mama always says I don't look a day over 18 — though that could be because she's always trying to convince people she's about three decades younger than she is. And Mr. Larkin — I don't know, fifty? How do wolves age?"

Drea and Atlas burst into laughter, and Robbie cringed.

I shook my head, and prepared to leave. Clearly, my comedian Shields could handle this from here.

I held out my hand for the camera Atlas had taken down, and he passed it over. "You two stay here with him until Zara gets here. When she gives the all clear, bring him into town. I'll send Leif out with some clothes."

I turned to head back to the house, and Robbie called out after me, "Thanks for your help, Mr. Larkin, dude! And hey, you're even cooler in person than on TV!"

I shook my head. Kids these days.

Chapter Twenty-Six

JADE

My neck ached from holding my shoulders so high, tension coiling in me after every minute spent with Jett. Balto hated the male, and while I didn't have a concrete reason against him, I trusted her. Something about him made us uncomfortable, but the same could be true of just about every male I'd met in the last few years.

"Okay, so I'm going to adjust the sketch a bit for the final plans," Aspen said as we reached Main Street again, and I forced myself to pay attention. "That'll be pretty boring for you, but feel free to hang out in the office if you want."

Music blasted out of Cruz Motors as we neared, and Aspen visibly prepared for battle. Sensing a repeat of this morning headed our way, I spun towards her. "How about I talk to Cruz and ask him to turn down the music while you get started?"

She heaved a heavy sigh, face morphing into a deep frown, but nodded. "Tell him he's getting much worse than a bath next time."

Aspen stomped up the stairs as I made my way to the last bay in the garage, where Cruz's feet stuck out from under an old Nissan coupe. The other cars in the lot were all classics, so the age of the vehicle wasn't surprising, but the rollbars inside were enough to tell me this wasn't a typical build. The painting details were stunning — most of it was a bold pearlescent red, but parts of it were matte black, looking as if the tires were smoking. Even if a giant number 86 wasn't painted on the side, I'd have known this was a race car, meant for speed.

"Excuse me?" I tried, but the music was so loud, he didn't seem to hear me. I knocked on the hood instead. "Hello?"

Cruz slid out from under the car and grinned up at me, black grease smeared across his cheek and hands.

"Miss me already, *mi amor*?"

I huffed. "Do you mind turning your music down? We need to get some work done upstairs."

Raising a brow, he got to his feet, wiping his hands on a rag. With a flick of his hand, the volume magically turned down. "*We*?"

"Thank you," I said about the music, then continued, "Well, Aspen will be drawing up new plans for a few hours, I think."

"Gotcha." Cruz wiped at his cheek, but the grease only smeared more. "What about you?"

I shifted on my feet. Honestly, I had no idea what to do now. I didn't want to head back to the empty pack house, but Aspen wouldn't need me while she was drafting.

Cruz tilted his head, eyes narrowing in thought. "You ever change a brake pad?"

)))●(((

Working with Cruz was more fun than I'd anticipated, even if it left me covered in grease. We changed out the brake pads on the Nissan while Cruz explained the differences between a regular car and a drift racer. I'd never seen a drift race outside of movies, but even his basic descriptions of it left me anxious. Flying around corners at full speed while your tires spun wildly out of control? No thanks.

The 1950's Chevy truck he pulled into the bay next, though — that was more my style.

"Who does your paint jobs?" I asked as I admired the

custom paint — baby blue, almost the color of the sky, with a white pinstripe feathered around the doors. The upholstery inside was also white with matching blue piping, and I almost drooled at how beautiful it was, if you could call a truck beautiful.

Cruz opened his mouth to answer right as Aspen called, "Jade, are you still here?"

I popped out from behind the truck and Aspen blinked back her shock at the sight of me.

"You better treat her good or I'm going to poach your assistant," Cruz said, holding his knuckles out for me to bump. I awkwardly did so, making him laugh again.

"I'm absolutely certain I can pay her more than you." Aspen smirked, turning to leave. "Jade, come have dinner at Summer's with me. You should have a break from that testerical pack house."

I grabbed one of the cleaner rags nearby, trying to work off the grease. "Oh, I don't want to be a bother —"

"Please. Summer always makes enough food for six people and then insists we need three different desserts, too." Aspen waved a hand, dismissing my concerns as she pointed to the sink at the back of the shop. For as much as she hated Cruz, she sure did know her way around his shop. "Besides, she says she wants to show you something."

Intrigued, I gave in, quickly washing my hands and waving goodbye to Cruz as Aspen and I headed out the door.

⟩⟩⟩●⟨⟨⟨

"Ta-da!" Summer beamed once we arrived, showing off her newly labeled bins. "I know you said *not* to get a label maker, but hey, I *was* a good little wolf who got her shit organized, so I deserved a reward. And I decided that reward was a label maker. And now," Summer preened, trailing a finger along all her matching labels, perfectly color-coordinated for her pastel sunrise color palette, "I have my *aesthetic* back."

"Oh, sheesh." Aspen rolled her eyes, and left the room to head back down the hall to the kitchen. "Are we cooking or ordering?"

"There's about a thousand pounds of ripe zucchini on the roof, so don't you dare think about ordering in," Summer shouted back, and Aspen grumbled something but didn't argue back. "And peaches!" Summer lowered her voice to speak to me, "I am determined to win the pie contest at the peach festival this year, so I've been trying out dozens of recipes."

"Peach festival?"

Summer nodded as we headed back out towards the kitchen. "It's at the end of the season. Peach everything — jam, wine, pie, danishes, honey, themed crafts, you name it. Lance started it a few years back when dad's peach farm started really producing and the whole town got on board."

"Lance," I paused. "You mean Lance Morgaine?"

"Yeah." Summer popped a peach slice in her mouth as she tied on an apron. "You know him?"

"Only through my sister," I said, resting against the counter. "She lives with his sister, Brigid Morgaine, in Deadlights Cove."

"That's right!" Summer smiled. "I forgot you had a sister! Is it just you two?"

I nodded, swallowing the lump that formed in my throat as I slid my hand into my pocket, feeling the phone there. Ruby had responded to my GIFs, but we hadn't talked much today. I'd long since gotten over most of my constant need to hover, but my nightmare had brought it all back. "Yes. Our parents died in an accident when I was 21. Ruby is 12 years younger than me though — she was nine at the time."

Summer's mouth turned down in a sympathetic frown. "I'm so sorry. I can't imagine losing both parents. One was bad enough."

Pushing off the counter, I moved towards the sliding glass doors to the patio, but I heard the sadness in her words. Somehow I'd forgotten this was something West and I shared, as terrible as it was. Nobody wanted to bond over grief. Leif hadn't volunteered what happened to his birth parents before West adopted him, but I wondered if we shared parenting a tween after loss, too. "It was a long time ago." Changing the subject I asked, "Need me to pick some zucchini?"

Summer tilted her head towards the apartment door. "Stairwell, take them up, be sure to prop the door open. Oh, and grab some roma tomatoes too. And an onion. And a red pepper."

I waited, hand on the doorknob to see if there was any more.

"That should do it." Summer nodded to herself, and I headed up the steps to the roof.

Propping the door open as instructed, I gasped at the space. Every available inch was covered in plants, neat garden beds spaced with gravel paths between them, most with tall trellises stretching the plants vertically for maximum use of space.

Summer, apparently, had been hard at work, since every vegetable was already neatly labeled on matching wooden garden stakes. There was a basket hanging by the door to the stairwell, which I grabbed and quickly filled with the produce Summer had designated.

Back in the kitchen, Aspen boiled pasta while Summer trimmed some fresh herbs. Wildly out of my depth, I handed off the basket and stepped back, not sure how I could contribute to this picture of domesticity.

"So, Jade," Summer started, a glint in her eye that put me on alert as she slid me a hard seltzer and started chopping the vegetables. "What's the deal with you and my brother?" She gave a pointed wiggle of her eyebrows.

I popped the top of the seltzer as I shook my head. "No deal. West helped me out a few years ago when I needed to find a witch to help my sister."

"You sure? Don't tell me you haven't noticed how he watches you."

"I've noticed," I deadpanned, thinking of all the times I'd not only seen but felt his eyes on me. A rush of heat washed through me at the thought, but I dismissed it, refusing to let my mind go there. "Doesn't mean anything other than he's an overbearing Alpha male with a staring problem. Not interested."

Summer chuckled. "You're not wrong, although I'm not sure that's all there is to it."

"Drop it," Aspen snapped, shooting her sister a glare. "She said she's not interested."

Holding up her hands, Summer said, "Okay, sorry. Subject dropped. I know it's only been a few days, but how are you liking life here in town?"

I thought about it, pondering my answer. Everyone seemed to know everyone, which was different for me. I'd kept a low profile for years — it was strange having people I didn't know immediately know who *I* was. But everyone had been friendly so far. Settling for honesty, I answered, "It's not as bad as I thought it would be."

"I'm so glad to hear that." Summer beamed. "I saw you laughing your ass off with Cruz when I walked by the shop earlier."

Aspen barked a laugh. "You're even less subtle than Dad, you know that?"

Summer shrugged. "I love love. Sue me."

I smiled. "Cruz is fun, but there's nothing else there, promise."

"Because she has taste." Aspen stirred the pasta so vigorously, water splashed out and sizzled on the stove. "And Cruz is a moron."

Summer raised her eyebrows, as if she didn't believe me, but when I didn't break, she let it go. "Okay, if not Cruz, anybody else? Oh! Have you met Atlas yet?"

I racked my brain for all the people who'd been at the job site, but the name didn't sound familiar. "I don't think so."

"Then no, you haven't. He's not the type of male you forget." Summer grinned. "He's — well, *huge*, for one —"

"Obviously the most important thing in a male," Aspen snorted.

"Sounds like maybe *you* should date him," I countered, trying to shift the conversation off of me, but Summer waved off the comment.

"Please," she laughed. "He and Cooper have been attached at the hip since they got back from the military. No way am I dating one of my brother's best friends. Also I'm pretty positive our brothers would murder any of their friends if they even looked twice in our direction. Aspen had a crush on—"

"Don't." Aspen pointed the wooden spoon at her sister. "You are a liar, and I did not."

I glanced between the sisters, trying and failing to hide the grin that crept up my lips. "Cruz, right? Tell me she had a crush on Cruz."

"Not true," Aspen said, a hint of anger rising in her voice, but Summer turned to me with an exaggerated wink. "Only an idiot could have a crush on that male, and I am no idiot. That's why I'm with Matthew. He's a sensible choice. Has a good head on his shoulders and a plan for the future. I know I can count on him."

Summer scrunched her nose in distaste as she turned away from Aspen, but I didn't say anything.

"What about you, Summer?"

"I think the last date I went on was two years ago," Summer grimaced. "I tried that supe dating site, OkCauldron, but nobody lives near here, and everyone that *does* live near here is pack. Not that there's anything wrong with dating in the pack, it's just a bit incestuous, you know? And also kind of boring. I need more adventure than that — someone who will really whisk me off my feet. And I'm pretty positive being known as the youngest Larkin girl is a curse. No one here would even consider dating me for fear of my brothers. Big family problems, right?"

I hummed in solidarity, but couldn't relate. No one had ever looked out for me, but that was a depressing topic I didn't want to go into.

"Are your brothers dating anyone?"

Summer and Aspen shared a bemused look before bursting into laughter.

"Cooper can barely string two sentences together before he has enough social interaction for the week," Summer said. "I haven't seen him interested in anyone since Eloise — this quirky little witch he knew when he was sixteen."

"I think West might spontaneously combust if he takes on one more thing in his life," Aspen added.

"Terran has barely recovered from River's mom leaving them."

"And Leif is a baby. Well, 20 I guess, but still. I don't think he's dating anyone."

"But you," Summer started again on me, "you should totally take advantage of being here for a while. Sow your wild oats and all that."

Aspen *tsk*ed. "You sound just like Dad."

"I'm not interested in dating right now," I said, hoping to end this conversation. "Or ever again, really."

The sisters turned slowly to stare at me.

"*There's* a story," Summer murmured, tilting her head.

Aspen hummed in agreement, the two of them ganging up on me.

"It's not a fun one," I warned them. I couldn't remember the last time I had someone to talk to like this, and suddenly the weight of carrying it all alone felt insufferable. Even if I left in a month, some intrinsic part of me knew I could trust the Larkins

ing, all of it. As Ruby got older, I started losing track of her for periods of time." I blinked at the moisture in my eyes. "He kept saying she was just running around with the other kids, but when I'd ask her later, she had no idea what I was talking about. Like she'd just lost that time, but had no awareness of losing it. Every-time I brought it up to Thaddeus, he told me to relax. Everything was fine. I was being hysterical."

"Ugh, *men*," Summer muttered.

"We had no money, nowhere to go, no way out. Nothing was as it seemed there, and the more I learned about what the Coven was really up to, the more desperate I was for a way out." I swallowed heavily, keeping the worst of my secrets, no matter how much I trusted these ladies. "Then, one day, Max showed up. Our dark avenging angel. And he got us out."

"Holy crap," Summer breathed.

I let the silence linger, fighting to breathe normally. My hands shook as I lifted my glass, taking a small sip. "Ruby has no memory of it," I whispered as guilt ate at me the way it had every day for the last five years. "I begged Max to wipe her memories of that entire time. She's still so young, has so much life ahead of her. She doesn't need to carry the trauma of our time there."

"But you do?"

My head snapped up, meeting Summer's sad eyes as my spine hardened into steel, washing away any lingering weakness. "Yes. So it will never, *ever* happen to us again."

Silence greeted the end of my tragic tale, until Aspen finally broke it.

"That's why you're so anti-pack," she stated, not as a question. "You don't want another cult situation."

"Can you blame her? Holy kumquats," Summer said, her eyes still wide with shock.

"What about the Coven?" Aspen asked, her eyes narrowed. "Do you still keep in touch with anyone there? Or is that why you've moved around so much?" She jerked back, then leaned over the table. "Did he hit you?"

I clenched my jaw, biting back the scream that wanted to rip free as memories surfaced. While Thaddeus never *hit* me, he'd done everything in his power to make sure I lived in a state of constant fear, submitting to him in all ways, and I'd forgiven him every time he asked for it, like an idiot. Rubbing at the wrists that had borne bruises for years, I said, "I haven't seen anyone from the Coven in years until Bram a few days ago."

I could feel Aspen's gaze on me before I even lifted my head, not missing the way I'd only answered one of her questions. She was smart — I'd given her plenty to go off of.

"What an asshole," Summer said, her usual smile wiped clean. "I hate him and I don't even know him. We should hunt him down and give him a taste of his own medicine. What's his favorite food? I could poison it."

I gave a noncommittal shrug. I'd been more concerned with leaving him in my rear view mirror than hunting him down again.

"That's one of the reasons I hate shifting. I have this irrational fear Thaddeus can somehow track my magical signature." I didn't bother explaining that the real reason I hated shifting was a lot more gruesome, and a memory I sometimes wished I'd let Max take from me.

"Is that possible?" Summer asked. "How powerful of a witch was he?"

"Not as far as I know, but I was never great at the witch stuff. And he was pretty powerful, but it was more than just him. There were dozens of witches in the Coven."

"Even if it were possible, you're safe to shift here," Aspen added matter-of-factly. "No one gets onto pack lands without West knowing about it, and he'd never let anything happen to you. Wolf out whenever you need to."

I offered a small smile, trying to defuse the tension I'd unintentionally caused. "Thanks, but I'm good. I never shift if I can help it."

Silence crashed down like a tsunami, both sister's mouths once again dropping open in shock. They exchanged a loaded, concerned look, and Aspen set her glass down with a clatter loud enough, I was afraid it had cracked.

"Jade," Summer began in a tone of forced calm, "Explain yourself."

I looked between the two sisters. "It's not a big deal. I shift when I can't stand it anymore, but even then, it's usually a short run."

They frowned, Summer's eyes near bugging out in alarm, and Aspen's mouth narrowing to a thin, disappointed line.

"That's not possible," Summer spluttered. "You *need* to shift — if you don't shift regularly, your wolf will go nuts!"

Aspen's eyes turned piercing as she tilted her head, studying me. "Your wolf is already losing it, isn't she?"

I didn't answer, but my silence was enough confirmation as Aspen shook her head.

"Jade, you can't do that to yourself. I know you're not as accustomed to everything about your wolf heritage as a shifter in a pack would be, but our magic stems from the soul — and we have two. If you're denying half of yourself like it sounds like you are, you'll get out of balance. Shifting regularly is important — even I manage it at least once a week, and I live in a human town."

Summer nodded. "Most of the pack here shifts two to three times a week, if not more. But it's more than that, too. As wolves, we're pack animals. We're not meant to be alone for long periods of time. Even Aspen comes home to us every once in a while to reconnect with that bond for her wolf."

I worried my lip, sitting back as I thought through their words. My father was a Lone wolf his whole life, so it couldn't be as dire as they made it out, but if I dredged up those blurry memories of long ago, I could recall how often he shifted, even if just to run the edges of our property.

Aspen's phone went off with a custom ringtone before I could ask any further questions, and she groaned like she already knew who it was before setting it on the table and hitting speakerphone. "What now, Westathan?"

"Who are you with?" his voice rumbled, low and hesitant in a way that immediately had me sitting straighter. Something was wrong.

Aspen frowned. "Summer and Jade, why?"

"Drea found cameras installed just beyond the territory, pointing at pack lands. Atlas and Nova went and took them down, but I need you to take a look at them."

"Cameras?" Summer scrunched her nose. "What? Why?"

"I don't know, but it can't be good." West sighed loudly. The sisters shared a look of concern I felt myself joining in on — West had too much on his plate, something I was beginning to understand was a recurring theme for the male. "Can you come check them out? See if there's anything you can figure out about where they came from, how long they've been recording, and who might be getting this footage."

Aspen was already pushing back from the table. "I'm on my way."

The call ended and the sisters exchanged a look, then leapt into action.

"I'll put a box together for him." Summer scrambled to her feet. "Dad's at the ranch and Terran's working today, so I doubt he ate anything that could legally be considered food for dinner."

As Aspen went off to her room, I followed Summer to the kitchen.

"Is West the one Larkin who can't cook?" I tried to joke as I recalled the nachos he'd made me, but Summer's pinched face betrayed her concern — though whether it was about the cameras or her brother was hard to say.

"He *can*," she hedged, starting to pile pasta and the vegetable sauce she made into a container, "but does he make time for it? No. He's too busy spending 110% of his time looking after everyone else, and then is so exhausted he has nothing left to take care of himself." Summer closed up the container, then pulled a pie out of the fridge and started slicing it up, adding a few large pieces into another container. "I've seen him eat two strips of elk jerky and a stray tomato he found on the counter and call it a meal. Hopeless. It's probably half the reason Dad's over there grilling as often as he is. West takes care of everyone else, so we take care of him."

Summer stacked the containers into a tote bag, then grabbed what looked like a homemade loaf of bread and wrapped it before putting it on top. She glanced over at me and asked, "I know you're in Aspen's old room — have you noticed if he's sleeping okay? Sometimes his insomnia gets bad, which just makes everything worse, but he never tells us anything."

I hesitated — if he didn't open up to his family about this stuff, would it be a betrayal if I told her about our late night video game nights? But luckily, Summer waved it off.

"Nevermind, forget I asked. Probably weird to ask you to spy on your host and all that."

Aspen appeared in the kitchen doorway, a bag of gear slung over her shoulder. "Is it ready? Jade, want to walk back over with me?"

Aspen's arms were full, so Summer held out the tote to me, filled to the brim with homemade food for their brother, who both sisters were more than willing to drop everything to help.

Chapter Twenty-Seven

WEST

"Anything?" I asked Atlas as I pulled out a barstool and sat down. He'd followed me home after Zara cleared Robbie, getting him settled in the basement.

"I called around, looking for any information on a Bram Rasmus, but haven't found much. He's a witch, but no one had any dirt on him. Kid's clean."

I rubbed at my temples, already expecting that to be true after Max's strange questioning, but for once, it would have been nice if *something* came easily.

"One notable thing did pop up though," Atlas said, and I lifted my head to eye the male. Atlas chewed on his lip, apprehension rolling off him in waves, not something I was used to seeing in one of my strongest men.

"Well?" I asked, impatience getting the better of me.

"Terran said something about one of Bram's tattoos, so I went back and looked at the footage, both from the barn and the restaurant. He has a large black rose with thirteen thorns on his forearm, and something about that seemed familiar, so I sent it to some buddies. Do you remember the Black Rose Coven?"

I sat back in my chair with a heavy sigh. "That's the one that was busted up a few years ago, right? The cult where someone went all murder-suicide and killed a bunch of people, and the whole Coven disappeared?"

Atlas hummed in agreement, his gaze shifting to the front door where we both sensed Aspen and Jade walking up the path.

"Something like that. Not sure if anyone knows the real story. Rumor has it they were up to some shady shit, too. She doesn't have any tattoos, does she?"

"No," I growled at his insinuation. "Just because Bram was involved with the Black Rose Coven doesn't mean that's how she knows him."

"Something to consider," Atlas said as he walked towards the back door and out onto the porch. "I'm headed to Coop's, but I'll keep you updated if I hear more."

I nodded vaguely, but my mind was already spinning through everything I knew about Jade, about Bram, this nefarious Coven as I left the kitchen and paced in the foyer. My agitation grew at the not-knowing, the missing puzzle pieces, Togo demanding Jade tell me everything again. He didn't care that it hadn't gone well last time. *How can we protect her like this?* he argued.

"Leif is in the basement with the cameras," I sent to Aspen through our pack bonds as they approached the house, knowing she would read between the lines that I wanted Jade alone.

The door opened and I snapped my head up, pausing where I was wearing a hole in the rug. A relieved sigh escaped me at having them back home.

"I'll let you know if I find anything," Aspen said, trying to catch my eye, but I was laser-focused on Jade.

I took a step forward, unable to stop myself, drawn towards her. Togo was riding me hard, frustrated with how much was out of our control right now. With how little we could do to fix her past — so he wanted to latch on to what we could do about her present, her future. *That* was something we could handle. The last time I'd seen her, she'd stood entirely too close to Jett. Would I scent him on her anywhere? I didn't have any right to care if I did — Jade was a grown woman, she could make her own decisions.

Just like I could tear Jett to shreds. Free country.

"Westeros?" Aspen's voice sounded almost muffled, my senses fully tuned on Jade.

Her pupils widened as I stepped closer. Her pulse sped up. Her lips slightly parted.

"Okay, great talk," Aspen huffed, then, much sharper in my mind, she added, *"She's got history with controlling assholes. Don't be a dick."*

My sister's words made me pause, wondering what Jade had told her to make her say that, but I couldn't take my attention off the woman in front of me. Jade still wore the same ripped jeans and black tank from earlier today, but something was different and I couldn't put my finger on it. Vaguely, I heard the basement door open, and Aspen's footsteps descending.

Togo was barely contained below the surface of my consciousness, pacing in my mind.

"Summer sent this over for you." Jade held out a bag, a loaf of bread sticking out of it, but I didn't care about food right now. Jade wasn't looking me in the eyes — she was studying my chin intently.

Someone had told her about the importance of body language in a pack.

This was the closest Jade had ever come to showing respect to me as an Alpha, and for some reason, I didn't like it. I missed the way her brown eyes settled on me in a challenge, not caring about status or pack norms. I wanted her fire, her grit back, not this watered down version of herself because of who I was.

"She said something about you not eating enough, which seems hypocritical if you ask me."

I reached out, brushing Jade's fingers as I took the bag from her. Even that small contact was enough to send a shock through me, needing more, needing to unlock that wild ferocity Jade usually wielded. With every ounce of control I had, I inclined my head for Jade to come with me to the kitchen.

"How was the rest of your day?" There, words. Human

words. I shoved the food on the counter — there was no way I could eat right now, as keyed up as I was.

"Better than yours by the sounds of it. Are you — Summer said something about —" Jade cut herself off, frowning.

Could I ask her directly about the Coven? Would she shut down again?

Before I even registered what I was doing, I had her pressed back against the kitchen counter, my hands resting on either side of her. Her breath caught, and her tongue darted out, licking her lips, as my gaze raked over her.

Leaning in, my nose trailed just above her skin, my wolf insistent on being in control, and dammit, with how hard my head pounded, I let him. Taking a slow, deep inhale, he cataloged the scents on her. Summer and Aspen — she'd been with them at Summer's apartment. I knew that already. The chemical tang of oil and grease — my eyes shot down to her hands, traces of black still tingeing the edges of her nails.

I cocked my head. "You worked with Cruz?"

"Um, yeah."

Jade didn't shove me away, but she definitely didn't understand what was happening right now. Togo was at the forefront, his primal need to stake claim and make her ours so we could protect her properly overwhelming in its intensity. I closed my eyes, hiding the glowing gold she'd see if I moved back, but was too tired to fight for control.

Thankfully, her wolf sensed how on edge mine was and was more than willing to comply. Happy, excited energy rippled off her towards me through the faint pack bonds, mixed with her more human wariness. I leaned in closer, stopping just short of licking over her pulse pounding in her neck.

Even without touching her, I could feel and scent the way her body reacted to mine. This attraction wasn't as one-sided as she wanted me to believe, and that sent a shiver of delight through my body.

She cleared her throat, but I smiled at the husky tone tingeing her voice. "We changed brake pads. It was surprisingly fun. How did you know?"

Cruz was harmless, even if he was a flirt, so my heart warmed to hear she'd made a friend.

I straightened up enough to bring my hand just below her elbow, wanting to cover her in my scent, but that wasn't the lesson I needed to teach her right now. My hand slid down her arm, fingers lacing with hers just for a moment as I pulled her small hand into mine and willed the glow in my eyes to subside. Togo didn't step completely back in my mind, but he relented in this, satisfied with what he'd found. Lifting our joined hands, I held them in front of her, pointing out her nails.

"Close your eyes." I covered the black streaks of her nail beds, wanting to show her how I'd truly known. After a slightly confused dip of her eyebrows, Jade complied, her eyes shutting.

I had to force myself to loosen my grip; it was almost painful to break this small contact. I studied the way her long dark lashes rested on her cheeks, the contours of her face, so beautiful she took my breath away every time I saw her.

Focusing on the task, I lifted her hand even more and brought it just below her nose. "Do you smell that? I can tell you've tried to wash the grease off — Summer is obsessed with that verbena soap — but it's hard to get rid of it completely."

Then I waited. I wanted her to practice scenting, wanted to see if she could identify what had given her away, wanted to teach her everything I could about our ways in hopes I could convince her to stay, or at least how to protect herself better if she left. Togo balked at that thought, but I shoved him aside.

Jade inhaled, tilting forward as her brow creased in concentration. A regular human wouldn't have noticed the grease at these trace amounts, all but washed off, but shifters? We'd be able to scent this for days, until nearly every molecule was gone. This was the most important part of tracking, and it also helped when you needed to cover your own scent, something Jade had never been trained to do.

Jade's eyes snapped back open, wide with delight. "I *can* smell that," she breathed, surprised at herself. The corner of my mouth tipped up, pleased that she was pleased. "I have to focus so hard to notice it, though — you do it so naturally."

I nodded, reluctantly letting go of her hand even though I didn't step away. Now that I had her this close, I couldn't. "It'll become easier if you practice."

"What else can you scent on me?"

My chest tightened as Togo rumbled his approval. She was *inviting* us to sniff her? We didn't need to be asked twice.

I leaned down, my nose barely skating the delicate skin of her neck this time, relishing in the shiver it sent through her body. I wanted to press my lips to it. Wanted to sink my teeth in it.

"You were in Summer's garden," I told her, my voice a low rumble. "You girls had tequila with your dinner — margaritas? I can smell the job site — pine and diesel. Cruz's shop, of course, and" — I trailed a finger across her bare shoulder — "where Cruz touched you here."

Jade blinked, looking down at her own shoulder. "You can tell where he touched me? Hours ago?"

"Yes. It's smoky — demons usually are. See if you can single it out."

Closing her eyes again, Jade took a deep inhale, scrunching her face up adorably in concentration as she turned her head towards her shoulder. The move brought her that much closer to me, her neck stretched long, and this time I almost gave in to the instinct to lick my way across her smooth skin, to taste her. Then she heaved a sigh and shook her head. "I can't tell."

She'd shifted her body with the motion, and suddenly my senses zeroed in on her arm, just above her elbow.

Jett. I fucking knew it. It was her arm, which was hardly scandalous, but that fucker had known exactly what he was doing.

Putting my hand under her elbow, I brought her arm across her chest to bring her elbow closer to her nose, tapping with my thumb just below the place he'd touched her.

"And here," I said, the muscle in my jaw twitching. My chest physically hurt with how badly I needed to erase all traces of him from her body, even though moments before I'd had no such impulse with Cruz's scent. Cruz was family.

Bending down, Jade tried to figure out what I indicated on her arm, but soon gave up, frowning at me.

I blinked, my eyes shifting between mine and my wolf, and Jade pulled back, startled. I had to get it together. I didn't want to *scare* her, but fuck. My exhausting day paired with this headache and how badly I wanted Jade was a deadly combination. I was losing it.

"Jett held your arm." I swiped my thumb over the spot, envisioning it wiping away all trace of him. "Here."

Jade's eyes shuttered at that. "He's a bit…" she trailed off, and I couldn't stop myself from moving even further into her space, desperate to hear the end of that sentence from her lips. I felt the moment her whole body stiffened, tension riding her as she thought back over her interaction with the male, and I hated him even more.

"What?"

"Overbearing." Her gaze flicked up to mine, and my stomach twisted. Like her word was a physical shove, I stepped back.

Fuck. I was being just as bad as he'd probably been. Worse, even. Turning my back to her, I ran my hand through my hair, trying to calm down and give her space. I forced myself to walk away, moving to the counter as I pulled out the food from Summer.

But Jade wasn't as attuned to her wolf senses as I was. Whoever had told her about our customs today had failed to mention I'd hear how fast her heart beat in her chest, sense the frustration that washed through her when I stepped away, smell the way my proximity had affected her.

Maybe I was just as overbearing as Jett, but the difference was Jade *liked* it from me. All of the lingering tension she'd held when talking about Jett was gone, replaced by disappointment when I put distance between us.

Keeping the self-satisfied smile off my face, I grabbed the pie slices and two forks, then pulled out a stool in front of Jade as well as the one next to it. "Sit. Eat with me."

Jade studied me, her heart still pounding while she slowly sat. My leg brushed against hers as I leaned over, holding out a fork. She took it, and as she had a bite of the peach pie, a soft moan of contentment left her that went straight to my dick.

Instantly, I was imagining all the ways I could draw that sound out of her again, thoughts of kidnappings and cameras and everything but her a distant memory as I pictured her tan skin laid bare beneath me, moaning my name. Each moment I spent with her, it was more difficult to determine if those were my wolf's thoughts or mine. Maybe both, if I was honest with myself. She made me feel like a horny teenager, lost to my lusty thoughts.

Clenching my jaw, I forced myself to focus. "If Jett ever does something that makes you uncomfortable, that crosses the line, you'll tell me."

"Who says he makes me uncomfortable?"

"You do." I waved a hand to indicate her body before spearing a slice of peach on my fork. "Your body language the entire time he was talking to you at the job site, and the fact that *he* didn't respect those signals already makes me want to rip his eyes out." The last few words came out as a growl.

Finally, Jade met my gaze head-on, her fierce independent streak taking over again, and damn if I didn't love to see it. "I can take care of myself, West. I don't need you or anyone fighting my battles for me."

I wanted to shake some sense into her. "What about *with* you?" I tossed my fork down more forcefully than I intended, the silver clattering onto the plate as I fought to rein in my temper. Shit, I couldn't remember the last time I'd let anyone under my skin the way Jade was, and I couldn't decide whether I loved or hated it. My attention on her was quickly turning into frustrated infatuation. "I understand you want to stand on your own two feet, but that doesn't mean someone can't stand beside you. Can't have your back."

That seemed to give her pause, but she recovered after a minute, focusing heavily on the pie rather than meeting my eyes again. "You have enough on your plate without worrying about me."

Irritation rose in me as I pushed the plate away, turning my body to face hers. She looked up, confusion clouding her face as I reached forward and lightly gripped her chin, forcing her to meet my eyes. Her pupils dilated at the touch, and her breath caught at our nearness, making my growing need for her that much worse.

"Listen to me, Jade. Hear the honesty in my words and remember it. You are not a burden. I would do anything to ensure you're happy and healthy with everything you ever needed or wanted. You make me want to forget about everything else on my plate until only *you* are on the menu."

Chapter Twenty-Eight

JADE

West left after his proclamation, leaving the rest of the pie uneaten and me in a flutter of confusion. What the hell was *that*?

He wanted me on his "menu"? Did that mean what I thought it meant?

Who was I kidding? Of course it did.

Sexual energy had rolled off West in waves, pulling me under in a way I hadn't felt in years. Maybe ever. I was torn between calling Ruby, emotionally scarring my baby sister forever, and melting into a puddle right there in the kitchen. Choices, choices.

My skin burned where he'd touched me — my face, my hands, my thigh, my elbow.

Without thinking, I lifted my fingers to my nose, seeing if I could scent him the way he'd smelled Cruz and Jett on me. The barest hint of pine lingered, mixed with Summer's soap and the smells of Cruz's shop, but it was enough to have me closing my eyes, savoring it for just a moment as my heart raced.

"You doing okay?" Aspen said and my eyes flew open. I quickly lowered my hand back to my lap as embarrassment pinked my cheeks.

"Yep, fine!" I grabbed the fork and shoveled a bite of pie into my mouth to keep myself from answering further. What was I supposed to say — *your brother just suggested he'd like to eat me and my brain short-circuited so I was sniffing my hands to hang on to him a little longer, wondering what his hands would feel like on the rest of my body?* We weren't *those* kinds of friends yet.

Aspen studied me, her eyes squinted as she grabbed a glass from the cabinet and filled it with water. "Word to the wise, our scents change when we're turned on. Summer's pie is excellent, could bring a girl to her knees, but the lingering smell of my brother in the room is too strong for me to believe that caused your reaction."

My eyes bugged out of my head as I stared at the counter. "Well, that's mortifying. Do wolves have no secrets from each other then?"

"You get used to it." Aspen lifted a shoulder. "And you'll get better at hiding it — most of the time. Though it's harder around your ma —" Aspen coughed "— main romantic interest."

Something made me think that hadn't been what she'd started to say, but I was too busy thinking about all the times I'd probably betrayed myself to West. "I'm not interested in your brother like that."

Aspen hummed, sipping her water then patted my hand. "Your heart rate just went up and your scent shifted again. Lying to a shifter is a hell of a lot harder than you think it is."

An uneasy laugh escaped me, and I pushed away from the counter. *Was* I interested in West? A few days ago, even a few hours ago, the answer would have been an easy *Hard pass*, not only for him, but all males. He'd been arrogant and demanding more times than I could count. But after my talk with his sisters, and with Cooper and Max too, I couldn't escape the dawning realization that he had intention behind his every action. When he'd said he'd do anything to ensure I was happy and healthy, I could feel how much he meant it.

Didn't mean I had to accept it, though.

"I think I'm just going up to bed." I pointed at the stairs stupidly, remembering afterwards that I was staying in Aspen's room — she knew where it was.

She grinned, barely holding back a laugh at my flustered

reaction. "Tomorrow's Sunday, so I'm not working. Be at the office at 8 Monday morning and enjoy a day off."

I gave her a thumbs up, heading towards the stairs, the idea of a *day off* jarring me back to the present. Other than between moves or while I was unemployed, I hadn't intentionally taken a day off in years.

"Hey Jade?" Aspen said, and I turned back towards her, one foot on the steps. "I'm not going to say anything. About your past, or about this." She waved a hand in my direction. "Whatever is going on is between you and West. It's not my business. But know there are no males better than him, and I say this as someone who has seen all her brothers bet each other how many chili dogs they could eat before puking. West lost terribly — I don't know if that's a pro or con for him — but he's as good and as real as they come. He would never treat you the way Thaddeus did. And if West ever found out about him, he would hunt him down and make him suffer."

I nodded, not knowing what to say to that, and turned to go as she added, "And don't do anything alone in your bed you don't want this whole shifter house hearing!"

Cheeks burning at her implication, I scurried up to my room.

)❭❭●❬❬(

Aspen and West's words swirled around my head as I tossed and turned that night.

I knew in my gut that what Aspen had said was the truth. West was a good guy, maybe one of the best. He wasn't Thaddeus, and nothing about this pack was anything like the Coven.

And after our dinner chat, I wondered if I was part of my own problem. Had my choice not to shift put me in such an imbalance between Balto's soul and my own that it caused this restlessness in me? But how did I even begin to overcome the crippling fear that swallowed me every time I thought of shifting voluntarily? I couldn't just up and decide not to be afraid — anxiety didn't work that way.

But being here, surrounded by the Larkins, I realized how much I'd missed out on these last few years. The thought of going back to that lonely existence, of leaving Summer and Aspen, Cruz, even Cooper and Terran behind, made my chest ache.

Then there was West.

After how suggestive he'd been earlier, did I dare sneak down for another video game night?

Would he take that as meaning I *wanted* to be on his menu?

I twisted over to my other side in the bed, trying to get comfortable despite the growing ache to be near him.

Did I want to be on his menu?

Being alone with him seemed dangerous, but I was tired of assessing every single breath I took. Just the thought of him had my skin tingling, remembering how it had felt when he'd gripped my chin, forcing me to hear his words.

The pull to him was undeniable, and I wanted to lean in.

Stomach fluttering, I swung my feet out of bed and sat up. I tiptoed out onto the landing and my heart leapt into my throat at the sight of West's open door, flickering blue light coming from within.

His bedroom. Balto was practically drooling.

I paused, looking at the stairs and then back to his room, indecision warring in me. Going into his room felt personal on a level we hadn't been yet, but then again, so had the way his nose had trailed across my neck earlier.

"This controller has your name on it," West's voice carried out from his room, quiet enough not to wake anyone else, but loud enough I heard it. The low rumble was like a shot straight down my spine, lighting my nerves on fire. Remembering what Aspen had said earlier about my scent changing, I thought of every unsexy thing I could, giving myself a mental cold shower as I stepped into his room.

Like most of the house, large floor-to-ceiling windows offered a stunning view of the mountains. My breath caught at the stars twinkling in the night sky, flecks of white among the dark matching the snow-capped mountain range. The room was large, a king-size bed positioned on the wall opposite the windows so West woke up to this view. A fireplace burned in the corner with a couch in front of it and a TV above the mantle. West was spread out on the couch, half-laying down as he lounged with his feet on the coffee table, controller in hand. With a raised brow, he held up the other one, but I couldn't focus on anything other than the massive expanse of West's naked chest.

A soft laugh escaped him as he turned his attention back to the TV, and I remembered I was standing in the doorway, mouth hanging open.

"We had a new shifter show up today. The basement is getting a bit crowded," he murmured by way of explanation for the relocation. "I think Robbie and Leif are having their own *Super Smash* tournament as we speak, but it's less the relaxing vibe I like and more college frat boys. I swear I even saw a six-pack of light beer, but I'm choosing to ignore that my underage son is drinking in my basement. He needs to turn 21 already so I can stop feeling shitty about this."

I smiled, and it was enough to pull me to attention and across the room to the couch, sinking onto the supple leather one cushion over from him.

Sitting this close to him, I couldn't ignore that same piney scent that lingered on my hand earlier, and a wave of heat spread through my body before I could stop it. I blinked, trying to clear my mind by focusing on the beer on the coffee table, remembering how this conversation had started. "Light beer not your taste?"

He turned towards me, his mouth a straight line. "Is it anyone's?"

"What are you drinking, then?" I accepted the offered controller with a surprisingly steady hand considering how fast my heart raced, nodding towards his pint glass on the table.

Sitting up, he took a sip, eyes lingering on me for a beat longer than necessary as a small smile tugged on his lips. Fuck. He knew exactly where my mind was. "Actual beer. You want one?"

"Sure."

I focused on the TV to keep myself from counting his abs or noticing the way his sweatpants rode low on his hips, that deep V carving a path straight down, as he grabbed a beer from a mini fridge by the TV and another glass.

Eight abs. *At least.*

Could a person have more than eight? West might.

"Mario Kart?" I asked as the game loaded and West handed me a pint glass. I took a sip of the beer, savoring the taste with a hint of fruit mixed in with the hops. "This is really good."

Sensing West moving closer, I looked up right as his thumb reached out, swiping the drop of foam that was on my lip. My mouth slipped open, my eyes widening, as his own hazel gaze bored into me. Without breaking our stare off, he lifted his hand and licked the drop off his thumb.

My stomach — or something lower — *swooped* as my face flushed. Everything about tonight felt different, from the dim light of the room to the smaller size of this couch in the intimacy of his *bedroom*, forcing us closer together. Even without our conversation earlier in the kitchen, this felt loaded in a new way.

West's eyes darkened as I licked my lips, his gaze tracking the movement and I had to fight not to lean towards him, not to close the small distance between his mouth and mine.

"The guys have Smash."

What? Oh, the game. Who fucking cared?

All I could think about now was climbing West like a —

I snapped back upright, realizing how far I'd moved towards him, and worked to shut down that line of thinking before West could scent every dirty thought I had about him.

"That's fine, I'll just kick your ass at this instead," I deflected, throwing out a challenge I knew he couldn't resist.

That same low laugh sounded as West settled back onto his spot on the couch, leaning forward with his elbows on his knees as they spread wide, his warm thigh touching mine.

I didn't pull away.

I willed myself to focus on the game, taking the lead early as we raced. Flying around corners, I launched turtle shells and threw out banana peels, showing no mercy. My pulse thundered as I neared the finish line, ready to leave him in the dust yet again when my Toad flew in the air, spinning out of control. My jaw dropped as Yoshi, West's player, sped past and crossed the finish line. He sat back, dropping the remote on the coffee table as he stretched his arms across the back of the couch, the cockiest grin I'd ever seen on his face.

"Did you just nuke me at the last second and pass me?"

West laughed, leaned forward to grab his beer, and turned his eyes toward me. "It's called strategy, Jade. I'm a pursuit predator. When I decide I want something, nothing can stop me. I'm not afraid to be patient and play the long game."

I tore my gaze away from him, feeling the heat of his words as surely as the flames off the fireplace in front of me. My phone buzzed in my pocket, but Ruby could wait. I had a score to settle with an arrogant Alpha. "Rematch."

Even without looking at him, I could *feel* his smug expression as the game reloaded. "However long it takes for you to understand I have no intention of losing."

My mouth went dry, and I took a long sip of my beer as West restarted the game.

We played several rounds until I could barely keep my eyes open.

"Headed to bed?" West said as he stood and grabbed our glasses.

I nodded sleepily, a yawn slipping free. "Thanks for this. I forgot how much I love Mario Kart, even though you're a cheater."

West chuckled, and the sound made me want to climb in his bed instead of my own.

His eyes flashed gold as he leaned down, his lips skimming my ear. "Sweet dreams, Jade."

I was frozen in place as he walked down the hall towards the stairs, my body and heart a wild mixture of energized and exhausted.

Eventually I made my feet move towards my own room as my phone buzzed in my pocket again. I pulled it out as I collapsed onto my bed, wondering what Ruby wanted so late at night.

Only the text wasn't from Ruby, and heavy, acidic dread flooded my stomach as I read the incoming text.

UNKNOWN NUMBER

Enjoying Colorado, baby? You always did love the mountains.

My heart leapt to my throat, darkness creeping in the edges of my vision, and I thought I might be sick.

Could that be Thaddeus?

Hands shaking, I quickly blocked the number and deleted the text, then threw my phone across the room onto a pile of clothes in the corner, like that could erase the weight of my panic.

How did he know where I was? And how did he have my new number?

Chapter Twenty-Nine

JADE

As exhausted as I'd been before heading to bed, sleep never found me, deeply unsettled by the mystery text message. I'd immediately jumped to the conclusion that the anonymous number belonged to Thaddeus, but I couldn't figure out how he got my brand new number — the one I'd had for *less than a day* — and how he knew even roughly where I was.

Max had said he'd erased Bram's memory of seeing me here, and I trusted him, didn't I? I vaguely remembered seeing Max around the Coven off and on before he'd rescued Ruby and me, but not enough to piece together what his position was with them. When he'd rescued us, I assumed he was working as some sort of undercover agent, sent to take down the Coven, but had he ever actually said that? Had I, once again, been wrong about a male? Had his valiant rescue been enough to blind me to a grander scheme?

Nausea roiled in my stomach at the thought, not sure who to trust, if anyone. I lay in my bed, staring at the ceiling as I decided my next course of action. If I left town, I was no better off than I was here. Worse, even, since I had no money and no place to go. I covered my face with my hands, letting out a silent scream as I let the anger and grief for my past swallow me.

My phone buzzed on the nightstand, and ice-cold dread shot through me. I held my breath as I stared at it, unwilling to reach across the bed to grab it for fear of what I'd find.

It buzzed again, then again, then again in rapid succession.

My brow furrowed, the rapid-fire texts not Thaddeus's style, and curiosity getting the best of me as I reached across and grabbed my phone.

Heath added Jade to the group chat

HEATH

Family meeting. Wake up, my sleepy pups.

SUMMER

Good morning, Dad.

Oh! Hi Jade! Welcome!

Wait, who are we discussing?

GASP

West isn't in here guys, WAKE UP. DAD WANTS TO GOSSIP.

ASPEN

You have my attention.

TERRAN

I swear, if it's not my kid waking me up before the sunrise it's you fools.

COOPER

Hi Jade

LEIF

Hey Jade! Welcome to the madhouse!

SUMMER

No sense denying that, she's been here for a couple days. If you didn't realize we're all nuts by now, well, that's on you, Jade.

But enough with the delay tactics.

What's going on with West?

Gimme the deets.

HEATH

He's working himself to the bone.

SUMMER

I've noticed that too. Jade, did he eat the food I sent home with you?

I read through the texts, shocked and overwhelmed at how quickly they rolled in, one after the next, unsure if I should respond, but they kept going without me.

ASPEN

He was practically feeding peach pie to her while I was there. There was moaning.

SUMMER

There's always moaning when my pie is involved.

TERRAN

Summer. Please don't.

HEATH

I'm laughing and I feel terrible about it.

COOPER

She's turning into you.

SUMMER

That sounded dirty, didn't it?

LEIF

Yes. I'm trying to powerwash my memory as we speak.

TERRAN

Let me know if it works. I have a few memories
I'd happily have powerwashed out of my brain.

SUMMER

Uh oh. Do we need to start a Terran gossip chain
next? Is this a cry for help?

ASPEN

If Terran's codependency with Cruz isn't a cry for
help, then I don't know what is.

TERRAN

It's not my fault I stole all the likability in the
womb and left none for you.

ASPEN

Too bad you forgot to take any brain cells.

COOPER

Burn.

Leif has left the chat

HEATH

Look what you two did? Scaring Leif off. You
know how much he hates confrontation.

TERRAN

Sorry.

Aspen added Leif to the chat

ASPEN

Sorry Leif. We'll be nice.

SUMMER

I have about a dozen hugs with your name on it later, Leif. Love you.

LEIF

I warned you, Jade.

She's probably muted us all by now, ready to throw her new phone away.

ASPEN

I think about doing just that daily.

TERRAN

I thought you were canning the snark? You lasted less than 30 seconds.

ASPEN

That's what your first girlfriend said about you.

COOPER

West?

HEATH

Right right. Thank you, Coop.

Anyway, I'm getting worried. Between the council and the pack, he's got too much on his plate. Terran, look at his calendar and see if we can't stealthily force him to take a day off. He needs a break and a chance to clear his mind, even if it means we all have to step up to take over for him.

My heart warmed at the sentiment, seeing in action just how much West's family cared about him. And after the last several nights spent up with him, I couldn't find it in me to argue with Heath's concerns.

TERRAN

Looking now

Shit, he hasn't had a day off in over a month.
How did I not notice that? There are back to back
meetings every single day of the week.

HEATH

That's what I was afraid of.

ASPEN

And he's not eating?

HEATH

Well, I've been trying to fix that without
commanding him. He's on edge, whether he can
see it or not, and the last thing he needs is
confusion over my wolf wanting to take back over
as Alpha.

TERRAN

… Do you?

HEATH

Absolutely not. I don't want to take that on again
when I can admire ripe peaches with my Willie
every day.

SUMMER

Good grief.

ASPEN

That was way too far, Dad.

TERRAN

I'm choking.

LEIF

Don't make me leave again.

COOPER

I'm following you out if you do.

HEATH

FOCUS.

ASPEN

Coming from you, that's really something.

TERRAN

Okay, Dad. Fill us in on the plan. How are we commandeering West's schedule and forcing this day off for West?

HEATH

I was hoping you all had ideas for how we can convince him not to just fill his schedule back up if we clear it.

ASPEN

I mean...

TERRAN

...

SUMMER

Oh. I see.

MWAHAHAHA

LEIF

I do not see. Tell me what I need to do and I'll make it happen.

ASPEN

You need to go make Jade look at her phone, that's what you need to do.

My heart stuttered, reading over the last few lines again, trying to understand where this was going.

LEIF

Hang on, I'll go upstairs.

JADE

I'm here.

HEATH

Oh good! Good morning, sweetheart.

My fingers lingered over the keyboard, wondering what the hell I was supposed to say, but decided to wait. Clearly, this family had no trouble filling silences.

ASPEN

Hey Jade. Have any plans today?

JADE

… I sense a trap coming, but no.

SUMMER

No trap!

Just fun!

Swing by the bakery in an hour, and I'll pack you a picnic lunch perfect for a hike.

Aspen, are your boots still in the mud room at the house, or should I go upstairs and find mine for her to borrow?

ASPEN

Mine should be there.

JADE

Why do I need hiking boots and a picnic lunch?

COOPER

You girls didn't even ask if she wanted to help.

SUMMER

Of course she does, right Jade? I mean, the weather is perfect for a hike today, and all of the wildflowers are in bloom. She can go up to the waterfall!

JADE

Sounds nice, but I have not the slightest clue where said waterfall is.

ASPEN

But West does.

TERRAN

Can you see how hard I'm shaking my head right now? Surely your phones are vibrating in your hands.

ASPEN

Oh, so that's why it looks like a tiny carwash is happening on my screen. That's just your mop swishing over the phone.

LEIF

Gonna leave again.

ASPEN

Sorry.

(No I'm not. T, get a haircut.)

HEATH

It is getting long, bruh.

SUMMER

Dad. No.

HEATH

No bruh?

The words on the screen blurred as my eyes focused on the words "But West does." West's family was trying to set me up with him, playing it off as him needing an escape from his responsibilities. After how little I'd seen him eat and sleep lately, they weren't wrong, but spending the day hiking with just the two of us was the opposite of ignoring him, which felt like the right thing to do after last night's tension-filled Mario Kart — who would have thought those words would ever go together?

I hesitated, my first instinct to say no, but couldn't when the "what do you say, Jade?" text came through from Heath. West's family was worried about him, and he'd helped me so much lately. Maybe I could help him with this, too.

Fuck.

JADE

Fine. I'm in.

ASPEN

I can hear the enthusiasm.

SUMMER

Hush, Aspen. Don't ruin this. It's gonna be GREAT!

HEATH

Thank you, sweetheart.

JADE

What makes you think he'll actually say yes if I ask him? You already said his schedule is full. He has every reason to say he's too busy.

A loud, booming laugh rang down the hall, and I lifted my head off the pillow and looked towards the door.

TERRAN

Sorry, just fell out of bed laughing so hard.

ASPEN

Trust us. He won't say no.

SUMMER

My face hurts I'm smiling so big.

COOPER

Remind me to disown you all.

SUMMER

Whatever, you love us.

Come get your cinnamon roll.

COOPER

Rude of you to bake kryptonite into those damn things.

HEATH

Just wait until you try my version of them. Summer said she might stock some for me!

ASPEN

Dammit, Summer, we talked about this. Stop encouraging him.

Leif has left the chat

TERRAN

Look what you did.

I bet he's crying in the basement on Dad's behalf.

ASPEN

Shut up.

HEATH

You leave that sensitive boy alone. It's not his fault he had no idea what love looked like until way too late in life.

COOPER

I'd hide too if I could get away with it.

HEATH

You have no excuse, kitty cat. Your mother and I dunked you in love repeatedly every damn day of your life.

SUMMER

You really are the best, Dad.

TERRAN

Agreed, love you.

ASPEN

We all do. Don't we, Coop?

COOPER

Yes.

HEATH

I'm the luckiest to have you all.

Jade, let us know if you need any help. Terran, clear his schedule.

TERRAN

On it.

SUMMER

Picnic is packed when you're ready!

ASPEN

Pack some peach pie. They can moan all they want up in the mountains alone, far from me.

TERRAN
Stop saying moan.

COOPER
Please. No more.

I fought back a nervous laugh as I set my phone back down on the nightstand, wondering how I'd landed myself in the middle of this plan.

Chapter Thirty

WEST

The headache from yesterday was back as I hung up the phone from the Council conference call. It was barely 8 in the morning on a Sunday, but once I'd reported Robbie's arrival and story, an emergency meeting had been called.

I had 20 minutes to regroup before my meeting with the Shields to discuss new protocol now all the cameras had been removed. We'd upped our patrols, as well as the frequency of our meetings to stay in touch about anything we'd found, making my already crammed schedule even busier. Setting my elbows on the desk, I let my head drop and closed my eyes.

Everything was overwhelming lately. The last five years had gotten progressively worse, but even before then, I'd had trouble saying no to most requests, especially when it regarded a shifter in need.

Turned out there were *a lot* of shifters in need.

A soft knock sounded on the door, and I picked my head up, a slow smile spreading at the sight of Jade leaning in my doorway.

She was dressed casually in fitted leggings and a gray tank top, her half-green hair in a ponytail, and tan hiking boots I recognized as Aspen's. That she was wearing my sister's boots loosened a knot in my chest, smug satisfaction filling me as I took this as another sign of her becoming part of my family and pack.

"You headed out?" I asked, eyes raking over her form as

Togo pushed forward, reminding me how comfortable she'd been on my couch last night.

Jade bit her lip, nose scrunched as she hesitated, and I frowned.

Pushing back in my chair, I came around the desk to stand in front of her, studying her more closely. Something was bothering her, but the tangled emotions she emanated were at odds. "Something wrong?"

"No." She shook her head, then took a deep breath, brown eyes lifting to meet mine. "And yes. I'm headed out. Summer packed me a picnic lunch I'm picking up, and then I'm going hiking. The girls mentioned a waterfall about a mile outside of town, and I thought it would be a good day for a hike."

Now I really frowned. "You're going alone? It's a straight shot out of town into the mountains, but it's steep, and not a clear path." I glanced down at her attire, then back up. "If you're taking a picnic and dressed like this, then you're not shifting to run there either. You're hiking."

"Gee." Jade cocked her head to the side in a sassy move. "Nothing gets past you. Must be those big eyes you have."

I chuckled, then reached forward and bopped her nose with a finger. "The better to see you with, Jade."

The moment I touched her skin, I knew I shouldn't have. All thoughts of kidnappings, politics, and pack went out the window, my mind zeroing in on the nearness of her body.

Her cheeks pinked with a hint of a blush, and I wanted to reach forward and feel the heat. I shoved my hands in my pockets to keep them in place, but couldn't bring myself to step away from her.

"Do you" — she stopped, swiping her tongue over her bottom lip as if she was nervous, and I couldn't look away — "Would you want to come with me?"

My mind stuttered, every thought coming to a standstill. I

took in the way she chewed on the corner of her lip, her eyes raking over me.

Did I want to go with her? Absolutely, I did. I wanted to do anything that put us alone like we'd been last night, snuggled up playing video games. I wanted to do anything that allowed me to stare at her ass as she climbed a hill in front of me for an hour. But the weight of my responsibilities was heavier than anything I wanted, and I had my pack meeting in 20 minutes.

In that moment, I resented my life. The path I'd chosen and all the sacrifices it required. My extremely limited availability had cost me Sarah's and my relationship eight years ago, and as I stood before Jade, I saw it happening again. In a blink, everything that could be with Jade disappeared, knowing I could never give her what she deserved. I had nothing left of myself to give.

But fuck, I didn't have a choice. My pack mattered more.

I opened my mouth to deny her just as my phone beeped on my desk. Frustration slammed through me in a wave as I reached behind me and grabbed it, looking at the screen.

"Canceled?" I read the calendar notification aloud, then flicked through the other ten notifications that followed it, trying to figure out what happened to cause the glitch.

My entire calendar for the day had been wiped clean.

"Something wrong?" Jade asked, a hint of mischief in her voice.

I narrowed my eyes at her. "My family put you up to this, didn't they?"

Jade grinned, then scratched her neck as she looked at the floor. "Honestly, I was steamrolled. I'm afraid of what will happen if we don't go. You Larkins are a force of nature."

My jaw worked, annoyed at my family for pushing this on her and stepping over the line with their demands. I refused to inspect that small part of me that was devastated to hear she'd only asked me at my family's encouragement. "I'll talk to them. We don't have to go."

I moved to walk out of the office, but Jade put her hand up, her palm resting on my chest.

Contact. Fuck, she was touching me by her own choice. It took all my self control not to lean into her touch.

"Wait," she said, her fingers moving slightly as if she wanted to dig her fingers into my skin as badly as I wanted her to. "Maybe we should go."

I shook my head, but I didn't pull away from her. "It's really fine. They're overstepping."

"When was the last time you took a day off?" she asked, then took her hand off my chest. Immediately, I wanted to step forward into her space and feel her warmth again, but I leashed the instinct and stood my ground.

"I don't know. Last week."

Her brows rose, disbelief written on every feature. "So *this* is what Aspen meant when she said lying was useless. I heard the way your heart rate changed just now. Who knew West Larkin was a little liar?"

I looked out the windows, needing to focus on anything but Jade as my head spun. The sun bounced off the swaying aspen leaves, the gorgeous day like a beacon, calling to me. My family thought they could step in and take over my life like this? Irritation fought with my desire to spend every waking moment in Jade's company, and today, I wasn't going to look a gift horse in the mouth. "You know what? Fuck it. Let's go. Terran can be me for a day."

Jade smiled, and her happiness radiated down the faint connection we shared in the pack bonds as she held out her hand. Before she realized what she'd done, I grabbed it, lacing our fingers together as I pulled her towards the front door.

Satisfaction coursed through me when she didn't pull her hand out of mine. I wasn't about to let go anytime soon.

)))●(((

Jade was quiet on the drive across town, but hopped out of the truck with a smile before I'd even parked in front of Summer's bakery. "I'll be right back. You stay in the truck."

She hurried into the store, and I sat back to wait, my gaze drifting over the street. This early on a Sunday morning meant the town was mostly empty, but a few inquisitive stares and thoughts of my pack came my way.

"*Shut it down,*" Terran's thoughts rang in my mind, and I tipped my head back against the headrest, closing my eyes. "*Close down your connection to the pack today and just leave it open for me. I've got you, brother.*"

I wanted to believe him, but memories of wildly immature Terran flitted through my mind. Sometimes it was hard to believe how much my brother had grown up in the past few years, but he had. I trusted him with my life, and I could trust him with the pack, too.

"*Just for a few hours,*" I sent back, making sure my gratitude rang through to him through our bond.

"*However long you need,*" Terran answered. "*Go. Recharge. Come back bossier than ever.*"

I shook my head, but did as he said. With a deep inhale, I raised my mental walls, blocking out the entire pack but Terran. The spiderweb connections were still there, just muted until I reopened the lines. Instantly, the pressure on my chest loosened, my headache fading to a dull pound as everything seemed *less*.

The bell above Summer's bakery door jingled and I opened my eyes as my sister held the door open for Jade, smiling and waving at me. When Jade passed her, Summer pulled her into a tight hug, then let her go.

I smiled at the startled expression on Jade's face, then looked back at my sister right in time for the exaggerated wink she shot me before blowing a kiss. I caught it, then mimed throwing it out the window before wiping my hands on my shirt. Summer laughed, and Jade turned to look back at her, hand on the truck's door handle. I reached across the center console and pushed the door open, taking the cooler backpack from her and setting it on the bench seat behind us.

"All set?" I asked as Jade climbed back in the truck.

"Yeah." She buckled her seatbelt, then met my eye for a split second before she dropped it, staring at my chin instead. "That thing weighs a ton. I don't know what she packed in there, but I'd say we have *options.*"

I grinned, then put the truck in reverse and headed out of town. Eyes on the road, I cleared my throat, thinking back to how she'd dropped her gaze minutes before.

"Did Aspen tell you about body language and pack dynamics?"

I heard Jade's heartbeat accelerate as she faced the window, away from me. "Yeah. I asked her some questions, and she gave me some tips. She figured it would make it easier for me in town so everyone doesn't think I'm throwing out some silent challenge."

I nodded, thinking through my next words carefully. "Good. But I'm giving you permission to ignore everything she told you when it's just us."

Her head whipped around, and I fought back a smile at her mouth hanging slightly open.

"I thought I annoyed you every time I rolled my eyes and beat you at a staring competition. And now you're *inviting* it?"

"For your own well-being, I need you to understand pack dynamics and where you fall into it, even if you're only here for a month. It's not just me it affects — it's the pack as a whole. And I think the record shows me beating *you* at every staring contest so far."

She scoffed at that but cut back to the thread. "So what does that mean, when you say I don't have to do that when it's just us?"

"Just that. I've seen the way you race in Mario Kart. If my

ego starts to feel bruised, I'll just turn on Rainbow Road, and all will be right with the world again." She let out an indignant huff I chuckled at, my headache fading more with every minute I put between us and the town as we neared the trailhead. "Besides, I want you to be comfortable just being yourself."

She squinted, studying me closely, then turned to look back out the window away from me. "Okay."

I turned off the main road shortly after, heading onto my father's land where we'd find the trailhead. We parked at the base of the mountain and I grabbed the backpack, slinging it on as Jade climbed out of the truck.

"Ready?" I grabbed a hat out of the backseat and put on my sunglasses. The morning was still chilly, but the sun was as bright as to be expected at 10,000 feet elevation. Jade squinted, hand over her eyes as she took in the trail before us, and I pulled my sunglasses back off and handed them to her. "Wear these."

She took them from my hand, and a wave of satisfaction rolled through me when she put them on.

I motioned towards the trail for her to lead the way, and we set off, working our way up into the forest.

A worn path wove between the pine trees, leading the way to the waterfall I'd visited dozens of times. I breathed deep, letting the fresh mountain air eat away the last of my headache as I moved to follow her.

We walked in silence for several minutes, Jade inspecting every mountain flower and vista we passed while I tried and failed not to inspect Jade's ass. Whoever invented leggings deserved a Nobel Prize.

"So, what's the deal with Leif?" Jade asked, pulling me from the gutter where my thoughts resided.

"What do you mean?" I hadn't talked to Leif this morning, and I was tempted to pull up the pack bonds to check on him, but resisted the urge. Terran was as intertwined in the pack bonds as I was — if Leif was in danger or distressed, he'd know.

"Nothing really. I just got the impression everyone tiptoes around him from the group texts this morning."

I grimaced, though she couldn't see it ahead of me. "I hate to break it to you, but once you're in a group text, you can't get out of them with my family. You're *in* now, whether you want to be or not."

Jade barked a laugh, coming to a stop at a break in the trees. I reached behind me, grabbed the water bottle out of the backpack side pocket, and handed it to her. A droplet of water dripped from her mouth down her chin and neck, slipping beneath the grey fabric of her shirt, and damn, I wanted to lean forward and lick it off.

"What's his story?" Jade prodded, and I forced myself to concentrate.

"Leif was abused by his last pack. His mom couldn't take care of him, and wouldn't say who his father was. She came to me when Leif was 7, practically begging me to take him. He's such a good kid and had an unfortunate hand dealt to him. I was in a position to help, so I did."

Jade nodded, but I could see the questions swimming in her expression. As reserved as she was with her own story, she was dying to hear more.

I stepped around her and started walking again, thinking back to 13 years ago. "Adoptions in shifter society aren't unheard of, but they're rare. Normally a pack will take in children in need, and it's more of a community raising the kid than a designated guardian. Because of Leif's past and parentage, his situation was different. She wouldn't tell me who his father was, but I read between the lines. Whoever it was, he was powerful, and she'd done her best to hide Leif from him. Bringing him into the pack would be protection in itself, but at 7, he needed a family. I adopted him, gave him my name, and his pack bonds are uncontestable. To come for him is a direct challenge to me, and not many shifters are stupid enough to do that."

The crunching of leaves behind me abruptly stopped, and I turned to look back at Jade, stalled in place. Her brow was furrowed, expression clouded. I lowered my wall blocking out the pack bonds enough to let her faint connection back in, trying to get a read on her feelings, but it was all a jumble.

"So you just adopted him and the pack took him in? Or you were like, his *dad?*"

"Both, honestly. I wasn't ready to be a dad to a first grader at 25, but I couldn't look at his little worried face and not try to make his life right, to give him everything I'd been lucky enough to have at his age, and that included a parent who loved him. A whole family who loved him." She frowned harder, and I back-tracked to stand in front of her. "Why?"

"Just like that, you gave up your whole life for him?"

A slightly bitter laugh escaped me as I tipped my head up to the sky, her words striking a nerve today. "Just like that."

"Do you resent it?" she asked, her voice quieter, and I looked back down at her. Suddenly, I was reminded we had this in common — a parental relationship thrust on us out of duty more than choice. "Not getting to choose your own life?"

I sighed, reaching forward slowly and tucking a strand of hair behind her ear. "I did choose it. And I chose him. Still do, every damn day because that kid is great and worth it and I'm proud to call him my son. But it doesn't mean I never think about the things I gave up. Not just with Leif, but as Alpha, and representa-tive to the Council. They all own a piece of me, and — some-times I can't tell if there are any pieces left."

Jade nodded, then reached out and gave my hand a squeeze before she dropped it and started walking again. Admitting that out loud had me rooted in place, reeling in the shock wave of what I'd just told her.

I refused to complain about the weight of my responsibilities — everything I did was too important to back away from, and idle complaints would get me nowhere.

"What's Ruby like?" I asked, hoping her questions about Leif meant she was open to getting to know me, and letting me know her. "As stubborn as you?"

Jade's head whipped over her shoulder as she scowled, but it lacked any real heat.

I grinned, then reached forward and grabbed the water bottle she still held in her hand and took a long sip as we continued to walk.

"How old is she?"

"Twenty," Jade answered, and I heard the hesitancy in her answer, but I was determined to wear her down.

"Same as Leif. They're at that *adult-but-not-really* age. It's annoying and great at the same time. They think they have everything figured out and don't need us anymore, but are still too naive about the world around them. Kind of like having a tweenager all over again."

Jade chuckled, and my chest loosened at the sound. "She has a job at a bar, and has learned so much in the last five years in Deadlights Cove. It's wild to think about how much of a life she has outside of me."

"Scallywags?"

"What?"

"The bar. I assume she's working for Blaze at Scallywags in Deadlights Cove?"

"Oh." Jade nodded. "Yeah, she works for Blaze. Do you know him?"

"Everyone knows Blaze." I laughed, thinking of the many run-ins I'd had with the chaotic demon. "Ask her about his game nights sometime and you're in for a hell of a story."

Jade side-eyed me, then nodded. I tried to put myself in her shoes, imagining sending Leif to the other side of the country to live without me, and my heart hurt at the thought.

Leif still lived under my roof, and the day he decided he was ready to be on his own would be tough. I wasn't too macho to admit I'd probably cry like a baby as I hugged him goodbye. Even the thought of the hypothetical situation had me feeling emotional.

Maybe that was why I said, "You made a great decision, sending Ruby to Morgaine. I don't know what the circumstances were when you two showed up here, but there's no one I trust more than that old witch and her crew. If I had to send Leif away, she would be my first choice."

A long sigh escaped Jade as her chin dipped. A wave of sadness radiated off her. Whether it was over missing her sister or what I'd said, I couldn't tell, but the urge to pull her into me for a hug was so strong, I barely stopped myself from reaching out and grabbing her.

She trudged up the path, her breaths coming faster as we rose in elevation, but we didn't stop for another break. I let the silence linger, turning my focus to the scenery. Summer was in full force in the mountains, everything a vibrant green with splashes of color from the many wildflowers intermixed. Already I could hear the water rushing ahead, about a quarter-mile in front of us.

The thought made me pause, thinking back to Jade's scenting ability and wondering how much she sensed compared to most wolves. I was bombarded with senses up here: the pine resin scent of the woods and Jade's own citrusy scent; the sound of the water, the trees rustling in the wind, the birdsong, leaves crumpling under Jade's boots; the feel of the packed dirt and rocks beneath my feet, the bark on the trees as I marked our passing. My wolf's senses added so much to the setting, and a wave of peaceful contentment settled over me I hadn't felt in a long time.

Would Jade let me help her learn how to embrace her wolf's senses?

Up here, away from all of my many responsibilities, was the first time in ages I felt true calm between me and my wolf. There was no fight for dominance, no urge to protect, no weight of responsibility dictating our every move. I could just... be.

That I was spending this moment of peaceful serenity with Jade didn't only make it better, it made it feel *right*.

Chapter Thirty-One

JADE

I heard the waterfall before I saw it, dense pine trees covering both sides of the path. Sun streamed through the branches in a clearing ahead and I moved towards it.

Hearing West talk about Leif made my mind shift to thoughts of Ruby, cataloging the similarities in West's and my life.

I wasn't sure why I'd asked if he resented his life. Nothing about the way he talked or acted made me think he did. Maybe I was just searching for a character flaw in this otherwise perfect male, Alpha bossiness aside. If he felt even an inkling like I did, maybe it would ease some of my guilt. But of course, his answer had been as perfect as he was.

The path brightened as the trees cleared closer to the waterfall, and I soaked in the warmth of the sun's rays. Luckily I'd chosen a tank top this morning even though it had been chilly when we left — I was plenty warm now.

A stream several feet wide crossed the path in front of me, rocks dotting the way across. The air was humid with the falling water, and I breathed deeply, inhaling the scent of pine and fresh air.

"The waterfall is up this way," West said as he laid a hand on my back, steering me to the right. My body tensed at the small contact, everything feeling like a livewire with him today. Between last night's comfort and following panic, everything had me on edge today. But this time, rather than pull away from him, I wanted to lean in. Balto surged forward, encouraging me to do just that, but I shoved her back down in my consciousness.

Just because she was touchy-feely didn't mean I was.

Usually.

Not so much lately.

West's fingers trailed across my back, separated only by the thin cotton of my tank top, and I wondered what it would feel like to have those rough and calloused hands on my bare skin.

I shivered, and West pulled his hand back, pointing the way. Frustrated with my own neediness, I hurried up the path along the water's edge, towards the sound of the waterfall.

Even knowing it was here didn't prepare me for the sight ahead. Water flowed over a cliff twenty feet above the path, crashing into a pool too wide to jump across before it descended down into the stream we'd walked along. Rainbows of light cast across the falling water, spraying up into the air, the whole scene magical.

Before I could overthink it, I pulled my boots and socks off, then rolled up my leggings.

"Careful, it's deeper than it looks and it's slippery," West said, standing behind me. I shot him my sassiest expression.

"Thank you, Captain Obvious. I never would have expected wet rocks to be slippery."

The rocks dug into my feet as I stepped closer, sinking my toes into the ice-cold water. I gasped, my muscles seizing instantly at the chill. Goosebumps broke out over my whole body, but the glacial water coursing over my skin sent my heart racing, needing more. I took another tentative step, curling my toes to grip on the slippery rock as I held out my arms for balance.

With each step from the shore, the water swept away all of my thoughts, dissolving the ever-present darkness that lingered in my mind. Gone were my nightmarish memories of Ruby's and my past, my worries over where I would go next, even the fear from the text message. None of it mattered as I focused on maintaining my balance in the rushing water, up to my knees now.

"I wouldn't go much—" I turned to glare at West, but the small movement was enough to throw off my balance. My foot lost purchase on the rock, and my arms windmilled as I tried to recover. In a split second, my whole body crashed down, head submerged under the water. Bubbles filled my vision until a large hand grasped my arm and pulled me up.

I gasped for air as I opened my eyes, sitting in water up to my collarbone. West stood in the middle of the stream, jeans wet to his knees as he stared wide-eyed down at me. He stepped forward, opening his mouth to say something, but he must have found the same moss-covered rock I had, and down he went.

Just as I had, West's arms windmilled to keep his balance, but it was no use. He disappeared beneath the water with a splash, boot-clad feet in the air before he resurfaced.

My jaw dropped. West shook his head, water flinging in all directions from the long dark strands as he sat in the water facing me.

Before I could stop it, a laugh escaped me, and West's eyes found mine, glowing molten gold.

"I warned you," West said, and I tossed my head back, laughing harder as my body shook in the frigid water.

"You did." I pointed at him, but couldn't stop laughing. "Why did you charge in after me? Afraid I was going to drown in two feet of water?"

"Instinct. I reacted before I thought better of it."

The image of his feet flying up in the air as he went under replayed, and I slapped my hand over my mouth, trying to muffle my hysterical laugh. "Oh god, that was funny. You rolled up the windows with the best of 'em, then *WHOOP* up went your feet and down went your head. Surprised your boots didn't go flying off into the trees they whipped up so fast."

I giggled harder, shaking violently in the water, as West sighed. "Are you recounting your own experience? Because that's exactly what happened."

"*I know.* Which makes it that much funnier that you were dumb enough to follow me out here and do it too."

West looked away, a grin spreading on his face that told me he was fighting back his own laughter. I put my hand down in the water, trying to push myself to standing, and slipped again, splashing back down in a tangled heap. A roar of laughter slipped free as my head tilted back, staring up at the sunny sky overhead.

"Easy there," West said, pushing carefully to his feet then reaching a hand out to me.

"Do you learn nothing? Move out of the way and I'll pick my feet up and float downstream to where it's shallower."

West reached down and grabbed my hand, moving us both back towards shore as he pulled me out of the water. We were both drenched, head to toe, and his shirt clung to every ridge on his stomach. I'd seen his naked chest several times already, but something about the wet fabric clinging to every muscle made it borderline indecent.

Every step out of the water had me shivering harder. The icy snowmelt water had sapped all the heat I'd worked up on the hike, and now the reality of the mountain-chill air hit me all over again..

"Shift," West said when we stood on dry ground. "Your wolf can warm your body faster while we wait for our clothes to dry in the sun."

The logic behind his statement made sense, but I froze, panic seizing me at the thought of shifting. It was only West and I in the woods, but I wasn't in a fight-or-flight situation, nor was I raging mad — the only ways I seemed to be able to override my bone-deep fear of my wolf lately.

"Nevermind." West tugged me into a sunny patch further down the stream. He dropped my hand long enough to pull off his wet t-shirt and toe off his boots, then bent to pull off his wet socks. My teeth chattered, body shivering violently as I watched him stand back up, undoing the button on his jeans.

A nervous giggle escaped me as he lowered the zipper, then stepped out of his jeans, laying them in the sun to dry with his other clothes. Even knowing what he was about to say didn't make it any less nerve-racking. "Strip."

My eyes flicked from him standing in front of me in only his boxers to the clothes discarded on the ground.

He stepped closer to me, hands lifting to rest on my hips. I gasped at the touch, and he picked his hands up, holding them away from my body. "We're not doing anything but getting warm. Your lips are turning blue, Jade. You need to get out of your wet clothes so I can warm up your body. If you're not willing to shift, then you need body heat. A fire is too dangerous in the forest right now, so those are your options."

My head bobbed, nodding more vigorously as I lifted my shaking hands to my waist and grabbed the hem of my tank top to lift it. The wet fabric stuck to my skin, making it more difficult to free myself, and West's jaw worked, his eyes focused heavily on my hands.

"Can I help?" he asked, eyes alight with warmth. If I hadn't been shaking so hard, I would have said no, but I was too cold to care. My small nod was enough for West to step forward, his warm hands settling on my chilled skin.

I sucked in a breath, eyes blown wide as heat spread through me with each inch he raised my shirt. The moment felt tortu-ously slow, my heart thrumming in my chest as I studied his face, lines showing how deeply he was concentrating on this task. The wet shirt plopped to the ground as he sank to his knees in front of me, hands resting on my hips.

"These too," he said, his voice raspier than before as his thumbs hooked under the waistband of my leggings. If I'd thought the sight of him in a wet t-shirt was indecent, then West on his knees before me, looking up at me with those bright hazel eyes was *obscene.* My breaths came heavier as I imagined him on his knees for other reasons, heat flushing my body as he worked the wet material down my hips. Instantly, I was desperate to be free of the fabric, grabbing it and helping him slide them down my wet skin. I rested my hand on his shoulder as I stepped out, standing before him in nothing but my sports bra and underwear.

The air was thick with tension around us, West's scent changing to a spicier undertone I hoped meant he was as turned on by this as I was.

He took my wet clothes to the sunny spot he'd left his own, then returned to sit on a log in the sun. I pulled heavy breaths in through my nose and out through my mouth as I willed my teeth to stop chattering. When he patted his thighs, eyes on mine, I stepped towards him.

"Sit on my lap, facing me. Chest to chest," he said, but the words were missing the usual command he issued freely, even if he hadn't asked. He wasn't ordering me to do what he said, just encouraging me to comply.

I should have run the opposite direction, should have let Balto come forward and take a nap in the sun, should have done anything but step towards him, straddling his legs. But I was tired of fighting whatever this was.

Heart racing, I lowered myself to his lap, loving how it felt when his hands laced behind my back and pulled me into his chest. I curled my hands up between us, pinned to my chest as he closed the last sliver of distance.

His heart beat beneath my hands, the steady rhythm lulling me into a sense of comfort. His arms squeezed tighter around me, pulling me closer until I rested my cheek on his chest, soaking in his warmth. "There you go, gem. Use me."

The words sent me into a fit of giggles again, the whole situation absurd. When Heath had asked me to get West to take a day off, I doubted he'd imagined our naked bodies pressed together for warmth after an unintentional swim in freezing waters.

"I can't tell whether to be offended by how much you've laughed at me in the last few minutes. Tell me what you're laughing at, at least."

I bit my cheeks, trying to hold in my laugh, but it only made me splutter. "Everyone in your family was positive you'd say yes if I asked you to take a day off, which I had a hard time believing. Yet, here you are, on your one day off, playing hero to my disastrous life as I'm pressed naked to your chest."

West's fingers tangled in my hair as he bent down to whisper in my ear, his hot breath fanning across my chilled skin. "I can think of worse ways to spend a day off than holding you naked. I'm kicking myself I didn't think of this ploy earlier. Terran would have, that's for sure. This has Cruz written all over it. Hell, I bet my dad would even have pulled a move like this intentionally."

I shook with laughter, feeling lighter than I had in years as I soaked in his warmth. West's chest rumbled as he laughed with me, hand cradling my head against him.

We lapsed into an easy silence, listening to the water rushing by as my teeth chattered less, warmth returning to my body.

"Thank you," West said, his broad hand stroking down my back, leaving a trail of warmth in its wake. "For today."

I pulled my head back to look up at him, studying his expression. "You're welcome. But I don't think I did anything other than get you out of the house."

West lifted his hands, bringing them to my neck, thumb trailing over my pulse point. The subtle touch paired with the warmth in his eyes had heat pooling low in my belly, making me aware of how little clothing remained between us.

"It's more than that. When I'm around you, everything else becomes background noise, my focus solely on you. It's infuriating — I can't lose focus, *ever* — and at the same time a breath of fresh air I didn't know I needed. Like I've been underwater for years and I'm finally coming up for air."

I searched his face, trying to understand what he meant, and why I felt the same. "What are we doing?" I asked, voicing my thought rather than letting it eat me alive. I wanted to kiss him, and that felt dangerous.

His thumb trailed across my jaw as his eyes fell to my lips, focused intently. "I don't know."

Just as Aspen taught me, I heard the lie for what it was. Maybe it was the heat of our bodies that had me feeling bold enough to lean forward, brushing my nose against his as my hands settled around his shoulders. "Yes, you do."

Instantly, West's fingers tightened, pulling me the last few inches closer to him as his lips touched down on mine. The gentleness of the kiss surprised me, and I could feel West holding himself back. But I'd had enough of that.

My fingers dug into the firm muscles of his back as I deepened the kiss, and it was the only invitation he needed. His hold on my face became greedy, steering me as he needed while his tongue brushed across my lips, urging me to open for him. Without hesitation, I did just that, and his tongue swept across mine. Unable to hold still, I squirmed in his lap, scooting closer until my whole body was pressed against his. Everywhere we touched left a fire in its wake, heat burning me with its intensity. His mouth drifted down the side of my jaw to my neck, and I arched up into his touch, loving the way his teeth scraped across my sensitive skin. Suddenly, I needed to feel his mouth *everywhere*.

"What are you doing to me?" West said against my skin, licking a path across my neck. I gasped at the touch, my eyes rolling back in my head as my heart threatened to break free from my chest. "I can't breathe, I want you so bad."

His words were gasoline on a fire, making me burn that much hotter. I couldn't stop myself from grinding down on his lap, feeling the honesty of his words in his thick length beneath me.

"It's never been like this before," I breathed, my fingers tangling in his hair as he kissed across my collar bone, his lips trailing the top of my sports bra. I couldn't stop myself from pushing my chest up into his mouth, needing to feel him everywhere. "I don't understand. I don't even like you."

West grabbed my neck and pulled my face back to his, pupils blown wide as he pushed up against me from below. I moaned at the feel of his hard cock rubbing against my most sensitive parts, both of us breathing heavily. "Don't lie to me, gem. You feel this connection the same as I do."

I wanted to deny him, but he was right. My wolf had known it before I did, choosing to run to him for safety, but the more I learned about West, the more I liked him. Our nights spent playing childish games were some of my favorites in recent years, the easy conversations meaning more to me than he'd ever understand. His life was full of people who loved him, filled with warmth and family, even when it was hard.

I'd been alone for so long, it was hard to trust myself. I wanted to dismiss my growing attachment to West as just me latching on to the first male who seemed safe and honest about his intentions, but I couldn't. There was an undeniable *something* here between us, and knowing he felt it too made me feral.

I couldn't find the words to say any of that, so I showed him instead. I ground down on him while I pulled his face to mine, locking my lips over his in a searing kiss. We moved in tandem, riding the wave of emotion and the heat of our bodies.

That West didn't try to remove the rest of my clothes and take this further spoke to his considerable patience. He could have slid his hands into the waistband of my underwear and pulled them off, and I would have let him. There wasn't anything I would deny him in the moment, but West never took more than I offered.

If I hadn't already admitted to myself I had feelings for the male, that would have done it.

"You are so fucking beautiful," he growled as his fingers bracketed my waist, pulling my hips across his lap while he ground into me. His lips trailed across my chest, sucking through the thin fabric. "I can't tell you how badly I've wanted to do this every time you walk in the room."

My core tightened with every move, pushing me closer to the edge. Dropping my head to his shoulder, I kissed along his neck as he'd done to me, sucking gently on the skin.

"Oh, fuck," he groaned, pulling me harder against him. "Do that again."

I did, each pass of his dick against me driving me wild. Everything inside me clenched, and I moaned his name, my whole body tensing.

"I can't wait to feel you squeeze me," West said in a breathy moan, pushing harder into me, "coming all over my cock."

That did it.

My forehead dropped to his shoulder as my body seized, my whole body shaking that had nothing to do with the freezing water behind us.

West kissed along my shoulder, his arms tightening around me. Somehow, that more than anything chipped away at the wall around my heart, cracks forming in the crumbling mortar as a sliver of magic slipped in, twining with mine.

"There you are, gem." West smiled against my skin, and I squeezed him tighter, the fight draining out of me. "Right where you need to be, at my side."

I should have fought back at his words, told him I was only here for a month and I wasn't anything to him, or that this didn't mean what he thought it did.

But those words would have been a lie.

For the first time in years, I didn't want to run. I wanted to stay right where I was.

I wanted to *live*, not hide.

And somehow, I was positive West could be the one to help me do just that.

Chapter Thirty-Two

WEST

I traced lazy circles over Jade's hip while she dozed, curled into me on the ground as we waited for our clothes to dry in the sun. As much as I wanted to go further, to do everything with her, she wasn't ready for that level of intimacy.

I could be patient. Even if every time she licked my neck, teasing the idea of a mate mark whether she knew it or not, drove me nearly feral with the need to sink inside her.

And now I was hard as a rock again. Great.

Closing my eyes, I exhaled slowly, willing my instincts and my wolf to calm the fuck down. Easier said than done.

Everything leading up to this moment flashed through my mind — the years I'd spent with Sarah waiting for a mate bond to show up. We'd known each other since we were toddlers, and she was a close friend. Everyone said we'd be together, that the mate bond was just slow in showing up because she was a witch, not a wolf, but that we were meant to be.

I'd believed them all, sure I'd lost my shot at a mated partner, until Jade walked into my life.

Even after so little time together, I couldn't deny it. Whether we put a name to it or not, claimed it or denied it, I was sure Jade was my mate, fated to be mine forever.

Mine, my wolf echoed my thoughts, a sentiment he'd never voiced with Sarah and now all but shouted at me repeatedly.

My father had always said *You just know* when any of us would ask about recognizing your mate. With Jade, that finally made sense.

But would Jade *just know*? And if she did, would she accept it, accept me? She'd obviously been through some trauma — could the mate bond overcome that?

Or would she run the other way, as she'd grown accustomed to doing?

Even if she did feel it and accept it, and chose to stay, she hadn't grown up in a pack. She might not understand the full scope of responsibilities I held. Would she grow to resent how much of my time, my energy, I had to give to everyone else — like Sarah had?

My stomach soured with the mere possibility of Jade choosing to leave me, to leave the pack, when a soft, contented sigh from beside me brought my attention laser-focusing back on Jade.

She squinted one eye open against the sunlight shining down on us, taking in where we lay.

"I fell asleep?"

"You fell asleep."

She scrunched her nose adorably, her eyebrows furrowing. "Well, that's embarrassing. One good dry humping and I'm done for, apparently."

I grinned. "I'll take it as a compliment and bear it in mind for the future."

"The future?"

I nodded and rolled her onto her back, covering her body with mine as I kept our skin just barely apart.

"Yes." I grazed my nose down her neck, sending a shiver through her as I lightly kissed her. "For the next time we do that, but without the clothes."

She let out an incoherent whimper of acknowledgment, and I gave her my weight for a second, teasing everything I had in mind. Her fingers dug into my waist, holding me in place, but her shoulders hitched, her body and mind at war with what she wanted.

Taking her cue whether she intended it or not, I pulled off her, drawing my knees up as I sat. Thinking fast to keep the conversation going before she shut down, I said, "Tell me something about you I don't know."

Her gaze swung up, studying me intently, and I forced myself not to reach for her. "Like what?"

"I don't know. Anything. Your favorite color?"

"Green. Yours?"

"Blue. What else?"

She was silent for a beat, chewing her lip as she looked down at her hands. "I have this old book that's the story of Balto, the sled dog. I got the paperback when I was a kid, and read it so much the spine fell apart and I had to Duct-tape it together. It seems silly to be sad I had to leave it behind when I ran, but I am. I'm sure my landlord has thrown it out by now, as well as all my other belongings."

"Is that your favorite book?" I asked, trying not to show how much the hurt in her words hurt *me*. I hated the hand she'd been dealt in life, but it had led her to me, so I couldn't bring myself to wish it away.

"Anything Balto, and a few Jack London's that were my dad's, but I haven't been able to read much else. It's kinda hard to have a library card when you're on the run."

"*Call of the Wild* and *White Fang*?" I said, unable to hold back the smile at the words. "Classic wolf books."

Her small hand thumped on my thigh as she smacked me, and I chuckled, liking this easy conversation we had going as much as her touch. "Personally, I've always identified more with_the *real* hero of Alaskan sled dogs. My wolf is named Togo."

Her brow wrinkled, but her lips tipped up in a smile. "Mine is Balto."

I grinned. "Yeah? I guess we were always meant to be best friends, then."

Her cheeks flushed, but from her smile, I knew that idea pleased her. I knocked into her gently with my shoulder. "What else?"

She sighed, tipping her head to look at me. "I don't know. You put me on the spot, and I'm not that complicated."

I arched a brow, meeting her gaze head-on in a challenge I knew I'd win. She shook her head, then turned to look back up at the sky.

"Okay, maybe I am."

Reaching across, I took her hand, lacing our fingers together as I squeezed in solidarity. "We all are."

Several beats of silence passed as the stream bubbled in front of us, trees swayed in the breeze, and birds chirped from their perches overhead. I rubbed my thumb over the back of her hand, savoring this quiet moment like I did all of our more fiery ones. For as many secrets as Jade kept, this was the easiest I'd felt around a woman in years, maybe ever.

"Sarah left me after I adopted Leif," I said before I could stop the words. It seemed stupid to talk about an ex when we were just starting up whatever this was, but I wanted this to be different between us. To be *more*. Jade turned on her side, bending her free arm under her head as those deep brown eyes studied me.

"Why?"

"She wanted more. A mate bond, status in my pack, a wedding, children, my time... the whole shebang."

"And you didn't?"

"I did," I said, then paused, my eyes dropping to her lips, imagining all of those things with Jade. "I still do. But it's not that simple for me. I can't just step back and let things go. Too many people rely on me, and I'll never be able to focus on my own family the way I want to."

"Seems like you did a good job as a father figure for Leif, if you ask me. He turned out pretty great, so maybe that was more Sarah's problem than yours. She wanted something you couldn't give her at the time, but that doesn't mean you have nothing to give."

Instantly, I rolled towards her, pulling her face to mine in a kiss far more tender than any of the ones we'd shared earlier. I couldn't find the words to tell her how much what she'd said meant to me, so I showed her instead.

Chapter Thirty-Three

JADE

"Sorry." West's eyes closed as he clenched his jaw, trying and failing to hold himself back from me. If I hadn't been desperate for him before, I was now. Knowing he was as helpless in this attraction as I was made me feel wanted in a way I never had before, and I loved it.

Before I could pull him back on top of me to continue our heady kisses, West pushed to his feet and walked towards our clothes. Every muscle in his back rippled as he wrung my leggings out, and the softest whimper left me at the sight. Of course, West heard it. He heard everything.

He looked over his shoulder, and I ducked my head to hide the blush heating my face. My wolf was ready to throw us at him, claiming him in every way we could until we were so deeply imprinted on his soul, he'd never look at another woman again. Human-me still had some reservations, mainly the hangup over my pesky wolf and our dark past.

If I pursued whatever this was with West, would I have to join the pack? What would that even look like?

And what happened when he found out exactly what I'd done? Why I'd been running for so long? West was *good* down to the marrow, and what I'd done... he'd never look at me the same.

"Careful," West said as he dropped back to sit on the ground at my side with the cooler full of food. "Your ears are about to start smoking with how hard you're thinking over there."

I exhaled, focusing on the waterfall as I fought to rein in my spiraling thoughts. Was I getting ahead of myself? "I just never expected…"

West bit into an apple and handed me one as well. "Can't say I planned on this either. But I'm not mad it happened."

"No?" I flipped the apple over in my hands, needing a distraction. Was *it* me humping him in the woods, or us flirting in general? Or did he think we were dating now? *Were* we?

His eyes flashed from their typical hazel to a more golden color as they raked over my body, heating me as sure as the sun high in the sky. "Not even a little."

I bit into my apple to occupy myself before I said anything dumb, savoring the crisp, sweet taste.

"Care to tell me what's making you nervous?"

A high-pitched giggle came out of my mouth as I fought to swallow without choking, and West reached across the distance between us and pulled me towards him. He settled me between his legs, my back to his front as he held me to his chest, leaving a tender kiss on my temple.

"If it's about how I feel about you, just know that I'm tempted to kidnap you and run off into the woods so this day never has to end."

My heart fluttered wildly as he peppered kisses from my temple to my neck and shoulder.

"Do you happen to know any witch magic to make it so our clothes never dry and I have to hold you in just your bra and underwear forever?"

I smiled, shaking my head. "Unfortunately, I know even less about being a witch than I do about being a wolf. And you're well aware of how little I know about that."

"That's a lie," West said, hands laced around my stomach as he traced small circles over my skin. "You wield some kind of magic to have me so thoroughly under your spell."

I smiled, nustling closer to his chest as I soaked in the feel of his hands on me. "Likewise."

"Good." West kissed my neck, pausing over where my pulse hammered under my skin. "I'd hate to be alone in this feeling."

My stomach grumbled, and West pulled away from me to open the cooler and inspect the contents. He pulled out a baguette and a wedge of brie cheese, as well as assorted meats, nuts, and fruits. Without asking me if I wanted any, he ripped off a chunk of the baguette and cut into the brie with a knife Summer had packed, all one-handed as he held my hip in the other, like he couldn't bear to let go of me.

"Eat," he said, holding the bread in front of my face. I turned my head to look at him over my shoulder, noticing the fierce set to his jaw as he wiggled the bread, urging me on.

I settled back looking over the stream again and took the bread from him, biting into the crunchy bread and soft cheese. A moan escaped me before I could stop it, eyes closing as I took a second bite. "I forgot how much I love brie."

West's hand tightened on my hip, his body rumbling content-edly against my back. "Careful with those moans or I'll be eating you instead."

I grinned, shoving the last of the bread into my mouth as a wave of heat spread through my body at his words. "Are you always this much of a dirty talker?"

"To you? Yes."

I swallowed the last of my bread, my breaths coming quick at how casually he'd said it. His lips skimmed across my neck, and my eyes shut, never wanting this to end.

"About your wolf," West said, and I froze, all traces of our easy conversation screeching to a halt. "I want to help you."

"I didn't ask for help."

His rough hands slid over my torso, pulling me tighter against him as he kissed my temple again, and my body relaxed like he was some sort of drug to my fight-or-flight response. "I know you didn't, but I can feel the imbalance in your connection with her, even before you refused to shift to get warm."

"Explain what you mean by that — you can *feel* me?"

"You're changing the subject, but I'll allow it," West mumbled against my temple. "Pack bonds form a connection between each of our wolves, connecting us across distances. Imagine a spiderweb, racing off in all directions from a central spot. The Alpha — me — is at the center, connected to everyone. We can send telepathic messages in short bursts, easier when we're in closer proximity, like yelling. It's easy to yell to someone in the same house as you, less so from here to town. Our pack bonds also make it so I have a general sense of everyone's well-being. If someone is in distress, I'll know."

"What constitutes *distress*?" I asked, realizing how over-whelming it must be to be an Alpha. There had to be hundreds of wolves here in Timber Creek.

"Physical pain, strong emotional reactions, things like that."

"So if Terran stepped on a LEGO in the middle of the night getting a glass of water, it'd wake you up?"

West's chest rumbled with laughter against my skin. "Terran only has one volume setting: Loud. I'd *hear* him step on a LEGO in the middle of the night without the pack bonds. But no, those kinds of instant reactions I can tune out and sort through to understand he's not in mortal danger. But if he broke a bone, I'd know. Even those outside of my pack I can feel to some extent, but more so with Lone wolves in my terri-tory, like you. You're unclaimed, not linked to any Alpha, so you exist like a bug flying outside of my web, just waiting to wander in."

Curiosity got the better of me, and I asked, "And what can you feel from me right now?"

West tightened his grip on my waist, pulling me firmly against him. "You're anxious, but I'm coming to realize that's just a base-level feeling for you all the time. You're content, which makes me happy. And you're horny, which makes me *very* happy."

I snorted, but couldn't deny any of those things. "Can I feel you through the same connection? I don't know if I've ever felt anyone through the type of magical link you're talking about. Maybe I don't have that ability in all of my brokenness."

"You're not broken, gem. You've just been lost. But I found you, and I never intend to let you go."

The words should have scared me, feeling far more permanent than anything I was willing to agree to, but instead, I felt a deep seated sense of belonging.

"Now, back to your wolf." His fingers traced lazily over my skin, soothing in their swirling patterns. "Why didn't you want to shift?"

My heart raced as he brought the topic back around to me, but now that he'd explained the connection between us, I realized hiding would be pointless. I opened my mouth to answer, but nothing came out. Licking my lips, I tried again, the words coming out in the faintest whisper, "I'm afraid."

"Afraid of what? Of your wolf?"

Just talking about Balto brought her to the forefront of my mind, and I had to fight the knee-jerk reaction to push her back in my consciousness to main control. But instead of forcing her way forward like she often did, she settled alongside me, sharing space like a loyal canine companion rather than an attack dog. And didn't that just figure — like taking your car to a mechanic for a weird sound and it stops as you pull into the bay. "I have a hard time maintaining control when I shift."

West's hands stilled, then started their tracing patterns again. "How often do you shift?"

"Not enough, according to your sisters. They seemed to think that might be part of my problem."

West hummed some sort of agreement, waiting for me to go on. As much as I wanted to hide my weaknesses, I was quickly realizing I'd never be able to fix my connection with my wolf on my own. And I trusted West, more than I had anyone in a long time.

"I don't always remember what I do when I shift," I admitted. "It's like Balto takes over, and I'm not in control or even aware until I wake up hours later, human again."

West tensed behind me, but if he was alarmed by my confession, it didn't show in his tone when he asked, "Has it always been like that?"

I swallowed heavily. "No."

He waited, sensing there was more, and I took a breath. "When I left Thaddeus, it was… bad." I grimaced at the understatement of the century, but there were some realities I couldn't bring myself to voice, even now, years later. "Balto took over. She protected Ruby." I blinked at the moisture in the corner of my eye. "We had to protect Ruby."

West's hand began its soothing motion on my hip again as he no doubt pieced together the parts I'd left out.

"And you're afraid, if you shift again…"

I gave the barest nod. "What if Balto sees everyone as a threat? I can't control her if I'm not really *there*. Not present. I can't be out of control like that, not again. Never again."

"That's understandable you wouldn't want to go through that again," West hummed. "Last question and I promise I'll drop it for today. Are you usually alone when you shift?"

"Always. I'd never risk shifting around other people."

The *not again* went understood.

But true to his word, West let it drop, even though it was obvious he had other questions, that he wanted to push and know everything.

Instead, he kissed my temple, helped me up, and packed up our picnic. We pulled on our mostly dry clothes, and made our way back to the trail.

As we headed back down to the truck, he pointed out all the

wildflowers we passed. Sometimes we stopped so I could smell them, memorizing their scents with surprising ease, Balto's senses and memory ready to assist.

For once, my wolf worked in partnership with me, and I decided to take that as a good sign.

As we neared the trailhead, I caught a new scent, and my nose wrinkled in disgust. "Oh my God, what is —"

West's arm shot around my waist, and I stuttered to a halt at the sight of a giant buffalo blocking our path.

A giant buffalo with a little purple bow braided between her eyes.

"Willie," West began, in a tone like he was chastising a misbehaving toddler, and not like we were facing down a thousand pound animal. "Did you escape the ranch again?"

Willie swung her huge head towards us, grunting and huffing through her snout.

"Dad's going to be worried about you," West continued, hands on his hips now, and I bit my lip to stifle a smile. He was acting like she could actually understand him, and it was ridiculous.

Willie took a step closer, scenting the air hard, and West sighed. He slung the backpack off his shoulder, unzipping it.

"Don't think I don't know you're on a diet, young lady." He held up a juicy red apple, and I could have sworn Willie's eyes twinkled. He rolled it over the ground to her, and after a thorough sniffing, Willie chomped it up.

"Go on home now." West took a slow but steady step towards her, and Willie, somewhat begrudgingly, turned and took off into the woods with another grunt.

"So that's a Willie."

West nodded. "That's a Willie."

"How many Willies are there?"

"Last I checked, about a dozen."

I hummed, knowing nothing about buffalo. "She had a braid?"

"River's current fixation. The girls all get braids and bows, the boy Willie's get mohawks."

"Hm. And you're just an old softie, apparently. She played you like a fiddle for that apple, big guy."

West shot me a scowl, but it lacked heat as he grabbed my hand, tugging me into his chest. "Softie, is it?" He kissed me deeply, pressing me into him, until I could feel just how *not* soft he was. "We'll see about that, gem."

Chapter Thirty-Four

WEST

Jade was quiet during the drive back, and it took everything in me not to push her for more of her story. She'd relaxed a little on the hike down as we practiced scenting flowers, but once we'd seen civilization again, she'd tensed back up, the weight of her past closing in on her.

After today, I was more convinced than ever that Jade was meant to be a part of our pack. The Balto to my Togo — I couldn't stop my grin at the knowledge of what she called her wolf, all the more proof of how well we fit together. I just needed her to see it, too.

I drummed my fingers on the steering wheel, darting a glance over to Jade as I tried to figure out how to approach the conversation of shifting together. She gazed out the window as we passed through town, but her eyes were glazed over, her thoughts clearly far away.

Maybe I'd ask Aspen or Summer to talk it over with her first.

Even with the long summer days, the sun was already sinking towards the mountains by the time we entered the gates on my property. Between the physical and emotional exertion of the day, Jade was exhausted, excusing herself to her room as soon as we went inside.

Togo urged me to follow her upstairs, to comfort her, to nuzzle into her neck, but it seemed like she wanted to decompress alone, so I forced him to back off.

After dropping the picnic basket in the kitchen to deal with later, I headed to my office, calling out to Terran on the way.

"Any issues?"

I could feel his sarcasm as he responded immediately, *"If you can believe it, the world managed to keep turning without you for six hours, big shot."*

I only sensed Jade in the house, so more than likely he and Leif were still at the restaurant, which was just as well. I didn't mind a little time to myself after the day's revelations, either.

But as soon as I booted up my laptop, I realized that was too much to hope for.

I scanned the long list of emails waiting for me, clicking on one labeled *Rob Yeung Inquiry.* I'd mentioned the panda shifter to Max, asking him to look into the male. Something seemed off about him, but I couldn't put my finger on what it was.

I skimmed his background check, reading through his family ties, recent addresses, and pack bonds. Or, in his case, lack thereof.

Robbie had been accepted into a small pack in California that was a mixed bag of shifters five years ago, but had been dropped from their registration two years later, listed as inactive. Vaughn Sawyer, the Alpha there, had been on my shit list for years, so this discrepancy wasn't wholly unexpected, even if the idea of an Alpha dropping a pack member so quickly set my teeth on edge.

I clicked on the file, hoping there was a paper trail to show where he'd gone next, but the link that should have been there was missing.

Picking up my phone, I dialed Max's number, listening to it ring as I tapped my fingers on my desk, questions running through my mind.

"Again, wolf?" Max sighed, resignation strong in his tone.

"Where did Robbie go after he left Sawyer's pack?"

"Nowhere. Unless he used an alias, — and I can't imagine

why or how he'd avoid the system entirely — this panda shifter of yours has been missing for two years."

I scrubbed a hand over my face, the headache from earlier resurfacing. "How is that possible? How did he not show up on the missing shifters reports? Why didn't we find this before now? And why the *hell* didn't Sawyer report his sudden absence? He didn't even list a reason for kicking Robbie out."

Max sighed. "Robbie's a hybrid. Not quite witch enough to show up on witch registries, and apparently not shifter enough for your people to keep track of him either. He fell through the cracks."

A low growl rumbled through me, hating the reality that was our world. While I'd worked tirelessly over the last five years as a representative for shifters on the Council, we still had a long way to go to get rid of outdated prejudices. Thinking back over my conversation with Robbie when he'd arrived, I tried to piece together anything useful. "Any chance he's had his memories tampered with? I didn't get the impression that he knows he's been gone for two years."

"I can't make that call without seeing him in person, but it's always a possibility."

I grumbled an acknowledgment, even though I already knew that would be his answer. "How many others have fallen through the cracks, Max? How many others have we failed?"

Max was silent for a beat. "Keep an eye on him for now. I'll get out there as soon as I can to check his memories and see what we find."

I shut my laptop after we hung up, the world hanging heavily on my shoulders once more.

"Robbie with you?" I sent out to Terran, feeling guilty I hadn't paid more attention to the newcomer.

"Yeah, he's with Leif. Good kid. What's up?" Terran answered, and I could feel the hesitancy in his mind.

"Nothing. Just watch him. We're keeping him for a while."

Exhaustion propelled me up the stairs, passing Jade's door and into my own room. Even if I wanted to pursue what we'd started earlier, the silence on the other side of her door told me she'd already fallen asleep, and I wouldn't be far behind.

)))●(((

I sensed her discomfort before I heard her.

The faint thread of the starting pack bond between Jade and I twitched, her wolf broadcasting her distress to me even if she didn't know it.

Togo was on the alert immediately, a growl rumbling in his throat even before we knew what the threat was.

I sat up, the sheet pooling around my waist as I cocked my head, tuning in to the pack bond for any clues as to what was wrong.

"RUBY—"

I was out of bed before I could register if the words had come from her mouth or her mind, hurrying to Jade's room.

Not wanting to startle her further, I eased the door open and closed it quietly behind me.

My heart wrenched at the sight of Jade flailing in the throes of a nightmare, muttering under her breath.

Kneeling beside her bed, I pulled her hand into mine, squeezing gently and pushing awareness through the pack bond, willing her to wake on her own. The faint thread glowed the tiniest bit brighter as her subconscious mind felt my intention, and slowly her muttering stopped.

"That's it, gem," I murmured, brushing her hair off her brow, the strands damp with sweat. "It's a nightmare. Come back to me."

Her thrashing slowed, her breaths evened out, and finally she let out a soft sigh, squeezing my hand back.

And if that didn't make my heart swell.

"West?"

"Right here."

My own blood was pounding, and I was desperate to wrap myself around her, but I stayed motionless as she came back into awareness.

Jade turned onto her side to face me, the whites of her eyes a soft blue in the faint moonlight as her gaze traced down her arm to where her hand held mine.

Mate. Comfort mate.

I clenched my jaw, willing control into my being.

"Are you all right now?"

The pillow rustled softly as she nodded. "Sorry I woke you up."

"Please. You know I don't sleep."

She moved to pull her hand back, but there was no way I was letting that happen. I *needed* to stay in contact with her, and for now, this was all I had. All I was allowing myself.

"It was just a bad dream, West," she said, trying to play it off, but she still trembled. Her heart raced like the night she'd asked for my phone. "You don't have to stay."

"Jade." I waited for her brown eyes to find mine again. "It's my fault you had a nightmare. I brought up all that stuff today. That's what the nightmare was, right? I heard you call for Ruby."

She tensed again, but before she could respond, I continued.

"Look, I can read between the lines to know something happened when you were protecting Ruby. You're afraid, and maybe you have reason to be. But *I'm* not afraid of you, or anything you've done in the name of protecting your pack. You won't get rid of me that easy. Understand?"

A look of confusion passed over her face, and my heart constricted at the sight. Had no one ever fought for her before?

"Now, I'll be staying the rest of the night, so either move over in that bed or toss me a pillow."

A long moment passed before she muttered, "Stubborn alpha wolf."

I grinned as she shuffled to the other side of her bed, allowing me to sink into the spot she'd just left, her scent rising from the sheets and sending Togo wild.

I wrapped an arm around her, nestling her face against my chest.

"You're suffocating me."

"Nice try."

"How am I supposed to sleep with your man smell all up in my face?"

I chuckled. "My man smell?"

A delicate finger poked my chest. "You know what I mean."

"Hm." I slipped a hand under her knee and pulled her leg up and over my hip, my thigh settling between her legs. "I have no idea what you're talking about."

A soft intake of breath brought a smug grin to my lips that I was glad she couldn't see.

"Go back to sleep, Jade." I pressed a kiss to her forehead. "I'll keep the nightmares away."

And sending feelings of warmth and safety and hope down the fragile pack bond between us, I did just that.

Her body sagged against me, face pressing into my chest as she drifted back to sleep, but I couldn't stop brushing my fingers through her hair.

Never had I felt this *right*.

I wasn't sure how I was going to convince her to spend every night in my bed, but no way was I going back to sleeping alone.

I closed my eyes, breathing in her citrus scent as plans formed in my mind.

The sun streaked through the blinds as Jade stirred in her sleep. Sometime in the night, she'd turned onto her side, and her ass was pressed into my crotch, scooting dangerously closer. I tightened my arm around her torso, the one under her head dead asleep, but there wasn't a chance in hell I'd move it unless she made me.

Without looking at a clock, I could already tell I'd slept in, something I hadn't done in ages. My phone was still in my bedroom across the hall, and nothing that might be waiting for me mattered as much as the woman in my arms, inching closer.

Jade peeked over her shoulder, a small smile playing on her lips. "Good morning," she said, her voice a sexy rasp.

I closed the distance between us and kissed her lightly. "Hi. How'd you sleep?"

"Great, actually. You?"

"Better than I have in years."

She blushed, eyes cast down away from me as she tangled her fingers with mine on her waist. That bashful look was enough to have me throw my leg over hers, pushing her flat to the bed as I rolled on top of her.

Her dark eyes flashed up at me in surprise, but closed the moment I kissed her, pushing it deeper this time as I let my hips drop into the cradle of hers. Her foot slid up the back of my calf as her arms rose around my neck, lips parting to let me in. Our tongues tangled as blood rushed south, her scent telling me she was just as needy as me.

My hand slid under her shirt, pushing it up as I grazed her warm skin, needing anything she'd give me. She squirmed under me, hands finding my waistband and pushing down. Just before her hands could slip inside and find out just how badly I wanted her, music blared from the hallway.

I pulled away from the kiss, glaring at the door as the intro to *Sexual Healing* blasted. Jade's hand pulled back, her face dumbstruck as her eyes blew wide. Before I could stop her, she scrambled out from under me and into the bathroom, slamming the door.

Falling back on the bed, I brushed a hand down my face as I willed the murderous thoughts down, then dropped my feet to the floor and wrenched open the door.

Terran stood in the hall, speaker held over his head as Cruz danced at his side in a solo jam session.

"Hello, brother," Terran said, a smug grin spreading ear to ear.

Cruz stopped dancing, winked, and disappeared into thin air a split second before I lunged for my brother.

Terran ran for it, my fingers just grazing his t-shirt as he slammed his door in my face.

I glared at his door, but mustered my self-respect enough not to bust in.

"You're evicted."

"Please," Terran scoffed through the door, shutting off the speaker as I made my way back towards my room. "You'd miss me and River way too much in this big ol' house all alone."

"Never know until I try." I slammed the door to my bedroom, needing a cold shower, but I could hear Terran laugh as he emerged back into the hall and headed downstairs.

Chapter Thirty-Five

JADE

I hesitated at the top of the landing. My face still felt flushed, my lips still tingled from our kiss, but how was I supposed to act today after I'd used him as my personal vibrator on our hike and given him nothing in return, then woken him up in the middle of the night with my nightmare?

Assuming it had been Terran outside my door this morning, there was no hiding where West had spent the night, or what we'd been doing this morning. Aspen had warned me about that, and yet, in the moment, I'd wanted him so badly it hadn't mattered.

My stomach rumbled so loud I was sure they could hear it in the kitchen. Food mattered more than my lingering embarrassment.

Putting on my best *She's a Strong, Independent Woman Who Don't Need No Male* face, I descended the stairs. I'd just play it cool and see how West acted, and then I'd adjust accordingly. It was a great plan, I'd be totally chill, and —

The sight of West at the kitchen table knocked the breath right out of me, one hand holding his steaming coffee mug in a way that made me want to lick the muscles in his tattooed forearm, the other scrolling on his tablet. He was still shirtless, and Balto wanted to rub her muzzle all over the muscles in his shoulders.

No, wait, that was me — I wanted to do that.

Maybe he heard my drool hitting the floor, because he set his tablet and mug down, turning to me.

"Hey-o," I said, super coolly, with a little fan wave for good measure. *Excellent start*, I mentally kicked myself, breaking eye contact and all but running for the coffee pot.

"Morning."

The sexy rumble of his raspy morning voice nearly made me whimper, and I gripped the mug I'd grabbed even tighter. That cold shower had done *nothing* to relieve how badly I wanted him.

"Yep, morning — what are you up to this week?" I blurted in one breath, setting the coffee pot back down without even spilling it. Being the brave, grown-up woman I was, I made my way to the table, pulling out a chair a few seats down from him, when the screech of West's chair pushing back made me pause.

"Jade." His voice, and gaze, were direct, and focused wholly on me. "Your seat is right here."

He widened his legs, making his meaning clear.

Balto leapt at his invitation, ready to launch herself into his lap. As if he could sense that, West gave me that cocky smirk that made my knees weak.

As though I was in a trance, I went to him. Setting my mug on the table, I moved between his legs, our eyes nearly level with him sitting. His hand wrapped around my waist, sending electricity through my body, and he tugged me closer until I sat in his lap. Nuzzling into my hair, then my neck, a contented rumble sounded from him that had me melting against his bare chest, wishing I could scent him as keenly as he could me.

"That's better," he murmured, pressing his lips to my temple and trailing his fingers across my low back. I'd forgotten how good it felt to share casual physical intimacy like this. "Now, you asked about my week. As it happens, we're getting ready for a pack run next Saturday, and I wanted to ask if you'd join us."

I stiffened, panic dousing any lingering arousal. West kept his hand on my back, moving in soothing strokes.

He waited in silence for me to speak, giving me time to think through my answer — something I appreciated. He placed a tender kiss on my shoulder, and my wolf all but purred in his proximity.

"Did you notice I asked, not demanded?"

That was enough to make me smile, turning slightly towards him. "Let me go find you a trophy for this epic show of restraint. Except I'd win it for holding back the eye roll that so desperately wants to make an appearance. But you're used to losing to me by now, surely."

West grinned, his eyes crinkling at the corners as he shook with silent laughter. His other arm came around my waist, tugging me more solidly into his chest. With a deep breath, I relaxed and let myself enjoy how steady and sure his grip felt as I rested my head on his chest. This didn't feel new or awkward — it felt right.

Listening to the steady thump of his heart, I asked, "Can you tell me about it first before I make a decision?"

His hand slipped under the oversized sweater I wore, but rested on my back in a gesture meant to calm me rather than ignite the heat between us. "What do you want to know?"

"Who else will be there? The whole pack?"

"Yes, although we spread out among our territory, so we'll be in smaller groups of about ten. You can go with my sisters if that would make you more comfortable."

Immediately I felt more at ease at the thought of running with Aspen and Summer than the whole pack. West's hands rubbed up my back, pushing my sweater up slightly, but I couldn't focus on his touch anymore as my anxiety over shifting dragged me down.

"Tell me what you're thinking, Jade. You're panicking. What are you worried about?"

"Will there be kids near me?"

His hands stilled and my breath caught, waiting for him to push me away at the insinuation.

"I'm sorry," I apologized, pulling away from him, needing space to breathe. "I'm not —"

But West didn't let me pull away. His hands slid up my arms, then settled on my neck, thumbs tracing across my jaw as his hazel gaze trapped me in place.

"You're afraid of hurting someone again."

My breath caught, tears pricking at my eyes at how close he was to the truth.

"You don't have to tell me what happened," he said, his voice low. "But if you choose to come, I'll stay with you the whole time. I won't let anything happen to you, and I won't let your wolf take over. Can you trust me to help you? To help your wolf?"

My heart raced at his words, but I knew deep down, no matter how terrified I was, that I needed this.

I gave him the tiniest of nods. "Okay."

West broke into a grin before he pulled me back into his chest, hugging me tight to his warm skin, and I let it soothe the years of worries, just for this moment.

He placed a kiss on the top of my head. "Thank you for trusting me. I know how much this means."

My fingers dug into his warm skin, pulling him closer to me in the only way I could.

He might think he knew how much this meant, but he had no idea.

Back in my room after breakfast, I steeled myself to do what I'd been dreading since we returned from the mountains — check my phone.

A breath of relief whooshed out of me as I scanned my missed messages — all from Ruby, no new unknown numbers.

Maybe the previous one had been a fluke? Just a wrong number I'd overreacted to?

With a shaky laugh, I set my phone on the dresser, plugging it in to charge, when something on the window caught my eye.

I pushed aside the gauzy curtain, and had to slap my palm over my mouth to stop my scream.

Deep paint scrawled across my window in a shape I'd never forget. A black rose, surrounded by thirteen thorns, blood dripping from each one.

Chapter Thirty-Six

JADE

"Um, Jade? You good?"

The gentle tap on my shoulder had my whole body flinching with a gasp, and Summer's eyes went wide as she lifted her arms in surrender.

"Easy, killer." She laughed, unaware of the way her teasing nickname churned my gut even further.

All week I'd gone through the motions working with Aspen, trying to forget the Coven's mark on my window. But no matter how hard I scrubbed the glass, I couldn't erase the image from my mind, couldn't face the implications of its presence.

The day after it had appeared, I almost convinced myself I'd imagined it — until I caught sight of lingering paint I'd missed, and the nausea came rushing back.

One question had haunted me for days: *How did they get up to the pack house undetected?*

I had no answers, so I had to shove it down. Everyone had noticed I'd tensed back up, but thankfully, they all seemed to be endlessly patient with my many quirks, none more so than West. He'd taken every touch and hug I'd given him, but never asked for more. Never asked for an explanation for my change in behavior, probably assuming it was over the pack run tonight.

Which wasn't entirely wrong.

I'd spent the day cleaning my already tidy room, trying to soothe the anxiety thrumming through me, but it was useless. The temperature dropped quickly here in the mountains as the sun set, but the chill wind of night air did nothing to stop my nervous sweating.

We stood behind the garage, waiting for the rest of the pack to gather. Already, this was more shifters than I'd ever seen in one place, at least a hundred people already milling around. They kept shooting glances my way, but with Summer and Aspen as my sentinels, no one approached to investigate me further.

A few children ran past, shrieking and chasing each other, and I gulped.

Blood splatter flashed in my mind, and I blinked, willing my mind to clear the images of my past.

Summer stepped closer, her brow furrowing, as she rubbed a hand over my back.

"It'll be okay, Jade. Have you not shifted in front of other wolves in a while?" she ventured.

I gave a shaky laugh, letting her think that was all this was. Nerves, stage fright, whatever. That was easier to live with than her knowing the truth. "It's been a good decade since I've shifted with anyone but my sister."

"We'll let everyone else get a head start," Aspen said from my other side, stepping close enough her arm leaned into mine, though she didn't outright touch me like Summer did. "Then it'll just be us, and West. He'll go out with the first group, but he'll circle back."

Nodding, I swallowed heavily, though my mouth was fully dry. I was vaguely aware of the people around me, laughing and joking and catching up, but all I could hear was my pulse pounding in my ears, and the static rush of my panic.

This was a bad idea. I couldn't do this, couldn't *risk* this. These people — they were innocent, they'd taken me in with open arms, and I was a liability. The black rose on my window was all the reminder I needed for just how out of control I was, how much of a risk I posed to these people.

My claws itched at my fingertips, and I clenched my fists hard enough to dent my palms.

The sisters kept an eye on me while they made light conversation, and I knew they were talking to try to ease my stress. Not forcing me to participate, but letting me be near them in case I wanted to.

Summer dropped her hand from my back, and my head jerked up, surprising myself at how much I missed her touch. I only had a minute to wonder why she'd taken a step away when West's pine scent filled my senses as he took her place.

And then, there was just West. He stepped in front of me wearing only a pair of black gym shorts, blocking my view of the rest of the pack. His warm hand cupped the back of my neck, his other hand tilting my chin up.

His voice was low, only for me, when he asked, "Still want to do this?" His hazel eyes bored into mine, searching my face.

Did I want to? No. And yes. I wanted to be good enough to be part of this, and I *knew* Aspen and Summer were right about Balto and I being all out of whack, but I was terrified.

I took a deep breath, blinking moisture from my eyes as I met West's steady gaze. I trusted him to protect his pack. He wouldn't let me hurt anyone here.

Shakily, I nodded. "You'll stay with me?"

"Of course. I have to get it started with the first group, but stay here with Summer and Aspen and I'll come back."

He held my eyes until I nodded again, then pressed a kiss to my forehead that nearly made my knees buckle as he whispered, "I can't wait to run with you."

My heart stuttered, but he was already striding away, leaping with agile grace to the top of a nearby boulder so the whole crowd could see him.

Summer took my hand again, her reassuring, warm presence helping to ground me as West started to speak.

"Pups, you know the deal." He looked at each of the children who jumped around eagerly at the base of the boulder, two already shifted into their small wolves. "Stay with your adults."

One of them — still human — let out a howl, and laughter echoed through the rest of the pack.

"I'll take that as agreement. Everyone else, stay safe and inside our territory, connect with your wolves and each other, and enjoy the night!"

The pack howled as West quickly and unceremoniously stripped, then leapt off the boulder, shifting mid-air. My jaw dropped to the ground, my brain needing several seconds to catch up with what I'd just seen. By the time I regathered myself, half the crowd around was naked or already wolfed out.

West's giant storm-grey wolf took off into the woods, the first group right on his tail, disappearing into the shadow of the trees.

Whether it was because West was gone or because being in wolf form made them bolder, a few wolves approached me now, sniffing hard as their sharp eyes assessed me. Anytime one got too close, though, Aspen stepped in front of me, clearly guarding me, and they shuffled off.

"Idiots," she muttered as she fended off another, the crowd all but dispersed now. "As if just because West is gone he doesn't know everything happening here."

A large, all-black wolf approached next, piercing blue eyes completely ignoring Aspen as it neared in a predatory crouch, gaze intent and unblinking.

"Jett," Aspen snapped, but he didn't even twitch, still inching closer to me, nostrils flaring as he sniffed my air.

A low chuff came from our right, and I hardly contained my shriek at the sight of the hulking brown bear lumbering over.

"Told you Atlas was huge," Summer whispered from my other side, squeezing my hand, and she wasn't kidding. Atlas in bear form was easily six feet tall, making Jett look like a pup. "He's just below Terran in rank —a Shield — and as loyal as they come. Cooper's best friend."

Jett and Atlas stared off for a long moment, Atlas rumbling a low growl and Jett utterly silent. Trees rustled in the woods behind them as West came trotting back out of the forest, teeth bared in a snarl. Jett's ears swiveled backwards as he turned and ran after the others.

With a huff, West came to a stop in front of me. The rest of the pack had cleared out, so now it was only us, the sisters, and Atlas.

Atlas ambled off, lingering at the edge of the forest. I got the sense he was giving us privacy while keeping an eye out for Jett.

A blink later, West was human again, and I started, still not used to seeing other wolves shift like that.

Not to mention, *naked West.*

Eyes north, Jade. For the love of all that is good and —

— Aaaand my gaze dipped. Heat flushed my face as West smirked, well aware of what he was packing. It wasn't the first time he'd been naked in front of me, but it was a whole different ball game after we'd humped each other like teenagers by the waterfall. Suddenly I hated the distance I'd put between us this past week.

Aspen rolled her eyes, and Summer stifled a laugh.

"Go wait with Atlas," West ordered them, his eyes never leaving mine.

Summer squeezed my hand one last time before she and Aspen moved away, nonchalantly dropping their clothes and shifting into their wolves with ease. They glanced back at us once before turning and trotting out to where Atlas now sat against a tree, scratching his back against the bark in a perfect imitation of Baloo.

West brushed a strand of hair out of my face, tucking it behind my ear. Even in his human form, his eyes seemed to glow brighter tonight. Was it the moonlight, or was his wolf riding closer to the surface?

"Ready?" His thumb brushed against my cheek, and I

nodded, even though my heart felt like it was about to crack open my chest and escape.

With a small grin, West turned, giving me privacy to lose my clothes. As I did, I became hyper-aware of every inch of skin I exposed to the night air. I'd been naked in front of him before, but that had been a night of desperation. This was different. This was a choice.

I fought not to cover myself with my hands when I was done, but wolves weren't prudes about nudity, and I wouldn't be either.

"Now what?"

West chuckled. "Now, you shift."

I cleared my throat. "Just like that?"

"Mmhmm."

He made it sound so simple. They *all* made it look so easy. But it wasn't either of those things. If I shifted, I could lose control. I could hurt someone.

"Jade," West's low rumble reached me, and I *felt* the Alpha command in it, though he kept it low. I could ignore him if I wanted to, or I could try to ease into my wolf by letting him take the lead. "Close your eyes."

I took a deep breath, then did as he asked. Instantly, the sounds of the forest were louder, the scents stronger. Crickets and frogs chirped all around us; pine resin and the scent of warm soil reached out from the woods.

He stepped closer, and I knew he was facing me now, but I kept my eyes shut.

"Do you hear the forest, Jade? Can you hear the pack out there, too?"

I tilted my head, concentrating hard until I *could* hear them — paws pounding on rocks and pine needles, wolves tussling together, yips and barks of the pups playing.

"What do you smell?"

"You," I blurted immediately, and West laughed. "And… the trees. The soil."

"What about the creek?"

I sniffed harder. Could he really smell the creek from here? I couldn't tell, and shook my head.

"What about your wolf? Balto can smell it, can't she?"

At his words, Balto, who had been pacing impatiently just below my consciousness, reared her head up. Our souls bled together for a minute, Balto taking over, scenting through my nose and easily picking out the scent of running water.

But losing control, even for a moment, had my panic soaring again, and without conscious thought, I stamped Balto back down, wrenching my eyes open.

"What just happened, Jade?" West's hand came to the back of my shoulder, and I tried not to show my body's reaction at having him so close to me while both of us were fully naked.

"I lost control." I gulped. "I can't do this."

"Hey, it's okay. Balto recognizes me — Togo — as Alpha, right?" I nodded, all too aware of this annoying little fact. Balto was ready to roll over and show her belly, salivating at the reminder of who was in charge here. "That means, if *anything* were to happen, I can make her stop."

I blinked up at him, still shaken from my loss of control. "Can we do a test? Just to be sure?"

"A test?"

"We'll shift, have your wolf order something at mine, and then we'll shift back. A test."

Slowly, West nodded, then stepped back to give me room to shift.

I bit my lip, but I wanted to try this. I didn't love the idea of him ordering me around, but it was better than losing control. If I could trust him not to let me hurt anyone, maybe I could try to enjoy myself.

Scrunching my eyes shut, I willed Balto up to the surface, and to my surprise, she answered. I couldn't remember the last time I'd managed a shift that wasn't out of desperation, but today it felt easy. She stepped up, gently taking over until the tell-tale signs of my shift shivered through my body.

In a blink, I was on all four paws, Balto's soul front and center as she stretched out, first leaning back, then pressing forward to stretch her long legs.

I hadn't even noticed West shifting, but he was already beside me as a wolf.

"Lie down."

I didn't have a chance to register his command before Balto happily complied, dropping her belly to the ground for him.

"Jade?" His voice echoed within my mind. *"You good?"*

I tilted my head up, meeting his eyes through my wolf's.

And then it dawned on me — Balto hadn't pushed me out. We were sharing consciousness, even while shifted.

Somehow, I was calmer now. My wolf trusted West implicitly. All I had to do was let her, let both of them, handle this.

"I'm good," I sent back, hoping he heard me.

He stepped closer, nuzzling into my neck, then trotted a few paces away before glancing back, a clear taunt of *You coming?*

I leapt to my paws, and ran after West into the woods. Atlas, Summer, and Aspen fell in around us as we raced through the trees and jumped over logs and boulders. My paws pounded, strong and sure, my eyesight and hearing sharper than I'd ever felt them before.

A pack. I was running with a pack, for the first time in my life.

And I was safe.

I was safe here.

I scented the creek again, stronger now, and let out a yip of joy as I picked up my speed, keeping pace side by side with West as we raced.

Chapter Thirty-Seven

WEST

My paws pounded in the dirt, trees a blur as we raced through the forest behind my house. Jade running beside me, keeping up with me and enjoying herself, made my heart soar. I wanted to do this with her every week, every day. Her wolf was smaller than me, but Balto was fast, and even when I put on a burst of speed, she met me stride for stride.

Creek, creek, creek — her wolf had a one-track mind ever since she'd scented it. I didn't think Jade knew her wolf was projecting her thoughts so clearly, but that could be a lesson for another time. Tonight, I just wanted her to enjoy being a wolf, among her kin.

I wanted her to see what it could mean to be in my pack.

And damn if it didn't make me puff my chest out to have her with us.

As we neared the creek, the sounds of the rest of the pack reached us, several groups already here. Jade's ears swiveled, hearing them, and she slowed, hanging back a little until her snout was in line with my shoulders.

Perfect mate, my wolf huffed his approval, and I had to agree.

We cleared the treeline upstream from where Terran stood with the rest of the pack, and I led the way, putting my snout down for a long drink of the cool mountain water. Jade joined me, subconsciously resting her shoulder against mine as she did, and internally, I beamed.

Aspen, Summer, and Atlas settled around us, keeping an eye on the rest of the pack so I could focus on Jade.

Some of the pack shifted back to human to lounge around or swim, but most stayed in animal form, as Jade and I did.

She bent down for another drink, stepping into the water.

I sank to the ground just on the shore, content to watch her jumping around and splashing, enjoying herself.

"Good first pack run?" I sent to her.

She turned, and ran back over to me before doing a full-body shake, spraying water all over me.

"Yes. Thank you."

She licked around my mouth, a sign of affection and deference among wolves that sent my hormones, already amped up, into overdrive.

I moved into a crouch, giving her a playful growl and nip that sent her scampering across the creek, waking up my prey drive as I dove after her.

With a pounce, I took her down, both of us rolling over each other until I stood over her, my teeth around her neck, but only in play, not clamping down. Her eyes met mine, and then she tilted her head, baring her neck even further. I couldn't stop the growl that left me.

The next thing I knew, four paws punched into my chest, throwing me off as Jade made her escape, laughing at me in our minds.

"That was cheating," I warned, stalking after her.

"It's only cheating if it doesn't work, but it did, so I win." Her wolf tossed what could only be described as a smirk at me, and I picked up my pace to a steady lope after her as she scampered into the woods.

She wanted a chase? Fine by me.

I trailed her through the trees, letting her have just enough of a head start to think she might be able to win.

Stalling behind a boulder, I waited as her steps grew quieter, letting her get even further away. When I couldn't hear her anymore, I put my nose to the ground, following her trail at a trot.

Fuck, this was so much fun. After a few minutes, I could scent her getting closer, and my heart raced at the anticipation of catching her.

Then a low snarl reached my ears, and I knew something was wrong.

In a burst of speed, I cleared the remaining distance to find Jade in a clearing, face to face with Jett.

I went to move between them, but Jade stepped in front of me, blocking me from this encounter.

"Jett, leave," I tried instead, turning my attention to the actual problem — the giant black wolf who wanted to claim Jade as his own — and infusing my words with as much Alpha command as I could.

Jett struggled, fighting my order, and my hackles rose.

But Jade surprised the shit out of both of us, lunging forward and snapping at him, teeth fully bared and snarling loud.

Shocked, Jett jumped back and froze. Jade rushed him again, snapping and snarling. I reached out along the thin pack bonds forming between Jade and myself, trying to sense if she had lost control to her wolf. But no — she and Balto shared control and were in full agreement as she went after him.

Snapping again, and again, until finally, Jett turned and ran.

Mate, my wolf rumbled, our excitement rising at seeing her take on Jett.

Jade stared after him for a long while, waiting until we couldn't hear him scampering off anymore, then turned to me, pride beaming off her.

"Run home, gemstone, before I make you mine here and now," I said, Togo vibrating with how hard I had to restrain him from leaping on her.

Jade swished her tail right under my nose. *"Catch me if you can, Togo."*

Fuck. I chased after her.

))) ● (((

We barely stepped foot on the back deck at the house before we shifted, and she had me pinned against the wall.

"Fuck, Jade —" I licked a long line up her neck, tugging at her sensitive skin gently with my teeth as she leaned into me, any hint of distance she'd kept this last week gone. My hands wrapped around her waist, sinking to her hips, pulling her against me. "You see what you do to me?" She gasped as I kicked her legs apart, making sure she could feel *all* of me. "What seeing you wolf out and put Jett in his place like that does to me?"

Her nails dug into my back as I sucked her nipple into my mouth, biting just hard enough to make her arch her back. "More," she groaned, and I flipped our positions.

Not missing a beat, she wrapped a leg around my hips, urging me closer, and I lifted my head up to plunge my tongue into her mouth.

Jade moaned, and I didn't let up, didn't give her a break as I devoured her, my hands roaming all over her beautiful body. I couldn't get close enough, even as she wrapped her other leg around me. I picked her up, my palms cupping her ass as I ground against her.

"West," she panted, a whimper leaving her as I rocked against her again. "I need —"

"What, gem?" I licked her jaw, bit her collarbone, sucked her breast. "What do you need?" The house rattled as I rocked against her hard. "Because what I need is to fuck you so hard the shingles fall off. I need to watch you take every inch of me inside you until you scream my name. I need to fill you up and claim every part of you while you come so hard you forget everyone but me." She was trembling, panting, her chest heaving. "How does that sound, gem?"

Her eyes flashed golden, then returned to that dark chocolate I loved so much as she nodded. I claimed her mouth again, not wasting a moment.

"River, let's go check out—" Heath's voice carried from the kitchen and we froze. My head snapped to the side as my father opened the sliding door from the kitchen. His eyes met mine long enough he knew we were out here, then his face morphed to feigned shock as he slapped a hand over his eyes and pushed River back inside. "Put it *away*, son. No need for puppies on the porch, right where everyone can see you."

"Puppies!" a tiny voice shrieked, and Jade's feet dropped to the floor as she buried her face in my chest.

Trying to steady my breathing, I half-turned, still covering Jade's body with mine as I glared at my father and the child popping her head out beside him.

River scrunched her nose. "I don't see any puppies, just Uncle West's gross naked booty. Where are they, Papa?"

"Yeah, West," my dad said, a smirk playing on his lips. "Where *are* the puppies?"

"River, I thought you were staying with Uncle Cruz?" I panted, still painfully hard against Jade's stomach, though it was fading the longer my family stared at us.

"He went to go pick up pizza," she said. "I wanted to finish my LEGOs instead so he left me with Papa."

I caught Jade's eye, her face gone bright red, and suddenly, I burst out laughing, my head dropping to her shoulder. It wasn't long before she joined me, covering her mouth to stifle her laugh.

"River, go inside, sweetie, we'll come help you with your LEGOs in a minute," Jade managed between laughter.

River scowled dubiously. "With clothes on?"

"Yes, with clothes on," I assured her, and with a dramatic

huff fit for the stage, River turned on her heel and stomped off. My father grinned, then followed her inside.

"Oh my God." Jade choked on another laugh as I eased back, moving to the clothing bin by the back door and tossing her some sweats. I grabbed some for myself and tugged them on too. "Your dad just saw me naked. And we scarred your niece for life."

"She'll get over it." I hoped. "Shifter kids are more used to nudity than humans."

"There's a big difference between nudity and what we were doing, West."

I cringed, already knowing Terran was going to chew me out for this later.

Jade went for the sliding door, but I stopped her with a hand to her shoulder. With a finger under her chin, I tilted her face up, admiring the flush that arousal and the night's excitement gave her.

"Hey. You okay?" Her eyes were bright with her wolf, almost glowing, and I brushed her dark hair away from her face, unable to stop touching her. "You did great tonight."

She broke into a grin. "I kind of thought I did."

I nodded back towards the wall where we'd been a few moments ago. "Sorry if that was a bit too much —"

Laying a soft fingertip on my lips, she stopped my apology. "Only be sorry we didn't get to finish it. Now, we have LEGOs to build, Togo, and mine are going to be so much better than yours."

She tapped my cheek playfully, then slid open the door and sauntered inside. I followed after her and slid it shut.

"LEGOs aren't a contest."

"Not for me and River, no. But you? On your own? Good luck beating us, Alpha."

Alpha. Togo and I liked the sound of that. We liked it a lot.

Chapter Thirty-Eight

JADE

I held my breath, and turned the key in the ignition. The truck rattled for a moment, and my heart squeezed, anticipation about to burst into disappointment, when the engine finally caught.

"Aha!" I grinned, and Cruz beamed back at me, clapping the roof of the baby blue truck I'd helped him with over the last couple weeks. "We did it!"

"Little elbow grease and a lot of patience can go a long way," Cruz said, his eyes moving past me to his shop office, where Aspen was finishing up lunch. She'd eaten upstairs every other day lately, but knowing Cruz and I were so close to finishing the truck, I'd pushed back my break, and she'd come down to watch.

Clearing his throat, he turned back to me, leaning down into the truck with a wide smile. "I promised if you got her running on your own before your month here was up, you could keep her, so she's all yours. You earned it, almost a week early, too. She just needs a name."

I turned off the truck, hopping out and taking the rag he offered me to wipe my hands. While I knew the work I'd put in wasn't nearly enough to pay for this truck, I couldn't find it in me to turn Cruz down. I couldn't remember the last time I loved an inanimate object like I'd come to love this little truck over the last two weeks working on it with him. "It's blue, so maybe Juneau."

"Juneau?"

"There are some glaciers around Juneau, they have this blue color. According to one of my old *Balto* books, anyway."

Cruz scrunched his face before chuckling again. "I've never met anyone as obsessed with that story as you. Except maybe West."

Like saying his name had summoned him, my phone buzzed in my pocket. Momentary panic flooded me as I smiled up at Cruz, trying to hide my reaction every time my phone went off lately. Since the rose incident, I hadn't seen or heard anything out of the ordinary, but the lingering fear never left my mind, not even after almost a month of safety here in Timber Creek.

Cruz waved a rag at me. "Go, have a break. You earned it, *chiquita.*"

My hands shook as I wiped them, then pulled out my phone, finding a crate to sit on by the open bay doors.

WEST

You ran out of the house pretty fast this morning after we were interrupted on the way to the shower. Hope you're not avoiding me, gem.

Instantly, the nerves changed to butterflies, a slow smile spreading. After the last two weeks of kisses and touches, I wasn't sure I could avoid him even if I tried. West's attention was addicting, his affection a cure to my soul. I'd never believed in the concept of mates before him, but the way he made me feel... Maybe there was some truth to it.

If anything could convince me, it might have been the full set of Balto and Alaskan history books books that showed up outside my room a few days after the pack run. They were well-worn, the spines cracked, and a few pages even had what I would have sworn were puppy teeth marks in them. Maybe West had read them with Leif? The thought still made me smile, picturing West cozy up in bed with a young Leif, reading to his son.

That West was willing to share these books — clearly well loved — with me nearly made my heart burst.

My month in Timber Creek was almost up, and the thought

of leaving was less and less appealing by the day. I didn't want to leave, didn't want to be alone again, didn't want to lose the feel of West's hands on my skin, especially since we'd started a terrible trend of being interrupted every time things started to progress.

JADE

Big day at the auto shop. We got the truck running!

WEST

Auto shop? Not with Aspen today?

JADE

Long story. What's up?

WEST

I have to go to Maine for a gala. It's all very political, but I need to be there to represent shifters for the Council. I leave this afternoon.

Excitement stirred at his words.

JADE

Maine?

Three dots popped up instantly, showing him typing back, then disappeared. My hopes fell, then the dots appeared again.

WEST

You'll come with me?

I wanted to agree immediately, jumping at the chance to see Ruby again. But what he was asking was more than just a social visit to my sister.

If I went with him, stood at his side in front of heads of

supernatural communities from all over the US, it would mean something. It was a declaration, loud and clear that we were together, and I shocked myself with how badly I wanted that.

JADE

Yes. I'll go with you.

WEST

I can't wait to get you alone, without half a dozen eavesdropping shifters.

A grin stole over my face, and I bit my lip as I typed back.

JADE

Oh? Why's that?

WEST

For all the things I plan to do with you, I want you to feel free to scream my name. We leave in a few hours, and we'll be sharing a room. Pack accordingly.

I tried to hide my smile as I looked up, but Cruz was busy on the far side of the shop, and Aspen must have gone back upstairs, because the office was empty.

When had this become my life? Fixing cars and flirting with an Alpha wolf over text?

I didn't hate it.

I stood, moving to slip my phone back in my pocket, when it buzzed again, my adrenaline already perking back up as I wondered what West had to say now.

Then my heart dropped to my stomach.

UNKNOWN NUMBER

I look forward to seeing you again soon, baby.
Have you missed me?

My pulse pounded, reading over the words.

He was coming after me? He would *dare*, even when I was surrounded by my —

My mind stuttered over the words *My pack*. Was that what they were now? My subconscious seemed to think so, though I wasn't sure when the change had happened.

I furiously deleted the message, heading for the stairs to tell Aspen I had to go pack, and tried to think of anything but the text's foreboding words. Now seemed like the perfect time to get out of town.

))) ● (((

With a quick goodbye, I tossed the truck keys to Cruz and promised to come pick it up later. Needing a minute to clear my head, I took a deep breath and started towards the packhouse.

Baby.

I'd always hated that pet name, and Thaddeus had laughed every time I brought it up. Balto snarled at the thought of him, but *baby* wasn't an uncommon moniker — it could still have been a wrong number.

I was too paranoid to think that was the truth, not after the rose on the window. Not after seeing Bram. Not after the secrets I kept.

Keying in the passcode to the gate, I slipped through and into the packhouse, headed straight for my bedroom to regroup and pack.

The door opened as I approached, and I leapt back, my fangs elongating without a thought.

Summer stood in my doorway, her hand over her heart. "Crap, I didn't mean to scare you. I figured you'd have scented me here already."

I blinked, my gums aching as my fangs receded, embarrassed by my reaction. "I'm so sorry. I didn't mean—"

"Nope." Summer shook her head, then pulled me into a hug,

gripping me tight until the last of the adrenaline faded from my system. "It was my fault. I scared you, and your wolf protected you, just like she should."

Closing my eyes, I let my arms wrap around her, soaking in her easy comfort as my mind returned to the present. "Why are you here?"

She pulled back, a bright smile on her face as she turned around and went into my room. A green suitcase lay on my bed, open but full of clothes I'd never seen before. "West thought you might need some help packing, so I did it for you. You can change out anything you don't like, but everything is in colors and cuts that should flatter your body."

I glanced between the suitcase and Summer. "Is there something in the water here?"

Summer chuckled. "What do you mean?"

"You're all so damn *nice.*"

"We take care of our own, and after the pack run, I'm pretty positive that includes you."

I winced. "Heard about that, did you?"

"We all did, honey." She smiled, her nose scrunched as she sorted through the clothes in the suitcase. "Maybe more than I ever needed to know about my brother, honestly. But let's skip to the part where you two are serious enough to go on this trip together now."

"Is it really that big of a deal for me to go with him?" I asked. "He said Maine and I jumped at the chance. I can see my sister while we're there."

Her hands stilled, and she turned to look at me, a sundress in her grip.

"Okay, I'm going to do this once and then never again, probably," Summer said, chewing on her lip as she looked to the door then back at me. "You're serious about him, right? I love you, but Jade... this is my brother. And he's way more fragile than he seems. He puts on this big tough-guy act, taking care of all of us, but he's *never* acted the way he did with you in front of our pack at the run. I can't think of a time he's publicly dated anyone after Sarah, ever. If you're not planning on staying… if this isn't serious for you, you need to walk away now. Even then, I'm not positive he won't chase you. Don't go with him on this trip if you don't want it to mean something, because it definitely does to him."

I dipped my chin as my cheeks heated, needing a moment to think over her words. I'd more or less come to the same conclusion, but hearing it confirmed so decisively from someone close to West made it more real.

I fingered the seam of my t-shirt, already rethinking all of our plans. "I don't know if I'm brave enough." I hadn't meant to say it outloud, but it slipped out.

Before I had time to go on, Summer stepped up to me, curling her arms around my shoulders as she hugged me tight once more.

"No one can know what anyone else feels, how they're affected by their past, but Jade," Summer whispered, gripping me so tight I was forced to hug her back, "West is so far from Thaddeus, you can't compare them. He'd never do any of the things you told us about, and if he did, Aspen and I would be the first ones in line to murder him. If you're ready to let him in, I promise you won't regret it. He's worth being brave for."

I nodded, hearing her words as my throat closed up at the well of emotions. I'd done nothing to earn this family's loyalty, and here they were, having my back at every turn, just like West said he would.

"This is more hugs than I've allowed in years," I said into her shoulder, and Summer laughed, pulling away.

"I warned you I'm a hugger. One last thing and then I'll leave you alone." She twirled her hand in the air, motioning for me to turn as she walked towards my en suite bathroom. "I bought a witch spell in town to redo your green dye, if you want."

I frowned. "There's a *witch spell* for hair dye?"

She hummed, tugging me the last few feet into the bathroom as I followed her. "It's pretty basic, and doesn't fade as fast as traditional dyes. Should we try it?"

Glancing in the mirror, I eyed my outgrown hair, far more black than the teal-green I preferred, and thought of the day I'd dyed Ruby's and my hair the first time. It was one of my favorite memories, and one I hoped she remembered too. "Let's do it."

Chapter Thirty-Nine

JADE

"Stunning," West said as I stepped out of my room, my hair dyed and styled in loose waves, hanging down my back.

Summer emerged from behind me, clapping her hands together. "Right? Green is your color, Jade. It turned out so good."

I grinned, in equal parts at Summer's exuberance and the heat in West's eyes as he took the suitcase from my hand and urged me towards the stairs.

My phone sat heavy in the pocket of my black floral jumpsuit Summer insisted I wear, but no more texts had come through and I'd blocked the new number. *Just a wrong number.*

"Thank you for coming with me." West's lips ghosted over the shell of my ear as we moved through the foyer, sending my body into a heady spiral of anticipation.

He reached in front of me to open the door, and—

"Step right up to Air de la Cruz, where the seatbelts are nonexistent, the vertigo guaranteed, the nausea probable, and the snacks a risk not worth taking — refer back to the nausea clause."

Cruz flourished a hand from the driveway as West and I exited the house. West shook his head at Cruz's antics while we descended the few steps down to the driveway to meet our demon transport.

"Ever traveled by flicker, Jade?" Cruz asked, stretching his neck side to side with a *crack.*

"Can't say I have," I admitted while he continued stretching out.

"Well, once you've had a ride on the Cruz Express —"

"Watch it." West's warning was a low growl, which Cruz ignored.

"— You'll probably think twice before hopping on again," he chuckled. "We travel in the in-between, disappearing and reappearing with a thought, to put it simply. It's not the most fun for non-demons, or so I've been told, but you'll be all right. Oh, almost forgot" — he bowed shallowly, handing me a brown paper bag — "for the lady."

I turned it over, then peeked inside. Empty. "What's this for?"

"The puking. All right, let's get this show on the road, *vamonos.*"

I shot West a hesitant look, but before I had time to voice any concerns, Cruz grabbed our arms. With a gut-churning yank, Colorado disappeared.

My feet slammed into the ground, and I pulled open the paper bag just in time to use it.

"We aim to anticipate your needs here at Cruz Air." He chuckled, and incinerated the bag with a snap of his fingers before I even finished closing it. "Tips are never expected but always appreciated, miss."

While I struggled to get my bearings, blinking the world back into focus after my brain had been swirled to mush, a glass shattered somewhere nearby and someone let out an ear-splitting shriek.

"JADE!"

I was body-slammed to the floor the next second, my balance still wobbly after demon-travel. My eyes finally focused enough to see bright red hair, and a familiar row of studs down the outside of an ear.

"Ruby!" I gripped my sister tight, not caring that we were on the floor in the middle of who knew where.

Within a breath, my sister openly sobbed, her whole body shaking as she clung to me. "Why didn't you tell me you were coming?"

I ran my hands over her hair as I tried to soothe her the way I had so many times before. "And miss being flat-tackled in public? Why would I do such a thing?"

She sat up, wiping the tears from her face as she laughed, pulling me upright. "You jerk."

We got to our feet, Ruby still clinging to my waist as if I'd disappear if she let me go. I pulled her head to me as I kissed her hair. "I missed you too, sis."

She sighed, then stepped back, and I looked around for the first time, noticing the number of people who sat nearby at the crowded rooftop bar. I recognized the classic white gazebo in the town square that marked this as Deadlights Cove, which meant this bar was Scallywags, where Ruby now worked.

"Really Cruz?" I turned to him with an eye roll. "You had to land us right in the middle of a restaurant?"

"And miss this happy reunion? I think not." He rubbed the back of his neck. "And in my defense, the last time I was here, this rooftop was empty." With a last wink, Cruz disappeared.

"West," someone called, and Orion, the mayor of Deadlights Cove, stepped towards us. "Good to see you."

They shook hands, and I cataloged the differences between the two males. Where West was rugged in a distinctly Mountain-y way, Orion was as buttoned-up as I remembered. His silver hair was combed neatly to the side, as pristine as his white wings and white button-down shirt, rolled up to the elbows. Everything about the angel was polished right down to his pressed pants and loafers, such a contrast to the other angel in my life, Max.

"Likewise," West said, a genuine smile lighting his face. He liked these people, and I was happy to see him at ease here. "You mentioned accommodations for us had changed?"

A small Black woman with bright blue hair slipped off a stool at the bar, draining the last of her whiskey glass as she stepped up to Orion's side. "I'm Devanna." She gave her empty cup to Orion as she held out a hand to me. "I've heard all about you from your sister."

"Jade," I said, shaking her hand briefly. "And same. Thanks for everything you've done for her. I'm always happy to hear how much you all look after your own."

Devanna smiled, then nodded. "Sorry to keep you guys on a tight schedule, but Orion has everything planned down to the minute for West while he's here."

Orion pinched the bridge of his nose. "Not the *minute*."

"Close enough," Devanna scoffed. "Don't worry, though. You and Ruby have a whole day *scheduled* to catch up tomorrow. I have the keys to the cabins, if you want to follow me."

West put his hand on my lower back, and together we followed her.

I looked over my shoulder at Ruby, whose eyes were laser-focused on the small of my back, studying West's hand and how I wasn't jumping away from him.

"What the hell?" she mouthed, then grinned, waggling her eyebrows.

I shook my head, then blew her a kiss. "I'll come find you tomorrow," I said, already feeling the few feet of distance between us. We walked down the stairs and into the main bar, loud with patrons sitting around the many tables. Everyone paused as we entered the room, turning slowly in our direction.

"Hey West!" came a voice from a booth, and I smiled at Nimue, a demon I'd met a few times before on visits to the town. She bounced a baby in her lap and wrangled a young boy next to her. "And Jade, it's been ages! Kit, do you know Ruby's sister?"

A bronze-skinned male in a plaid flannel rose from the bench across from her, a girl the same age as the young boy clinging to his hand.

"West," he said, awkwardly offering his free left hand to

shake instead, which West took with a smile. "Jade, nice to meet you. I'm Kit. Akil's brother."

My eyes widened in acknowledgment.

"Am I missing something?" West asked.

"Ruby's dating Akil," I explained.

West laughed. "Ah, I see."

"He'll be around this weekend if you want to interrogate him." Kit grinned, his daughter already tugging his hand to get his attention back. "But it was nice to meet you."

We barely made it another two steps before we were stopped again.

"Larkin," came a deep rumble, and a man I could only describe as a Viking appeared, arms crossed as he inspected us. I knew Ryker by reputation, and his intimidating presence certainly lived up to it.

We crossed the whole restaurant like that, stopping every few feet for someone else to greet West. He was pleasant with all of them, greeting everyone by name and introducing me, too.

Devanna waited for us by the far end of the bar by the door, giving me an exasperated, *What can you do?* look, and signaled the blonde bartender for another whiskey while she waited.

Finally, we reached her, and she led the way out of the bar and up the street. The air was significantly more humid here than Colorado, the town square and streets alive and green with plants and flowers. We walked along Ocean Avenue, the waves crashing beside us and harbor bell ringing out in the distance, until a trail veered off the main road, taking a few winding turns into the woods.

Every step raised my pulse as West's texts from earlier echoed in my mind.

Can't wait to get you alone.

We're sharing a room.

Plan accordingly.

Risking a glance at the male, his dark eyes met mine, and I knew he was thinking the same thing.

When the trail ended, the trees cleared to reveal a little white cabin only a few steps up from a rocky beach.

"The gala is at the hall at the Last Resort tomorrow night," Devanna said as she unlocked the blue door. "But I'm sure people will be at Scallywags before and after if you're looking to socialize, Jade. West, Orion sent you a full itinerary, so check your email."

She glanced between us behind her thick black framed glasses, tilting her head. "Will you need a second cabin, or —"

West snatched the keys from her hand. "No."

Devanna didn't even look at him, only waiting for me to confirm the same for her.

I swallowed, my words stuck in my throat, not because I didn't want to say them, but this was my chance to back out. I met West's nearly molten eyes as I said, "One cabin is good."

"Okay, well, at least wait until I'm out of earshot before you start tearing clothes off," Devanna muttered, putting her hands up. She stepped off the cabin's little porch, stomping off back through the woods towards the main street.

"After you." West nodded towards the open door, and I walked in, him following after me with our bags. He set them just inside the door, closing it behind him with an ominous *click*.

Feeling very much like I was trapped in here with a feral wolf, which I was, goosebumps rose on my skin as West turned his full attention on me, taking slow steps over.

"So, Jade," he started conversationally, like he wasn't making my heart race and my stomach flutter and my *other* things squirm as he stalked closer. "Let's recap. We've had two weeks of interruptions by my meddling family — I wish I could say they'll leave us alone in the future, but I can't make promises where they're concerned. This morning, I made myself, hopefully, very clear —"

I nodded, my hands finding a countertop behind me and holding on for dear life as he stopped in front of me, mere inches away. "You did."

"And today, I know you spoke with Summer." West tilted his head, gauging my reaction. "Yet you're still here. With me." I was pretty sure they could still hear my heart at Scallywags, it was so loud. "Alone."

I nodded again, and West's hand came up under my jaw, tilting my face up to his. "Yes, I'm here."

His hazel eyes searched mine, his chest rising and falling more rapidly too. The idea that I, Jade, just Jade, affected him, when he was practically shifter royalty, as much as he affected me was enough to make my head spin.

"Jade." He pressed closer, but still not close enough. Our only point of contact was his fingers on my chin, but I was desperate for more. "If we do this, there's no going back. My wolf is positive you're his mate, and I can't argue with him anymore. We want you, we want the mate bond, we want to claim you, and for you to claim us. Do you understand?"

"That you're a possessive alphahole?" I teased, a brow rising in challenge as I held back a smirk, adding a beat of levity so I had a moment to process. His words sent a rush through me, because I felt it, and Balto felt it too. She'd been trying to tell me from the beginning, but I hadn't wanted to hear it. Couldn't process the extent of everything this meant.

Forever.

A family.

A *home*.

Everything I'd ever wanted, and never allowed for myself. But I was tired of fighting, tired of believing I didn't deserve it. I couldn't let him go.

"That's a given." His head tilted down towards me and to the side. The feel of his nose trailing across my jaw was salacious, sending a shiver down my spine. "I don't share. Especially not you, Jade. It's all or nothing."

I mumbled incoherent babble as my fingers dug into his shirt, holding on for purchase as a tidal wave of lust and emotion threatened to pull me under.

"Are you on birth control? Our healing magic prevents the spread of diseases, so I'm clean."

I nodded, digging my fingers in more. "Yes. I'm good."

"Good." He licked a trail across my pulsepoint and my knees trembled.

He's worth being brave for, Summer had said, and even if it terrified the living daylights out of me, I felt the truth of it in my soul. West was worth everything.

"I don't share either," I breathed, heart racing.

He hummed against my skin, the vibrations sending a wash of heat over my body. "No one matters but you. If you run again, I'll chase you." He nipped my neck. "You already know how good I am at finding you, gem. You're mine forever."

After everything I'd been through the last few years with Thaddeus, that should have terrified me, but it didn't. From him, it wasn't threatening. It was protective.

I'd seen first hand how hard he worked to keep his family safe, seen how hard they loved each other. And that was the best proof of all.

West pulled back, searching my eyes, waiting. He was so patient, more than I could ever hope to be, but I was done waiting.

I licked my lips, my gaze darting down to his mouth and back up. "I won't run," I said, and hoped I meant it. I held his gaze — for most wolves, a challenge, but not between us. Not like this. "I'm all in, mate."

With a groan, West picked me up, crashing his lips to mine as he guided my legs around his waist. His kiss was possessive, demanding I give him everything, but I gave as good as I got. He started walking us down the hall to the bedroom, and I tugged on his hair, earning another groan.

The next breath, my back hit the wall so West could grind into me, items clattering to the floor beside us as my foot swept over a hall table.

He pulled back just enough that we could see what had fallen — shards of decorative seashells now littered the floor, and I bit my lip to stifle a chuckle.

West shrugged. "I'll hide those from Devanna before we leave."

I shot him a look. "You'll replace them."

His eyes flashed golden, his lips pulling back in a wolfish grin. He shifted his hips tantalizingly between us, pressing on me just right. "Order me again, gem."

My face heated, and I smirked. "Carry me to the bedroom, Alpha."

"Yes, mate."

A screech left me as I was suddenly upside down, tossed over West's shoulder as he jogged down the rest of the hallway. "I should have listened to my brothers sooner," he said as he slapped my ass.

My back hit the mattress, the antique iron bed frame squeaking in protest. "Don't break the bed. Devanna is a little terrifying."

"No promises." Teeth nipped at my shoulder as West rolled us, settling between my legs then pushing the straps of my jumpsuit down my arms.

"Remember when I chased you in that parking lot?" he panted, groaning and rocking into me as I found his belt. "This was all I could think about for days."

My fingers grappled with his jeans, needing to get them off, until West reached down and grabbed my wrist, pinning it over my head.

"Mine," he said as his mouth slid down my neck, tongue

trailing as he licked between my breasts, then lavished each one with attention. I arched up into him, my mouth falling open as desperation set in.

"Alpha."

His head dropped down to my chest, pulling in a deep breath. "*Fuck.*"

When he lifted his face back up, his hazel eyes had gone bright gold, Togo at the forefront. Balto rose to greet him, pushing forward in my mind. "Mate."

In seconds, we ripped each other's clothes off, our wolves in complete agreement with this plan. I wrapped my legs around him, urging him closer, and whimpered when his body slid down mine.

"I need to taste you," West said as he nipped my inner thigh, pushing my knees apart to make space for his broad shoulders. My eyes squeezed shut as his tongue slid across my skin, moving closer to where I needed him.

A gasp escaped as he finally swiped across my center, licking and swirling just right. My hand flew to his head, fingers grappling in his hair as I held on through the torrent of heat washing over my body. His fingers joined his tongue, pressing into me, and my back arched high, leaving the bed.

No one had done *this* with me in — I couldn't even remember how long — and no one had made it feel as good as West.

I moaned his name as I tugged on his hair, trying to pull him up before this was over too soon.

He growled, grabbing my wrist and pinning it down.

"I don't want to come without —"

"You're going to come on my mouth, mate, at least once before I'm inside you. Cover me in your scent so everyone knows I'm yours." I whimpered, and his golden eyes lifted to mine. "Because our first time? I won't be able to be gentle, and I need you ready for me."

My jaw went slack, then his mouth was back on me, fingers curling just right, and my head dropped back.

He wanted me to — twice? Three times? Never in my —

But I couldn't stop it if I wanted to, my body quickly ascending to that peak at his expert attention. Then he added a perfect suction, and I went over the edge, panting his name.

Spots dotted my vision as my heart pounded, reeling as West pressed a kiss to my thigh then rose to his knees, looking down on me. My eyes widened at the sight of his beard — so damp. From *me*.

But the smug, feral look in West's eyes said he didn't mind, not one bit.

His hand moved slowly over himself and my gaze dropped, saliva pooling in my mouth at the sight of his thick shaft. I reached forward, wanting to touch him, but he batted my hand to the side, pushing me back down on the bed.

"We have our whole lives to play, mate," he said as his weight settled between my hips. He lifted my thighs as he gripped himself, sliding through my wetness.

"I need you."

His eyes met mine as he pushed in, both of us groaning at finally being connected in this way. I tangled my fingers in his hair, pulling him down on me. His mouth found mine, kissing me deeply as he moved, but it wasn't enough. The last few weeks had been slow torture, building towards this moment, and I needed everything he had to give me.

I pushed my hips up into his, meeting him as he thrust deeper, and West pulled back from the kiss, his eyes molten gold. A hand settled on my hip as he held me in place and snapped his hips forward, my mouth falling open in a gasp.

"I told you I wouldn't be gentle," he said as he licked across my neck. My head fell to the side as I moaned his name. "You feel so damn good. So damn *mine.*"

Teeth scraped my neck, my thoughts an incoherent rush as

he continued to slam into me. This was the most whole I'd ever felt, and I never wanted it to end. "Say you're mine, Jade."

"I'm yours."

"*Fuck*," he muttered before teeth — no, *fangs* — sank into my neck, and my nerves exploded, my vision blacking out for the second time. West groaned, teeth still in my skin, as he followed me over the edge.

Our movements slowed, and as my senses came back online, I felt him licking my neck, faintly aware of a slow trickle of blood from the wound. But instead of pain, tingles of pleasure raced through me again, and I shuddered.

Still connected, West pushed up on his forearms, admiring my neck with a smug male pride before meeting my eyes. He pushed my hair out of my face, then pressed his lips to mine, the slight tang of copper on his tongue.

"Mine," he breathed, pressing his forehead to mine.

As the world came back into focus around me, I looked up at him — my mate. My senses seemed sharper, the smell of West's pine scent mixing with my own as I fought to even my breathing.

West had claimed me, and he was mine.

Chapter Forty

WEST

With Jade's citrus scent wrapped around me, I could hardly focus on the quarterly updates the Premier angel Malachi and the other heads of species covered.

I'd found and claimed my mate. She hadn't claimed me in return, but I didn't want to push it, not when I knew I held her heart in my hands. Balto's instincts would tell her what to do in time, and we had our whole lives ahead of us.

Besides, I wasn't here for these updates — I was well aware of them all already. I'd come to this meeting to talk with Malachi and Max afterwards. Headquarters had been frustratingly slow in acknowledging the shifter crisis, and I was done waiting. We needed decisions, we needed action, *yesterday*. If they weren't ready to make the next move, I'd start without them.

I fiddled with my phone, checking for messages from Jade, the distance between us feeling monumental, even though she was just across town.

I should have been listening, but my thoughts drifted back to Jade for the hundredth time this morning. The feel of her smooth skin under my hands, the sounds she'd made as we'd moved together, the taste of her as I made her mine.

"You shouldn't be out in public until you're decent," came a low grumble from my left, and I blinked myself out of the filthy memories.

"What?"

Ryker waved his hand in my direction. "You newly mated wolves — your pheromones are suffocating all of us. Obscene."

I shrugged, unable to stop the grin from taking over my face. He wasn't wrong. This was one of the reasons newly mated wolves usually spent a good week together, working off some of those pheromones.

"You and Selene have been miserable to be around for years. Not so sure it's a *newly* mated problem, Scales."

He grunted, but my mind was already wandering again, picturing all the ways I still wanted to claim my mate, and suddenly my jeans were too tight.

"For the love of the gods, stop thinking about her or get the fuck out," Ryker hissed, covering his face with his hand to hide our whispered discussion from the other supes in the room, who were shooting glances our way.

Maybe he had a point.

Luckily, it seemed the meeting had wrapped up. Not that I had any idea what they'd gone over, but I'd hear about it eventually anyway.

I pushed back from the table, trying to refocus back on the room. Representatives from each supernatural species were here, the meeting a mixed bag of angels, witches, shifters, nymphs, and one demon. Noticeably, there was still no leader for the vampires; their species had been reluctant to come out of the shadows since we'd learned about them five years ago.

I shook hands with the people I knew, pulling from the depths of my control to contribute small talk when my mind wanted to be wholly focused elsewhere.

"I suppose congratulations are in order," Kit said with a knowing grin.

I shook my head, but couldn't hide my smile. "Not the greatest timing, but a mate bond wasn't about to be ignored."

He laughed, clapping me on the shoulder as he moved past, and my gaze snapped up as Togo's hackles rose.

"I'm surprised you're here," a voice sneered from behind me, and I turned, barely hiding my dislike as Vaughn Sawyer approached me. "Any real male wouldn't leave his mate so soon after initiating the bond."

I breathed deep, fighting the urge to shove this asshole against the wall. Even without prodding me when I was highly distracted, I hated this sad excuse for an Alpha.

It was no secret that Sawyer fought dirty, the story of how he'd become Alpha of the Redwood pack as gruesome as any I'd ever heard. No one in his pack had ever filed a formal complaint against him though, so my hands were tied unless I wanted to challenge him outright, then absorb his pack into my own. I was spread too thin as it was, but I knew I couldn't put off dealing with him forever.

"See, I earn this thing called loyalty in my people, something you know nothing about. I'm not worried about my mate, nor any of my pack. Considering you can't keep tabs on your own, you can shut your damn mouth."

Sawyer held my gaze, arms crossed over his chest. The look alone was a challenge, but he didn't pose a threat to me, no matter how much I despised him. My wolf was stronger than his, if push came to shove.

"What are you trying to say, Larkin? What do you know of my pack?" Sawyer asked, cold eyes glinting.

I opened my mouth to respond, but someone called my name from across the room.

"West." Max's voice was sharper than I was used to hearing from him, and he nodded his head towards a side room. "You wanted to speak with the Premier?"

The way his gaze slid to Sawyer told me there was something between the lines here. Clenching my jaw to stop the barbs I had locked and loaded for Sawyer, I left him without a word, striding after Max into an adjoining room.

He closed the door behind us, Malachi already seated at the

small conference table, his wings glimmering behind him. Unusual among angels, Malachi's wings weren't full-white, but darkened to a storm-grey by the bottom feathers.

With a wave of his hand, magic encased the room, sealing us into a sound-proof bubble. I looked between the two males, then frowned at Max.

"What was that about?"

Max sighed, taking a seat. "We don't think Sawyer *lost* Robbie." I approached the table, but was too keyed up to sit myself. "We think Robbie escaped, and for the kid's safety, let's not alert Sawyer he's been found."

His words hit me like a gut punch. "What are you talking about? I know Sawyer's an asshole, but —"

"Way worse than that," Max cut in. "We're still gathering evidence, but all signs point to Sawyer running an underground fight ring."

I was stunned.

"Tragic as that is, that's not why you wanted to meet with me," Malachi said, tapping his fingers impatiently on the table.

"Actually, I think that's exactly why. This is what I keep talking about." I gave Max a pointed look. "Missing shifters. Whether they're escaping a — fuck, a fight ring? — or not. Who is tracking them? Helping them?"

"What are you proposing? Microchips?" Malachi raised an eyebrow, and I fought the snarl in my throat.

"Not all shifters *want* to be tracked, West," Max added, then held up his hands when I turned my glare on him. "Just to point out all sides here."

"I don't have the answers yet, but this can't keep happening. The reason we restructured the Council was to even the scales and make sure we're taking care of *all* supernaturals, and I'm telling you, you're fucking failing. We all get those missing shifter reports, and the numbers are going up. But then what happens? Who is going after them, looking for them? Maybe not all of them want to be found, but what about the ones that *do*? That have been taken by fight rings or human kidnappers or fuck knows what, and who need someone to rescue them? I'm not going to shut up about this until something is done, Malachi."

The Premier held up his hands. "You're right. And it hasn't escaped my notice the lengths you're going to to make Timber Creek a welcome home to the lost shifters, but it can't just be you." His grey eyes slid to his son, his brow furrowing in thought. "Massimo, you know some of those circles. Perhaps this should be your next task."

Max scoffed. "Now that you were finally able to bust me out of prison, you mean?" My head tilted at that revelation, but Max pressed on. "Besides, everyone I know in *'those circles,'* as you put it, is pretty angry with me, either for betraying them or just being related to you. Nevermind what they'd do if it ever got out about my" — Max darted a look at me as his black wings shifted — "heritage."

Malachi waved a hand. "Larkin is trustworthy, son." Turning to me, the Premier said, "Massimo is half-vampire."

I blinked, trying and failing to hide my surprise. After the magic I'd seen him wield during the interrogation in my barn, I'd suspected Max was something more than angel. Not to mention his unusual dark hair and wings, different from any other angel I'd seen But it wasn't any of my business. I hadn't asked, and he'd never explained.

Max grumbled as he held up a hand, ticking off on his fingers. "Ex-con, half-vamp, related to *you*, half-angel and therefore associated with the PRICs, not even a shifter." He cocked his head in mock thought. "Did I forget any? Yes, I can see why you think I'd be perfect for this."

While I might have agreed with him, the truth was, we were desperate. I met Max's gaze. "Someone's got to do it."

Max frowned, finding himself outnumbered here.

"This has become too necessary to worry about who is *perfect* for it," Malachi said. "West is right. We can't let this go on any longer without addressing it. Maybe we need a shifter to partner you up with, to increase their trust." Turning to me, he gave a nod. "We'll figure something out."

I glanced between them, Max still looking less than convinced, but I knew he was a good male, and for all his faults, Malachi was usually a male of his word. "I'll hold you to that."

"Good." Malachi pushed back from the table, striding towards the door. "Then we'll see you tonight at the gala."

Chapter Forty-One

JADE

My fist hovered in the air to knock on the carriage house door, but Ruby yanked it open before I made contact.

"Took you long enough."

She crushed me in a hug on her front porch.

"Since when are you a morning person? I had to drag you out of bed to get you to school on time."

"Since my sister quite literally dropped into town and will leave again before I have enough time with her."

She tugged me into the carriage house and up the stairs to the apartment above Morgaine's garage.

I stopped on the landing, taking in the space. The walls were dark gray with white trim, but with the windows open to let in the ocean breeze, everything seemed alive and airy. Throw pillows were tossed across the teal couch, a variety of colors and floral patterns that all mixed perfectly with Ruby's feminine goth style she'd rocked for years.

Everything about the small apartment screamed *Ruby's Home* and emotion flooded me that she had this place to herself.

Ruby twisted a lock of her red-dyed hair around her finger. "Do you like it? Once I mentioned redecorating to Mo, she went overboard. A bunch of demons arrived the next day with Blaze and renovated it faster than I knew was possible."

Their generosity rendered me at a loss for words until my gaze landed on a glaringly bright tie-dye tapestry on the back wall. Extending a finger, I pointed, one eyebrow raised.

"Mo made it on a Tequila and Tie-Dye Tuesday." Ruby grimaced. "After everything she's done for me, I couldn't say no."

Throwing myself on the couch, I patted the seat next to me. Ruby dropped down into it, tossing an arm across my waist as she laid her head on my shoulder. Unable to help myself, I kissed the top of her hair, squeezing her back. She'd always been more touchy-feely than me, but seeing her here had unlocked how much I'd truly missed her. I'd been alone for so long, I'd forgotten what it felt like to have her near.

"You smell," Ruby said, voice muffled as she snuggled me.

I shoved at her face, pushing her off me with a laugh. "Really? Already ditching the niceties. Should I comment about the pile of clothes on the floor of your closet? Or that your drawers are shoved so full of clothes, the wood is warping as it tries to contain your mess? Maybe you're not as grown up as I thought."

Ruby slapped my arm and I clutched it, faking injury as she launched a pillow at me. Like no time had passed, I grabbed a handful of pretzels off the coffee table and tossed them at her.

"Don't mess up my home! I just cleaned it!"

"And now it all makes sense. That's why you're up early, right? Panic cleaning because I was coming over?"

Ruby picked a pretzel off the couch and ate it. "It's amazing how fast you can clean when you know your super organized big sister is on her way. If I leave you alone in here, you'll be alphabetizing my books in no time."

I rolled my eyes, but smiled. "Damn, I've missed you, you twerp."

Ruby grinned, hugging me again. "Same, jerk. And you really do smell. Why has your scent changed? It has this weird pine-y note to it now. Not bad, just different than I remember."

I fought not to lift my arm and sniff myself, wondering what she was talking about. If anything, I probably smelled like sex after the marathon West and I had last night and this morning, but I'd showered before coming over here. Maybe it was part of the whole mate bond thing, which I needed to ask West to explain better. I didn't regret it, not one bit, but I also didn't fully understand it. I wanted to be with him, and that was all that mattered.

With a shrug, I changed the conversation. "Tell me everything. I know we talk all the time, but it's different being together. I want to hear all about your life here."

Ruby hugged a magenta pillow to her chest, smiling as she told me all about her boyfriend Akil, working at Scallywags, all of Mo's many shenanigans, and her life here in Deadlights Cove. Ruby was genuinely happy, and our past wasn't weighing her down at all.

I'd questioned my decision to have Max remove her memories of our time with the Coven so many times, I'd beaten not only the dead horse but the flies hovering over it. No one can know how anyone else will handle their trauma, and I worried constantly that by taking Ruby's memories, I'd opened her up to walking into a similar situation someday.

But there was a huge difference between Ruby at 20 now and me when I'd met Thaddeus at 23. She had a community of people supporting her, guiding her, and loving her through whatever decisions she made. If she fell, there were people to pick her back up. If she got hurt, she had friends who would line up to take care of her. If she went missing, it wouldn't go unnoticed.

She'd never be vulnerable the way I'd been, solely because it was impossible not to love my quirky, emotional little sister once you got to know her. She was a bright light, despite our past.

"Why are you teary?" Ruby asked, stopping her storytelling as she reached across to grab my hand. "That's my job, not yours."

I gave her a watery smile. "Nothing. I'm just really happy you're here and finding a life perfect for you. Moving you to

Deadlights Cove was the right decision. Maybe I didn't do everything wrong."

Ruby frowned, squeezing my hand. "Jade. You've never done anything wrong by me. We were dealt a shitty hand, losing our parents so young, and you stepped up in every way you knew how. I can't imagine having a nine-year-old thrust on me right now, and yet, you did at my age. You raised me to the best of your abilities, and not a day goes by that I don't think how lucky I am to have you. I know how hard you worked to provide for me, and I'm so grateful I had you in my corner, always."

I pressed my palms into my eyes, my heart shattering and remaking itself at her words. Ruby had no memory of how bad I'd ruined everything, and yet she sat here thanking me for the life she had.

But that was a secret I intended to take to the grave.

Not only did she not know how terrible it had become in those years, she had no idea what I'd done in a fit of rage. It was bad enough she'd been involved — my sister, the empath she was, would never recover if she knew the brutality I'd resorted to. The blood that coated my hands.

She'd never look at me the same.

"Jade." She scooted forward to wrap her arms around me when I didn't recover fast enough, weighed down by the guilt of my past. "Hey. What's wrong? Why are you upset?"

I wrapped my hands around her, squeezing. Just the feel of her, whole, was enough to banish the memories of that day, to push them back to the recesses of my mind where they belonged. "I'm just really happy you're happy."

"These don't feel like happy tears. And I know all about the different kinds of tears."

A laugh bubbled out of me at that. "You do cry a lot."

"I do." Ruby chuckled. "Sue me."

After I didn't respond, she asked, "How is Timber Creek? Are you liking it there? You seemed pretty *chummy* with West last night, who, by the way, is just as much of a snack as I remembered."

I ducked my head, chin down as I bit back my smile at the mention of his name. "It's not bad."

Ruby's dark eyebrows climbed as she stared wide-eyed at me. "I'm going to need a heck of a lot more than that. At the very least, what's his secret guilty pleasure? And are you going to marry him and have his babies? Because they'd be cute as hell and I'd be a great aunt."

I side-eyed her, not sure how to answer the latter part. "It's possible he has a soft spot for *Super Smash* and *Mario Kart*."

"Ooh." Ruby grinned. "So you've been breaking out the Kirby power moves to put him in his place, then. I like it."

"I didn't even confirm we were together."

"Please," Ruby scoffed. "That's why you stink. His scent is all over you." Her eyes expanded as she leaned forward, sniffing me so aggressively compared to how I'd seen River scent things, it was like a slap in the face, a reminder of everything Ruby had lost because of me. "Are you his mate? Is that why you smell different?"

I jerked back, surprise clouding my thoughts. "What makes you think that?"

"I spend a lot of time around Akil and his family. There are a whole bunch of mated pairs and their scents kind of mingle, like what yours is doing. I don't know, maybe I'm wrong though. You know my wolf is pretty much non-existent these days."

There wasn't bitterness in her words, just resignation, but it still twisted the guilt even tighter in my chest. Forcing myself to focus on the topic at hand rather than let the past drag me under, I grinned.

"He just fucked me into next week yesterday and again this morning."

Ruby lifted her hands, shoving her fingers in her ears. "La la la la la. I can't hear you."

I smirked. "You asked."

"Yoohoo!" a voice called from downstairs. "Good morning girls! Anyone want to join me for pancakes?"

Ruby grabbed my hand, pulling me up from the couch. "Come on. Mo makes the best pancakes. Though whatever you do, don't eat any of the ones that have green flecks in them."

"Why?"

Ruby shuddered. "Trust me."

Mo was gone by the time we made it downstairs, but I followed Ruby across the backyard to the main house, stepping through the back door into the kitchen. A rainbow of color assaulted my senses — yellow cabinets, turquoise vintage appliances, a wooden table with twelve chairs, each a different color, around it.

"Welcome!" Mo said, a smile as bright as the hot pink floral kimono she wore over her yellow polka-dot pants. She lifted her arms, pulling me into a hug as she crushed me against her. Planting a kiss on my cheek, she grabbed both sides of my face, pulling back to study me. As uncomfortable as the move made me, this witch had done more for my family than I'd ever be able to repay her for, so I let her study me behind those big teal glasses that made her eyes double the size. Despite the fact that Mo looked to be in her mid-seventies, with wrinkles and a white bob of hair, I'd heard enough stories from Ruby to know the witch was at least several hundred years old.

"Mmm," she hummed contentedly, patting my cheek lightly before she let me go. "I don't even need to meddle here, do I?"

"See if you can put a spell on her that makes her not run for the hills the moment she feels comfortable," Ruby said as she pulled back the blue chair on the far side of the table. "We just need her to stay in one place long enough to make this relationship stick, rather than act like the wild wolf she is."

I shot Ruby a deadpan look, more annoyed than hurt by her words, because she wasn't wrong. And after our talk that day at

Cooper's house, I knew how much my running affected her. She just didn't understand *why*, but I had no intention of admitting the details of our past to her.

"Timber Creek has a way of weaving its own sort of spells," Mo said, taking the seat next to Ruby as she smiled at me, the look full of emotion that made me squirm. I knew mind-reading wasn't a power witches could have, but Brigid Morgaine was no ordinary witch. "I think your sister will be just fine."

Chapter Forty-Two

JADE

As the afternoon wore on, I glanced at the clock on Ruby's wall, Balto and I both feeling antsy the longer we spent apart from West. A few orgasms and I was already addicted.

"What time is the gala?" Ruby asked, combing through her closet to find something appropriately "formal" that wasn't also goth punk. Summer had thrown in a few sundresses for me, but they weren't *gala* material and I was getting nervous about my options.

"Seven. I need to start getting ready."

"How about this?" She twirled a red dress on its hanger.

I winced. "Red? With my green hair? What is it, Christmas in July?"

Holding it up to my neck, Ruby scrunched her nose. "Yeah, no. That's bad." She stuffed it back among her other dresses, rifling through them again. "And I'm guessing knee-length skater dresses don't count as formal."

"I highly doubt it."

A knock came from the exterior door downstairs, and Ruby and I exchanged a confused look.

"Mo again?" I asked, that same anxiety I'd felt for years surfacing. No one knew I was in Maine, and this was the farthest I'd ever been from the Coven's old stomping grounds, so I pushed my panic aside, trusting Balto's lack of response.

"I doubt it. She usually calls out." Ruby headed for the stairs to answer the door and pointed at another corner of the closet. "Try the skirts, maybe we can mix and match something."

I didn't want to alert Ruby, so I did as she asked, searching through her many skirts for something decent as she bounded down the stairs.

Then she shrieked, and I bolted for the stairs.

"*Ruby?!*"

"Oh, my GOD," came her reply in her best Janice-from-*Friends* impression as she raced back up the steps, and I ran to meet her at the top.

"Are you okay?"

Dramatically gasping, she presented the matte black box to me. A *dress* box.

"*Heboughtyouadress!*" she squealed in one breath.

My brows furrowed as I took the box from her, setting it on the coffee table to take a look.

Unease gripped me as I studied it, letting Balto's senses check it for anything suspicious, but West's pine scent was the only thing I could smell.

Ruby kept up a steady stream of excited giggles as I opened it, unfolding the tissue paper inside to find the dress of my wildest dreams.

It was a flowing, midnight blue maxi dress, overlaid with thin emerald green chiffon embroidered with leaves, the green a perfect match to my hair when it caught the light.

I pulled it out, holding it up to my chest and turning to Ruby.

"This is insane, right? Who the hell gets a dress delivered in real life?"

"Princesses!" Ruby shrieked when she looked back in the box. "There's a note! And shoes! Oh, my goddess, Akil better step up his game."

She shoved the note at me as she tried on the shoes, a pair of simple green velvet heels to match the leaves.

Gem,
I can't wait to take this dress off you tonight.
West

"Holy." I gulped, blinking at the card.

"What did he say?"

"Nothing!"

Ruby made a disgusted sound in her throat, clearly reading between the lines, and laughed. "Okay, well let's see it!"

With slightly wobbly knees, I went to change.

The fabric was silky smooth as it slipped over my skin, and I squeezed my eyes shut to let the moment linger. Savored this. Whether he'd chosen the dress or had Summer choose it for me, I couldn't have picked something more perfect for myself if I'd tried. Never had anyone made me feel seen like West did, understood and safe in a way that stole my breath.

Without knowing any of my horrible past, he accepted me as I was, made me feel wanted on a soul-deep level. I just had to hope that he'd still feel that way once he knew the truth, knew all the secrets I kept.

The thought of losing him was unbearable, hurting in a way I'd never seen coming.

I studied myself in the mirror. For the first time in years, I allowed myself to *want*, even for just this one moment.

I wanted to let West in.

I wanted to be the one he turned to when the world felt too heavy, to help shoulder his burdens.

I wanted to give him all of my ugly broken pieces, to let him see the real me, and still want me.

I wanted to be done hiding.

I wanted a pack, a family.

I wanted to be his mate.

I wanted *him.*

With a deep breath, I straightened my spine, accepting that

in order to have any of the things I wanted, I needed to trust him.

And that started tonight.

)))●(((

"Stop fiddling with your hair, woman!" Ruby slapped my hand down. "I did not spend an hour perfecting your curls and spelling them against this Goddess-awful Maine humidity for you to flatten them with your finger oils before you even leave the house."

Why was I nervous? Oh, right, because West bought me this super fancy dress and shoes that probably cost more than my old abandoned truck and I was about to go to an event with all the high-falutin folk of the supernatural world and meet *the* Premier of our world.

Your typical Friday night.

Ruby really had done a wonderful job on my hair and makeup. My curls were half-up in a twist secured with an opalescent crescent moon pin, the rest left to cascade over my shoulders. My makeup was understated, almost natural, with the main emphasis on my lips, which she'd done in a rich berry to contrast my hair and dress.

"I don't know where you learned all this, but thank you." I met her eyes in the mirror. "Now I just have to figure out how to walk in these shoes and hopefully remember I have lipstick on so I don't accidentally smudge it and look like a fool, and maybe I should stop hyperventilating."

"You'll have a big strapping male on your arm, so don't worry about tripping — he'll catch you." Ruby smirked. "As for the lipstick, this stuff is smudge-proof, so you'll be fine."

"Look at you, thinking of everything."

A knock sounded from downstairs, and I knew it was West.

Butterflies reignited in my stomach as I turned to Ruby again, our eyes widening.

"There's my ride," I offered, voice shaky, then shook my head as I realized how that sounded. "I didn't mean it like that."

Ruby snorted. "I've heard it both ways. This is a sex-positive space. Now let's go greet your gentleman caller. Wait, let me get my disposable camera! That's what you do for prom, right?"

"Don't you dare." I swatted her arm, but she was already laughing.

"Kidding. I'll leave you kids alone, but I *will* be spying out the window. And just because he buys you dinner does not mean you owe him anything, young lady!"

Shaking my head, I left Ruby in her bedroom — scurrying over to the window, as promised — and headed down to meet West.

My heart pounded loud enough, he could probably hear it through the door as I turned the handle. I pulled it open, and my lips parted at the sight of him in a crisp navy suit, white button-down, and a dark green tie that was the perfect match to my dress. His hair was styled back away from his face, tamed in a way I'd never seen it, his beard neatly trimmed.

West's eyes blazed from hazel to gold as he took me in, reaching for my hand to pull me outside and close the door. In an instant, his other hand was on my waist, tugging me closer until my body was flush against his, his pine scent extra strong tonight, intoxicating my senses.

"You look good enough to devour, mate," he breathed in my ear, nibbling the shell of it. "I can't wait to ruin this dress."

I gasped, pulling back to slap him on the chest even as my body responded to his words, fire lighting in my veins. "Absolutely not, Alpha. This dress is way too beautiful to ruin. I won't allow it."

West raised a brow in challenge, a smirk pulling on his lips in a decidedly delicious way. "Are you trying to order me around again?"

He raised a hand to thread it through my hair, but before he could, a voice called out from above, "Do *not* ruin those curls, West Larkin!"

I rolled my eyes. "Stop spying on us!"

"Never! This is for your own good!"

Pressing his lips together, West tried and failed to smother a laugh, but pointedly dropped his hand, wrapping my arm through his instead.

As we stepped off Ruby's porch and started down the street, I could have sworn a curtain swung closed inside Mo's house, as though someone had just been peering out the window. West must have noticed it too, because he chuckled and leaned down to whisper, "And you thought Timber Creek folks were nosy."

I hummed. "Maybe it's all supes?"

Chapter Forty-Three

JADE

Soft acoustic music played in the hall as we entered, the space illuminated with chandeliers, casting soft warm light over the guests mingling at high-top tables. Everything was classy and beautiful in a way I hadn't expected at "The Last Resort" motel.

Glances flitted our way from dozens of strangers, and my nerves kicked up again at being surrounded by this many unknown supernaturals. I leaned into West, needing to remind myself I was safe as long as I was with him. "Why The Last Resort? Seems like a terrible name for a hotel, especially one as beautiful as this."

West bent to speak in my ear. "You should have seen this place a few years ago." His warm breath over my skin was enough to have me gripping him tighter, my hormones in over-drive around this male, especially now that I knew exactly how he could use his body. "It's been a dump for years, but Orion and Devanna took over the property and redid it. I heard he wanted to change the name, but got hung up with some sort of kerfuffle with the Historical Society. Which is run by Devanna."

I frowned, turning to look up at West. "Aren't they together?"

West kissed me on the temple, and slipped his hand around my back, guiding me through the crowd. "Yes. Arguing is like foreplay for those two. I've learned it's best not to ask questions where they're involved."

We wound our way through the crowd to the bar along the far wall, grabbing drinks before turning to look over the room.

"Do you know all these people?" I asked, taking a sip of my wine.

West nodded, and began to point out various people around the room. "That's Darius, Alpha of the local pack here. Over there, in the bolo tie, is Tulok — he's something like the Orion to a small supe town in Alaska. You probably know Ostara, she was the head of Coven here, but her son Lysander runs it now — he's the one speaking with Devanna."

I tried to keep up with all the names, but quickly lost track as West pointed out one supe leader after another from all over the country. It was clear, though, that West had known these people for a long time — this was as much his social circle as his pack, and that fact sent me reeling. The upper levels of supe society were so far outside my comfort zone, it gave me a whole new view of the life West led outside of his pack.

"And this" — West wrapped an arm around my waist, turning us to face two approaching angels — "is Malachi Russo, and of course you already know his son Max."

I took a steadying breath as I offered a polite smile to the Premier, leader of the Council and head of all supernatural society. Where Max's wings were fully black, along with his hair, Malachi's wings were a grey ombré from light to dark. There was a distinct familial resemblance between them, though Malachi had the silver hair typical of angels and looked a few decades older than Max. With the way angels aged, that could mean he was anywhere from thirty to three hundred years older than his son.

"Ms. Rodriguez, a pleasure to meet you at last," Malachi said, extending a hand. I shook it, still bewildered he knew who I was. "Though of course, not under the best circumstances."

My eyes darted to West, then Max, before returning to Malachi, wondering how much Max had told him.

"Should we go somewhere quieter?" Max asked, and when

Malachi and West nodded, led the way out of the main ballroom and into a smaller meeting room down a short hallway.

"Massimo and West have been telling me you went through an attempted kidnapping recently," Malachi started, taking a seat at the conference table and motioning me into a chair. West took the seat beside me, and Max sat on the other side of the table. "But what we need to know is, what is the connection between that attempted kidnapping and your history with the Black Rose Coven."

My heart lurched just hearing the name of Thaddeus's Coven again, and I swallowed heavily. West shifted in his seat, his brow furrowing as he sensed my distress, but I kept my eyes fixed on Malachi.

"Why would you think there's any connection between them?" I asked, my mouth dry.

Malachi's gaze slid to Max before returning to me. "It seems highly unlikely for you, a witch-shifter hybrid, to be kidnapped at random, when there is a known Coven who needs supernaturals exactly like you for their experiments, and with whom you were previously affiliated."

Tensing, I tried not to flinch as I felt the weight of West's stare. I didn't want all that history rehashed here, in front of him. *I* wanted to be the one who told him my story.

Malachi waved a hand in the air dismissively. "The how of it doesn't matter. I'd like to bring you to Headquarters to consult with us on how to bring down the Black Rose Coven, once and for all. But I understand you've just mated with West, so I'll give you time to adjust to this new bond." He smiled, his eyes glancing between us, but ice slid down my spine at his words.

I didn't want to go anywhere near headquarters or have anything to do with the Coven ever again. I wanted to leave it all in my past and start anew in Timber Creek with West.

The three of them talked logistics as my mind raced. West's hand slid to my thigh under the table and squeezed in solidarity, supporting me, even without knowing all the details of my horrific past.

My phone buzzed while they were talking, and I slipped it out of my bag under the table, not wanting Malachi to think I was being rude.

Then I read the message, and had to fight to keep my face neutral.

UNKNOWN NUMBER

It's time, baby. Ditch the body guards and meet me behind the motel.

What followed was a long range image of Ruby sitting on her porch, wearing the outfit I had left her in.

My stalker had found my sister.

If it was Thaddeus — it *had* to be — I knew just how much danger she was in.

My vision darkened as panic took over, narrowing to pinpricks before I remembered to breathe.

"Jade? Are you all right?"

I nearly leapt out of my skin when West's palm gently squeezed my thigh. My hands shook, maybe my entire body was shaking, but I couldn't let him know. Couldn't let him see me like this.

Balto snarled at me, insisting I let her help, or let West help, but there was nothing either of them could do. I couldn't let anything bad happen to my sister, never again.

She mattered more than anything else, always.

I had no choice.

"Just feeling a little unsettled — rehashing it all," I managed to say, forcing a smile. My mind disconnected from my body in an all-to-familiar way, excuses rising easily to my tongue. "I'm going to run to the bathroom and maybe grab a glass of water."

West started to stand, but I waved him to sit back down. "Honestly, I'm fine. I'll be back in a minute."

Before he could argue, I gave them a tiny wave and hurried out of the room, heading towards the bathroom first in case anyone saw me. Instead of going inside, I kept walking past it, down the hallway, then through the lobby, and outside.

My heart thundered in my chest as I slipped into the shadows around the side of the motel, then hesitated at the corner, my back pressed firmly against the wall.

This was the part in the horror movie where everyone yelled at the main character for being an idiot. I knew that. But I also knew that I'd do anything to protect my sister, and this fucker had proved he knew exactly where to find her.

With a deep breath, I clenched my fists at my sides and forced myself to take the final step around the corner.

Nothing. There was no one waiting. Not Thaddeus, or anyone else.

I frowned, looking around the wooded area behind the motel, peering into the darkness. Were they just messing with me, and they'd never been here? Were they actually with Ruby right now?

Arms clamped around my sides from behind me. I took a breath to scream, but a palm slapped down over my mouth.

Hot breath swept over my ear as a voice I'd never wanted to hear again crooned, "Long time no see, baby."

Chapter Forty-Four

JADE

Thaddeus.

I thrashed in his arms, trying to wrench myself free, but a stinging burst of magic sparked across my skin, binding my wolf and most of my strength. He laughed darkly against my back at my attempts, only ramping up my rage. I sank my teeth into his hand until he hissed and lowered it.

"Let me *go*." I aimed to stamp my heel into the top of his foot, but he moved it just in time.

"Don't be like this, baby," he murmured, nipping at my ear. At one point, I'd loved the sound of his deep voice, the feel of his lips on my skin, but now everything in me recoiled from him. "I've been waiting to have my hands on you again for five years. I won't let you go so easily."

His arms tightened around my chest until I struggled to fill my lungs. Balto's teeth were fully bared in my mind's eye, froth dripping from her snarling jaws, begging me to let her shift and tear Thaddeus apart. For once, I was ready to let her have her way, but whatever spell Thad had cast on me made it impossible.

"Thaddeus —" I gasped, batting at his hands as my heart raced. "Can't — breathe —"

"If I let you go, will you be good for me, baby?"

The snarl that escaped my throat at his repeated use of *baby* told me my wolf felt the same.

Another bitter chuckle rumbled against my back, and his grip tightened. "Apparently not."

"Please —" I was getting lightheaded as I fought to pull in anything more than a shallow breath as his arms squeezed against my torso. "Thaddeus —"

"I missed hearing you say my name." He placed a kiss far too tender for the moment below my ear. But finally, he loosened his hold.

Staggering forward, I doubled over as I gasped for air, planting one hand on the wall to steady myself. I barely caught my breath before Thaddeus shoved me up against the rough brick, grasping my wrists in one hand and holding them above my head, the other hand going around my throat.

"Here's what's going to happen, baby," he said, his eerily light blue eyes almost white in the darkness. I wished his outside matched his inside, but Thaddeus was as stunningly handsome as he'd been when I met him nine years ago. Nothing about the golden-blond man towering over me said *monster*, but I knew better now. He'd lured me in with a promise of safety and security, and I'd gone to him like a bug drawn to the bright colors of a venus fly trap. "You're coming with me, back to the Coven where you belong."

I glared, furious not only with him, but at myself for ever believing he was anything but poisonous. "Are you out of your —"

His grip tightened around my neck, and I snapped my mouth shut as he sank his weight onto me, pinning me in place even more. Thaddeus had always gotten off on controlling me, and this was his favorite game to play.

I should have been afraid, but anger boiled in me and I wanted to lose myself in my rage.

Bringing his lips to my ear, his cheek pressed against mine. "If you fight me, we'll go after that ridiculous town you've been hiding away in. Timber Creek? Don't think I haven't noticed how West has his hands all over you and how you think you can fit in with his little family. I have eyes everywhere, Jade. I've seen how happy you are there, without me. It's time for that to end. No one gets your smiles but me."

My heart galloped, fear overshadowing the rage I'd felt moments before at the thought of harm coming to Timber Creek. I wasn't stupid enough to underestimate Thaddeus and the Coven again — they were far more powerful than I'd ever understood.

"We'll take West's wolves out one by one — keeping anyone who might be useful for us — and then we'll level the whole place to the ground. How convenient that West's niece is only half-wolf. She'd make an excellent candidate for us, don't you think? And so young. So much potential. You wouldn't make me go after her, would you?"

Panic rose in me as I struggled against his hold, desperation taking over as my mind painted a gruesome picture of little River in the same shape I'd found Ruby in years ago. Another burst of magic tingled across my skin, ruining any ability I had to push him off, but I shook with barely contained energy. "If you go anywhere near her, West will slaughter you."

Thaddeus chuckled, the dark rumble ominous as his fingers flexed on my neck, his grip turning painful. "You have so much faith in him. But do you think he'd protect you the way I did? I kept the Coven from using you for years, my sweet Jade. So broken, so lonely, so desperate to please. I've missed you so much."

His lips trailed across my jaw and I jerked in his hold, repulsed.

"In case that isn't incentive enough," he kissed just below my ear, "if you agree to come with me now, if you don't fight me, we'll leave Ruby alone for good. A failed experiment that should be eliminated, but I'll hide her from our records."

He pulled back to meet my eyes. How could I have not seen the crazy in them when we'd first met? Or had he gotten worse over the years?

"How could I ever trust you?"

The corner of his brow lifted. "I'll pledge it."

A magical pledge was binding spellwork — as long as I made sure he worded it correctly, it would be foolproof. He would never be able to go after Ruby again.

"Ruby — or Timber Creek — ever again. The Larkins are untouchable. You'll leave all of them alone. You, *and* the whole Coven." My mind raced, needing to make sure I had everything covered.

Was I really doing this? Considering giving myself back over to the Coven — to *Thaddeus* — in exchange for Ruby and Timber Creek's safety?

Moonlight glinted against his eyes as his gaze traced over my face, then lower, all over my body, still flush against his.

"I'll swear it, Jade." He moved his hand from my throat to caress my jaw, brushing his thumb over my chin, his touch now tender. "You're the one I need."

I nodded, and when my heart wanted to shatter, I coated it in steel.

"I knew you'd see reason. Trust me, baby. This is for the best."

"Vow it. Now, or I'll fight you every inch of the way back to the Coven."

That low, poisonous laugh cut through the night air as Thaddeus leaned in. "You say that as if you have a choice. But I'm a man of my word."

I bit the insides of my cheeks to keep from antagonizing him. "Vow it."

Thaddeus smiled, but it didn't meet his cold eyes. He pulled back enough to hold out his hand and I placed mine in his. The flash of metal in the moonlight was my only warning before his blade cut into my palm, and I hissed at the sharp pain. He shot me a look full of condescension, like I was weak for acknowledging the pain, then cut his own palm and pressed it to mine. The buzz of magic passed between us when he spoke.

"I vow to keep Ruby Rodriguez and the town of Timber Creek out of the reach of the Coven, including myself."

"And the Larkins."

His eyebrow hitched up. "Are they not in Timber Creek?"

"Vow it."

Magic tingled over my hand again, and Thaddeus's blue eyes settled on mine. "I vow it."

I dropped his hand the moment the magic was done, wiping mine on the wall at my back, a desperate attempt to get him off me.

Thaddeus stepped away from me as a black SUV rolled to a stop feet from us. He held a hand out to help me walk across the uneven ground, but I pulled away from him.

I was done with needing anything from Thaddeus.

A grin tipped the corner of his mouth as I stepped into the car, and I saw a hint of the man who had charmed his way into my life, once upon a time.

What a fool I'd been.

Chapter Forty-Five

WEST

Minutes ticked by after Jade left, Malachi and Max discussing how they planned to try to take down the Black Rose Coven, but I was too distracted to follow their conversation.

After Atlas dug up everything he could on Bram, I'd suspected Jade might have been involved, but the angels made it sound like she'd been in pretty deep with the Coven. Yet she didn't wear their tattoo — so how involved could she have been?

I couldn't focus, finally dismissing myself from the conversation as I headed the direction Jade had gone.

"Jade?" I called as I pushed the women's bathroom door slightly ajar. No one answered, and I didn't scent her either, which was strange. Had she never made it here?

Senses alert, Togo came forward in my mind, sniffing the air. We caught her scent, but only a trace — she'd been here, but had gone past the bathroom. I moved towards the exit door at the end of the hall, following her trail. The moment I stepped outside, I knew something was wrong.

Her usual citrus scent turned sour. My head snapped in all directions, looking for her, but I couldn't see her.

Moving quickly, I tracked her around the side of the building. It wasn't just her scent here — there was another scent as well — *male*, which Togo growled at. Jade's had turned pungent with fear, and the thought she was in danger had my vision flickering between Togo's and mine.

Then — blood. I scented her blood, and nearly shifted on the spot.

Find him. Kill him, Togo snarled, slamming into the barrier between us.

Reaching into my pack bonds, I felt for her mate bond. While she'd let me mark her, she hadn't reciprocated yet and she still wasn't pack, so the connection wasn't as strong. I could sense her panic, but couldn't trace the bond to her exact location.

My heart raced as I fumbled to loosen my tie, my claws itching to punch out, ready to let my wolf out when I spotted the cabins in the distance. I took off at a sprint, telling myself I was overreacting and I'd find her inside, safe and sound.

The door banged against the wall as I threw it open, claws almost distended as I prepared to rip whoever had hurt her to shreds.

But she wasn't here, and her scent was stale. She hadn't returned since we'd left this morning. I stormed back outside, pulling my phone out.

"Dammit, pick up, Jade," I grumbled as it rang through, going to her voicemail. Ending the call, I raced back to where I'd last caught her trail at the motel.

Now I saw the tire tracks streaking the grass, leading back to the road. I spun in the direction they'd gone, desperate panic seizing me at my helplessness.

My heart slammed in my chest as I took off at a run down the road, not caring that there was no way I could find her on foot. Standing in the middle of the road, I stared in both directions, but their scents disappeared beneath gasoline.

Fuck.

Whipping my phone out again, I dialed the one person who might be able to help me locate them.

"You're getting needy, West."

"Max," I snapped, then took a steadying breath. This wasn't

his fault, and I needed his help. "Sorry. Get out here. Jade is gone."

Rustling on his end. "Gone?"

"I'm on the main road. Her scent disappeared by the motel, and there are tire tracks. I need you to use whatever angel-vamp magic you have to try to find her, and then I need you to tell me *everything*."

My eyes shifted between my wolf and mine, and I blinked hard, fighting him down. My muscles spasmed with the urge to shift, my teeth ached to punch into fangs fit for shredding flesh. But I needed to be human right now, no matter how much Togo wanted to take over and track Jade down. "I think Jade's secrets caught up with her."

)>>●《《(

"His name is Thaddeus Webb," Max began wearily, pouring himself a large, steaming mug of black coffee from the motel samovar in the breakfast room. Despite whatever angel-vamp powers he had, he hadn't been able to garner any information from the scene about what might have happened, or where Jade had gone. Only who she'd been with. "If anyone from the Coven would be able to manipulate her, it's him."

My knuckles whitened where I gripped the back of a wooden chair, the wood creaking under my palms.

Thaddeus Webb. Finally, my target had a full name.

"Go on," I growled, pushing off the chair to pace the vacant room again, the gala still going on in the ballroom down the hall.

"After the leaders of the Black Rose Coven were murdered five years ago, he became the de facto leader. As far as I know, he found Jade when she was young and vulnerable, and made her dependent on him."

"Why isn't he in fucking jail? How could you and the PRICs have let the Coven go? You and Malachi made it sound like

they're behind at least some of the missing shifters, and you just
—"

"We were working on it," Max continued. "I'd been undercover for a while, gathering evidence to put them away for a long
time. Then one night, it all went to shit." He gave me a pointed
look, and I fought not to bare my teeth at him. "The Coven
experiments on supernaturals, specifically hybrid shifters. The
idea was to create a supernatural who could be both parts of
their genetics to their fullest extent. Typically, half-shifters are
one or the other — they can shift but not access the magic from
their other genes, or they can't shift but can use their other
magic. The Coven wants both — in Jade's case, a half-wolf half-
witch who can heal and fight like a shifter *and* perform magic at
the same level as a full witch. Imagine the possibilities, West.
They're creating an army."

I swore under my breath, thinking of the hybrid shifters listed
on every email from Headquarters. They knew, and they'd been
withholding information.

"Ruby had a stronger connection to both her wolf and her
witch magic from the start, so they'd been experimenting on her
for a while, but something went wrong. Whatever the Coven did
left Ruby's wolf dead, and Ruby herself not far behind. Ruby will
never access her wolf again, and Jade begged me to take away
the knowledge that she'd ever been able to shift. To erase the
worst memories of her abuse."

I blinked, a mixture of despair and rage filling me for everything Jade and her sister had been through.

"Jade didn't know any of the experiments were going on;
Thaddeus purposefully kept her out of the loop and she was too
low-powered in her witch abilities to ever be admitted into the
Coven. When she found Ruby almost dead —" Max scrubbed a
hand over his face. "You can imagine. She lost her mind, lost
herself to her wolf, and it was chaos. She killed eight witches that
day, West, and injured more. I had to make a call."

I stopped pacing to stare at him, desperate for the next words out of his mouth, so much of Jade's hesitancy towards her wolf and my pack clicking into place. My heart tore that my mate had had to go through that without me at her side.

"If I hadn't gotten them out that night, the Coven would have killed her for what she did. I made it to the scene when she'd taken out everyone else — the other witches were on their way but hadn't arrived yet. I could hear their footsteps. Jade was growling at me, still a wolf, ready to lash out and try to take me too."

A tiny twinge of pride flared in my chest for the ferocity of my mate.

"She didn't deserve to die, and neither did Ruby. I knew I could get them out, but I didn't have time to second-guess it. I knocked her out with magic, grabbed them, and vanished us the fuck out of there."

He lifted his head, and I raised a brow at this new term he used.

"Vanishing is sort of like flickering but for vampires, where we can become shadow." I nodded as Max let out a deep sigh, his black wings shifting behind him, completely nonchalant about revealing that startling tidbit of information about his species. "By the time anyone from the PRICs was able to get to the compound, the Coven was gone without a trace."

"Okay." I lowered myself into a chair, turning over the information about Jade and her past. "But that was five years ago, right? How have you not found them by now? Where would they be hiding?"

Max raised a brow. "They're a group of very powerful witches, West. They're smart. They've stayed on the move, and they use magic to cloak themselves. When I questioned Bram Rasmus, I encountered one of the strongest cloaking spells in his mind I've ever felt. If I'd attempted to pry any deeper, I would have scrambled his mind irrevocably, probably without even breaking through the spell. We've gotten close a few other times, but without someone on the inside anymore…" He lifted a shoulder. "I blew my cover. But every time I see those Rodriguez girls alive, I can't bring myself to regret it."

So much of his story made sense, putting together the missing puzzle pieces to Jade's story. Her paranoia. Her anxiety. Her distrust of my pack. Her nightmares. Her guilt. Her hero worship of the male before me.

Letting my head hang between my shoulders, I ran through the information again. And again. Trying to see a way through this, a way to find her.

"I doubt he'll hurt her, if that's what you're worried about."

I scowled at him. "He already did."

"What?"

I pushed to my feet again, feeling the trace of pain in my connection to Jade. "I scented her blood out there. I can feel her pain. But she's fucking *gone*, and something is messing with my ability to get a read on her location."

"Her blood?"

My pulse pounded in my ears, my vision shifting rapidly.

"We'll find her, West. We'll find her, and the Coven, and this time, we'll make sure they don't get away."

My head jerked up at his words, and I glared at him. "What the fuck are you talking about? You just said you haven't been able to find them in five years. Now, magically, you can?"

A dangerous grin crept over Max's face as he nodded. "Exactly."

"What's the plan, then?"

"We can amp up your mate bond with a little help from a witch. The Coven notoriously underestimates shifters, especially a mate bond. They don't have a similar concept, and the majority of the Coven is more interested in pure bloodlines for everything but their experiments. Whatever spell they've put on her, I bet we can overpower it and track her down through your bond," he explained, annoyingly calm.

"Who said she's my mate?"

He gestured to my entire being. "Witches can't scent a mate bond, but I can." Draining the last of his coffee, he stood and clapped me on the shoulder. "I'm going to find Malachi and get a team from HQ assembled and ready to go. Find Brigid Morgaine and tell her you need to trace your mate bond. She'll know what to do. Text me once you know where we're going."

I stared at him, dumbfounded it could be so simple. Sure, I could faintly sense Jade through the pack bonds, but depending on how far away she was now, who knew if this could actually work? And without her in my pack yet, would the bond be strong enough to —

"Hey. Less panicking, more witchcraft." Max gave my shoulder a squeeze and strolled off for the hallway back to the ballroom.

Right. Mo. I needed to find Mo.

Chapter Forty-Six

JADE

I flinched as Thaddeus's hand landed on my thigh and gave it a squeeze before he stroked up and down my leg. There was a time when I'd lived for his touch, but that ship had sailed long ago, then burned and sank to the depths of the ocean when he'd taken everything from Ruby. Now, I compared the cold touch that made me recoil to the one I'd spent last night in.

I thought I'd been in love with Thaddeus once upon a time, but it didn't even compare to the way I felt about West.

Loving West was an all-encompassing feeling, inescapable in its intensity.

No matter how painful it was to be back here with Thaddeus, putting myself through this again, I would do anything to keep the Coven as far as possible from West and Ruby.

"Relax, baby. You'll be home safe soon."

I fought the full-body shudder his words incurred, turning my attention to the heavily tinted windows in the back of the SUV. A partition separated us from the driver, and I wasn't familiar enough with Deadlights Cove to have a good handle on where I was, even if I could make out any of my surroundings in the dark.

I was well and truly trapped.

Balto paced in my consciousness, teeth bared in a silent snarl at being locked inside my head. I wrapped my arms around my waist and inched as far away from Thaddeus on the bench seat as I could. Despite the heat of summer outside the vehicle, it was winter cold inside.

Thaddeus shot me a disdainful look but pulled his hand back, draping his arm over the back of the seat instead.

"Where are we going? Where's" — I choked over the word — "*home?*"

The lines around his eyes softened at my words, though I knew he wasn't stupid enough to believe I'd come around so quickly.

"You'll see." He turned earnest, pale blue eyes on me. Eyes I'd once found beautiful, that I'd once compared to glacier ice. If only I'd realized at the time how apt that analogy was. "Jade, I want us to start over. I didn't want to be so rough with you earlier, but you don't understand how much I missed you, baby. The last thing I'd ever want is to scare away or hurt the woman I love. Knowing you were here with another man was too much for me to handle, and my emotions took over. I know how you left was upsetting —"

My nose wrinkled in disdain, not buying a single word of the shit spewing out of his mouth.

"— But things are different now. What happened back then — it was a wake-up call. We don't practice like that anymore."

"Yeah, right."

"You'll see," he repeated, his tone just short of patronizing. "I know we have a long way — *I* have a long way — to go before I regain your trust." The corner of his mouth quirked up, just barely. It made him look younger, almost boyish, especially with his surprising black lashes against his pale skin. Even now, I couldn't deny he knew how to make himself charming. "But it'll be worth it, I know it will."

We pulled off the highway, and I realized we were heading to a small airstrip. A ball of lead dropped into my stomach as the reality of my situation hit me.

We were leaving.

I was leaving with Thaddeus.

I'd been running from this exact moment for five years, and it had all been for nothing.

Well, maybe not *nothing*. Ruby was safe, I reminded myself. That was all that mattered.

The car parked, and I moved for the door, but Thaddeus cleared his throat, halting my movements.

"Give me your bag."

I glanced down at the purse in my lap, which I'd been clutching for dear life, not that it would save me now. With a heavy swallow, I passed it over to him.

Thaddeus ripped it open, digging through it, and as I should have expected, fished out my phone. My brand new phone from West.

Lowering the window, Thaddeus handed the phone off to the driver, who'd left the vehicle and come around the side of the car.

"That's mine," I choked out uselessly, my one lifeline to the outside world vanishing into some Coven stooge's suit jacket after he'd powered it down. Unable to be traced.

"And when you show me I can trust you again, maybe I'll get you a new one." Thaddeus finished looking through my bag for anything else he might deem unacceptable, then shoved it back at me. "It's not safe for you to run off again, Jade. So be a good little girl, and you can have phone time to call your sister."

Nausea swirling in my gut, I hugged my bag to my chest and wordlessly followed Thaddeus onto the private plane.

)))●(((

Thaddeus still wouldn't say where we were headed, so I kept my eyes peeled to the window, trying to take note of any geographical features that might help me orient myself. But at some point, the lack of sleep and stress got to me, and I fell asleep, dreams of wolves in cages haunting me.

It was dark when Thaddeus shook me awake, the plane already taxiing down a runway.

"There's a toiletry kit in the bathroom if you want to clean up." He nodded towards the back of the plane. "And there's a set of fresh clothes for you."

He shot a glance down at my dress, the most beautiful thing I'd ever worn and my last tie to West. Before he could make some remark about it, I headed for the bathroom, grabbing the bundle of clothes on the seat and bringing it in with me.

I knew the real meaning under his words.

Clean up? *Don't embarrass me by looking a mess in front of the rest of the Coven.*

New clothes? *Don't you dare wear something another man bought you while you're with me.*

I stared at my reflection in the tiny mirror, my hair a mess after the way he'd handled me, my makeup smudged. I wiped at my face, clearing any trace of our altercation as I stared at the bite mark on my shoulder. Tracing my fingers over it, I held the memories of my month with West, locking them inside me.

I wouldn't let Thaddeus break me, not this time. I could wear his stupid clothes and follow his rules, but he'd never get his hands on my heart again. It wasn't mine to give anymore.

When I emerged from the bathroom in the simple black dress he'd given me, Thaddeus broke into a smile, carelessly taking my bundled dress and tossing it aside like garbage before cupping my face.

"You're always so beautiful, baby." He pressed a soft kiss to my forehead before pulling back. "I can't wait to show you every-thing we've been doing, all the progress we've made. And everyone will be so happy to see you again."

I found that hard to believe, seeing as I'd killed eight of their nearest and dearest friends, but kept my mouth shut. I wasn't sure how much the others knew about the events of that day, and wasn't about to make myself a target needlessly. When Bram had seen me in Timber Creek, there'd been no hint that he saw me as a mass-murderer, so my bet was that Thaddeus had pinned the murders on someone other than me to protect his own reputation.

Fine by me. They could all underestimate me, once again.

After I took my seat again, Thaddeus opened his suit jacket and pulled out a small box. My stomach dropped at the sight, knowing what lay within.

"Can't forget this," Thaddeus said, pulling out the diamond solitaire ring he'd given me six years ago. Balto slammed against the barrier in my mind, but she was still magically contained as he lifted my left hand, sliding the ring onto my finger. My hand shook even though I tried to hide the tremor, but Thaddeus squeezed my fingers, then lifted my hand to his mouth, kissing my knuckles. As he dropped my hand, I tried to remind myself that it was just a ring, not the shackle it felt.

Off the plane, all I could see besides the airport hangar was forest, which didn't help me identify where we were. An hour or so drive through winding back roads brought us to a giant, wrought-iron gate that opened when the driver hit a buzzer on the side of the driveway.

"Looks like you've leveled up from the old dorms."

Thaddeus hummed noncommittally as the car made its way up a winding, elegant cobblestone drive, a large Victorian-style mansion coming into view.

"Before we go inside," Thaddeus began, pausing until I turned to face him, "I want to make sure you remember how this works."

I could feel my blood pressure rising, but clenched my jaw against any outward sign of my anger.

"Do yourself a favor, baby." He gave me a sympathetic

grimace, patting my hand. "Your life here can be so easy if your behavior meets my expectations. You know that, right?"

The air was cool outside the car, much less humid than it had been in Maine, and the scent in the air made me think we were back in the Rocky Mountains. Thaddeus ran a hand through his golden-blond hair, giving it that effortlessly messy look as his smile widened. Without waiting for my answer, he held the carved oak front door open for me, gesturing me inside.

"I told the others to join us in the meeting room." His palm found the small of my back, guiding me down a maze of hallways, the sound of conversation increasing the further we went until the hall opened into a large, overly bright space.

The room fell silent, all heads swiveling to us in the entrance. I wanted to crawl into a hole and never come out, but Thaddeus had other plans.

His arm wrapped around my waist, tugging me into his side as he grinned and pressed a kiss to my cheek.

"She's back!" he announced, and a chorus of welcome rose from the others that did nothing to ease my nerves. "After all these years, my little wandering wolf is safe back home. I trust you all to make her feel welcome and part of the family again in no time. For now, let's celebrate the return of this goddess among us mere mortals!"

One of the kids brought over a tray of champagne, and Thaddeus handed me one before taking one for himself.

"To Jade!"

The others echoed the toast, and Thaddeus clinked my glass before twining his arm around mine, nodding at me to do the same, and we drank to a round of cheers. I downed mine in one.

Thaddeus only smiled, and gestured for the kid to bring me another, before tugging me along with him to make the rounds to the others individually.

Many of his lead witches were new — unsurprising, since I'd

killed most of the old ones — and I wondered how he'd explained the many vacancies to them.

"So Jade, we've heard all about you," one of the witches said, eyeing me shrewdly over the rim of her champagne glass. "Where did you run off to all these years?"

His hand tightened on my waist, and he answered before I had to. "My Jade is a free spirit. I sent her off to rediscover her wolf, but she's home for good now."

The witch shot me a dubious look, but didn't comment on that, and moved on after a few more minutes of idle chit chat.

"Jade?"

My head turned at the familiar voice, and I watched Bram carefully as he worked his way towards me, trying to discern if his memory of our last encounter was well and truly gone the way Max had told me it was. If Bram wasn't the one to track me to Timber Creek, who was?

"You look so good. And your hair is longer. I love it." Thaddeus dropped my hand as Bram pulled me into a hug, and I searched for any of the tells Aspen and I had talked about to know if someone was lying. Bram's heart was even, his breathing normal. As easy as it would be to believe it had been him who betrayed me, I didn't think it was.

I lifted a hand to his waist, hoping whatever goodness in Bram I'd known back then still existed.

"I've been so worried about you," he said, pulling back from me as he dropped his hands to his sides.

I feigned a smile. I doubted it convinced anyone. "I'm back."

Bram pulled me deeper into the room, introducing me to new members I didn't know, but I felt Thaddeus's eyes following me as we wandered through the crowded space.

I lost count of the number of champagne glasses I drained, of the false smiles I plastered on my face, and soon I was fighting back yawns.

"Hey, Thaddeus?" I turned to him when another witch

drifted off, pressing a hand to his warm chest, and blinking at the deja vu of it all. "I'm pretty tired. Do you mind —"

His hand closed over mine on his chest. "Of course, baby. Let's get you to bed."

I dreaded those implications, but I was dead on my feet, and sighed in relief as we left the bright lights of the meeting room.

"Watch your step, these old stairs aren't even."

Right on cue, I tripped, and Thaddeus scooped me up.

He chuckled, his voice rumbling in his chest as he carried me up the stairs. "I almost forgot what a lightweight you are."

"I blame your fancy-ass champagne."

Setting me down just inside a room, he steadied me on my feet before flicking on a light switch, soft warm lighting illuminating —

"I hope you like it, baby."

My mouth dropped open as I took in the room that only faintly spun. Propping myself up on the wall with one hand, I blinked to clear the haze from my vision.

He'd designed this room for me. The walls were a rich forest green — my favorite color — with the ceiling painted like a night sky, black and sparkling with stars. A suede couch faced a TV, and beside it was a bookcase with old books and movies. An elegant, free-standing clothes rack was filled with stylish, no doubt expensive, pieces that I was sure would fit me perfectly, even if they were too fancy for my style. Everything was elegant, from the thick area rug under my feet, to the embroidered emerald duvet on the bed.

Thaddeus nodded for me to explore, and I kicked off my shoes so I wouldn't get the rug dirty, before gingerly stepping over to the clothes rack, fingering through the hangers mindlessly.

It was beautiful, all of it, but it made bile creep up the back of my throat. Even with five years separating us, he'd clearly never given up on me.

A door creaked, and I turned to Thaddeus pushing open a door in the side wall of the room.

"My room is right through here if you need anything," he said, and a wave of tension left me at the meaning. "I understand you might need time."

Time before I end up back in his bed, was the rest of his unspoken implication.

Yeah. I'd need time all right. A whole fucking lifetime.

Still, I was relieved he let me have my own room.

Oh, how low the bar had fallen.

Stepping up to me again, he clasped my shoulders, pressing his forehead to mine.

"You did great tonight, Jade."

I hesitated only a breath before deciding it was worth pushing my luck. "Can I call Ruby?" His eyes sharpened instantly, so I rushed on. "Just to let her know everything is okay? I didn't get to say goodbye —"

"Shh," Thaddeus cut me off, brushing his thumb over my cheek. "Let's get you settled in first, all right? We can talk about you calling her again in a few days."

I clenched my fists to stop from scratching his face, bit my tongue to stop myself from protesting. His mind was made up, and any argument would only make him postpone it longer.

"Anything you need, anything you want, let me know and we'll get it, okay? I take care of what's mine, baby." His lips caressed my forehead, his hands rubbed over my shoulders. "You're home, and you belong to me again. Everything will be okay now."

Numbing my emotions, steeling my heart, I swallowed and nodded. Thaddeus wrapped me in a hug, then pulled back to give me one last smile before disappearing through the door adjoining our rooms.

"Goodnight, Jade."

I wet my lips to reply, my mouth dry as sandpaper, but when I tried to speak, no sound came out.

Chapter Forty-Seven

JADE

Despite how tired I was, I couldn't sleep, tossing and turning in that giant, cold bed, sick to my stomach.

I'd already thrown up twice.

Whatever kindnesses or gentleness Thaddeus had shown wouldn't last. Taking my phone was only the tip of the iceberg of his controlling tendencies, and I couldn't do it.

I couldn't live like this again.

Not after I knew the opposite, the freedom and safety and self-determination I'd known with West, with the whole pack.

Flopping onto my back, I stared up at the painted night sky on my ceiling, feeling helpless.

But I wasn't the same girl, the same wolf I'd been the last time the Coven had me. I'd been on my own for years, taking care of myself even before West and his pack came into my life. And being with the pack had made me feel *more* powerful, not less. *More* independent, *more* authentic.

Aspen and Summer had helped me learn how to connect with the powers of my wolf, even in human form. They'd pulled me into their circle, welcoming me as a sister, no questions asked.

Heath, Terran, Cooper, Leif, and even River had shown me I didn't have to be anything other than myself to be accepted.

Cruz had put my hands to work, gifting me a distraction and a feeling of accomplishment, all while never judging me, never pushing me.

And West. Our wolves called to each other, that much was

obvious from day one, but it was so much more than that. He never stopped fighting for me — to be with him and the pack, yes, but also to find my own strength. His selflessness showed in everything he did, and I couldn't forget how wonderful it felt to be on the receiving end of his time and attention. Everyone in his circle knew just how lucky they were to be there, and I had finally gotten the memo.

No one compared to West Larkin.

But the best part about West wasn't how he made me feel wanted and accepted. He made me feel like *me*. A better, stronger version of myself, sure, but me, all the same.

I'd fallen for him in all of the little moments we'd shared, and I'd do anything to protect him, to return everything he'd so freely given me.

I refused to forget myself this time, refused to let Thaddeus and the Coven wear me down into nothingness. Besides, he'd made the vow. Ruby, the Larkins, Timber Creek — he couldn't touch them. That meant if I could just get out and get back to Timber Creek, I'd be safe too.

And if I could somehow set up the Coven to go down when I did? So much the better.

)))●(((

The first two days, I bided my time. I "behaved" to let Thaddeus think I was playing nice — kept quiet and kept my eyes and ears open. Thaddeus watched me that first day, but he'd shirked his usual responsibilities to be with me — something I was sure couldn't last long.

I tried to memorize the layout of the large house as he showed me around, though I wasn't allowed to wander off on my own to explore it. Still, I saw enough to realize the Coven "experiments" must be taking place in another building.

The second morning, Thaddeus assigned Bram as my guard, and I hid the glimmer of hope that stirred.

Thaddeus clapped us both on the shoulders as he turned to leave us. "I'm sure you'll have no trouble getting along for a few hours. Take good care of my baby, Bram."

Bram gave him a nod, and Thaddeus leaned down towards me. I hid my wince as he pressed a kiss to my cheek before strolling off, leaving Bram and I alone.

"Why are you giving me that look?"

Bram blinked. "I'm not."

I squinted, and he sighed, rubbing the back of his neck.

"I didn't think you were coming back," he admitted. "And I have this vague feeling like — I don't know, like maybe I saw you in passing? But I can't quite remember when, or where…" He shook his head, letting it go, and I let out a breath. "Maybe it was a dream, or someone who looked like you. Anyway, I'm just surprised to see you here."

I shrugged. "Well, here I am."

He stared at me a moment longer before nodding towards the hallway. "I have a few tinctures to finish up."

We wound through the house, the others ignoring us as Bram led the way to the laboratory-like room that faced the woods behind the house. Bookcases filled with jars and boxes scrawled with handwritten labels lined one wall of the room, and tiers of growing herbs and flowers greened the light coming in through the windows, casting the room in an eerie glow.

The witchy scents — comfrey and myrrh, heather and valerian — that permeated the room sent a jolt of warning through me, the memories tied to the smells too sharp. But luckily, Bram wasn't a shifter, and missed my subtle flinch as he moved behind a countertop and started igniting the Bunsen burners.

A pang struck my chest at how familiar his movements were. How many hours had I spent with him just like this, helping him work while utterly oblivious to what his tinctures and potions were used for?

Comfrey and myrrh for cleaning and healing wounds. Heather and valerian to put their victims to sleep.

I'd looked them up once I'd learned the truth about the Coven, about the experiments, suddenly curious why Bram had always made the same things, over and over. Why his potions always ran out.

A mortar and pestle scraped across the counter a moment before Bram dropped a bundle of herbs beside it, a silent request for my help.

I raised my gaze from the flasks bubbling above the flames, but Bram had already moved to the plants at the window, snipping off leaves and flowers as he went.

Following his movements, I looked out the window behind him, spotting another outbuilding further back on the property, almost hidden behind huge brambling rhododendrons. Thaddeus hadn't included that building on my tour yesterday. I focused in on it, pulling my wolf senses to the forefront. Balto's eyesight was far better than my own, and she zeroed in on the building, feeling my intention.

My breath caught as Thaddeus emerged from the trees around the building with four witches at his side, deep in conversation. They paused at the building, frustration on Thaddeus's face as he ripped open a door. The other witches followed him inside, and I frowned.

Mechanically, I grasped the cool stone of the pestle, dropping a few leaves into the mortar.

"What is this for?" I ventured. Testing him.

"Comfrey?" He raised an eyebrow in suspicion, like surely everyone knew what comfrey was for.

Like everyone here, he gave me a sad smile. "I always forget how weak your witch powers are and how little you know."

I ignored the familiar jab, using it to my benefit. I needed him to talk to me, to find our way back to the easy friendship we'd had before.

"Comfrey is for wounds."

"Okay, so why all the wound care? Are we at war or something?"

Bram turned back to the plants, but I saw the slight tensing of his shoulders at my questions.

"Let me guess." I rolled my eyes, willing playfulness into my tone. If I was going to get Bram on my side, I had to put him at ease first. "Thaddeus doesn't want me knowing too much. Right?"

Returning to the bench with a bundle of plants in his hands, Bram shrugged, at least having the decency to look apologetic. "Not yet." Setting down the foliage, he leaned his palms on the countertop. "You did leave."

Remembering Thaddeus's words from the night before, I parroted them. "Thaddeus wanted me to reconnect with my wolf."

The muscle in Bram's jaw twitched, betraying just how much he believed *that*. "Sure."

I held up the herb paste I'd made, and Bram took it, scooping the contents into a container before handing it back for me to keep going.

"I missed you, though," I blurted, the words more honest than I'd meant to share, and he looked up with a start, blinking. Until I said it, I hadn't realized how much it was true. I *had* missed my one friend from here, when I managed to separate those memories from all the *other* ones.

"I missed you, too," he finally stammered, then cleared his throat. "At first, I thought maybe you'd been one of the ones who, uh, didn't make it. I thought—" He broke off, eyes darting to me then back to his boiling concoctions.

"What?"

A long pause, long enough I worried he'd closed up on me again, and then —

"I thought — if you'd actually left of your own free will — that you would've told me first." A flash of hurt crossed his face, quickly hidden.

"I didn't have time to," I said, another not-lie. "Or I would have."

Bram gave a stiff nod.

Biting my lip, I warred with myself — to push him, or to let him come to me?

"And did you? Reconnect with your wolf?"

It was an olive branch, and I grasped onto it for dear life, my lips breaking into a true smile as I told my only old friend what I could about running with my wolf.

Chapter Forty-Eight

JADE

I couldn't get the outbuilding out of my mind. The rest of the afternoon with Bram, I forced myself to avoid looking at it, not wanting to alert him to my interest. But now, lying in bed, it was all I could think about.

How many shifters were in cages out there?

How many of them were kids?

How many of them didn't have much time left, no matter how the Coven tried to patch them up with Bram's tinctures?

And most importantly, were they under guard, or did the Coven feel a cage was sufficient?

That last question, I told myself, was irrelevant. That only mattered if I was about to bust in there and try to free them.

Which I wasn't. Because that would be stupid.

It would be stupid to slip out of my covers, and pull on my sweater and socks. To tiptoe to my door, sneakers in my hands, and try to open it silently.

To pad down the uneven, creaky staircase, holding my breath, and slink to the backdoor.

It was a good thing I'd been living with shifters, and thus all the more aware of every sound I made, because apparently I was stupid.

Somehow, I made it out of the house without making a noise or running into anyone. My heart thundered so loudly, I couldn't believe no one had heard me. This never would have worked in the pack house.

My hands shook so much, I could hardly tie my shoes.

But then the memory of Ruby, broken and bloody, flooded my mind, and suddenly I didn't care if anyone caught me. If there were shifters out there, I had to help them.

The first step was knowing the truth, and how many there were.

Despite it being summer, it was chilly here at night. I pulled my sleeves over my hands as I stalked towards the outbuilding, thankful for the clouds overhead darkening the sky. I stuck to the shadows when possible, creeping along the trees, wincing at every branch and leaf that crunched beneath my shoes.

With every step, I was sure a beam of light would find me, and the jig would be up. That a voice would call out and I'd be done for. But five years of paranoia made Balto and I as alert as I'd ever been.

I wanted to look behind me, but I kept my gaze locked forward, intent on the dingy grey building growing closer with each breath.

I paused in the shadow of a cluster of trees a few paces from the building, tuning in to my enhanced senses. I couldn't hear or scent anyone outside the building, so at least out here, it was unguarded.

Taking a breath, I made it the last few feet to the door, and quietly slipped inside.

The smell hit me first — blood and urine and despair. Balto pushed at the boundary between us, the memory of the last time we'd scented that still too sharp, and I was surprised by how close to the surface she felt now. Thaddeus's magic had kept her locked away for the past two days, her soul muffled, but now her rage cracked the bonds that held her. No matter her anger, we couldn't lose control this time.

The interior was dark, but my eyes shifted seamlessly, Balto's eyesight clicking in until I could see nearly as well as in daylight.

Boxes and crates were piled high, this entryway merely a

storage room, so I moved further inside, following the scent of misery.

Turning a corner, my hand flew over my mouth as I gasped, taking in the sight.

Rows upon rows of iron cages and cells lined the room, the building clearly a converted stable. One by one, a few heads lifted, hopeless eyes looking my way, then blinking at me. There were more that didn't turn to me — too beaten down physically or emotionally to bother.

"You're not a witch."

I jolted at the squeaky voice, tracking it down to the third cage, a tiny redheaded girl furrowing her brow at me. A scar cut across her face, a jagged line of pink.

"Shh! Don't talk to her!" The shifter in the cell next to her hissed, and the girl backed away from the front of her cage, chastised.

My eyes watered to see this, to see them, and my stomach twisted at the truth I'd suspected from the start. Bile rose in my throat as I looked at the other cages, seeing how young most of these shifters were, wondering how desperate they were, just like I'd been so many years ago when I'd been caught in the Coven's net.

"I'm not a witch," I whispered, not even sure who I was speaking to. "I want to help you. Get you out of here. Are there keys?"

The one who had hushed the girl stepped forward, peering at me between the bars of her cell. She was older, but still in her teens — far too young to have gone missing without a trace. Her jeans and tee were dirty, but I didn't see any wounds, so maybe she hadn't been here long.

"Yes, but some of the cages are spelled, too," she said, wary as she assessed me. She must have been satisfied with whatever she saw in me because she nodded to the far end of the room.

Keys.

I ran for them, pulling the ring and flipping through them. No labels, but two different sizes — for the cells, and for the smaller cages, I assumed.

I went for the little girl's cage first, her huge blue eyes tracking my every move.

This wasn't the plan. I hadn't meant to try to free anyone tonight. I'd meant to assess the situation, then double back to my room and make a plan on the best course of action to get them out safely.

But then I saw that girl, saw the reality of these people, and how could I leave them?

I fumbled with the keys, wincing with every clink of the metal as I tried key after key, until finally, it clicked.

When the lock fell away, no magic on this one, I let out a breath, swinging the door open and beckoning to the girl.

She glanced between me and the teen beside her, unsure who to trust.

"Oh, Jade. You disappoint me."

I froze. *No.*

"Not because you're here," Thaddeus continued, and I bit my lip to stop the cry that threatened to escape me. "I figured you'd try, sooner or later. I just hoped you'd go for *later*, to be less predictable."

He sighed dramatically, and I locked eyes with the teen in the cage as I rose slowly to my feet, then turned to face him.

In a flash, his hand gripped my jaw, squeezing painfully tight.

"Did you really think I wouldn't have this place spelled for intruders?" he sneered, disappointment and disgust on his face as he leaned over me. "I knew the second you stepped foot inside. I only waited to see what you would do."

"Thaddeus —"

Wrenching my arm, he dragged me down the row of cells, until we reached a few at the end that were empty, their doors open, and he threw me in. My palms scraped on the concrete as

I caught myself, my knees smarting, but I jumped back up and whirled around in an instant, not allowing myself a moment to quell the pain.

He stalked after me, crowding me in the corner, the cell bars pressing into my back. It burned where it touched the skin exposed between my leggings and my sweater, the iron instantly dulling Balto's senses as it counteracted the magic in me.

"I gave you everything you needed. Everything you could have wanted. I kept you out of here all those years, and this is how you repay me?" He shook his head. "I suppose I'm the fool. I wanted to believe you when you said you'd behave this time."

I swallowed, desperately trying to think of a way out of this, to get *all* of us out of this.

With the barest movement of my arm, my fingers wound around the bars, my palm stinging in pain.

"I'm sorry," I breathed, willing sincerity into my voice as I shifted my fingers to claws, scraping the metal as silently as I could. "You said the Coven was different now, and I was curious —"

"Don't lie to me," Thaddeus snarled, his eyes dark with anger as he pushed into my space.

I put my free hand on his chest, hoping the contact might calm him. Blinking up at him, I willed tears to form, thinking of that scar on the little girl's face, knowing no one had been here to protect her. My voice shook with genuine sadness as I said, "You're right. I shouldn't have come out here alone. I should have waited until you decided I was ready."

I nearly choked on the words, but it didn't matter what I said, as long as I kept him distracted and didn't escalate the situation.

Thaddeus glared at me, trying to decide if he should trust me. I slid my hand from his chest to his jaw, giving him a caress that made him shudder, his eyes fluttering closed.

"Please forgive me?" I glanced up at him through my eyelashes, pushing out my bottom lip just the barest amount.

It didn't take much to turn his anger to heat, and he licked his lips.

As he leaned towards me, I heard it. The faint crunch of boots on gravel.

My heart gave a flutter, but I didn't break Thaddeus's stare, needing him to focus on me.

Mate, came a rumbled growl in my mind, and I swallowed my sob of relief at that voice. *You have some explaining to do.*

I couldn't stop the quirk of my lips, but luckily, Thaddeus thought it was for him. Closing his eyes, he pressed his mouth to mine, breathing me in like his first gulp of fresh air in five years.

With a slash, my claws raked across his neck.

He staggered back, hissing at the pain as he gripped his neck. "You *bitch.*"

But his second of shock cost him, and when he lunged for me, I'd already sprinted out of the cell. I whipped around to crash the door closed, using every ounce of shifter strength I had to hold it shut as Thaddeus barrelled into the other side.

He frowned as he realized I was stronger than him — realized I had broken through his spell on my wolf. He reached for his magic instead, and I twisted the lock.

But his magic didn't answer him, and his eyes widened in horror.

"How did you —"

I held up my hand, now human again, but the scrape of black still stained my fingertips.

His shock turned, his temper flaring as he put it together, and a satisfied smirk crept over my face.

"Fuck, Jade! This isn't over! You think you can take on the entire Coven this time? You might have taken out eight witches last time, but you can't beat us all alone. You'll never win." He thrashed himself into the bars, scrabbling with the lock, but with his magic temporarily deadened by the iron shavings I'd shoved into his blood, he was only a human trapped in a cell.

The back door to the building smashed open, floodlights filling the space with startling brightness before a large shadow stepped into view.

"She's not alone this time, witch," came a rumbled voice, and my heart swelled, relief sweeping through me at the sight of my mate. He tossed me something I only caught thanks to my shifter reflexes. "Blue shell, gem."

I looked at the taser he'd given me — good enough.

Chapter Forty-Nine

WEST

Two days.

Two fucking days Jade was lost to me.

As much as I wanted to step inside Thaddeus's cell and rip him to shreds, I had to wait. Once Mo and the Deadlights Cove Coven had dialed in to my mate bond, adding power to override whatever blocking spell Thaddeus had put on Jade, it had been a matter of moments for me to pinpoint her location in Wyoming. While I'd been ready to hold a blade to the closest demon's neck until they flickered me there, I couldn't do that, and it killed me.

Max had taken her location intel back to the PRICs, and the size of the campus the Black Rose Coven was running became evident. We needed a better plan than to just rush in and hope for the best.

"Did you come alone?" Jade's voice was muffled as I clutched her to my chest, both Togo and I needing contact to ensure she was okay. I glanced around the barn, cataloging the number of shifters and how I could make these fuckers pay for what they'd done. "We need to get them out of here."

"The whole team is here." I kissed her forehead, not ready to let go. "Cooper is going to hand my ass to me for breaking rank. I was supposed to wait, but the moment this asshole touched you, I was done."

Her fingers curled into my chest while Thaddeus spat profanities at us until I slammed my hand against the bar, rattling his cage. The witch fell back, landing on his ass as my eyes turned pure gold, teeth elongating.

"Did he hurt you?" My voice rumbled with my wolf, his ears pricking up as Jade gave a dark chuckle, scoffing down at Thaddeus.

"I'd like to see him try."

I smirked, my pride glowing for my fierce mate. Blood dripped from the slashes along Thaddeus's neck, showing how controlled she'd been. She'd come so far. Before I could tell her so, an explosion sounded outside, and that was my cue.

"What the hell was that?" Jade's eyes snapped to the door, and I grabbed her hand, pulling her down the hallway past the cages, shifters huddled within for safety.

"Cooper."

Her mouth hung open, and I couldn't stop myself from covering it with mine, even if this split second wasn't enough.

"Time to make them pay."

A second explosion sounded, then shouts as chaos ensued. By the time we pushed open the barn doors, the Victorian house was in flames, the side facing the barn missing.

My brother stood in full combat gear with a dozen shifters, some wolves, some wearing the same camo fatigues as him from their days in the military together. As one, they moved, descending on the house as anyone left inside ran to escape. A mixture of gunfire and gut-churning snarls filled the air as, one by one, the leaders of Black Rose Coven were destroyed.

Beside me, Jade's eyes were wide, her hand shaking in mine evidence of her shock, even if I hadn't felt it through our bond.

"There are kids in there."

"We know," I said, and pointed to the far side of the house.

Out the side door, Max appeared with a small group of the Coven's children, as well as a handful of adults. How he could tell who could be trusted, he hadn't explained except to say it was a "vamp thing."

Something I would be sure to ask him about someday, but for now, we needed innocents safe and justice served.

Witches fled from the building, right into the waiting arms of my wolves, including one I recognized.

"*Krista!*"

Her head snapped up, face paling as she backed away, looking for an exit. Atlas stood behind her, clamping a hand around her shoulder. "Are you the one who told them where Jade was?"

"I didn't know!" She was stupid enough to lie to me, shaking her head violently. "I swear I didn't know about the experiments. Thaddeus said he just wanted to know Jade was safe. Let me talk to Max. He can explain."

The dark angel appeared between us, his jaw tight. "There's nothing to explain."

"Please!" She tried to pull herself free of Atlas's grip, lurching towards Max. "I love you Max, I always have. I did it for you. If Thaddeus was happy with me, then maybe he'd let you come back."

Max nodded to Atlas, who let Krista go, the witch rushing over to clutch Max's shirt.

With a tired sigh, Max planted a hand at her temple, and Krista went slack in his arms. The whites of his eyes darkened in that way I'd learned indicated his vampire magic, inky blackness seeping from his fingertips and across Krista's face.

We all held our breath, watching this display of his magic, and then he blinked it away. The shadows disappeared.

He stepped away, the unconscious witch sliding to the ground without his support, and joined me and Jade.

"She's been feeding the Coven intel for a while. Garnered some locations for cameras you might not notice around the property, and the Coven hired out the same anti-shifter group that's been hunting and kidnapping us to sell to the highest bidder," he confirmed, and my teeth ground together. "They've been watching Timber Creek, looking for a way in."

Turning to Jade, he added, "She enchanted Leif for your number, and spelled that rose onto your window."

"She did *what* to my son?" Then I frowned at the rest of his words, turning to Jade. "Your number? Has he been contacting you? And what window? *My* window? At the pack house?"

Hesitantly, Jade nodded, then looked at the incapacitated witch at our feet. "None of it matters now. It's over. They can't taunt me anymore."

"It was just a temporary spell on Leif. Would have worn off in a few moments." With a nod, Max moved off to deal with the rest of the witches.

Quicker than it seemed possible, it was over, silence descending over the forest around us again.

A flash of light, and a group of angels appeared, ready to take any remaining Coven members to Headquarters for questioning and assessment.

Jade glanced between the angels and the outbuilding. "What about —"

"Cooper has a shifter healer on the way to check them out. We figured they'd be more comfortable with that than a witch or a doctor, or going to Headquarters," I said, and Jade noticeably relaxed. "Then we'll work on getting them back where they belong."

Jade blinked, her eyes bright, and she nodded. "Good. And if they don't have anywhere to go?"

I nipped at her ear. "You know the answer to that already, mate. What did you think the dorm building was for?"

"Just checking." Jade smiled, pinching my arm, before turning more serious again. "And Thaddeus?"

The growl left my throat before I could stop it, the mere mention of that asshole's name enough to raise my hackles.

Over her head, I nodded to Cooper, who gave a salute and

disappeared into the building. I tugged Jade around the back of it, out of sight of the angels and anyone else who might feel the need to write an official report.

"That's up to you, gem." My hands rested on her neck as she tilted her chin up towards me. "You did beautifully locking him in that cell, so if you'd like, we can leave him there to rot."

The back door creaked, and Cooper reemerged, marching a handcuffed and gagged Thaddeus in front of him.

"If you'd rather the angels get him, we can arrange that, too. Or if you want it to be over, here and now, say the word and it's done."

Thaddeus muttered behind his gag and writhed in his restraints, but he was no match for Cooper, who whacked him over the head, producing a satisfying grunt of pain.

Looking between us, Jade frowned as she considered my offer. I didn't think of myself as a killer, but for her, I'd tear his head from his body with no remorse.

Jade's expression turned cold as she made up her mind. "He doesn't deserve to have it over quickly." Shifting her gaze to Cooper, she added, "Send him to the angels. Let them have him for the rest of his miserable life."

Cooper raised a brow, and Jade turned away, walking back around to the front of the building without a backwards glance at her abuser.

Raising an eyebrow at me, Cooper waited.

Smug bastard.

But he was right, I had one last thing to say to Thaddeus.

Well, my fist did.

A few moments later, shaking out my smarting hand, I rejoined Jade around the other side, pulling her into my arms and inhaling her scent like a drug.

"Let's get you home, mate."

Chapter Fifty

JADE

Home.

It was still hard to wrap my mind around the idea that I had one, even as I sat curled up in West's lap on the short plane ride back to Colorado. Cooper and Atlas were apparently a one-stop-shop rescue organization, the two of them piloting the private plane with ease.

In the back, West had barely been able to let go of me.

The first thing he'd done once we boarded was hand me a satellite phone, the call already ringing through to Ruby. Luckily, Ruby hadn't known the full extent of my circumstances, but it was a relief to hear her voice all the same, to hear her playful admonishment for leaving Deadlights Cove without saying goodbye.

The moment I said I ran into Thaddeus, the line went silent.

"You're not talking to him again, are you?" The pained tone of her voice told me she still remembered him and how he'd manipulated me, even if the details of our years with the Coven were fuzzy.

West's hand slid under my shirt, rubbing across my skin, and I leaned into him. "No. He was arrested today. I don't think I'll ever hear from him again." Suddenly, I was laughing. The stress and relief mixing up inside me and finally bubbling over.

"You're anxious laughing," Ruby said. "Never a good sign. Do I need to come to Colorado? Or are you moving again? Tell me where I need to come find you and I'm there."

West's hand stilled on my back, and I turned to look at him. His hazel eyes focused on me, hearing every word she'd said even though I didn't have it on speakerphone. Nothing was private with shifter hearing. The hesitancy in his eyes had me lifting my hand to rest on his chest, feeling his steady heartbeat under my fingertips.

"I'm fine," I said, answering both Ruby and the unspoken concern on West's face. "I'm better than fine. And I'm going back to Timber Creek, with no intention of moving. Might even join the pack."

Ruby screeched, and I held the phone away from my face to escape the loud noise followed by tears of happiness, if I knew my little sister.

West reached for the phone, holding it to his ear momentarily as he said bye to my sister and hung up, his eyes never leaving mine.

I turned to straddle his lap, cupping his face as I kissed him, pouring every ounce of how much I loved him into our mate bond. My heart beat in time with his as heat washed over my body. His tongue slipped inside my mouth, tangling with mine, and my fingers flexed as I pulled myself closer, needing this connection.

"Just a reminder you're not alone in this plane, boss," Atlas shouted back at us. I jerked back, but West tightened his grip on me, not letting me go. "If you can possibly keep it in your pants for twenty more minutes."

My face flushed, hiding against West's chest in mortification, but he only slapped my ass.

"I can be patient," he murmured low enough only I could hear. "I have a lifetime of loving you ahead of me."

I smiled. I liked the sound of that.

When we landed back in Colorado, something felt different than before, or maybe I was. Either way, Balto was more alert than ever, a different kind of magic tingling through my nerves and heightening all my senses.

The drive from the airstrip to the pack house was a blur, my focus on West's hand on my knee in the car, on his woodsy scent.

He must have sent out a warning for everyone to vacate the house, because it was uncharacteristically silent as we entered. I opened my mouth to comment on it, but my words quickly turned to a yelp as West scooped me up, and bounded up the stairs.

"Two days, mate," he grumbled against my ear, then scraped his teeth along it.

"Too long."

He hummed his agreement as he kicked his door closed behind us, then tossed me on the bed. His eyes met mine, burning with hunger and adoration in equal measure as I peeled off my sweater, needing him just as badly as he needed me.

West's tongue trailed over my skin, filling me with a desire that I couldn't resist. He licked over the lace of my bra, teeth grazing my nipples as I tipped my head up, gripping the back of his head. My fingers tangled in his hair as his hands slipped behind my back, undoing the clasp. The moment his warm tongue lapped at me, I gasped, unable to control my reactions to him.

"So responsive." West's voice rumbled across my skin as his beard scraped across my chest. "I love that."

I clawed at his shoulders, needing more than these tantalizing touches. Sliding my hand down his back, I reached into the back of his jeans, palming his ass through his boxers, and squeezed.

A low, seductive laugh escaped him as I pulled his hips into mine. "Tell me what you need, gem."

"You." My voice was breathy as he ground his hips into me,

his neediness evident in his body and our mate bond. "All of you. Now. Forever. I thought I gave you up. Remind me that I didn't."

He chuckled again, then moved down my body, leaving a trail of kisses across my skin as he pulled off my jeans and toyed with the lace of my thong. "Do you know how beautiful you are, Jade? How you fill my waking and subconscious thoughts? You can't give me up. You own my soul." His gaze met mine before he pressed his mouth between my legs, a moan leaving me even though there was still a layer of fabric between us.

Taking matters into my own hands, I pushed my thong down my hips and West ripped it off my legs. Then he was back, his beard scratching the inside of my thighs, and his palms wrapped around my ass, lifting me slightly to meet his tongue.

"Fuck, you're so wet, Jade. So wet for your mate." His tongue swiped through me, making my breath catch as a hand slid up my body, fingers circling my breast. "You're perfect."

I had to fight the urge to lock my knees around his head, to pull him closer as he worked me. My legs shook as his hands and tongue worked in unison to elicit the deepest moans I'd ever heard come from my mouth.

"More," I breathed, eyes squeezed shut against the rush of sensations taking over my body. "I need more. I think " — I gasped when I felt my canines itching, but Balto was thrilled — "I need to bite you."

West's eyes *glowed*. "Bite me then, mate."

I lurched up, twisting us until West was under me and I straddled his hips. Sliding my hands under his shirt, I pushed it over his head and tossed it aside. Our lips crashed together while West undid his belt and pushed his jeans down, baring himself to me.

We moved in a familiar dance, our bodies guiding us more than any conscious thought as he pulled my hips down, sinking himself into me.

I gasped at the stretch, a shiver racing through my spine as I leaned forward and bit him where his neck met his shoulder.

Copper coated my tongue as colors danced against my eyelids, a Rainbow Road forming between his soul and mine in my mind. A mate bond, tying us together forever.

Mate, Togo said in my head.

Mine, Balto answered, and I grinned, pulling my mouth free of West's skin. I rose above him, wiping my mouth as West pounded into me from below.

"Forever," West said, his fingers digging into my hips as he moved, his eyes glowing bright.

I moaned his name, unable to hold back before my body shattered into a million pieces, shaking with the crush of emotions it brought. West waited until my body slumped before lifting me off him.

"Turn around, on your hands and knees."

Heat zinged through my body, wanting everything he had to give. I settled on my hands and knees as his palm landed softly on my lower back, pressing slowly until I arched.

"You look so fucking beautiful like this, gem." The mattress dipped as he moved behind me, his hands gripping my hips and drifting over my ass, down the backs of my thighs, and back. "Showing me how wet you are."

He dipped fingers inside me, and I pushed back against him, needing more.

Just as I was about to insist, he removed his fingers and swiped himself through my wetness, hovering over where I needed him most. His hand slipped under me, sliding over my belly as he leaned down over me to whisper in my ear. "Someday you'll carry our children. I can't wait to have a family with you. I love you so damn much, mate. I'm yours forever."

I whimpered at his words, then groaned as he pushed back inside me. My arms gave out as he moved, shoulders dropping to the mattress as I clawed at the sheets, holding on for dear life. His grip was firm on my hips as he rose over me, drawing out every sensation in a delicious torture.

With our bond in place, I not only felt my own ecstasy, but his. It was intoxicating, a drug I couldn't resist. In no time at all, my body tightened around his again. He hauled me up against him, curling his arms around my chest as he tilted my face towards his. The kiss was a searing claim, a one-way ticket to a life I never imagined in the arms of West Larkin.

"Come for me, gem," West said as he held my jaw, thrusting deep inside me again. I reached behind me, holding his head to my shoulder as he licked where he'd marked me before, then bit down on the same spot, our bond glowing warm again.

I cried out as my body seized, his lips stealing the sound from my mouth as he kissed me. I'd have slumped forward on the bed if his grip on me wasn't so tight, but he kept me upright, eyes on mine as his hips jerked, then his gaze shuttered as he groaned my name.

Heart racing, I felt more whole than I ever had, knowing I'd found a part of me I didn't know was missing in West. We belonged together.

His body slumped to the bed as he turned me in his arms, tugging me down to his chest. Under my ear, his heart thundered, beating in sync with mine.

"I love you," he whispered, kissing my head as his hands traced over my back.

"I love you, too. More than anything."

Chapter Fifty-One

WEST

I hid my surprise as Max materialized a few feet above the back porch the next morning, but he must have sensed my wince anyway, judging by his smirk.

With a flap of his black wings, he touched down, rattling the railing enough to jostle my coffee, and I shot him a scowl as I shook the drops off my hand. Any other supe, I would have sensed half a mile away, but something about his vampire abilities made him undetectable until he wanted to be detected.

"Is it done?"

Max leaned on the railing next to me, looking over the rolling mountains in the distance.

"Thaddeus Webb has been sentenced to life in the Iron Keep for illegal experiments on supernatural beings, kidnapping supernaturals, and several supe deaths previously unaccounted for."

"Good fucking riddance."

Max hummed in agreement.

"What of the other Coven members? The kids, and the adults we didn't kill?"

"We're tracking down if the kids have any supernatural family in other, upstanding Covens we can send them to," Max said. "If not, we'll reach out to Covens who might be willing to take in some fosters, or adopt. Morgaine is taking over organizing placements for both the Coven kids as well as the hybrids they held in captivity, although some of them are going to need a strong Alpha."

Max turned to me, and I hummed as I sipped my coffee, already thinking through plans for Aspen to make the dorms more kid-friendly. No way in hell was I letting a single one of those kids end up alone.

"They'll be well-cared for, wherever they end up, we'll make sure of it," he mirrored my thoughts. "The adults, including Jade's friend Bram, were on the whole given prison sentences ranging from three to ten years, based on how involved they were in the operations. Most of them were more than happy to provide us with evidence against Thaddeus as well."

I nodded, knowing that was more than fair, even if Jade might not like the idea of Bram in prison. He'd still been a part of it, had known what was going on, and hadn't tried to stop any of it, even if he wasn't evil to his core like Thaddeus was.

"What now?" I asked.

Max rested his elbows on the porch railing, hanging his head as he sighed. "Now, we make sure this can't happen again. The Black Rose Coven is gone, but that doesn't excuse the fact that this many hybrid shifters went missing for this long and no one bothered hunting them down."

I raised a brow. "You're taking that on like Malachi asked?"

His gaze swung to me, a flat glare. "He's not exactly the easiest to say no to."

I chuckled, clapping him on the back. "Let me know how I can help, and you know I'm in."

Max stood, turning his back to the railing as he looked into the house. "She staying?"

"Yes." I looked up to the window above me where she was still asleep in my bed. *Our* bed. "Yes, she is."

"Good." Max smiled, holding a hand out for me to shake. "Take care of her. They don't get much better than Jade."

I gripped his hand, agreeing wholeheartedly, when someone shouted as they came around the side of the house.

"Is it safe? Are you clothed? Because I swear to the moon, Westion Mark, if I have to see one more inch of naked — oh."

Summer frowned, peering through the tiniest gap between the fingers she held over her eyes, before dropping her hand. "I expected you to be out here with Jade, what with the whole *mating* thing."

I rolled my eyes. "If Jade was out here with me, believe me, you'd know long before you made it this close."

"Gross." Summer pretended to gag, then held out the basket she'd brought with her, as friendly as ever. "Anyway, I came bearing gifts. For *Jade*," she added, cutting me a sharp glance. "I assumed you probably hadn't let her sleep, nevermind stop for sustenance, since you'd gotten her back, and I can't have her thinking the pack isn't ecstatic she's here."

"Well, you were wrong." We'd stopped to shower, which turned heated, then made it to the kitchen for a snack, where I ate her on the counter like I'd promised weeks ago. But I was famished, and Jade would be too when she woke up.

Ignoring me, she turned a smile on Max. "You can have one, because you helped get our girl back."

Max tried and failed to hide a grin as he peeked into the basket, swiping a muffin a split second before I snatched the basket from Summer, and he took a triumphant bite.

"Sorry to eat and run, wolves, but duty calls," Max said, brushing crumbs off his hands, black wings unfurling beside him.

"Where to now?"

Max scowled. "Now it's back to Headquarters so dear old Dad and I can brainstorm how to fix vampire PR so I'm not shunned on sight while I try to help supe communities all over the country." He grimaced, but I didn't miss Summer's eyes widening with excitement.

"His last idea was to glamour my wings white." Max shuddered at the thought, and I chuckled.

"Bring baked goods." Summer gestured to her basket, as if it was that simple. It was, for her. Everyone loved Summer. Her easy-going personality was impossible to resist, and I'd seen her work her magic on even the toughest shifters for years. "Always works for me."

Max shook his head, clapping her on the shoulder. For a split second, he frowned, his gaze moving from Summer's face to his hand on her shoulder, but then he dropped it, backing half a step away. "No offense, but I think we'll see what else we can come up with so I'm not hauling pallets of muffins around with me every-where. But if we can't think of anything else, I know who to call."

With one last glance at Summer, Max leapt up on the railing, giving me a nod before launching into the air. His wings beat once, twice, and then he vanished, like he'd never been there at all.

Summer snorted. "Ten bucks says he brings a box of donuts to his next visit." She turned to me, pointing to the basket. "You make sure Jade gets those."

"I will."

"And a decent meal."

"Summer —"

"No, don't *Summer* me. A burger patty and a handful of berries is *not* a real meal. I've seen what you eat when left to your own devices."

"You can go now." Putting my hands on her shoulders, I spun her around, marching her back across the deck the way she'd come.

"Fine! Fine. But no one can say I didn't try to do a wellness check."

I gave her one final shove. "Thank you for the pastries."

She raised a hand, waving off my thanks, before disappearing around the corner of the house.

I smiled, thinking of my worn out mate upstairs, and grabbed the basket, taking the stairs two at a time.

Jade had to keep up her energy. I was nowhere near done with her.

>>>●(((

Not ready to say goodbye to Timber Creek? Summer Larkins stumbles into espionage, chaos, and questionable disguises as the world's worst sidekick to a dangerously broody vampire, Max Russo. Love Bites, out now!

WEST

Two Months Later

I savored the breeze kicking up as we waited for the pack to assemble. It was only a matter of time before the mountains turned gold for the fall, and the scent on the wind said it would be sooner than later this year.

I stood with Terran, letting Jade have a moment with Ruby, who'd come out for a visit and to see Jade's new life here. As far as Ruby knew, this was her first time in Timber Creek, and the sisters had been exploring the town and having fun together the past few days.

Seeing how she took care of her sister, Leif, and River, plus all of the new hybrid shifter children we'd absorbed into our pack over the last two months, made me nearly feral, ready for our future to start. This woman was my whole world, and I wanted to spend my life surrounding her with as much love as possible.

"You know, you almost make it look worth it," Terran commented, arms crossed over his chest, and I resisted the urge to knock off his backwards baseball cap.

"What?"

He nodded at Jade. "The whole mate thing."

I knew what he wasn't saying. After our mom died, seeing how wrecked our dad was had done a number on all of us. But with Jade, that wasn't even a passing thought.

"It is worth it." I shrugged. "Come what may."

He eyed me dubiously, then shook his head, heading off to track down Cruz and River.

His skepticism didn't bother me. I might have been cynical too, before it happened to me. I could only hope if he found his mate, he'd have the courage to face it.

Jade and Ruby wandered over, and a grin stole over my face as they laughed at some joke I'd missed.

"Ready for this, gem?" I pulled Jade into my arms, tipping her face up to mine.

Excitement shivered through her, maybe a little nerves too, but her eyes glowed. "As long as you're there with me, mate."

Mate. Yes, we liked that word on her tongue.

"Then let's do this. Ruby, get ready to see your sister lead this pack."

"Go get 'em, sis." Ruby grinned, pulling Jade from me to wrap her in a hug of her own, then sauntering off to join her boyfriend Akil and his brother Emerson, who had both come out with her for the visit.

I pulled Jade up onto the boulder with me, addressing the crowd.

"Tonight, we welcome our newest pack member, and my mate, Jade," I called, and the pack took up a howl that had Jade chuckling semi-nervously. Turning to her, I lowered my voice. "After you, gem."

Jade took a breath, and reached for the hem of her shirt. Knowing this was still uncomfortable for her, I quickly followed, stepping in front of her to block most of the pack's view until she shifted, and the others followed suit.

She leapt off the boulder, and I was only a split second behind her, shifting to stay right at her hip. With a howl, she called the rest of the pack to us, and soon we were surrounded by animals of all types, sizes, and colors, before she took off into the trees.

We ran after her, my chest bursting with pride to have her embracing this side of herself, to have our pack embracing her. Right here where she belonged, in these woods, these mountains, free and strong and *mine*.

My wild, wild wolf.

THE END

Acknowledgments

What in the *world?* It's hard for us to believe we're here, in a new town, in this same crazy universe we created. *Deadlights Cove* was the journey of a lifetime, and to find so many of you along the way who loved it as much as we did… It's wonderful.

To the Wild Willies: You are the best street team around, and your excitement and enthusiasm constantly blows us away. (We might need to come up with a better name than this though.) Thank you for screaming from the rooftops with us!

Amy, Brit, Elle, and Lex: There aren't enough thank you's in the world to tell you how much you mean to us. You keep signing up for this chaotic journey, time and time again, and we adore you for it.

From B:

To J, for your constant support every step of the way.

To Aimee, for pushing me to keep going every time I'm ready to give up on our books. Bringing stories to life with you is the hardest I've worked and the most fun I've had. Cheers to launching our second series.

And to my mom, for your support in reading every single one of my books.

From Aimee:

To Chris, for believing in me more than anyone. I love you, I love you, I love you.

To B. Making magic with you has been the most fulfilling

thing I've ever done, and I never want it to stop. Gonna hug you until you forcibly extract me.

To Brit, for pushing me to be better while telling me I'm fabulous, on repeat. Every day.

To Lex, for constantly keeping me on track with *all of the things* while we make our dreams come true. You're the real MVP.

And to my girls and Magnus, loving you is the easiest thing in the world.

XO,
Aimee and B.

About B. Perkins

B. has been making up stories about magic since she learned how to write words on paper. When not immersed in fictional worlds, she enjoys spending time in nature. She has several degrees in various things, and if all they're good for is to provide background in creating fantasy worlds and systems, then maybe they were worth it.

instagram.com/b.p.writes

About Aimee Vance

Aimee Vance writes heartfelt and hilarious romance featuring sassy heroines, grumpy heroes, and small-town happily-ever-afters—preferably with a Diet Coke nearby. Her romcoms blend humor and heart with sharp banter, big feelings, and love stories designed to make readers laugh, swoon, and feel right at home.

A lifelong fantasy and romance reader, Aimee studied public relations at Texas Christian University. She lives in Texas with her husband, two young daughters, and a Labrador Retriever. When she's not writing, she's usually rereading her favorite romances or cheering from the sidelines of her kids' sporting events—occasionally at the same time.

facebook.com/aimeevancebooks

instagram.com/aimeevancebooks

goodreads.com/aimeevancebooks

amazon.com/author/aimeevancebooks

bookbub.com/authors/aimee-vance